I0526445

The Omega Jon Christ – The Last Illest

The author, Brooklyn born Shakim Bio, is an Official Street General, who was raised in Far Rockawa; a heavily impoverished and extremely dangerous section of the borough of Queens, New York. Sha came of age earning his stripes while engulfed in a whirlwind of criminal thoughts, drug dealing, violence, women and partying. His reputation is ironclad and his respect echos throughout the streets of New York City, the streets of various towns and cities across the United States as well as Federal Penitentiaries and State Prison Systems. Before committing himself to a life of crime, which he does not glorify, however, real is real, Shakim was touched by the artistic expressions that blossomed and bloomed from the culture he and so many others around him lived daily; a culture where the have-nots instinctively made-do with very little, making something from nothing while surviving harsh living conditions. Shakim Bio fell in love with the culture of Hip Hop! While reflecting on his life, after being confined to a 40 year federal prison sentence, Shakim came to overstand that his unconditional love for Hip Hop Music and culture, collided with the drama of his street ventures and he was a product of "Street Hop", which is the result of REAL street life merging with Hip Hop culture. This novel takes you through one dimension of Shakim's true story…

Copyright © 2006, 2013 by Shakim Bio
Written by: Shakim Bio
Typed by: Greg Martin
Edited / Book Design: Greg Martin
Typeset: Pam Quigley
Cover Concept: Shakim Bio
Cover Design: Cedric "CKillz" Killings and Greg Martin

Warning! Sale of this book without a front cover may be unauthorized. If this book was purchased without a cover it may have been reported to the publisher as "unsold or destroyed." Neither the author nor the publisher may have received payment for sale of this book.

All rights reserved under international and Pan – American Conventions, including the right to reproduction of this work in whole or in part, in any form except with written consent from Mikahs 7 Publishing, with the exception of reviewers, whom may quote brief passages in their reviews.

Published in the United States by: Mikahs 7 Publishing
736D St. Andrews Rd. PMB 143
Colombia, SC 29210

Mikahspublishing@yahoo.com

ISBN: 9780984659623 (ebook)

Acknowledgments

Peace to the Nation of Gods and Earths all over the world, to every God Body I ever built and added on with, to all real deejays and emcees who still respect and represent the foundation; still standing tall and remaining tru. To all my true Generals, comrades and soldiers all over the world, to my family, Mom for putting up with all the noise and accepting all my bullshit, my sisters, aunts, cousins, my seeds; DaQuan Original, its your turn! Much love to my youngest, Shamel, The Brown Family, Guice Family and Tanner Family. All the hoods I been through building or destroying. Sonya Yeargin for believing in my movement when everybody doubted me, Greg "G: Ali" a.k.a. "G: Millionz" Martin you are the true definition of a friend, one Love, lets get this paper. To all my Mikahs 7 Fam, all haters that prayed for my failure and downfall you know who you are. Edgmere, Forties, Redfern, Ocean Village, The Sixties, 71-15, Arverne, Wavecrest, Bayswater, Hammels PJ's (ONE LOVE), The whole Far Rock, All my peeps from Farmers Blvd, my peeps from Rochdale, Baisley, the whole Queens JFK side to the LaGuardia side, Brooklyn, Bronx, Staten Island, Manhattan, Uptown and Upstate; I rep N.Y. very well! All my peeps in Lorain Ohio, Columbia, S.C., ATL, Florida, D.C., Philly, VA, N.C., Detroit, Baltimore, I was in so many states gettin' money, Shit's crazy! Al Monday, Benson, Lenny, Big Tiz, Spice, Cee, Sha-Born, Kelly Blue, Rich Kid (KA), Lance, Rasheem Supreme, Ronald Tucker & Manumit Publishing, Seth & Diane Ferranti at Gorilla Convict Publishing, Book Gang Media, all my true comrades and warriors locked up in the Feds and State Pens. My East Coast, West Coast, Mid-West and Dirty South peeps, my N.O. peeps, my Yardie Massiave Fam "Gangsta fuh life." Seen?! Xtra thanks to: the Five Percenter Newspaper, Dave "Ice" Cook, King Tut, Junglist, Bloody Sparkz, AB God, Ramega, Boom Bash Preme, Kobe (Twin from D.C.), Quasim (Hollis), Devin X (Black) for understanding my vision and capturing it on paper, CED "Ckillz" Killings for his part in bringing my book covers to life. Don Won Pablo a.k.a. Chino

Gambino (Ohio), Daymond John from Fubu the collection - I appreciate all that you've done for me and I appreciate all that you didn't do too, it's still love. DJ Premier for birthing Street Hop, Jay-Z for the inspiration thru moves and music, Nas, you still Nasty Nas no doubt, Kool G Rap and all true lyricists, you know who you are. To both my baby moms, to my past, present and future females that still show love and support, even the ones that express hate, thank you. To Tamekia, I love you, to all legal hustlers, 9 to 5 heads, school goers, all my gun shooters, money getters, kidnappers, car thieves, stick-up kids, grimey heads, paper chasers, boosting chicks, sack chasers, whatever your hustle is, lets get legit and get legal money. Yo, if I missed you, sorry, I got you on the next one. This is dedicated to all those who recognize and appreciate realness, I told my story for you, we are Hip Hop; only a few of us are Street Hop!

Salutes!

Omega Jon Christ Speaks:

It wasn't easy penning this novel but it wasn't hard either. I started this joint while I was sittin' in the box, June of 2003... It took a while for me to finish this because I started, gave up, threw tantrums, screamed at and threatened heads, ripped pages, leaked certain pages, released certain elements of certain chapters, built up a lot of hype, then gave up again. I had to be pushed, convinced and motivated, I lashed out at those who gave constructive criticism and went through a whole bunch of other shit during the writing process of my story, all the while, I was duckin' new indictments (I got acquitted in 03'), waitin' out prison investigations and prison charges (I beat them too). I've been told that I have too much influence beyond prison's control and how much of a threat I am. I've argued with comrades, made new associates, new enemies and I've been in the greatest war one could ever be in, **the war with self**; somehow I manage to maintain sanity. I've put the pen down for months at a time, being caught up in my legal issues or sprayin' ink to my comrades in other prisons, in the streets and the entertainment industry. I've been through the ups and downs... some days I felt inspired, other days, I was fed up with everything; the writing, the back and forth riffing, my team fallin' apart out there then getting' it back together, all the networking on phones or through letters, the **"Please Sha don't do it!"**, the Murder Inc. investigation, during which I decided not to produce this book to the **"Fuck that shit, it's on and poppin'!"**, Yea, sooner or later I would always get back to writing what you are reading right now.

This is for all those who love me or hate me... either way, you still gotta feel my realness. You may love it... you may hate it... but you will recognize it and know it's real. I may not be seen or heard but I'm definitely felt. A real niggah like me is still doin' real things, I'm the last of the dying breed. Niggahs aint gotta know me or like me... but you gon' respect my Gangsta!

This novel is some true shit! A lot of names have been crossed out or purposely left out. All references to real events, businesses and organizations are all factual, real and true. Any resemblance to actual persons, living or dead, is entirely intentional and on point. If I exposed you and you don't like it, **FUCK YOU!** I'm still the Illest, **I just don't shoot guns now… I shoot ink**.

Salutes!!!

The General Monk – Monk of Illness

The Omega Jon Christ.

Queen's Illest!

The Last Illest!!

Pieces and whole parts of the following published songs are illustrated in the free bonus chapter titled "Jay-z vs Nas, Nas vs Jay-z, Me vs You, You vs Me". The Author, song, titles and albums are listed as follows:

"Live at the BBQ" – Main Source feat. Nasty Nas, Akinyele, Joe Fatal and the Large Professor, Album: Breaking Atoms.
"Halftime" – Nasty Nas, Album: Zebrahead Soundtrack / Illmatic.
"One Love"- Nas, Album: Illmatic.
"The Message"- Nas, Album: It Was Written.
"New York State of Mind" - (a few lines) Album: Illmatic.
"Memory Lane" – Nas, Album: Illmatic.
"Life's a Bitch" – Nas feat. AZ, Album: Illmatic.
"Street Dreams" – Nas, Album: It Was Written.
"Affirmative Action" – Nas feat. AZ, Cormega, Foxy Brown- Album: It Was Written.
"I Gave You Power" – Nas, Album: It Was Written.
"Black Girl Lost" – Nas, Album: It Was Written.
"One Mic" (few lines) – Nas, Album: It Was Written.
"Verbal Intercourse" – Raekwon & Ghostface ft. Nas Album: Only Built 4 Cuban Linx.
"Ether" – Nas Album: Stillmatic
"Déjà vu" (few lines) – Lord Tariq & Peter Gunz.
"Reservoir Dogs" – Jadakiss, Beanie Segal & Jay-z Album: Vol.2 Hard Knock Life.
"Men at Work" (few lines) – Kool G Rap & DJ Polo Album: Road to the Riches.
"Poison" (few lines) - Kool G Rap & DJ Polo -Album: Road to the Riches.
"Rated R" (few lines) – RedMan, Album: Whut? … The Album.
"Yes You May" Remix (few lines) – Big L
"Dead Presidents pt. II" (few lines) – Jay-z, Album: Reasonable Doubt.
"Brooklyn's Finest" – Jay-z feat. Notorious B.I.G., Album: Reasonable Doubt.
"Can I Live?" (few lines) Jay-z, Album: Reasonable Doubt.
"Where I'm From" – Jay-z, Album: In My Lifetime, Vol. 1.

"A Million And One Questions" – Jay-Z, Album: In My Lifetime, Vol. 1.

"Rhyme No More" – Jay-z, Album: In My Lifetime, Vol. 1.

"Imaginary Player" – Jay-z, Album: In My Lifetime, Vol. 1.

"Friend or Foe pt. I" – Jay-z, Album: Reasonable Doubt.

"Who You Wit?" – Jay-z, Album: In My Lifetime, Vol. 1

"A Week Ago" – Jay-z feat. Too Short, Album: Vol. 2… Hard Knock Life.

"Do It Again (Throw Your Hands Up)" – Jay-z ft. Beanie Segal & Amil, Album: Roc La Familia.

"D'evils" – Jay-z, Album: Reasonable Doubt.

"Best of Me" Remix – Mya feat. Jay-z, Album: DJ Clue Presents… Backstage.

"Itz Murda" – Ja Rule feat. DMX & Jay-z, Album: Vinni Vetti Vecci.

CHAPTER 1

SINS OF MY SONS / WHO IS REALLY BUILT LIKE THAT?

Summer of 1991 Lorain, Ohio

Phone rings four times; a female answers...

Female: "Hello?"

Caller: "Hello? Yo what's up? Is Shakim in?"

Female: "Hold on a minute... Shakim get the phone!"

I get on the phone.

ME: "Yo!"

Caller: "Yo, what up niggah?"

ME: "Yo ███████ what up son, what's goin' on?"

Caller: "Nothin', nothin' niggah, I'm just callin' to see what's up, you know?"

ME: "Nah niggah, I don't know. You called me long distance from N. Y. to see what's up?"

Caller: (laughing) "Ha, ha, ha, ha! You a funny niggah! What, I can't call my niggahs? I aint tell you no bullshit when you were callin' me from jail with the war stories niggah."

We both laughed.

ME: "Yo ██████ what up though?"

Caller: "Yo, where our niggah at? I need to talk to him."

ME: "Our niggah don't live here."

Caller: "I know, I know, I just need to talk to that niggah."

ME: "What's up?"

Caller: "Yo Sha, let me ask you somethin'... do you have anything comin' down?"

ME: "Nah son, why?"

Caller: "Do that niggah got somethin' comin' down, is he expectin' somethin'?"

ME: "Not that I know of..."

Caller: "You sure?"

ME: "Yeah niggah, why?"

Caller: "Yo, I'ma tell you some ill shit. (hard exhale) Yo, I know someone who got some THINGS and they're tryna get rid of 'em, like... now!"

ME: "Yeah? Who?"

Caller: "Niggah, between me and you, I just robbed my main man Irving."

ME: "Huh?"

Caller: "Man, it's fucked up in N.Y. I got a wife and kids... I'm tryna get dough too."

ME: "fuck is you talkin' about?"

Caller: "Man that niggah Irv put me on to some game about him bringin' work down for y'all, he tells me about every trip. Your manz won't fuck with me and he knows I got a car and need to make dough."

ME: "What you mean, you robbed Irv?"

Caller: "Niggah told me about how y'all put the joints in the front and back bumpers, nigga told me everything. You know he talks too much, he tells me when he's goin' and everything. So I was with your manz last weekend and mentioned how I could drive and he said he was straight... said he don't need no shit nowhere. I asked him if he needed shit moved anytime soon and he said nah but Irv told me he's comin' down with some shit. So if it aint y'all shit its ███████ shit, unless your manz lied to me."

ME: "I'm not understandin' you, how you robbed him?"

Caller: "Listen Sha, shut the fuck up and let me finish tellin' you the shit, crazy ass niggah! Anyways, I'm in N.Y. fucked up, this nigga keeps tellin' me he's drivin' to Ohio with some shit...talkin' 'bout the bumpers got work in them so last night me and ███████ came through Irv's block with some tools. I don't know how to steal no car like y'all thievin' ass niggahs, you know y'all some thievin' ass niggas, right? But anyways, I took the bumpers off, shit was crazy. I took three of them things, I put the back bumper back on but when I put the front bumper back on I didn't tighten it up because Irv's lights (in the house) came on. Man, I feel fucked up for doin' that... I robbed my own manz. He about to go out there and it aint gon' be no shit, ha ha! He's drivin' down there for nothin'! Yo, you wanna buy this shit from me?"

ME: "Yo, you lyin' son."

Caller: "Word to my seeds, I took that shit. Ask ███████ if he wanna buy it. That niggah aint call me back and I beeped him twenty times. I know he's out there, I'm tryna get rid of this shit."

ME: "You a dirty niggah son!"

Caller: "Niggah, I'll rob you too! Ha, ha, ha, ha, ha!"

ME: "Niggah, I will blast you, bitch ass niggah."

We laughed.
ME: "Yo, give the shit back ███████. You gotta give it back to him, that's your manz."

Caller: "Fuck that! That's my manz and I'm out here starvin'! I got kids to feed, fuck that!"

ME: "Fuck you!"

Caller: "Yo, call me back, I'm tryna make moves in the rotten apple, I'm a king pin now!"

-click.

* * * * *

"I'm the flyest... Always ranked highest...
when it comes to kickin' lyrics I could never be the dryest"

1985

CHAPTER 2

The Underground Rap scene in Queens was definitely crazy and off the scale. You had some real raw cats that could spit and they were reppin' Queens to the fullest. This was around the 1984 – 1988 era and a fella like me was tryna be in the middle of it all. I'm not screamin' I was the illest emcee but I was ill in my own kind of way. Back in 83' – 84', I was kickin' "God Body rhymes", had my battle joints but I was more into kickin' righteous raps that dealt with the "120 Lessons" and sciences of that nature... believe me, **NOBODY** could see me in that league. Once I got kicked out of Murray Bergtraum High School in Manhattan, I went to Beach Channel High in Rockaway Beach, Queens. It was a couple cats that could spit but none of them was fuckin' with the kid (me). My deejay back then, was Master Born Cee a.k.a. "Thunder Cuts" went to school there as well as my manz Master Dee from Bay Towers.

I got kicked out of Beach Channel too so next I went to Far Rockaway High School. The underground rap scene there was bananas, we used to go to different schools lookin' for a battle; a fight with lyrics. We would go ten, sometimes twenty deep to any high school lookin' for "elite" emcees. It was always three or four dudes who claimed to possess some kinda rhyme ability, only to get destroyed. It was crowds outside like a fight was about to go down; all the B-Boys, B-Girls and whoever wanted to eyewitness and hear the exchange of verbal wordplay would be out there. Sometimes, we got brave and went inside the school's cafeteria or in the staircases to spit, on some "Fame" (old school television show and recently remade film). Niggahs, was serious like that back then, me and my clique was so ill that after the battle or... skills display, we would wild out by snatchin' jewelry such as chains, name brand frame glasses, earrings and whatever... we were ill like that.

There were different wordsmith assassins in Queens who were known back in the mid-eighties. Holdin' down Far Rock was a cat named "Father M.C.", who later became my associate and sometimes he was my rhyme partner; Son (Father) was vicious and had the whole Far Rockaway on his dick, he was a rap God. Jamaica, Queens had a few ill spitters like L.L. Cool J, who went to Andrew Jackson High School and held Farmers Boulevard down. In the Laurelton section (Merrick Blvd) was a cat named "Mikey Dee" and his LA (Laurelton) Posse, son was a light-skinned, grey-eyed, pretty boy thug niggah that was ill with the lyrics. He and L.L. had some personal shit between them and had been goin' at it for years before "L" even got a record deal. There was another cat named "Vitamin C" or "Vitamin B", I don't recall exactly which one or what school he went to but I used to see him up at other schools lookin' for battles. One time I bumped into him in front of Hillcrest High and I had to scorch him. There was another Emcee from Hollis, Queens named "MC Romeo", he later changed his name to "Roe Dog"; son was ill too. Roe had a deejay named "DJ Irv", who was also from Hollis. Roe was an olive colored, curly haired cat, who thought he was a pretty boy so much that he called himself "Romeo". I heard son spit a few times and he had big props in Hollis, even Run-DMC recognized him and gave him props. Roe had mega juice and it wasn't long before he ran into me "**Sha Bio**".

I was battlin' crazily as part of a rap group out of Far Rock, Edgemere Projects. God Supreme and General Born Gee were the "**Almighty 2 MC's**" and they had a lot of homemade tapes floatin' around. I was spittin' with Master Dee but the deal was I was also penning son's rhymes at the time. We were makin' tapes at Master Born Cee's crib because he had deejay equipment. I ran into the Almighty 2 and we were buildin' on some mathematics, we later exchanged lyrics and they felt my shit so much that we became the "**Almighty 3 MC's**" but that shit aint last long because they had their routine and I wasn't with tryna fit in with them or with them hoggin' the mic, exchangin' their routines so when it was my turn I went dolo (solo) and kicked ten straight raps back to back. To keep the peace, I slid from the group but we later linked back up.

Born Cee had a crew, I forgot their name but it consisted of "Rasheem Supreme", "Knowledge-Power" and "Master Freak". I used to sit at Born Cee's crib and watch them makin' tapes and doin' their thing; they used to let me rock there from time to time. Hammels projects had "**Mr. T and the funky A-Team**", which consisted of Just-Ice's half-brother "B.I. Self Allah", "Everlasting" and "Lord Imperial". They were doin' parties at the Police Athletic League in Far Rockaway and at the trade school in Five Towns. Redfern p.j's had the "**True and Living MC's**" and Father MC had a deejay from Far Rock's "40 Projects" named "Shamel Shateek".

I used to listen to 98.7 Kiss FM's Red Alert and Chuck ChillOut. I listened to 107.5 WBLS' Mr. Magic (R.I.P.) and Marley Marl. I also caught Mr. Magic when he was on WHBI 105.9 along with "The Awesome 2 Special K and Teddy Ted", The Hank Love Radio Show, The World Famous Supreme Team Show with "Just Allah the superstar" and "Cee Divine the Mastermind" and all the rap shows on 88.1. I would be up late nights tapin' shit, keepin' up with everything that had to do with the Underground Rap Scene. One night I heard a broadcast of a talent show where they were lookin' for the best rappers from the five boroughs to battle for five hundred dollars and a recording contract. I wrote the number down and I said "I'ma be there!" My mom was givin' a fella a headache for real around this time, not understanding my life, culture, art and love for the streets. Both my parents are natives of the island of Jamaica and worked very hard to get where they are. Moms couldn't put up with my shit and I was gettin' tired of her strict rules and bullshit that came along so a fella was on very thin ice at home.

One day after ridin' around with my enlightener "Lord Shaheim Wise", we bumped into "Lord Imperial", who was a member of the Funky A-Team, me and the God were tight like family. I wanted him to hear my shit and he was already on Ghetto Celeb Status in the hood and beyond so I spitted 2 raps and left him so fucked up he told me to call him the next day, we were cuttin' school to go to Born Cee's to make a tape in his house and that particular homemade demo tape ended up spreadin' all over Queens. I had tapes with Father MC, Lord Imperial and Rasheem Supreme, these cats had demo tapes in the mix; I was just a street spitter trying to shine. I gave myself a title that I introduced on the beginning of all homemade tapes. I spitted **"Check 1-2, 1-2, yes, yes, y'all you are now listening to the sounds of the latest, greatest, freshest, highest, flyest, divinest, New York's Finest rhyme designest and royal microphone's highness, the Lord Shakim Bio-Chemical Wise, with Master Dee and the most incredible Deejay Master Born Cee a.k.a. Thunder Cuts!"**. I brought these tapes along with Master Dee to mid-town Manhattan to meet the promoter of the talent show that I heard on the radio show. The promoter's name was "**Mr. Squeeze**" and the name of the hip hop club was "**The Beat Street Squeeze**" on 42nd street (the deuce) between 7th & 8th ave above a bodega (store). Around this time I also became acquainted with Mr. Squeeze's daughter, we used to talk on the phone and she thought she could rap. I spitted for her and shorty was in love from then on but anyway, the Beat Street Squeeze was a nice big space that held about fifteen hundred to two thousand people maybe more; it was some real fire hazard shit at that time.

I showed up to audition one night with Master Dee, there was a long ass line with so many heads but I had called twenty times, finally got through and convinced Mr. Squeeze to sign me up for the talent show so we didn't have to wait on the line cause he was waiting for me. I had been to Squeeze's Manhattan Condo before I even signed up for the talent show, he let me skip like fifty acts that were waiting to audition so I was there in front of Squeeze and some other cats. I spitted like three raps for Squeeze, he shook my hand and was like "you are in!" Master Dee aint have to say shit (not even "Check 1-2"). Then after talkin' about Hip Hop, I pulled out the tape and we went in the back to listen to it. After listening, Squeeze begged me to let him keep the tape, he asked "Can you get these people down here to rhyme like this?" I told him "you motherfuckin' right!!!" so he changed my shit from bein' part of the talent show to puttin' my name on the flyer. I later got a job at his next jump-off "**The Rap Attack**" in Brooklyn and I got my name "**Shakim Bio-Chemical**" and the Almighty 2 MC's on the Rap Attack grand opening flyer. On the Beat Street Squeeze flyer it was "**The Magnetic Peace Brothers**", which was me and Master Dee, we were on the flyer and that shit was all over the radio in N.Y.C. The only thing was, I couldn't get Father MC to come, he couldn't come due to his grandmoms wasn't havin' him goin' to a night club to rock and we were "kids" (in her mind).

My mom wasn't feelin' the idea of me goin' to an N.Y.C. club either, she wasn't havin' it... I played our tape for her and she thought it was a real record until I told her it was **me**. I couldn't get Imperial to come to the show either, he was workin' a job and hustlin' on the side but he did give me money to get a sweat suit to match my new sneakers and I already had a sterling silver name plate that read "Wise", short for my attribute, "**Lord Shakim Bio-Chemical Wise**"; Imperial also gave me a pair of gold glasses to rep hard. I got Born Cee to deejay and at the last minute, Rasheem Supreme came through with us. We went to the show like ten deep and the spot was packed, this was the first time I was gonna spit and be heard in a real club in front of the five boroughs. Mr. Squeeze was sweatin' me all night and at the last minute, DJ Born Cee couldn't get on because he didn't know how to use the knob mixer; he didn't want to mess up our set. They only gave us ten minutes so we had to use the house deejay but we brought our own records, we came through with real classic break beats. Before we went on, one of the members of the "**DisMaster Crew**" from Brooklyn pulled me to the side and asked me to keep it straight lyrics **no dissing,** he kept shakin' my hand and all that. When they introduced us... **WE ROCKED THAT BITCH!!!** We had the crowd open as me and Dee did our rap routine, then I spitted crazily and gave Rasheem his shine. Rah tore shit down, all the ladies was like "**AAAHHH!!**" Niggahs was like "**HOOOOO!!!!**" I went on and tore up the break beat "**Pussy Footer**", we had that spot fucked up, we just knew we won!!!

Man, the DisMaster Crew got their ten minutes and it turned into twenty. They rocked it and then flipped, got the deejay to turn the music down and they asked the crowd **"Who's the Magnetic Peace Brothers?"** **"They're from Queens!"** Man it was HECK-O my NECK THOUGH after they said **"QUEENS"**. Queens wasn't gettin' no props in the mid-eighties, especially from a BK crowd. Not only did we lose but my mom had to drive her Benz up to Manhattan to pick us up cause shit was kind of ill outside the club after all that. Regardless, niggahs knew my name, respected my handle and Mr. Squeeze respected my gangster, he still put me on when he opened **"The Rap Attack"** in BK. Like a year or two later, the DisMaster Crew came out with a record called "Small Time Hustler", which got airplay on WBLS / Mr. Magic's rap show. The shit was "alright", yeah I was hatin' on them and I still am cause WE WON that MC battle! The only reason DisMasters got over was cause they screamed **"BROOKLYN!!!"** and we were from Queens... **Fuck dem niggahs,** they wasn't really like that and their **one hit wonder** wasn't even a hit, they never came out again, they probably started smokin' crack or some shit.

* * * * *

CHAPTER 3

I got kicked out of school and transferred to August Martin High School in Jamaica, Queens. I crushed like ten emcees on my first day there. The word was out, they were sweatin' the kid (me) cause I rocked with Father MC and held mine down at a five borough battle (even though I lost). I started walkin' around the school like I was an **All Star** and I hooked up with cats from Rochdale Village on Guy R. Brewer Blvd. My dogs from section five; David, Cletus and a couple heads, my manz NaQuan and my next manz the God La-Be from Ocean Village in Far Rock. I was comin' to school all laced up with gold frames, gold teeth, leather pants, Kangols, I was all that and then some, I stayed dipped. Then shit got ugly, after battlin' in the lunchroom, with Rochdale holdin' my back (La-Bee didn't come to school that day), I came out the door and a kid hit me in the face with a fucking chair, WWF style! I whooped his ass but still, my face was like "whoa!" I had the crazy black eye, swollen lip, crazy shit in front of the chicks. I held it down though, after that we both got suspended, it was a Hollis – Southside beef.

The kid I fucked up was from Hollis and he thought I was from Southside. Every day after that, I had a crew in front of the school waitin' on me (most of the time). I was all jeweled up, still rockin' with a black eye and all. I held it down as a young thug. Me and my team was goin' up to Springfield High School, Jamaica high, Hillcrest, Bayside, Edison and John Adams yo, I did my thing but dough was low. I was failing in school and pussy was getting' me into a lot of trouble. I didn't have no record contract, my manz Master Supreme moved from my old hood in Brooklyn to my hood in Queens. We knew each other from the BK, he used to roll with some of my BK fam so when he moved to Queens, I gave him knowledge of self. I named him Master Supreme Cee Allah. Master Supreme Cee had equipment; that up to date shit but niggahs was broke and the streets was callin'.

A lot of shit changed up for the kid in the middle of 86'. I fell back for a minute but still was doin' my thing. I started gettin' caught up on catchin' cases; assaults, robberies, little bullshits and I wasn't kickin' no God Body raps no more either, I was on some street shit and shit was official. Then out of nowhere, I went into fulltime hustlin'. I had been pushin' nicks and dime bags of weed and slingin' little tens, twenties and fifties of powder since late 84'-85' but now I was rockin' the hood with the crack game and you couldn't tell a niggah **NATHAN**! Around this time, I was pushin' work for my manz in Far Rock in a housing project called "Hammels". A niggah had spots all over that bitch (Hammels PJ's)! I also had shit in the sixties and I just started tryna pump on Farmers Blvd. Around this time I was runnin' with a cat from Farmers named **Al Monday**, who I met through my student Master Supreme. Me and that cat Al built a solid relationship and was grindin' crazily. Son was a vicious car thief who could push cars and get away in any kind of speed chase. I kept the guns that were supposed to hold the Far Rock crack spots down. I had heaters, Al had the cars... you smell what I smell? **ROBBERIES**!

Me and Monday was light-weight illing, touchin' every borough at night fall, goin' from **Uptown to your town. FUCK YOU! Gimme the loot and ya' fuckin' jewels!** I was pullin' guns for fun, takin' niggah's walkmans **Fuck that!** All this and I still had work on the block and held spots down. Remember, I said you couldn't tell the kid **Nathan**? Well at that time, Nathan better not talk or he was gettin' it too! Through that niggah Al Monday, I met a lot of good cats. I met Harold "Hype" Williams, who was a light-skinned fly guy and graffiti niggah sprayin' up every wall with "HYPE", son was good peeps. I met Daymond John, who is now the C.E.O. of FUBU. We called that nigga "Leery Dee" cause he was down with whatever but he was always leery. I met Carl Brown and J. Alexander Martin, who we called "Jalex", all from FUBU (wasn't no FUBU in 85'-86'). Back in 87', Me and Jalex got arrested together on The Duece (42nd st in Mid-Town) on some assault on a police officer, criminal damaging and some next shit. I met quite a few niggahs, we were taggin' along, comin' through rap concerts while they (rappers) were on tour. We would drive out of state to catch up with certain rappers like L.L. Cool J and Run-DMC, we had the hook-ups through either Big Mookie from Hollis, who was body guarding niggahs or through "L" himself. Niggahs was showin' mad love so we would come through and rep. We bagged mad honies and started comin' through like "what!" in Philadelphia, D.C., Baltimore, wherever.

Around this time big "dooky" gold ropes was it and that was what we were takin' off of your neck; that and nugget bracelets, rings and watches and we was pawnin' all that bullshit, we kept some of it though. I was heavy on the neck, niggahs around me was callin' me "Forty" cause I always kept a forty ounce of beer (Old English 800). You could drive by a thousand times and see me on the corner slingin' with a forty in my hand. Niggahs would be amongst themselves bettin' I had the same forty from an hour ago, only to lose by askin' me for a sip and when I'd hand it to them, it was ice cold. I drank maybe fifteen – twenty forty ounces a day (seriously), my line was "My name is Shakim Bio-Chemical, how you livin'?" Niggahs used to bug out cause I always said that shit. "My name is Shakim Bio-Chemical, How you livin'? cause I'm livin' like every day is Thanksgiving!" Niggahs eyes used to pop open as I said "Yo! Let's go get a forty!"

I can't recall if it was Queens Day or what, I just knew they had some kind of summer jam or show at Roy Wilkins Park on Merrick Boulevard so I jumped in the 300E Benz with my manz and we was out. It was some free, outdoor shit and I came through with a forty oz. It was females everywhere and a lot of vendors sellin' shit. I had on a big dooky gold rope, a four finger ring (stolen) and brand new kicks on. My manz & dem King Kasheem, Nike and Funky Phade from the Almighty Shirt Kings was there sellin' shirts and shit, those was my niggahs. I left the park about four or five times to go to the store to buy ice cold forties. That cat from X-Clan who says "This is Protected by the Red, the Black and the Green, with a KEY… Sissssyyy!" was there with Daddy – O of Stetsasonic, who was hostin' a talent show in the park. It wasn't all that but mad females was there, mad cats from all over was out there. I saw L.L.'s Benz out there so I knew Farmers Blvd was out there too. Mad cars was goin' up and down the streets, they even had ill backgrounds to take photos in front of for $5 a pop. I was everywhere, Yo! The talent show had mad honies in it and there was a step show jumpin' off. Daddy – O and that X Clan cat were givin' out free records and by then, I was drunk and charged up. I ran into my manz & dem from Farmers, Ralo (Bumps), Flo and about twenty other Farmers representatives was there, they hugged me, showed me mad love and it was mad fortics bein' passed around.

We were a few feet from the stage, makin' so much noise, screamin' "**FARRRMERRRS!!!**" that I never heard Daddy – O ask us to quiet down... like a hundred times. He even got live and told us to **shut up**. I was guzzlin' a forty when all of a sudden, Daddy – O screamed "**You with the 40 ounce!**" The whole park looked at me and the music went off. I'm lookin' around with my forty in hand like "huh?" Daddy – O pointed at me and said "**Yea you! Come up here!**" I'm like "what!? Nah!" Farmers crew was like "**GO! GO! GO! GO! GO! GO! GO! GO! GO! GO! GO! GO!!**" It sounded like the whole park was sayin' "GO" so I said "Fuck it!" I snatched me a fresh cold forty from one of the Farmers crew and made my way up on stage. Daddy – O was pointin' to me, tellin' the crowd some b.s. about how blacks be reppin' us and Hip Hop wrong and that's why we can't get shows now and blah, blah blah. I took a guzzle of my forty and the whole park went crazy. I took the mic and told son he was wack and I would battle him and blaze him in front of everybody. Daddy – O had a look on his face like "who?" I took another guzzle and said "My name is Shakim Bio-Chemical, how you livin'?" Daddy – O looked at me and asked "You righteous?" I said "yea and I know and understand 120 lessons, now how you livin'? Cause I'm livin' like every day is Thanksgiving!" the crowd was screamin' as I proceeded to guzzle my forty, suds and all right there on stage.

Far Rock niggahs and Farmers niggahs was yellin' "**GO! GO! GO! Shakim GO!**" I started takin' the free records out of the jackets and throwin' them like frisbies, then everybody started doin' it, it was crazy! Daddy – O and that X Clan niggah started screamin' for the crowd to chill. After a while the crowd cooled down, I was still on stage standin' there... the X Clan cat said "If one more record is thrown the show is over!!!" Why did he say that? Cause out of nowhere, about fifty records flew at him on stage. Daddy – O said "That's it, the show is over!!!" Niggahs started walkin' away from the stage towards the vendors and other attractions. Daddy – O came towards me with his hand outreached for a handshake. Man, I dropped the mic, looked at him, turned my back and left. He was lucky cause I had a hundred street stories and I was livin' it, I was a G Rap / ODB (Ol' Dirty Bastard) mixed up in one niggah, I would have crushed him for "Talking all that Jazz".

I've always been a Kool G Rap fan, still am, WORD LIFE! Yo, I remember G Rap used to be in Lamour East, a big club like Latin Quarters but it was in Flushing, Queens. It was G Rap, Super Lover Cee and Casanova Rudd, Kid & Play, they were always in that club. Around that time I was messin' with one of Kid & Play's dancers named Erin Washington, shorty was on my dick hard but was frontin'. This particular day me and Monday went to the Coliseum on Jamaica ave to do some light weight shoppin' cause I was tryna get him to go to Lamour East to see G Rap and dem. While we were there I got my new cable (fat gold chain), got my gold teeth cleaned and I got crazy dipped with the new kicks; I kept brand new kicks on every day. I had a shorty who worked in the Coliseum, which is a flea market mall with mad vendors sellin' clothes, kicks, jewelry, food, music, everything! They even had a barber shop and beauty salon in there, shit, they probably had coke down there too. My shorty's name was Vicky Jackson, her pops owned the photo spot downstairs in the Coliseum and everybody took flicks there. If you wanted your face spray painted on your shirt or gear by the Almighty Shirt Kings they were also in the Coliseum. Vicky was two or three years younger than me but you couldn't tell because she looked older, she was mature and she could stay out all night. I loved shorty like cooked food, she was "all of it".

Me and Monday got right at the mall and got back to the crib, showered and got geared. I'm like "what's up for tonight my niggah?" He was like "whatever" I'm like "Lamour East to see G Rap!" He said "yea, yea, yeah" but the only catch to it was Vicky wanted to go and Monday aint have no chick that wanted to go hear no Kool G Rap so me bein' the ill niggah and pimp that I am, got Vicky's sister to go up there with him. She was kind of workin' with somethin' but she was a few months pregnant, she wasn't showin' though. We ill niggahs, that shit aint mean nothin', we was gon' bag mad shorties up there anyway and we was goin' with chicks, "what!!" Anyway, we got to the club and I left the heater (gun) in the whip cause wasn't no gettin' it in. Super Lover Cee and dem was cool, Kid & Play did a little somethin'. Then out of nowhere, MC Romeo came up on stage. Yea, that niggah from Hollis, he went up there with a motorcycle helmet in his hand and started spittin' with no beat. Hollis was screamin' **"GO! GO! GO! GO!"**

Some niggahs wasn't feelin' Roe as he was onstage givin' dap to niggahs who was reachin' out to him. Out of nowhere, Roe threw the mic down and smacked a niggah with the motorcycle helmet. That's some foul shit, **getting' smacked by a helmet at the club in front of about three thousand people.** Hollis was screamin' **"Hollis! Hollis!"** Security had to calm shit down, me and Monday looked at each other. Wasn't long before G Rap and Polo tore the spot down and I sang along with all that G Rap shit. I had on a grey Champion sweat suit, some Nikes, a blue Yankee cap and a Yankee Starter jacket with my cable hanging out like **"What!"** Monday had the black Champion jump off. Yo, after G Rap did his thing, he threw the mic down, jumped off the stage with his crew and left. Everybody started walkin' towards the back, I was standin' there in the middle of everything like I'm "like that" (I am!), when a little short niggah walked by and bumped into me... I grabbed shorty on some "yo you can't say sorry?" Yo, a BIG niggah who was with shorty just swung and I was fightin' like fifty niggahs! Shit was crazy! Vicky ran for shelter as Sha Bio fought and repped (I got mine but I also got stomped).

Monday came out of nowhere like we was Batman and Robin niggahs until security came in and pushed us outside. I saw twenty niggahs from Farmers, I'm like "Yo, we got beef!" Niggahs was like "whatever, let's do it!" My manz said "Yo, where's your chain?" I felt my neck and my chain was gone, I FLIPPED!! "Yo!!!" That night Lamour East got shut down for GOOD. It was mad shootin' and even after the police came the shots wouldn't stop, we were wildin'; shit made the papers. People were runnin' every where. I snatched about a hundred earrings and came home with ten fat gold ropes. We were bruised up and sore but I took Vicky to the hotel and wore that ass out. The next day, I was all sore and hurt, I went to the Coliseum to get the stolen jewelry fixed and cleaned and then I went to O'connor Park off of 198th / 199th st and Murdock ave to see what was happenin'. As I was walkin' with the Farmers crew, I had on like five of the dooky ropes I caught the previous night at Lamour East. When we got Farners and 112th, I saw niggahs standin' on the block, a fat light-skinned cat screamed and pointed at me... "That's him! That's that ill niggah from last night! That niggah is ill!!!" The fat cat was DJ Irv and in the mix of niggahs was MC Romeo (Roe Dog), who approached me "Yo, what's up Sha? I saw you last night, you got busy!" I said "Yo what up, I'm Shakim Bio-Chemical, how you livin'? Let's go get a forty!" From there... it was **ON**.

* * * * *

CHAPTER 4

At a later date, on the phone with ████████

ME: "Yo what up doe? You still king pin of the Rotten Apple?"

████████: "Yo, my niggah, I sold a half a brick! I'm happy now, the kid got some money so my wife and kids could stop the mothafuckin' cryin' and shut the fuck up!"

ME: "Damn ██████, you went and bust open one of dem things and sold half? You know you put Irv in a situation where niggahs may have to smash him, shit is crazy!"

████████: "I know, I know, I feel fucked up about it Sha... my niggah... but ya manz is fucked up out here. I been told that I'm a niggah so long that I became one and started acting like one. That niggah "Bunz" called me last night on some give the shit back shit but I was like, what shit? Ha, Ha, Ha, Ha! Now I'm one of him now, I can play games too. I know you told that niggah I got that shit too cause now he is callin' me talkin' 'bout give it back. I'm not givin' a mothafuckin' crumb back niggah! Ha, Ha!"

ME: "Duke, you called me lookin' for him plus you said you was beepin' him."

████████: "Right, right, niggah you're right about that plus that niggah Irv been callin' my crib like crazy buggin' my wife and he called my mom's crib. He probably done lost like fifty pounds sweatin' like crazy but ██████ is ass and he aint gonna hurt that niggah."

ME: "Yo ██████ said it was four joints, you told me you found three, which is it?"

████: "It was three joints, I'm a thirsty niggah and I was hungry, I aint gotta lie about what I took. I would have been happy with one but the niggah side of me got greedy plus I had ████ and ████ with me so I had to give them one to split."

ME: "Damn kid, you gave ████ one too? You fuckin' sick son!"

████: Yea, yea, I know but I aint broke no more so shit is good. Yo, call me back, my beeper is beepin'… I'm a busy niggah now… here take my beeper number niggah! Beep me and wait in line for me to call you back, 7-1-8-6-4-4-6-2-█-█, you got that?

ME: "6-2-█-█ yea, I got it. I will be at you. Later!"

-click.

* * * * *

Roe was a thug cat on the sly… he really wanted to put his hands in with the ill shit that we were into so without further delay, son was runnin' around doin' this and that. I am not the kind of man to put son out there on what exactly went down or what role he played but son was definitely official and I can vouch for his street credibility (whatever the fuck that means) to a certain extent. I've seen him pull some cowardly acts as well, which I told him I wouldn't expose but anyway Romeo was a niggah who had dreams of makin' it as the illest MC, he was the ladies' Romeo. He was respected throughout Jamaica, Queens by his peers, he was a part of the younger Hollis crew and son was family too. He got his long time, childhood love pregnant and was put in a situation by both his and her parents, who were tellin' him to marry her. That was how his family got down so by like eighteen or nineteen years old, son was married; a family man with a wife and children to take care of and feed but he was still tryna stay a street niggah and live up to bein' the illest MC. I saw Run of "Run DMC" give this niggah Ro props and Jam Master Jay showed this niggah crazy love. Roe was supposed to be "that niggah" but he wasn't, he was in the streets livin' that street life, tryna get on and keep money so crimes was committed and shit got funky.

Roe's manz Irv was another story... Irv was a deejay, nothing more, nothin' less. He made beats by sampling and looping then he made mix tapes; he was good at what he did, music. When shit went down, he was reliable because he had a car but he was a regular ass cat from Hollis and was known for his deejay skills. He later got recognition for fuckin' with real live niggahs (US!) cause he looked up to Al Monday. Al let Irv in and accepted him or should I say... formed his own circle and made Irv a part of it where Irv felt secure bein' in the midst of real live niggahs. Don't get me wrong, he wasn't actually a soft cat, there were potentials for him to become an ill cat but it wasn't his type or in him at the time. Irv's thing was bein' in the presence of ill cats that made shit happen so he got up close and personal with some of the struggles and experiences niggahs went through.

Now remember, I was hustlin' hard so me and Monday went out of state for a week or two. We hit places like Philadelphia tryna make shit happen but nothin' really jumped off like we thought it would. We even hit Florida for a few weeks but ended up getting' locked up in Jacksonville, we did like a month or so in the county jail down there. I had the same respect in jail as I did on the streets, I was a real live cat and very likeable; I'm a "**Brooklyn nigga from Queens**". I was born in Brooklyn and raised in Queens but a lot of the Brooklyn griminess can be seen in my ways and actions. I used to call Roe from Jails and hit him with war stories, which he incorporated into his raps. He had a joint where he spit "I been on Rikers Island and never been razor bladed!!" Knowin' that niggah aint NEVER go nowhere near the Island, not even on a visit. I called Roe while I was in numerous Ohio, South Carolina and Baltimore jails, even called him once when I was in jail in Minnesota; been callin' him since I've been in the Federal system.

I was the only one in our circle who stayed in jail (nothin' to brag about, just sayin'). I been on the island (Rikers) three or four times for charges ranging from gun possession, assaults, drugs, robberies, whatever... I been a jail niggah and always called

Roe to tell him I was holding it down and how when I went back home to those mean N.Y. streets I was gonna step my game back up. I was pushin' weight in coke and cracks so I journeyed with my manz and dem from Far Rockaway to a little town in Ohio called "Lorain". That shit was "La la land" to a fella like me so we went in head first and took over the crack trade immediately. You know how them N.Y. niggahs is, "**when the east is in the house, oh my god!!**"

Monday, Ro and dem was still up in N.Y. and Sha-Bio was in Lorain, Ohio **BUBBLING**! It wasn't long before I became homesick though, I missed my niggahs and my niggahs missed me. I was goin' back to N.Y. every now and then but more then than now so a lot of things changed; objectives and goals were different. Around this time Monday wanted to be an emcee, while I was a full time thug. Niggahs was still thuggin' but goals changed. I wanted to be the illest drug dealer with the fame and fortune, other cats wanted to use rap as an outlet to release their illness and get dough that way. It wasn't about props no more it was all about the dough. Props couldn't feed, clothe you or pay the fuckin' bills so now with Monday steppin' up his rhyme game and Roe still spittin' more… more crimes had to be committed cause niggahs wanted money for studio time. Yea, believe it or not, those cats was usin' dough for studio time to cut demos and shit. "Crime about it, rhyme about it, shine about it," shit was real. Monday was the illest car thief so cars was stolen and used as getaway joints. Niggahs hit the studio most of the day, settin' shit up and crimin' at night but I didn't wanna be an emcee no more, I still had the gift but I was huggin' the block out of town too much so for a minute, niggahs was out of tune cause one was a thug MC and the others was MC thugs (what's the difference?) but we were still niggahs for life.

* * * * *

When I would go back to N.Y. for personal issues and shit, sometimes I would go up to Farmers Blvd to check up on old associates and catch up on shit. I always heard my peeps and dem was into some ill shit and at the same time they had demo tapes buzzin' around the hood. I would see Monday come around with his entourage; my manz Phat Jon, Stoney, Terrell from O.V., Roe Dog and every now and then Irv would be there. You could tell these niggahs was on some bullshit, lookin' around like they were duckin' somethin' and they would bounce real quick on some "Yo kid what's up? Yo, meet me on the block though, we out!" These niggahs was tryna remain unseen during the day as much as possible. When and if you saw them, they were comin' through on the low. These cats was either splittin' up the money made from the last lick, gettin' rid of jewels and whatever, then plannin' on hittin' the studios to put together tracks and lyrics for demos. I was still in and out of town doin' what I was doin' but I understood the seriousness of what they were doin'.

One time, Monday, my manz "Hi-C" and a couple of heads were on their way to Chicago and they came through Ohio to see me. Hi-C had just started rhymin' and was makin' his bones; he was later featured on a posse cut called "Comin' Back to Farmers" on L.L. Cool J's "Mama said Knock You Out" album. It was L.L, Hi-C, my other manz "Big Money Grip", who was another cat who was comin' up on the underground scene, they were spittin' on a Marley Marl track. The cut was butta cause the cats on it repped the hood but for real, for real... that joint aint make it nowhere. Hi-C was still doin' crime and got locked up north before "L" even started his tour. Anyway, dem cats came through and told me of their mission, I was like "Yeah?" I was so impressed that on the low, I started pennin' new lyrics but the drug money was lovely and I quickly forgot about writin' rhymes again for a minute, I still kept up with the music though.

When I went back to N.Y.C. for the summer of 1990 I was on the run, duckin' a bullshit case I had in Ohio; it was only six months jail time. I was chillin' back and forth between Far Rock and Farmers. I would link up with a cat named Ivan a.k.a.

"Connivin" a.k.a. "Ive" (R.I.P.). "Ive" was official, known for bein' buck wild and lettin' his guns buss. Sometimes I would be be up on Farmers sittin' on the "Flo" can with Ralo, Flo, Takim and Donald, talkin' mad shit, drinkin' forties like it was still "88" and L.L. would pull up in his white Benz and kick it with us for a few hours. He would let us hear some of his new material and we used to give him our opinions. Rappers were just getting' out of that X Clan, De La Soul, Public Enemy, Native Tongue, leather medallion era rap thing. Now the props was goin' to whoever had the most money and shit, it was all about the dough. One night we were mixin' forty ounces of Old English with Guinness Stout (Cano'E) and I told "L" that fuckin' with me, I'd have him on B.E.T. sittin' with Donnie Simpson and he was laughin', not takin' me seriously, like I was jokin' or something but I was dead-ass. I wrote some ill shit and "L" needed a hit, we guzzled our forties and just left it at that but I could see he was peepin' me out of the corner of his eye. I pointed to myself and said "yeah" he laughed and said I had "more game than Parker Brothers". Years later, in November 1993, I was again tellin' "L" about DJ Irv from Hollis, who had an underground track out called "Shit Is Real" and on the B side "Hemmin' Heads" with an MC called "Mic Geronimo". I was helpin' Monday and Irv promote the joint.

One late night, me and "L" was in "King Georges" diner in Flushing, Queens. I was with my shorty Danielle, he was already in there with his manager at the time, Brian Latiure. I told him about DJ Irv, L's manager heard of Irv but "L" said he never heard of him and that he was comfortable with Marley Marl. He asked me if Irv made mix tapes and gave me his business card, which read "Uncle L Records"; he was tryna establish his own label and joint called "MurderGram" with Big Money Grip bein' his first artist. I know later in life when Irv blew up and became one of Def Jam's greatest assets with his Murder Inc. Label and all his acts and production, "L" probably was mumblin' to himself "**Damn! I was told about that niggah years ago...**" He may act like he don't remember but after readin' this shit he will. "L" was a real niggah when we were around each other and he kept the jokes but overall he was cool.

* * * * *

CHAPTER 5

Back it up to 1990… Monday had a song called "This is for my niggahs"; shit was tight for that time. Irv did the production, shit… Monday had a few joints that was buzzin' around the hood and throughout Queens. The only cats that could get the songs was niggahs from the hood cause his demo tape wasn't put out there for anything but the streets. Al Monday, the downtown car thief, even had a song with that title, word life! I was in Ohio with a copy of his shit. I made up my mind to start fuckin' with my niggahs again especially after hearin' a cut with Monday and Roe called "Street Life", **shit was bananas**! Then to make it more official, at the end of the song he said "**My manz Shakim Bio-Chemical is in Lorain, Ohio livin' that Street Life!**" I called around the way and sent word that Sha Bio was lookin' for him and within minutes I had his beeper, cellular and home numbers. Al was my manz, we always stayed in touch even after I was gettin' on with my thing and catchin' cases out of town. One time after I called him from jail, son (Monday) sold his Acura Legend to send me money to bail out; he was left with a motorcycle as transportation. After he sent me the dough, I called him he told me someone stole his bike the night before. That was crazy… a car thief's shit gettin' stolen?

After a while, we were in Lorain, Ohio on some street life shit, Monday had another joint called "Throw Em Off The Roof"… shit was the best shit he ever made. The chorus was sayin' "**Throw Em Off The Roof Al, Throw Em Off The Roof Al!**" Shit was crazy! He invited me to do a posse cut called "**The Back of the Barn**" that we never got to do. He had a cut called "Same Ol' Thing", Irv did all the production, these niggahs had stolen equipment and I'm not talkin' 'bout no little key board shit either. I'm screamin' some D&D Studios shit (No I can't spill the real on that epp). Moves was definitely bein' made but money wasn't flowin' regularly in big amounts because the licks they were pullin' would vary, some big, some small. Shit wasn't lookin' too good so niggahs depended on Monday to come up with some big moves and it just so happened that Shakim Bio-Chemical had "La La Land" open and love for his dogs so the Farmers occupation went from "Stickin' up" to the "Food department" where Sha-Bio was the manz.

Bein' around Irv more often, I got to witness and be a part of his genius music production skills and I gave ideas when needed. I had access to beats too; I'd hear a song, tell Irv, "Yo, I like that beat or I dig that bass line". A couple days later, son would have a tape with that beat or bass line sampled but he flipped it in his own way. Whatever it was you liked in the song you heard on the previous record, Irv made it stand out more, we had tapes of various beats, we had Mic Geronimo's "Shit is Real" and "Hemming Heads" beats like two years before Mic Geronimo came out with those records. I didn't know where Mic Geronimo even came from until Irv popped up with that niggah. Irv was doin' a lot of beats, makin' mix tapes, productions, engineering for Monday and his crew, outside crews and he had front row seats or back stage passes to the illest thug niggahs he ever met (US!) and it was always love when he came around. He was takin' mental notes, son wanted to be down and around us so much that he broke laws to make our cause more successful. He was doin' all the production plus hangin' around when niggahs was countin' cash and loadin' up heaters... he heard conversations before the drama went down, he knew a little inside information. I might be pushin' a whip down Farmers Blvd. or Jamaica Ave and Irv may be driving' in the other direction with whoever, he wouldn't honk the horn, he would turn around, get behind me and flash the high beams, signaling for me to pull over, then we'd get out, show love and kick it and no matter what, he would hit me with a tape with an ill beat. I'd promise to write somethin' ill to the beat, only to forget after getting' caught up in the everyday street life.

One thing a niggah gotta give Irv mad props on is that he was so ill with his shit, a lot of cats wanted to fuck with son. I remember back in 1992 – 93' I was listening to a demo tape by an ill spitter with a rough, grimey voice. He had a joint where the chorus went **"Fuck that, I aint goin' back! Fuck that, I aint goin' back!"** I liked the joint, then son had one that went **"On & on and on & on, the shit don't stop, it goes on & on"**. When listenin' to this cat spit about jail shit, sickin' his pits on niggahs and how he bumped into a cat from jail on the bricks who brags about a block and how he's runnin' it but he remembered how up north this niggah was "sonnin' it". Shit was bananas but me and Monday could never catch this niggahs name until we heard him say **"Dark Man X"**, this niggah finally came out years later while I was in the Feds. **"DMX"**, I remember hearin' son's shit from Irv bein' around us.

Irv was fuckin' with son (DMX), he also was doin' some production and engineering for a Brooklyn cat named **"Big Jazz"** (**Jaz-O**) from a group called **"Original Flavor"**. This was the niggah who put Jay-z on but this was when Jaz was tryna do his thing in the early 90's. He hit Irv with a box shaped BMW 325 or maybe it was a 318 (I can't really recall but it was a BMW) for Irv's help and input. I don't even know if son's shit ever came out cause we never heard his shit. Irv was puttin' in major hours in Dr. York's studio, fuckin' with niggahs when they were broke and not famous on the rap level. Irv was Monday's peeps first; he was a loud chubby cat who loved to gamble. Just being around us made son happy but he learned a lot cause he made history later on in life.

Roe was steppin' his rhymes up, he thought he was gonna be that next niggah, the new G. Rap or Jay-z before Jay-z. Son had a joint about the feds kickin' in the crib when he was in there with bricks… **"I flushed one key but I refuse to flush one more/ fuck it/ lock the door cause we goin' to war!!!/ Bussin' it/ and duckin' it/ screamin' "who the fuck did these feds think they were fuckin' with?"** You had to hear the shit, how son put it down, son refused to flush the drugs, got into a vicious shoot out with feds, got away, now he was **"Cabbin' it/not havin' it/ lookin' for the niggah who was blabbin' it"**. He had a next joint talkin' 'bout robbin' the whole world, screamin' **"If I catch you with your girl I'm harmin' her/ Stickin' my glock in her butt**

cheeks like a mothafuckin' thermometer!" Roe was bananas with it.

I used to be in Baltimore in 1991-93' doing my thing and at the same time, Roe was livin' out there with his wife and kids. I used to go get son and we'd ride around listenin' to music, drinkin' bottle after bottle of Moet; talkin' 'bout "when niggahs blow up on this rap shit". I was a vicious Hennessey monster, on some drunk shit, I gave Roe a free show by lettin' him see me smack a bum with a glock. This niggah used to go back and tell his wife about how wild a fella (ME) was. He praised my "illness" and witnessed my gunz bark on several occasions plus he remembered all the jail stories I gave him back in the days. We used to drink, drive around while I handled my business, attack the mall and get dipped, I would lace him, drink some more, blaze my guns and then go to my son's mom crib where we kept mixin' equipment to make tapes spittin' about shit. Roe was a journalist because he witnessed shit first hand and then put it in his rhymes. Even though I expected son to blow up on that rap shit, he didn't. Even after the success of his deejay and main man Irv. Roe later co-wrote the movie "**Belly**" with **Harold "Hype" Williams**. In the movie, son still used stories and shit he knew from first -hand knowledge and witnessin' moves and events that occurred in our real life situations. He was definitely lettin' us know he still remembered his true, real niggahs, even though he didn't blow up crazily… yet!

* * * * *

CHAPTER 6

On the phone...

A.M.: "Yo, Sha Catch the next flight up! Call the Airlines and make reservations, call me back and let me know what time you're landing and if it's Kennedy or LaGuardia".

ME: "Yo, what's up?"

A.M.: "Dem niggahs ████████ and dem came through like six deep, there was lookin' for your manz ████████. They know he took those thangs. It aint nothin' though, I got Irv with me now I just need you to come through so we can handle our thing and at the same time go holla at ████████. Shit is gettin' too ridiculous now, you know?"

ME: Yeah, I'm hip ████████ been calling and kickin' it with me. Niggahs is on some next shit. What I don't dig is everybody was supposed to be on one page but everybody wants to do their own thing and they're cuttin' the throats of niggahs they fuck with. ████████ wasn't supposed to fuck with Irv and Irv told ████████, ████████ fucks with ████████, who fucks with us. Shit is crazy God, next thing you know I'll be tryna rob you or you'll try to rob me".

A.M.: "No, No, No, I'ma be tryna kill you, know what I mean?!"

ME: "Ha, Ha, Ha! Cut the jokes! I'ma call and make reservations with U.S. Air, I'll hit you back and let you know when and where, most likely I'll fly out in the morning.

A.M.: "Alright do that, I need you to come through".

ME: "Yea and bring a gun with you, it's your best time to try to kill me".

A.M.: "Ha, Ha, Ha! Okay, make sure you wear a vest niggah!"

We was crackin' up.

-click.

One of my most memorable stories from being with Roe took place in early 1993 in Baltimore, MD when we was ridin' around and we heard RUN DMC was in town to perform in a club called "Hammer Jacks" that night. Run DMC are from Hollis, Queens (Like you don't know), they know Roe's reputation for spittin' rhymes and he was now with a cat who spit slugs (ME). I went and got fly for the night but I kinda played myself by rockin' a long sleeved, multi-colored, silk shirt with a black leather vest and some Timberland Chukkas. The shirt was a little bit too much for the occasion and me wearin' Timbs let you know I was tryna be fly but stay thugged out at the same time. Niggahs wasn't rockin' it like that in early 93' (No they wasn't), niggahs wasn't wearin' silk with Timbs like that. I was rockin' silk shirts with ninety dollar jeans, a leather vest and Timbs. That night, me and Roe were with Michelle McClain, who was Jackie McClain's daughter. Jackie McClain was some kind of Treasurer or held some high rank in the city of Baltimore but regardless of her position, her daughter was rollin' with us.

We set it off that day drinkin' and smokin'... I may have downed four bottles of Moet before we even went to Hammer Jacks that night. I remember when we went in, the spot was packed, I attacked the bar and got Henney'd up. It was mad honics in that piece and mad cats I knew was up in there too cause I was hittin' a lot of cats with work in different parts of the city around that time. Roe got lost in the crowd for a minute, son had to go to work later that night so he really didn't feel like comin' to the club in the first place. Also headlining with RUN DMC was Naughty by Nature and Apache, who had his hit "Gangsta Bitch" out at the time. Baltimore is or was on that house music with techno music, that house with eighty beats per minute type shit. They were rockin' that and throwin' in Hip Hop here and there. Everything was lovely and the bar was on BLAST, I got Michelle a few drinks, she and I got down like that, when we ordered drinks it was like it was for six heads when it was just us two. Roe came back to the bar area with Jam Master Jay from Run DMC, we ordered more drinks, Jay probably took a soda or some shit. Roe introduced us, even though we had met several times before at shows in different cities. He probably didn't remember, maybe he did but one thing is for sure, he was in for a hell of a night that night.

JMJ (Jam Master Jay) told us to roll back stage with him cause people were startin' to notice him by the bar. You don't see too many entertainers mingle in the crowd like a regular cat like that but here was JMJ at the bar fuckin' with me and Roe. Michelle wanted to stay in the crowd so we respected that, I dug in my pockets and hit her off with more than enough money for drinks. As we headed backstage, mad cats was stoppin' me, shakin' my hand, tryna be seen talkin' to a niggah and tryna get a good look at JMJ. We made it through the crowd, Jay let the big security niggahs know that we were with him, they hit us off with all access stickers so we wouldn't have any problems movin' around back there. Backstage had a V.I.P. bar so you know we touched that. JMJ explained to us that they were a part of the show and to stick by the dressin' room cause security was buggin'.

Jay also put us on point about Naughty by Nature and their entourage. For some reason, Naughty wanted the hallways cleared when they came out of their rooms. They didn't wanna be flocked by fans, groupies or whoever made it backstage. There was only a handful of people back there, maybe twenty at the most and believe me duke, Sha-Bio aint no groupie nigga nor do I be sweatin' no rappers or anybody for that matter. Anyway, we went in the Run DMC dressing room where Run was yappin' away on the phone. DMC was just chillin' and when Run saw Roe, he jumped up and gave him a big hug, shook my hand and kept on yappin' on his cell phone, DMC shook both of our hands and went back to chillin'. Me and Roe kept walkin' around, observing everything and playin' the V.I.P. bar backstage. I don't remember how but between me and Roe, one of us went outside to the car and got the .40 Glock in the club, I remember it ended up in the waist of my pants where it belonged. There were some cats who formed a cypher and started rhymin'; some freestylin'. Me and Roe enjoyed that shit as each cat did his thing, JMJ stood close by.

I met some N.Y. cats named Donald and Dougie, we were messin' with the same shorty. We talked about exactly where in N.Y.C. we were from then Roe said "fuck it" and started spittin' his vicious raps. Niggahs gathered around again and nodded their heads, listenin' to my manz. JMJ smiled as Roe schooled niggahs, he gave me some shine as I blew the spot up with my "**Wrecking mics for a living**" and my first verse of "**I Even Kill Kids**", Roe shook his head when I spit that and I even reached to pull out the .40 but Roe grabbed me, the Henney was takin' over. Roe walked me towards the V.I.P. bar tellin' me to "Chill, its mad security up in here and Jay and dem don't know we got heat in here, we can't mess it up". I said "Yea, yea, right, right Roe, let's get some drinks". Now understand somethin'... **I trust this niggah Roe**, had a lot of ups and downs with this niggah, met his family, I was friends with his wife at the time, Shonda and his children so you could say I was a close family friend. Roe was my niggah, I dressed him, fed him, gave him dough, did mad dirt with him and dramatized for son by blastin' my guns. Roe's seen my work; he's even seen me bloodied with black eyes and stitches all in my head; he's seen me broke before, he had to feed me on several occasions and I remember when this niggah crashed his Jetta while drivin' mad drunk. He crashed his shit, killin' the passenger who was ridin' with him and Roe himself ended up in a coma for a while. Here we were, drinkin' away, he was drivin' with no license because of that ill car accident he was in and he was on probation or some shit meanwhile, I was on the run for murders I didn't know nothin' about and I was still floodin' hoods with work in mad states.

We was drunk as hell in Club Hammer Jacks, backstage with a .40 Glock, Roe was talkin' and I wasn't listenin'. Next thing you know, security was tellin' everybody to find somewhere to go cause Naughty by Nature was comin' out of their room just to walk around and shit. We went back to Run DMC's room, Run was chillin' on the leather couch with boxes of Adidas sneakers and boxes of Black Timberland Boots. Run and "D" had a new record out called "Down with the King" and they changed their look to bald heads, all black khakis, black Timbs and black crosses. Roe was talkin' to JMJ and DMC; JMJ told Run about the rap skill display that just went on in the hallway and how Roe did his thing. Run said "Fuck that!" and Roe started laughin' along with everybody else. Run had an ill ego and knew he was "like that" and believe me, son could spit.

Old School or not, Run still had it in him and he had the arrogance as he should. **This is DJ Run from Run DMC, multi-platinum stats, worldwide recognition, merged Hip Hop with Rock & Roll, toured all around the world, helped bring Hip Hop to where it was and put Hollis Queens on the map worldwide.** Everybody was laughin', Roe responded "Yo, niggah you know I'm like that!" Run says "yea, you were like that but you couldn't fuck with me then like you can't fuck with me now!" Everybody got quiet, Roe was like "Nigga I will eat you up and you know it!" Run was like "so what's up then?" **Now those were some BATTLING WORDS, Run called my man Roe out right there in the dressing room in Club Hammer Jacks in Baltimore MD.** Roe was on the spot and Run knew he had him. I felt Roe could take him but Roe was standin' there with a smirk on his face. Run was like **"what's up Tony? You wanna try me or what?"** Run was still sittin' on the leather couch, **he got up, stood in his famous B-Boy stance and said** "How much money you got? We can put it up". Roe backed down on some "Come on Run" shit. I was drunk and witnessin' **some shit** so I dug in my pockets, pulled out like three or four gees, threw it on the floor in front of me and said "Yo, I got ten gees (**frontin'**) on my manz... Roe tear that niggah up!!" Roe looked crazy, he picked up my money and handed it back to me on some "Chill the fuck out" shit. To this day I still bring up how Run chumped my manz Roe in Baltimore. Run was on some "Thought so" type shit but he was studyin' me. He asked me "Yo, what do you do, you rap? That's a lot of money to be walkin' around with." Before I could say a word, Roe put his arm around me and pushed me toward the door on some "let's go get a drink and chill".

We went to the bar and got some drinks, I was like "Yo, why you faked jacks (backed down)?" Roe said "I will eat that niggah and he knows it, he always does that bullshit." I could tell son was embarrassed and vexed; he kept lookin' at his watch. "Yo, I can't go to work drunk either, I might call in sick or some shit so I can chill with you". I just looked at him, **son was mad that I saw Run do that. Run screamed on him! Called him out and Roe didn't do nada, shit was crucial**. It aint like I've never seen Roe fake jacks but rhymin' was his thing, he put in mad time and hard work so battlin' wasn't nothin' to him.

Out of nowhere, security came out again tellin' us to "Get somewhere!" I don't know how but we ended up in Apache's room. Apache (**R.I.P**) was sittin' down gettin' his hair braided by some chick. The next day someone told me the chick was Nikki D but anyway, we was up in Apache's dressing room with like three other cats, I said "what's up?" to him and made myself at home while Roe sat next to me explainin' how he was "always better than Run and Run knows it". I was just drunk listenin' to Roe and lookin' at Apache thinkin' "how the fuck did we end up in this niggah's room?" I downed my drink, got up and say "Yo, I'm getting' us somethin' to drink!" Apache pointed to a big ice cooler in the corner and said "Yo there's some drinks in there!" I'm like "Word?" So I goes to the cooler, open it and see like twelve Heinekens and two bottles of Moet. The other three cats put their hands out so I passed them a bottle of beer, I took both bottles of Moet out, passed one to Roe and I took the foil off and "**POP!!!**" Shit was foamin' crazily. Apache was like "**Yo! Yo! That wasn't for y'all to open! That was for after my performance!!!**" Roe looked at me then returned the bottle he was holdin' back to the cooler on ice. I took a few drinks of MY Moet then passed the bottle to Roe, who took it, shrugged and drank some too. I could tell by the expression on Apache's face he wasn't feelin' that. Here we were, two strange ass niggahs, one with a multi-colored silk shirt, a Jodeci leather vest, jeans and Timbs drinkin' his Moet when he only offered us beer. I know he was thinkin', "Who the fuck is these niggahs? One is talkin' 'bout he better than Run from Run DMC and Run knows it, the other is just poppin' my Moet like it's his and passin' it to the nigga who thinks he's a better rapper than Run from Run DMC... what the fuck?" We just invaded duke's dressing room and drank his shit, shit was crazy.

My head started spinnin' like crazy, Roe said he was goin' out in the crowd up front to check up on Michelle and told me to sit tight. Yo, I don't know how or why, maybe it was to use the bathroom, I don't know but I was in the hallway and shorties was sweatin' me. Now remember, I was in the rap cypher, I repped, I was in Run DMC's dressing room, I came through with JMJ and I just left Apache's dressing room. Who knows who these shorties thought I was, to them... I coulda been a big promoting cat or the next uprisin' rapper, I had that look, bald head, diamond imbedded gold fronts in my mouth, shorties always loved the kid, you know! Anyway, security comes out of nowhere and told everybody in the hallway to "Get somewhere!" again. Me? I stood right there like "What!?" so the shorties thought everything was everything and stood there with a niggah. Yo, this big Tony Atlas lookin' niggah came over to me, pointin' his finger, screamin' for me to get the fuck out of the hallway and sayin' some other shit. I was like "Huh? This niggah must not know who I am! I'm Sha-kim Bio-Chemical!!!" This big niggah grabs me by my leather vest, tryna manhandle me in front of the chicks and everything. Roe walked right in on it and ran over tellin' the security dude to chill and get the fuck off a niggah.

The commotion brought Naughty by Nature's Vinnie and Run DMC's JMJ out of their rooms. Vinnie was tellin' Roe that they need the hallways clear of "fans and groupies" JMJ said "Nah, Nah, these are my peoples", by then me and big man had had some serious words. He was looking down at me, I was grittin (my teeth) at him. He told me "What's up?" I was like "What!" He said "we can take this outside and see what's what then" Now remember this: I'm in Hammer Jacks Night Club with a sixteen shot in the clip, one in the chamber .40 Glock and this big, goofy dude is talkin' nuff shit not knowin' him soon get brush by di brusher zeen?!!? Vinnie's talkin' some bullshit about "fans and groupies" Yo, I couldn't take it so I told big man "C'mon, let's go outside". He looked at me, I'm 5'10", 161 pounds… he was 6'4" and looked like he weighed about 320 lbs. he told me "you aint tryna go outside, I'ma beat you up in the alley". He even had another big niggah with him, jumpin' in on some "C'mon, let's go outside!" JMJ, Roe and Vinnie was talkin', tryna straighten shit out amongst each other, while I was with these two big country lookin' niggahs. **I reached for my .40** and fear came cross dem face **QUICK.** Roe grabbed me and pushed me toward Run DMC's room, JMJ told me to lay down on the couch and sleep shit off. Roe was scared and tried to take Glock from its master. After an on & off tussle I give up Glock and lay down, my head was spinnin' so I jumped up and ran to the restroom to throw up, on the way, I saw big man, who looked down towards the ground.

Before long, my breath was twisted but I was still headed towards the bar and once again, security told everyone to "Get somewhere!" Vinnie emerged from his dressing room but I stayed at the bar so he came towards me on some "Yo, I thought you was someone who came in with the crowd, we have that problem all the time." I wasn't even payin' attention to him cause he thought I was a groupie. Funny shit is… we later saw each other in numerous spots, where I was with numerous rappers. One day backstage on the Budweiser tour in Virginia, Vinnie approached me with one of dem "**Wrecks in Effect**" dudes. I was with some of L.L.'s entourage and he wanted to know if I rapped or somethin' cause he'd seen my face around a few times. I was like "nah, I used to spit, I just come through; I'm known like that". Don't you know he tried to give me a "Naughty by Nature" T-shirt? "Nah, I'm good son". That aint even the last time I saw Vinnie either, we shook hands then the B-more thing came up and again and he said he didn't know I was with JMJ, he mistook me for a "Groupie". I gave him that same look (and this time, I had two Glocks on me plus my niggahs was loaded) but it was all love but… back to that actual night in B-more… I was drunk at the bar, Vinnie spoke and left, I went back towards the dressing room.

Run DMC just finished an interview and were sayin' the prayer they say before each show so me and Roe went back to the backstage area and Roe told me "We're gonna be on the side of the stage when Run DMC perform". My head was still spinnin' and my Glock was gone but I was like "Fuck it!" There was a small crowd, mostly big Hammer Jack white security cats because Hammer Jacks was a white owned establishment. The spot looked like it held twenty-five hundred people max, maybe three thousand, it was a nice sized place. This was like my third or fourth time in there but it was still hard to tell because I never really thought about it like that, security was beefed up. I wasn't sure if anyone had performed yet but you could hear the crowd, me and Roe walked toward security and they were like "**You gotta clear and make way, Run DMC is on in one minute!**" JMJ pointed to us and tells security "They're goin' on stage with us". Roe gave JMJ dap and said "Go do your thing and rep Hollis!" As Run DMC came to the backstage area they were gettin' pounds and high fives from all of us. Yo duke, I was so drunk and hyped that when JMJ came towards me with his fist out, I stuck my hands out towards his face like I was really checkin' him but that wasn't the case. I didn't know he took it the wrong way until the next day. We heard the crowd screamin', I didn't know what the fuck was happenin', Run DMC was standin' next to me waitin' to be introduced. As JMJ got his records in order, Run grabbed the mic and from backstage he screamed "I WANT TO KNOW WHO'S MOTHAFUCKIN' HOUSE THIS IS!!" The crowd was really screamin' amd JMJ entered the stage from a different way to get behind his equipment so me and Roe went up with him. At the end of the stage, there was a real big speaker, it was like six feet or taller. I climbed up on that shit and when I looked, I was so close to the mothafuckin' crowd, somebody coulda snatched me by my feet and pulled me down type shit.

As I was sittin' on the top of the speaker with my feet dangling, JMJ was cuttin' shit up on the 1's and 2's then Run asked the crowd "**Who's House? I want to know who's house?**" As part of their routine, DMC came out and started rhymin' his part of the song; the crowd went crazy and Run hadn't even come out yet. I can't really recall every detail but Run came out on "Run's house" then somewhere during their set, JMJ stepped down while Run was kickin' it to the crowd, came to me and said "Yo, watch how you move because you can make the needles jump, don't mess my cue up!!!" I said "You got that son". I respected what Jay said because I was up there movin' around a lot, frontin' with Apache's bottle of Moet, takin' baby sips because I was already drunk out of my mind. Crazy bass was thumpin' out of that speaker so my movin' around on it could cause Jay's needles to jump off cue and I didn't want to fuck up the show. Run DMC captivated the crowd with old songs then they got into "Down with the King". Mad honies was tryna get a fella's attention as I sat up on the speaker coolin'. Run screamed "I got the HOLLIS CREW with me!" and I thought for a second "Hollis?" Roe was chillin' against the speaker smilin', I tapped him, bent down to speak in his ear and I said "I aint from no fuckin' Hollis!!!" He said "Chill, chill Sha you from Hollis until the set is over!"

After the show, it was all hugs and pounds and shorties were everywhere. I bagged like twenty numbers and smoked one last blunt with Donald and Dougie; after that duke, I don't know what happened. I woke up the next day in me and Monday's rented condo, I had the ill headache, my clothes was off, money and Glock on the table… I figured Roe and Michelle must have brought me home last night. I had no shorty in the bed, I was so fucked up, I just laid there and cats was beepin' me off the hook, all fuckin' day the convo was like… "Yo, I seen you on stage" and blah, blah, blah, yeah yeah yeah and "No I'm not from Hollis" type shit. Later that night, Roe came through tellin' me how JMJ wanted to swing on me and knock my lights out for puttin' my hands in his face and tellin' him he "better represent!" I didn't know I did it like that but Roe said it looked ill how I did JMJ right before their set. He thought that shit was so funny, he kept sayin' "Yo, you had your hands all in Jay's face" and he showed me how I did it. I was like "Nah, I didn't do that". He told me that as he and Michelle dragged me to the car, I kept askin' for my Glock back cause I wanted to shoot up Hammer Jacks and I wanted to fight in the parkin' lot. I was like "Nah, nah!" Shit was crazy!

* * * * *

A couple weeks later, I was back up top in N.Y.C. with my peoples "Preme", Monday, Isreal and a few other Farmers cats; we were in this warehouse / club called either "Tribeca" or "Trafalgar Square", whatever it was called, it was a new spot in Jamaica, Queens right off of Jamaica ave. and it was mad big and off the hook, some check your coat at the door type shit. Police was on horses in front of that club, shit was illiotic, for real duke! Run DMC and Onyx was there on this particular night, I don't know who else but we came to see dem niggahs. We came in on some ill fly shit and everybody went in different directions once we got in cause everybody had their own shine and cats knew we who we were and we were ill niggahs. I touched the bar to get that Henney in me, Onyx just got off the stage, JMJ was tellin' everybody to come out to Hollis Park (Haggerty Park) for the shooting of Run DMC's new video "Never Let A Punk Get-away With Murder, buckshot, buckshots is all you hearda, ooooh what you gonna do? Ooooh what you gonna do?!" That shit and Onyx was doin' "Shifty" but he wanted heads to come enjoy Run DMC at Hollis Park that Saturday. I was at the bar with JMJ's manz "Runny Ray" (the cat who got killed in "Tougher than Leather" and died with a smile on his face… that niggah).

Me and Ray was at the bar pollyin', I was glad to see him, there was a rumor goin' around that he got killed and here he was standin' at the bar with his traditional Run DMC hat on. We were jokin', I don't know him like that but I know him enough that we shook hands and talked; Ray was a Hollis celeb and JMJ's manz for real. JMJ had a reputation for being a real street niggah; he was the thug part of the Run DMC trio. He was respected on the street level before this rap shit (and I had my hands all in his face, I be buggin' sometimes) and he rolled with known street niggahs that held it down, "Runny Ray" was one of them. We was kickin' it and jokin' by the bar (This spot had like three or more bars) and shorties was everywhere. They just put on some Ce Ce Peniston / Robin S., club / house music type shit (what y'all niggahs know about that Colonel Abrams type shit?) and shorties was on the dance floor goin' in. Me and Runny Ray was choppin' it up about street shit and I had a few cats with me when JMJ came over and shook hands. Jay was right at home, Jamaica, Queens with Hollis right, right there so he was around the way to say the least and he was Famous. He shook my hand, looked again and saw it was me. "Ah man! You definitely don't need to be drinking! Yo, Ray, this cat here is crazy and that aint the word!" I was like "What's up Jay?" He said "Yo for real, you was out of control in B-more, almost fucked up my show. If you wasn't peoples, I was gonna do those security dudes a favor, I really was kinda upset at you, you was out of control… wanted to kill everybody, you really need to stop drinkin' if you can't hold it." I was like "yeah, you're right, I was tipsy!" Jay said "No, you were beyond tipsy, you were a loose cannon". It was all love, we shook hands and hugged "ahite, ahite" as he gave everybody dap and Runny Ray gave us daps and hugs then rolled out. My niggahs was askin' "yo, what went down, son?" I explained "man, y'all niggahs don't wanna know, shit was crazy! Yo! Let's get some Henney!"

R.I.P. Jam Master Jay, shouts to his wife, family and seeds.

* * * * *

Phone rings, I answer…

████████ : "Yo, where you at?"

ME: "I'm chillin' in the lobby of the Executive telly on North Conduit but I'm shootin' through Farmers in a second, why what's up?"

████████ : "Man, I really didn't wanna do that sit down and look Irv in his face like that son, I didn't wanna give back shit. That's ill how ████████ and dem gave back their shit and tried to flip it like I'm the bad guy, like I did the shit by myself."

ME: "It's over now, fuck it!"

████ : "Shit can never be over! I heard ████████ is takin' and dem to "O" to get their hustle on. Dem cats was down with me on the lick but they changed roles, gave shit back and they turnin' workers for a soft niggah?"

ME: "Chill son, chill!"

████████ : "Fuck chillin'! This soft ass niggah said he gon' see me about takin' **his shit…** I didn't take it from him, I took it from **Irv**".

ME: "Dem niggahs aint gonna do nothin', it's all talk, you know he gotta keep his image on point, keep niggahs thinkin' he gangsta. Now he gotta try to get that money up cause when you did that, you put dem cats in a hell of a situation. Cats fucked with you and you did that crazy shit so ████ and ████████ gotta get that money up cause it was fronted to him and you stole the whole shipment, some crazy shit!"

████████ : "Dem cats aint fuck with me, everybody gettin' dough, pushin' Seven Series and Porshes and I'm out here strugglin' with a wife and kids in crazy cold, hard and fast N.Y.C. How I'm seein' my niggahs blow and I'm not? We supposed to be "**Family**" I'm ready to set this rap shit off Sha. Aint no niggah seein me in this rap shit but NO, everybody wanna see me sittin' on the side while they "gettin' it". Aint nobody thinkin' about me but a few, what happened to it being about **US**? We brought ill shit to the table, the world aint ready! Now money is involved, how niggahs gon' act when we blow for real? Huh? Seriously Sha, my niggah... **Who is really built like that other than us**? Answer that!! Everybody's thinkin' about self, FUCK THAT! Believe me, niggahs will even **flip and shit on YOU Sha, MARK MY WORDS**!

ME: "Yo, son, you're right...."

* * * * *

"Who The Fuck Is Shakim Bio-Chemical???"

I crush the strong and prey on the weak / so fuck you and your manz, y'all both butt cheeks/ I been steppin' on reps / ever since I left my front steps / from rockin' ten dollar Pro Keds/ to bussin' techs with hollow heads/ I tame and stain heads/ I was already known in the Feds/ way before I even came in the Feds/

So niggah, **who the fuck is you?"**

CHAPTER 7

That phone conversation with my manz still replays in my mind every day, even now as I write this. I remember his exact words... **"Niggahs will even flip and shit on you Sha, mark my words!"** I'm not tryna point out this and that because in reality, **niggahs don't owe me anything** and they have no obligations to do anything for me but I'm big on **loyalty and sincerity.** Whenever I was in a position to help someone out, especially my dogs, I did it without hesitation but you will see how certain things played out and how true colors surfaced. My manz knew what he was sayin' when he told me "... mark my words!" way back in 1991'. I remember back in 1992 or 93' niggahs had big plans to take over the rap game. Irv was makin' so many beats, Daymond was pushin' his FUBU hats and Hype was shootin' videos. Me, Monday, Monday's brother Richie, Roe and Irv were dreamin' and talkin' about our future, I still had my hands in mad dirt fuckin' with the drug game but niggahs was talkin' about "we aint gonna need that in a minute". Monday and Roe were puttin' in time in the studio with Irv and I kept shit movin' accordingly, kept my rhymes tight too. I was penning about day to day shit I was doin' and thinkin'. Niggahs was really grindin', we'd be pushin' a 750I one week and be parked up uptown in some stolen shit, waitin' for you and your manz to come out the next week, shit was real like that duke.

I remember how serious niggahs was when dealin' with Monday's song "Throw Em off the Roof", everybody on Farmers had a copy of that joint and around this time Hype was doin' a lot of photography shit too. Monday had promo snaps for the single; shit was sick, he had pics of him hangin' a niggah off a roof and the way it was shot made it look ill. The kid in the pic had make up on to look like he just took a serious ass whoopin'. Shit was ill like that, I seen the negatives, slides and all, niggahs was tryna pop off, **seriously**. To make shit more iller, one day while we were puffin' blunts, Monday came up with an idea and said' "Sha, since you been in so many towns and states, we should push you first. You dealt with a lot of different cats on different levels, from p.j's to major niggahs so if you came out with a joint and just put your face on the cover you'll probably push some serious numbers in sales". We laughed like crazy on that idea but Monday was dead serious cause a lot of cats knew me and recognized my face, felt my realness and knew our struggles but the idea was never pushed out there because I didn't take it seriously, I was so caught up in that street life but that was something that could have popped off and probably would have worked. I definitely had the power to attract and repel with my street swag and supreme charisma.

I remember thousands of occasions where my power to attract and repel was manifested. One time back in 92', we went clubbin' in Atlanta and we touched Club 112 in Buck head County. We were flossin' crazily, buyin' up the bar; it was me, Monday, Isreal, Tyheme, Shateek, Jamal and a few other Queens cats. Monday brought me a diamond pinky ring that cost a couple gees, that was my manz and we were gettin' a little paper at the time. I was always the flashy one; I used to rock two or three rings on every finger, thumbs and all that. I rocked big chains and even had cables wrapped around my wrist with my teeth flooded ever since back in the 80's. Monday toned me down with the excessive jewels cause I was killin' it even when Eric B and Rakim wasn't rockin' like that no more. Monday said a chain and a nice ring speaks for itself, all that other shit was kind of over-doin' it, especially in 1992 so I took the advice and toned it down with the jewelry. After that, I was rockin' hundred dollar jeans, ill shirts and one chain plus the pinky ring, so anyway, we were in Club 112 doin' it, shorties was everywhere, I was playin' the wall with a full bottle of Dom and I notice a cat in a Run DMC hat clockin' me so I gave him the famous "Sha Bio Grit" with gold fronts shinin'. The dude approached me and introduced himself as an owner of another ATL hot spot called "Frozen Paradise", he wanted to know if I was a rapper or something, of course he was attracted to the diamond ring I was blingin'. I showed it to him, we spoke for a while, I introduced him to Monday and he invited our whole crew to his club; later down the road he came in handy as he was goin' to claim eighty gees we lost in 92', we almost got it back but that's another story.

Another time, Me and Monday, bein' the ill cats we were, was eatin' and drinkin' at an expensive sea food spot at the Harbor in Baltimore. Again, we were decked in ill gear and expensive jewels, I pardoned myself to go take a leak and on my way to the bathroom, I passed two cats who looked me up and down; I return the glare and went in the bathroom. Upon my return, I passed them dudes again, they motion me to come over to them, I step to their table and they ask me to sit, we talked and exchanged numbers.They were some big boys and wanted to deal with a fella on the street level of things. My style attracts and it also repels for many times I used my swagger to ward off stick up cats and all that. I definitely had the look and was real with mine, on the street level I was ill and I did a lot of ill things.

I think back to my Far Rockaway, Queens days; how hard I had it bein' the only male with sisters in my family… I stayed in fights every day. I had to step up to the plate, be a man and get it how I live when all the kids my age were still bein' kids. I come from a middle class family with strong morals and principles but me bein' a young boy, I had no time to be under Mom dukes, I got caught up in the street life as soon as I was able to go outside. Even with my mom's strict rules, I still went out, ducked a few curfews and ran with the wild crowd. I have a sister who's nine years older than me, she was caught up in the disco era so I always was in tune with music. It was strange comin' up in a Jamaican family where all I heard in the house was Bob Marley and John Holt. When mom was at work, sis played all the shit that was happening; this later broadened my knowledge of break beats and old school classics.

Sis used to take me to park jams at P.S. 42 Park, instead of runnin' wild like the other kids, I would hang around her watching her and her crowd. I used to stand by the equipment watchin' the deejay do his thing and I observed the crowd reaction when certain records came on. This was back in 1977, 78', 79' and I got my first dose of early Hip Hop with MC's sayin' nursery rhymes that had the crowd screamin' along with them. I just fell in love with how the MC controlled the crowd, back then, MC's had MC voices and would be on some sing along shit "**Just clap your hands to the beat**" sayings like they were ridin' the beat and had voices like early Busy Bee, Super Rhymes, Love Bug Star Ski type voices, you know that Kurtis Blow type shit. In 77' or 78' when I came home from school I had to go to my next door neighbor's house until my sister came home. My neighbors were a family, it was Ms. Minnie and Mr. Jobson... they had 3 sons who were older, two were teenagers like seventeen, one was my sister's age, ███████ and ███████ and they had a sister named Carmen, who I always had a crush on. I was drawn to the two brothers, who were always in the basement messin' with studio equipment. They had two turntables, a mixer, amps, big speakers and crates upon crates of records. They stayed playin' disco, house and break beats and they would smoke weed and drink all day. They didn't scratch or cut records though, they just blended them or caught the breaks. One of the brothers was datin' my sister, we were like family and I would sit around them listenin' to music, watchin' them do dirt and learnin' shit until Sis came home.

I learned slang and peeped how the brothers carried themselves, when I went to school I mimicked them to the "T". I held my first gun due to bein' around these brothers because they were on some stick up shit back in 1979 – 80'. I used to carry their gun home for them in a leather bag and all they had to do was let me mess with their mixing equipment whenever I wanted and I would lust over my make believe girl, Carmen. I used to watch her dance and just stare at her, she had chocolate dark skin and was so fine, I still love her to this day. So I started messin' with the equipment and learnin' where to catch the break beats without scratchin'. I knew how to do it by ear, after listenin' to the records so many times I just knew where the breaks were. Rap wasn't on vinyl yet so King Tim the third and the Fat Back Band was the first record I heard on a little green and white forty five. I knew all the words to that record, then Sugar Hill's "Rapper's Delite" came out in 1979 and it was on.

My neighbors had a cousin named ███████, who was three or four years older than me, I used to be with him every day, eatin' ham and cheese sandwiches. He used to get the new rap records, come over and play them; back then there was no rap on the radio except Rapper's Delight. I got put on to Spoony G, The Treacherous 3, Grand Master Flash and the Furious Five, The Cold Crush Brothers and Kurtis Blow through ███████, he and I were inseparable back then. He brought me around the older crowd in the park, they used to rough me up and make me slap box with them. Picture a nine or ten year old slap boxin' a sixteen or seventeen year old, I was gettin' my ass whooped but this was preparin' me to be who I am today and I loved it. I got to listen to Hip Hop, chill with the elder cats who were "like that" at that time. Who would have guessed I would be the first one to open up P.S. 42 Park to the crack trade? I put my thing down in 85' but we aint up to that point yet so slow down youngster.

Anyway, between like 79' – 80', everybody was changin' their names to colorful shit like "Lord Divine", "Born Justice", "Supreme" and "Prince". My next door neighbors even did it for a minute, niggah told me his name is "Education" and would smack the shit out of me for callin' him by his real name. This niggah didn't even finish school but his name was "Education", what the fuck? Yeah, right! Their cousin changed his name to "Lord Shaheen Wise". I was thinkin' "What the fuck is going on?" I came around the older cats, they were greetin' each other with "Peace God!" callin' each other "Lord" or "God" and speakin' in scientific terms based on the sun, moon and stars. I thought the shit was crazy, shit... I was still eatin' my ham sandwiches every day. I remember a conversation one day that went like this "Yo Shaheen!" "What's the science God?" "Why don't you civilize this young savage (me) and enlighten him?" Everybody was lookin' at me, I guess after smackin' me around for months, they had some type of love for me, plus I was beginning to throw my hands up, block blows and tag them back with "lucky" smacks. I wasn't ready yet but I was easily whoopin' kids my age and before you knew it, I was given the "Supreme Mathematics" one at a time. I didn't even have an attribute (name) yet and I was still eatin' ham sandwiches like "whut!!" Every day when I came out, I had to know a lesson by heart, back and forth or I got punched on. Before I knew it, I was mastering my "Supreme Alphabet" and the ham sandwiches were gone.

My mom got married and my curfew got ill… so did the ass whoopins, therefore, I couldn't really hang out but I saw the gods in the park after school and I got to be around them for an hour or two. I couldn't go next door anymore either, step pops wasn't havin' that. One day, Born Justice, who later changed his name to Kashon, said, "Yo Young God, I got an attribute for you". Born Justice would who either give knowledge of self to everybody in my hood or he would direct one of his students to enlighten us but he gave out all the names. He said "I got your name written out for you so you better know this the next time I see you! Your attribute is **Lord Master Shakim God Allah** so you answer to **Shakim**! If I hear anyone call you John I'ma kick your ass if you don't kick theirs and don't let me see you again until you know your name". That's how it was back then, you were given your name, lessons were given piece by piece and you better know your shit or you'd get beat up, there was no escaping it. Everybody was "**God Body**" **aka Five Percenters**, it was everywhere in Far Rockaway. So, it was the end of 1979, an ill and very important year as two things were born, **Hip Hop on wax and "Lord Master Shakim God Allah**"…b**y name**.

"Peace to the Gods and Peace to the Earths, Peace to the babies of the Universe" **-1983**

* * * * *

CHAPTER 8

I can't remember exactly when I started writin' rhymes but when I started, I was writin' strictly "God Body" joints. Moms had me in the house like I was doin' a prison bid so I knowledged the 120 Lessons in no time. I'm talkin' about 1982, when I was gettin' kicked out of school after school, which started in elementary P.S. 42 to P.S. 197, then graduated to I.S. 53 and from there I graduated and went to Murray Bergtruam H.S., then to Beach Channel, Far Rock then August Martin and various summer schools and night schools even "600" school, which is special education.

Everywhere I went I made a lot of friends and few enemies, I changed my name a few times; I was always "**Shakim**", "**Lord Shakim**", "**Master Shakim**" or "**Lord Shakim Wise**". I had too many names to mention but around 1983 or 84' after readin' a plus degree (advanced lesson) with the question "**What is the Bio-chemical reconstruction terms of mathematics?**", I came up with the name "**Shakim Bio-Chemical**". I liked that question and the word "Bio-Chemical" so I added it to my name not knowin' around this time, another cat from Far Rock was using the name "Bio-chemical". Who was first to incorporate the word into their name? We will never know but his name was "**Lord Imperial Bio-Chemical**", we later hooked up and became the "**Bio-Chemical Brothers**" and he turned me onto the drug game in late 85'. We were sparkin' other God Bodies, "sparkin'" is when you question another God to the point where he admits he doesn't know and is learnin' from you. We had questions that were almost impossible to answer and we **specialized** in askin' "**Why is the sky blue?**" and "**Why is water wet?**" I had rhymes that were based on these lessons and I was also a break beat fanatic.

No matter where I was, mixing equipment was always available to me from next door to Born Cee's crib, my student Master Supreme's crib to anyone I knew like Master Dee, Justice and Divine. Even in our crack spots and cut up house at

██████'s had equipment so I always had access to shit from as early as I can remember and I'm talkin' from 1979 until my incarceration. I used to sneak out my mom's crib by climbin' out the window to go to Born Cee's crib to watch Sun cut shit up. He was "**Thunder Cuts**", Sun used to let me mix and fuck shit up, I couldn't fuck with Sun though; he was the nicest cat I knew at the time. He and his crew was raw, I used to tape his shit, go home and study it like my lessons so I knew every break. I would write rhymes to the breaks then I'd go back to his house with these rhymes to make tapes. Around this time, tapes was very important because hearin' any kind of raw or pure Hip Hop was like gettin' raw dope. The radio was playin' shit but not like that, Hip Hop was only gettin' a little play. I was in the basement with the "**Yes, yes y'all!**"

In 84' – 85' and I knew every Underground Hip Hop station whether major or minor. I had tapes of the **Kool Moe Dee vs. Chief Rocker Busy Bee** Battle and I was sellin' copies but niggahs was broke back then so I gave away a lot of freebees. I got a clear copy in the Bronx from my God Mother's next door neighbor, he laced me with it so I ran back to Queens with it and I know the words to the battle until this day. I eventually met Busy Bee back in 1989, when we were both locked up in Minnesota's Hennipen County Jail. I had the **Cold Crush Brothers vs. Dr. Rock and the Force MC's** battle on tape too. People don't remember that or that the Force MD's were once the Force MC's from Staten Island, who rapped and harmonized over break beats in the early 80's before they turned into an R&B group. Niggah, I was there pushin' tapes of raw Father MC, Thunder Cutz Born Cee, Mr. T and the Funky A Team to early B.I. Self and Just-Ice tapes. I had the ill collections and while niggahs was tradin' basketball and baseball cards, I had Hip Hop tapes. Me and Master Supreme made tapes that I kept at home, I had **Mr. Magic tapes, Red Alert, Chuck Chillout and World Famous Supreme Team** shit that I taped on the underground late night station WHBI (105.9). I was studyin' rhymes, break beats, cuts and scratches while niggahs was break dancing and pop lockin'. What's so ill was that I was known on every block, hood and project in Far

Rockaway, **I put my life on this "B"**. From 1983 to the day I got knocked (arrested; locked up) in 1993, I could walk in any project in Far Rockaway from Redfern, 40's, Edgemere, Nordack, Arverne, Ocean Village, 71-15, Hammels, wherever and I was known as the "**ill God**" with the lessons. Now remember, I went to five different schools in Far Rock so I basically knew everybody. I knew all the good guys, the bad guys, the bullies, the God Bodies, the emcees, the deejays, the dancin' niggahs, **I knew everybody** and I was "**GOOD**" no matter where I went. I was known for emceeing, stickin' heads up, shootin' cribs up, smackin' niggahs up, holdin' cyphers, the kid been through it all. I got niggahs who can and will vouch for this as bein' actual facts duke, **aint no extra mayo on this baby**!

We aint even gonna talk about when the drug game came into the picture, I dripped so much blood in Hammels projects in Far Rock for comin' on their turf between 1983 and 84', way before the guns; I'm talkin' about when you had to have hand skills to sell drugs. I went through so much shit to earn my respect in those p.j's, I went through the ranks to talk this shit and it got to the point where I could walk through any pj's with jewels drippin', pockets bulgin' and no worries. Back in '85, I got stuck up by an older stick up cat named "Zay" a.k.a. "Zig Knot", who is mentioned in Just-Ice's song "Goin' Way Back". What's so ill is a few weeks later I gave son a fair one and earned my braggin' rights. I'm talkin' about I fought a grown niggah who was known for runnin' shit in prisons up north… I fought him straight up, I got mines and lasted. I was fifteen years old, I had stick-up kids robbin' ill niggahs, sellin' me the jewels and I would rock 'em 24-7 from 1986 to 1988… all Far Rock ill niggahs knew me.

I was goin' to Jamaica, Queens too, I went up to Farmers Boulevard and got my props and they had me down as a "**FB**" rep and one of the realest, check the hood corners, **ask dem niggahs**! I was goin' up to schools laced up in jewelry, wearin' two-hundred dollar gold frames. I chased some Sutphin Boulevard cats across Baisley Pond back in 85'. In the winter time, niggahs used to walk across the frozen pond as a short cut to get to Sutphin Boulevard so one day, I went to school with a baby axe and chased cats, they ran like **bitches**! I'm a known niggah in the "60's", where I'm originally from in Far Rock. I opened up P.S. 42 Park with crack there, some Spanish cats had it locked on the coke tip, no, no, no, no that shit got shut down. **Sha-Bio put it down dun**. You had to ask permission to move a five dollar rock, ask my niggahs. I'm not sayin' I was the niggah who ran things with an iron fist because a few cats tried their hand so don't get it twisted but at the same time, **guess who was still shining**. When the ill cats from the p.j's came through the "60's" to house parties or park jams, **guess who never had to tuck his shit in**! I saw mad cats tuckin' their jewels and they were in their own hood. If your shit got took, **guess who got that shit back for you**! I had my ups and downs too though, I lost quite a few fist fights but I was known to fight big grown ass niggahs, a few my age put hands on me too but **guess who directed the ill beat down comebacks**! Here are two examples of your manz… First, one night I was drinkin' with my manz and dem in front of our buildings in the p.j.'s; Me, Gunja (Admiral Shipwreck) and a few other cats were drinkin' bottles of E&J crazily. My manz ██████████ baby mom's brother just came home from doin' a bid up north, his name was "Big Sha". Big Sha was a big monkey lookin' niggah, who had some size but anyway, Sha came in our midst, we were like twenty deep in front of the buildings, drinkin' and poppin' big shit. I was like sixteen years old, Big Sha joined in and I flipped askin' the God today's mathematics, he answered but he couldn't elaborate so I applied more pressure by quizzing the God on all kinds of degrees. Big Sha got frustrated and admitted he hadn't been studyin' so me, bein' drunk, strapped and not givin' a fuck where this niggah came from, Sing-Sing or Attica, bitched slapped him and told him to get the fuck out of here and don't let me see him until he knew his lessons; he took the slap like a champ and broke out with everybody laughin'.

Twenty minutes later we strolled to the boulevard and got more drinks. On the way back, we saw mad crack heads outside and Big Sha was standin' out there with his mom, pops, two brothers, a sister ,who was my manz baby moms and she had their two kids out there. They were waitin' for me so I walked through and asked Sha "what the fuck are you doin' outside, you studied your shit and know it that quick?" I heard laughter every where, Sha responded "I'm tryna see you on a fair one God". I asked "You're tryna see... me? What's the whole fam out here for, to watch me smack you again?" My niggahs laughed again. Why did I pull my 9mm and hand it to my manz and say "watch this"? We went in the building lobby and son did some "52 blocks" shit and beat my ass. I couldn't do nothin' with him, couldn't see son at all.

I still blame my drunkenness for why Big Sha got me but the reality of it was I just couldn't see son with the hands. I was out of his league, he made a punching bag out of my face, bloodied my nose, mouth and he closed one of my eyes. Shit happened in front of my niggahs, crack heads and on top of that, this niggah had his whole fam front row seein' this shit. Man, **fuck that**! I put my hands down, I wasn't even drunk anymore, by now, I was sober as shit. I went to my manz and said "Yo gimme that joint!" He was lookin' at me like I was crazy. This niggah had two kids by Big Sha's sister, who was standin' there with her family and kids. She was watchin' to see if this niggah would give me the gun. I had him under pressure cause he was my peeps, we were gettin' money together and I lived with him and his sisters. As he reached to give me the pistol, I saw in his eyes that he couldn't do it. I gave him a pass and hollered to my other manz "Yo, Admiral Shipwreck, give me your burner God, cause this niggah is fakin' for these bitches". With no hesitation, my manz gave me his joint, it was a .25 auto but fuck it. Yo, mom, pop, kids, brothers, sis and Big Sha all started screamin' and runnin' towards the elevator, which wasn't there so they ran up the staircase five at a time. I'm not gonna sit here and lie, I busted like five or six shots at Sha and his whole family. They ran up the steps fast as shit with me chasin' them but they had me by like two flights, they were gone. I came back downstairs, niggahs was dyin' laughin'. I shot at my manz baby mom's whole family and he was standin' there fucked up at me and the situation. It took a few weeks for him to even be able to go back and see his kids, then he straightened shit out and brought Sha and his brothers to me one night and I apologized, told him I was drunk and I was wrong. He got that and shook my hand, we drunk a forty ounce together and left it at that.

About two months later, when my manz ████████ from Farmers came to scoop me up at the spot for our late night sprees, we were in the lobby about to leave the building and guess who came in the lobby… Big Sha… he saw me and shouted "Peace Shakim!" but I could see fear in his face. "Peace Sha" I responded as me and ████████ exited the building. I said "Yo gimme your burner, son!" Without hesitation, ████████ passed me a nickel plated chrome .357 revolver, I tucked it and went back in the building with ████████ following me. I went toward the elevator, Sha was still standin' there. "Ay yo Sha, I forgot to give you this" I pull out and pistol whip him crazily, he was screamin' "wait, it is squashed!" I was like "Fuck all that!" As I beat him on the top of his head, he fell to the floor and started shakin'. I stomped him out a little and he wasn't movin', I had blood all over my TImbs as ████████ watched and said "come on Sha-Bio, let's be out!" We exited the building, I handed my manz his burner and I looked back to see Sha layin' there in a pool of blood with his leg shakin'. That's right, **fuck that**! What you thought? I had to let him know shit was real so **52 block that nigga**! Ha ha! Don't you know the bitch ass niggah told and police went to my mom's crib lookin' for me, askin' questions? I didn't live there and only went to see my mom once a week on late nights and shit, she knew I was all good. She didn't approve of my way of livin' but she knew her only son would take care of himself as she heard the stories from neighbors, who while drivin' by, saw me in areas and hoods.

Another "epp" was when I was chillin' in 42 Park by the handball court, where all the girls would be. I was with Master Supreme and Imperial Bio on a hot ass summer day; Imperial had the triple black 300E Benz sittin' on Lorenzos and I was a part of his team. We were chillin' out there and talkin' shit when my manz ████████ pulled up in his Jetta and jumped out like "Yo Sha, let me see you God!" I was like "Yo, what's up?" He asked me for a burner. Now this is my manz right here, he was the one who gave me the chrome joint to beat Big Sha down with, fuck that, this was my manz Al Monday. "What's up Allah Love (AL)?" He said "I got beef sun". That's all Al had to say to me and it was on. As I got in Al's Jetta, I told Preme and Imperial I'd be right back and we sped off to Ocean Village. The drama was with Monday's girl, who lived in Ocean Village (O.V.) and had a problem with this pretty boy ass cat from Edgemere, a notorious housing project in Far Rock. This pretty boy niggah was named "Petey" a.k.a. "Fendi". Petey was a light-skinned niggah with curly hair, high top fade, jumpin' up and down niggah who used to be dancin' and all that fly shit. He eventually became one of **EPMD's** main dancers and he's in many of their videos. At one time, this pretty ass niggah was Father MC's' dancer, he could dance and had mad bitches on his dick. Dem dancin' niggahs was gettin' the girls back then but anyway, Monday roughed Petey up a bit, you know, Monday smacked him up crazily, showin' him not to mess with his wifey. The thing was, Petey had as sister named Teresa, who was not only gorgeous and glamorous but she was also well respected in Edgemere.

Teresa was Raheim's girl... Raheim (R.I.P.) was one of Edgemere's most notorious cats and had shit on smash back in the day; I respected Raheim crazily. When I got robbed by "Zig Knot", he brought crazy heads to Hammels to hold me down. He came more on the strength of Lord Imperial Bio, who he was well acquainted with but I knew of Raheim before that and after the Hammels episode, we became cool from there. Niggahs was scared to death of Raheim... he had a brother name "Big Dad", who was another ill cat who eventually became head of Father MC's security and his main man. Raheim and his team of goons was so ill that niggahs was scared to walk thru Edgemere, wouldn't go up on the five – four (beach 54th st) and would tuck their jewels but **not me**. I had a pass because I knew Raheim and his crew, Shaheen (R.I.P.), Everlasting Science, C-God and a few others. Unfortunately, Raheim got murked in Teresa's building after leavin' her crib. Niggahs was so scared and respected Raheim so much that even after his death, niggahs was still afraid of his name, they looked out for his girl and his crew was still active. So Petey being Teresa's little brother meant one thing for Al Monday... **BIG TROUBLE!**

Monday is from Jamaica, Queens and would come out to Far Rock every day to see his girl, if he wasn't with his girl he was with me makin' moves so I was the only one he could come get. This was a very serious situation and me and Al were both kinda nervous as we headed back to O.V., which was a couple of blocks away from the "60's". I had two burners on me but that aint shit, as soon as we hit the parking lot, there were crazy Edgemere niggahs out there. The boardwalk to the beach was right there so niggahs was on the boardwalk, in the parking lot and all; we were in some trouble. As we got out, Petey pointed to the car and yelled "**There he is right there!!**" Mad niggahs walked up as we walked towards Monday's girl's building. I saw all the Gods from Edgemere I fucked with; Powerful, Barsha, Shamdu, Barlove, Wise, Father, Ramel and Teresa was in the middle like the Queen of England and lookin' so beautiful (yep, I said it). They walked up like "Yo, what's up money? Oh shit, Sha Bio, Peace God!!! What's up, this your manz?" They were all givin' me pounds and hugs while Petey was standin' there lookin' stupid. I kicked the Bo-Bo "Yeah God, this is my manz, duke disrespected his Queen" and blah, blah, blah.

Yo, shit was squashed within minutes and to make shit more iller, I stepped to Teresa in front of niggahs. "Excuse me, can I talk to you for a minute?" As she stepped to the side, I couldn't even look her in her beautiful eyes. "Listen, I know and understand you was Ra's Queen, you may not have noticed me but I went to Far Rock High for a minute while you went there and I used to ride the train with you way back. I used to see you all the time when you worked the cash register at C-Town across from Hammels. I would come in there just to look at you Teresa" I looked up at her and she was staring and smilin' at me. "I know who you are Shakim but I didn't know you was clockin' me like that". We made small talk and she gave me her telephone number, I still remember that shit to this day. I was an ill nigga, my manz had beef with these wild ass Edgemere niggahs and I squashed it with words alone cause they had major love for me and I pulled Ra's queen in front of them Edgemere niggahs, Whut!!! I had the big head after that and ever since then you couldn't tell me shit; a long way from gettin' chased and bullied by O.V.'s Derrick Fox (R.I.P. Rest in Piss Nigga!). I was comin' through O.V., Edgemere, Nordack, Arverne and I never had to tuck my jewels, hide my money, none of that. I got love and showed love. I used to be on the Five-Four, in buildings drinkin', smokin' and rollin' dice with these niggahs; cats I'd known by their birth names since kindergarten. These cats knew me by name and face and I knew them all from the twins, Barsha and Jamal to my manz Shabazz (Jon Smiley) and God Cee, all my dogs in the double buildings, three the hard way, Pac Man and his crew… I knew all the Dons, Hoods, thieves, killers, everybody… and they all showed love. I had a few run-ins but I was good. Big shout to Drack, Cardell, Dutchie, my manz Malik (in the wheel chair), Shabar, all my niggahs in the back buildings and double buildings.

I recall havin' beef with a niggah who robbed one of my peoples… The niggah lived in Edgemere on the 5-4 building 410, where my manz Shameek Champion is from. Me and two of my dogs took a cab to O.V. to plan shit out, my two menz was kinda nervous cause we were goin' to Edgemere to holla. I was like "Dog look, I got mega love over there but I'm Sha Bio" niggahs aint believe me. We had two 9mms and a .44 bulldog so we walked to Edgemere to the 5-4. When we got there, I got mad pounds and hugs, niggahs knew somethin' wasn't right cause they saw me on foot with two cats from Hammels p.j.'s but I told them "Nah, everything is everything, we came to see some bitches from the back building". I saw my manz Asiactic (A.Z.), God was crazy nice with the verbals on the mic; I knew him for a while and I loved his sister Karen. "Yo A. Z, let me build with you" He's gave me universal greetings "Peace God!" I ask "Yo A.Z what's the science?" "Nothin' much Sha, constant elevation, what's the science wit you Lord?" I asked him "Yo, where ██████ live at?" A.Z. was like, "Whoooooa, that's serious right there, why what's up?" I told him "Nah, duke disrespected my manz, came through Hammels, robbed and shot him" "yeah?" "Word Life!" "Yo Sha, I love you God, I'ma tell you but you can't let nobody know I told you, cause it will be mad beef… ███████ is feared out here". I was like "I got you A.Z." he then told me "He rest in apt █G, he's up there now cause he don't come out until 11p.m. or midnight type shit". I dug in my pocket and gave him $200 "Okay God, good lookin'!" He repeated "Now remember Sha, don't let no one know how you know where he's at!" I repeated "I got you baby!" then bounced toward my niggahs "Yo I know where he's at!"

When we entered the building, the deal was I had to be the one to knock on the door and ask for ██████████ unless he opened the door himself cause me and him wasn't beefin' and he knew my face. When I knocked on the door, an old ass lady answered "Yes?" I ask "Is ██████████ in?" "Who are you?" she asks and I said "Bobby". "Wait a minute, ██████████, door!" We all positioned ourselves, pulled out, cocked back and waited for duke to come to the door. Yo, as soon as that door opened, son eyes got big and he tried to shut the door. My manz .44 made a crazy roar as we let off our nines and riddled ██████████ door with bullets. We ran like shit down the steps, through the building, to the 5-4 back to O.V. I saw A.Z. as we bounced cause everybody heard that .44 and rapid gunfire. Niggahs was lookin' crazy as we hurriedly walked by, tryna get out of there. "Shakim Bio! Y'all niggahs is fuckin' crazy! What the fuck was that, a cannon!" We kept it movin' and ran off toward O.V.

* * * * *

A few days later, I got word that we missed ██████████ but he was really shook and he knew what the bullets were for. He didn't understand how or why I got with it until he found out I was a Hammels Red Coat. Lord Imperial had Hammels in a smash back in 1983 through 89'; the ill cats of Hammels like Born Unique,

Raheim from Hammels, Nanfu, B.I. Self, my manz Born Supreme. Lord, Supreme, Sha King, ShyHeim, Magnetic, Dahwu, Ever, Big Knowledge, Elton, Ralo, man it's just too many to name but they were all down with Lord Imperial. At one point, we all used to rock red, goose down, winter coats with the fur on the collars so a crack head started screamin' **"The Red Coats are comin'! The Red Coats are comin'!!"** and the Red Coats were born from there, ██████████ was second in command and I was third. Now remember, I had to go through major drama to be accepted by these niggahs and now I was part of runnin' niggahs out of the p.j.'s. Me and my manz Born Supreme used to round niggahs up to go shoot up the boardwalk parties and take jewels and cash, I used to come through both sides of the p.j.'s laced up in jewels and all. Niggah, me and Born went to go buy some big gold cables one day and ended up robbin' the jewelry store for like four cables a piece, around this time the whole p.j.'s went to the "March of Dimes Marathon" and went bananas. Niggahs was smashin' jewelry store windows, comin' back to the hood all jeweled up and shit then they started sticking each other up amongst themselves, shit was crazy!

I was there when "Razzi" from Brooklyn was stickin' everybody up when he would come through Hammels to see his peeps "Life" and "Young God". Razzi was a tall, dark-skinned, skinny cat, who was smokin' crack in cigarettes and weed. He had niggahs scared to wear their shit in their own p.j.'s. He was stickin' niggahs and bringin' me the jewels for sale or tradin' them for jumbs (cracks). I was there for all of that, runnin' outsiders out of the projects if they tried to open up spots plus we was holdin' the "60's" down. This shit was around my way, way back before I started goin' out of town but then I started branchin' out to Jamaica, Queens, connectin' with real cats like Al Monday and others. I can't even speak on one millionth of the shit I did while nowadays, niggahs be screamin' that b.s in rap songs but couldn't walk through my end of town. I stayed in more shit than flies, I was a street nigga from the beginning of time, even when I was a house niggah who couldn't come outside. I read every Donald Goines novel before 1984 and used to go to school talkin' that shit;

I read most of Ice Berg Slim's novels amongst others. I'm not sayin' that I was a terrible dude, nah not at all but I was there and in the mix of shit and my names rang bells amongst my peers, enemies or whatever, whoever! Niggahs still respect the handle from my 85'-88' shit. So if you wanna know who Shakim Bio-Chemical is, it aint hard to find out. If I was out there now, they'd probably have a statue of me in the middle of P.S. 42 Park in the "Sixties". Nah, seriously, I was molded and taught by the best, beat some of the best and stood by the best so that made me one of the best, if not the best.

Note: Let me make some things clear and let understanding be understood because I don't' want people to think the God Shakim Bio-Chemical was negative. Everybody didn't see me in the same light that I'm presenting. There was a time when I was all about my lessons, showing & proving and livin' it out. A lot of God Bodies know me in a more positive light, like the God GaMel, who had the "God Van" and sold cologne, hats, purses and what knots outside Beach 60th train station. I used to sell balloons on the boardwalk and could be found at Playland's Amusement Park building with the God ShaBorn from 71-15. Back then, I wore my crown with matching gear every day, I could show and prove every color I had on. I rarely missed a rally or parliament in Mecca (Uptown [Harlem]) or Medina (Brooklyn) and still today I have knowledge of self and I know and understand my lessons. Universal Greetings to all God Cypher Divines, Earths and our seeds! I always did and still will find time to build. I could never forget the Gods and Earths I know and have met throughout N.Y.C. nor the ones I met and built with out of state in the streets and the Prison System. P.E.A.C.E! I'm **ShaKim Bio-Chemical**!!!

* * * * *

CHAPTER 9

Summer of 1985 was the year I was moving up in the ranks. I wasn't playin' spots anymore I was outside movin' work in the lobbies and it wasn't two weeks before I got robbed for the first and only time. Bein' in spots and movin' around outside is completely different like "high and low". Bein' in a spot, I never had to open the door I'd just look out the peep hole and push the top lock out, I rigged it so the customer put the money through the hole and I returned the product. I was in the spot sometimes six to eight hours before my manz came up, he had to have a combination of special knocks on the door and even if I saw him through the peep hole, he had knocks to let me know no one was with him but regardless of all that, I always kept my gun in hand.

Housing police knocked on the door on my first day in the spot, I looked through the peep hole and got shook. I had all the work and a toolie ready to go out of the window. Police was like **"Open up!"** I shouted **"My mommy is not home, she said don't open the door for anyone, not even Uncle Nick!"** Police fell for that one even though it was the wrong apartment. After that, I was so shook I didn't serve anyone for four or five hours. I was gettin' a hundred and fifty dollars a week, not including weekly shopping sprees, eatin' out every day and the barber shop on Saturdays. I stayed fresh from head to toe and in school, niggahs couldn't see me. Man I had the gold teeth and every pair of designer frames out cause whenever my manz got a new pair, his old pair went straight to me and I kept a new pair (every joint you can think of) every two weeks. Bein' outside means once the customer got your attention, you directed him in the building to do the transaction and this left you open for all kinds of dangerous possibilities.

After a while, I knew who was who in the building so I was workin' the lobby mailboxes. I used to jimmy an old lady's or somebody's mailbox and would use it to stash crack bottles and dough. There were many times Police ran up on me, they even knew me by "Shakim"; they just couldn't catch me. I was in and out of all the buildings, Hammels p.j's had close to twenty buildings, I can't think of one building we didn't have a spot in during the mid to late 1980's. We even had spots in the rent building, the tenant patrol building and the Housing Police building. Niggahs was bold like that, we used to play the outside of buildings, rollin' dice, playin' the benches, the p.j.'s park or the boulevard. It was nothin' to be upstairs in someone's crib makin' a tape as niggahs was cuttin' and scratchin' and we took turns rhymin'. The next day or maybe that night, niggahs would be outside with the tape blastin' in their box radios and before you knew it, copies was made. I remember when we used to go twenty deep to the ave to get new kicks or haircuts, on Easter everybody who was somebody got fresh and we all rode the last car of the train all the way to "The Deuce" (42nd st) in Midtown Manhattan, I have many photos from those days. I remember goin' to school every now and then, bein' dropped off and picked up in rental cars in front of everyone. I would play homeroom class then go outside to showboat, get with Father MC and run around. I was the only one who kept money, we used to sweat the honies; pushin' up on bad bitches like Stephanie Taylor or Rosalyn Mason, we would run the halls or cut school, smokin' blunts, drinkin' forties out in Bayswater Park. Some days we would cut school and go make tapes or just say "Fuck it" and we'd stay in the p.j.'s all day makin' that dough.

When I started movin' outside, my pay was different; first two months, I got three hundred dollars off of every thousand I made, had to give back seven hundred so my money all depended on how fast I moved that "G pack". I was movin' like two "G packs" a day so I started gettin' four hundred dollars and gave back the six on every thousand and I still ran the spots. I had to make sure spots never ran out, me and my manz graduated to gettin' ten "G packs" and sometimes I had to cut and bottle them up with my manz. What was ill about the whole situation was my manz, who was hittin' us with work knew where we kept shit stashed in the safe house so every now and then, he would retrace steps after hittin' us off with work and he'd steal back two or three gees so we would be "short", that way, we always owed him and stayed on his team. It was some funny shit cause we were always "short" and this niggah gave us speeches about how we gotta work off what we "owed" him. I wrote a rhyme about it and wrote parts for everybody, chorus and all. The rhyme was called "Workin' for Free". The rhyme was ill and we did it in front of him; that was our protest to get off of his team. We left but came back a hundred times, it was **Crew Love**.

I remember the dude we worked for gave us his car to go shoppin' on the "ave" and he gave us three hours to get back. He had this "77" Cutlass Supreme, triple black, tinted windows, sittin' on "Trues and Vogues" with a boomerang antenna on the back trunk and he had a Puerto Rican horn in that piece. We had the Alpine, pullout "Benzi-box" and the car's nickname was the "Lion" because we had two or three cats down with us who had cars and we were on some "Transformer – Thunder Cat" shit. Everybody named their car a name and we transformed when we all got together to drive around.

Me and my manz ██████ went up to Jamaica ave, drivin' around and shit; we run up in a couple spots, got the latest, illest wears then cruised the streets blastin' music. We went up on Rockaway Blvd and saw DMC from Run DMC right next to us in his car, stopped at a red light. He was rockin' his trademark hat, he looked over at us and nodded his head and we nodded back. We were rockin' big gold ropes and four finger rings but still lookin' at DMC like **"Oh shit, there go DMC!"** So when the light turned green we let him pull off first then we gunned our shit passed him; music blastin' as we ran all the red lights up the long stretch by JFK airport. We was doin' like a "buck, buck ten" type shit laughin' cause we burnt DMC, left him ten blocks back. All of a sudden and out of nowhere, the car's engine started smokin', under the hood there was a furry like mesh material and it caught on fire, we thought the whole car was ablaze so we jumped out thinkin' shit was gonna blow the fuck up. The car was still mobile after we figured out what the problem was but certain hoses had melted and the paint job on the hood was all the way fucked up. The three hours turned into seven hours, we brought the car back at night so duke couldn't see the damage until morning. **Damn sun, we were workin' for free for real, for real now**!!

I was the smallest one in our crew so other rivals used to call me out. I had no problem throwin' my hands up but I seemed to always take an "L" (a Loss). I remember fightin' grown men and these niggahs weren't playin' or slap boxin' with me either. It got to the point where every time I went on the other side of the projects, I was fightin' a niggah every day. My manz thought up a plan, he was nice with his hands so he took me to Kings Plaza Shopping Mall in Brooklyn and brought me some forearm and ankle weights. We bought five pound joints for each wrist and ten pounds for each leg, I put them on in the mall and never took them off. I ate, slept, shitted, showered and fucked with those weights on. I had to run the boardwalk and slap box every member of our crew out on the beach in the sand, shit was hectic. I was being trained for three, four hours straight with the weights on then I was taught fighting techniques and combinations. I trained harder than Mike Tyson's training work out, I sparred for hours but I couldn't swing back. I was learnin' to duck dip and weave with the weights on and when I punched, the weights made my punches crazy slow. After about a month and a half, I was catchin' niggahs, blockin' everything thrown at me and mind you, I was still wearin' the weights on my arms and legs.

We went through the projects one day and my manz picked my first fight with one of the bully niggahs who could really fight. I was like "**Damn Dog**!!" Once my manz took the weights off my arms and legs, my shit was superfast. I was taught boxing and punching techiques with names like "The 5th Elements – Gold, fire, water, wind and wood", then "Batman and Robin", the "Butterfly"; back then, cats was fightin' with pretty styles and moves on some "52 Blocks" type shit. So when I had the weights taken off and my crew was standin' on the sidelines plus mad project niggahs was watchin', I was hyped. My manz started callin' out moves and combinations and I executed them, shit was crazy, I was weaving, ducking, shootin' jabs and everytime he yelled out a move, I did it all the way. He would say "**Butterfly!**" and I'd do the "Butterfly". He yelled "**Wood!!**" "**Fire, that's right Sha Bio!**" "**Batman and Robin**", everything he called out, I put it to good use. After the fight, we put the weights back on, shit was crazy but niggahs wasn't tryna see me with the hands and wasn't callin' me out any more. I stayed drunk and popped mad shit and I was the first to pop off on shit.

* * * * *

"I don't bug out or chill or be actin' ill / no tricks in 86' it's time to build / Eric be easy on the cut / no mistakes allowed/ cause to me/ M.C. means 'move the crowd' "

"Eric B for President"

Eric B & Rakim   1986

CHAPTER 10

1986 came and the crack epidemic was bananas! Niggahs was now on some different shit and guns was bein' used, all the fist fights, outside park jams and all that was changed up. Niggahs was now blastin' "dem thangs" and every housing project was against each other; it was always like that with Hip Hop and fights but everyone was God Body so at least we got along. The crack game was on full blast and changed all of that shit, your God Body attribute was nothin' but a name now. Cats named "Supreme" and "Born" was now beefin' with each other over buildings, yeah, it was like that now. Supreme mathematics and alphabets were used as codes... Gods were still building but not how they were in the past. This was a new year and there was dough to get, however, I stayed in tune with my lessons, built with Gods and tried to attend monthly rallies but I was also out there gettin' that dough.

We started packin' guns, coppin' any gun that was for sale and in N.Y. guns was hard to get so if someone came around with heat for sale we paid the price no matter what it was. Niggahs was gettin' robbed, shot and killed and shit was too real so we got armed and were ready for war at all times. Niggahs was beefin' over turf and goin' at each other in their own projects. We still had shit in the smash but cats was gettin' it on their own and others was movin' in so we ran niggahs out or we teamed up and ran other niggahs out. Some of us formed an alliance where we broke down and divided the P.J.'s and buildings, shit was divided where we kept one side and controlled ten buildings with three other cats and his boys and you controlled the other ten buildings with four cats and their boys but **we crossed the line regularly**. That was just the way shit was, niggahs was gettin' robbed and shot every day and night; I remember a few times shit got real ugly.

One day I bought two guns from ███████ , we needed them joints and anything else niggahs was tryna sell, shit was real like that. My manz █████ had an alliance with these next cats from way back so one day I was in front of a building shooting dice, talkin' shit when ███████ and another kid walk up. I was like "What's up?" he was like "What's up Sha? Yo, let me talk to you for a minute". We went in the building and again I ask "What's up?" He said, "Yo I'm havin' a problem with ███████ and them. They been fuckin' up my money every day. I gotta let this niggah know I aint no joke, you got a gun on you?" I said "Yeah, why?" He said "yo, you and ███████ come upstairs with me, I want to hold your gun to scare these niggahs, I'm not gonna shoot ███████ I just wanna scare his ass so they know I aint playin', you got me or what?" I thought about it "Yeah, hold up… Yo ███████ come here!" We all got on the elevator and went up to the crack spot that ███████ and dem was runnin'. I knew these niggahs was smokin' shit and all but I aint say nothin'. I passed ███████ a small Smith & Wesson .38 revolver, we got off the elevator on the fifth floor and knocked on the door a few times. We stood there for a few minutes then the door opened and ███████ was in there with three of his boys. He let us all in, I went in the kitchen with my manz and sat down. I heard ███████ in the livin' room yellin' at niggahs, he was talkin' crazy shit so I went to look… he was wavin' the .38 and screamin' at niggahs, dem cats was scared to death. I went back in the kitchen and sat down, I knew ███████ wasn't stupid cause when we came in, the apartment smelled like niggahs was smokin' crack in cigarettes or maybe this niggah was stupid cause he started talkin' low like everything was okay. They all came in the kitchen, me and my manz got up and this dumb ass niggah passed the .38 back to me right in front of everybody. Everybody in the apartment was watchin' me tuck the gun and these niggahs knew I wasn't down with ███████'s crew. "Yo, beep me later and have my money!" They said "Okay ███████ we will call you as soon as we are done." We all got up and walked toward the door, ███████ opened the door to let us out and as we went out the door, ███████'s eyes met mine… I could tell he was mad because he realized I gave ███████ the gun so as I walked out, he punched me in the side of my face and slammed the door. Right after he did that sucka shit, I heard every lock on the door lockin'; I put all six shots in that door.

Two weeks passed and this niggah ███████ (the one who stole on me) wouldn't come out of that spot. I sent crack heads up there and all but that door wouldn't open. I even had cats on post in front of their building to watch for this nigga. My spots were run by walkie-talkie headgear but man, fuck that... I had niggahs usin' the equipment to signal me if this clown came out. I knew he would try to sneak in and out late at night cause he had to eat plus this niggah was a down low crack head. What's so ill is I had known this niggah since like 1977-78', we were in school together and went on camping trips and cook outs back in the days. His baby mom was a Spanish chick and down low fiend too so I said to myself "next time I'ma fuck her and let her suck my dick for crumbs". I was so mad I wanted to kill this bitch ass niggah... he swung on me and slammed the door like a broad; he lucky none of them shots aint hit his ass.

Two more weeks passed and I still couldn't catch this niggah, we were even makin' jokes about it; he had to be caught out there some way, somehow. He didn't know how I move so eventually, he would slip up. Another month or so went by, it was a hot summer night and we were all outside by the middle buildings. It was like ten o'clock p.m. and everybody was out; females were by the benches, little kids were runnin' around, we were drinkin' forties and talkin' shit by the back entrance when out of nowhere, this niggah ████████ crept out of his building like a mouse. I saw him, he saw me and tried to run but I caught him and pulled out. Everybody was staring at me like I was crazy, shorties was runnin', grabbin' their kids and niggahs was gettin' out of the way. I had been talkin' about killin' this niggah for about two months now so everybody believed he was a dead man walking or... a dead man creepin'. His cousin ██████ had just shot and killed a female in front of niggahs two weeks ago so everybody was ready to witness another body. Holdin' my strap, I said "Yo bitch ass niggah, what's up now?" He was coppin' pleas "Yo Sha, listen God, you know I was mad at you, how could you give

██████████ a gun to bust at us? We supposed to be cool, I sold you that same gun!" That shit was so true. I gave a niggah a gun to see the same niggah I bought the gun from. I was like "Man fuck all that!" and I slapped him in his face, "I should kill you" everybody was so quiet, you could hear the leaves watchin' me. I smacked him again and said "Get the fuck outta here!" He saw I wasn't gonna shoot him and he said "Peace Shakim, Peace!" and he walked away. I walked over to niggahs and I saw in their faces they were waitin' for me to body that niggah. They started sayin' "You was supposed to kill that nigga Sha". I was like "Yeah, in front of all these people like ██████ did, right? Fuck it he aint nothin'". Niggahs was still tryna argue on some "True but he got out on you and in front of ██████ and dem. They are pussy, they wouldn't have gone upstairs if you gave them that gun, they did all that cause you and ██████ went up there with them. Sha... Damn Sha you should have blasted ████████ ".

The next morning, news of me givin' that niggah two slap and a pass was all over the P.J.'s "Sha said he was gonna kill ██████ when he caught him but when he caught him, he didn't do shit." Just that quick, the story had about a thousand different versions; I was "scared" and blah, blah, blah but seriously, I'm glad I didn't shoot him or kill him because there were like ten thousand eye witnesses out there. Trust me though, shit was far from over, about a week later I was comin' from my shorty's crib in Lefrak City, Queens, all the main cats was outside and there were some Jamaicans tryna open up a spot in the horse shoe by the middle buildings. Niggahs wasn't havin' that shit at all so I was comin' through and I saw niggahs out there mad deep. They told me the situation so I headed to the stash to get armed and niggahs was buggin' because I didn't have a gun on me, talkin' bout "Yo wait a minute, you just pulled out and smacked ██████ and you aint right? You're walkin' around, jewels and all and you aint holdin' (not strapped)? What are you stupid? Where the fuck you think you at, back in the soft ass sixties?"

By now the Jamaicans was headin' out, a niggah came out givin' us the signal, someone passed me a long revolver, I took it

"Yo Sha, you gotta cock it back before firing or it won't blast". I was like "I got this!" Nobody told me that it was a .44 long magnum; one of them Clint Eastwood "Dirty Harry" joints; the one where you gotta spin the chamber to load it, dump it, pull the hammer, cock it back to shoot and oh yeah… you gotta hold it with both hands when you shoot it. I ran in front of the building, niggahs was screamin' for me to back up as they surround the front of the building, I cocked back and niggahs was screamin' somethin' to me but I couldn't understand with everybody yellin' at once. I saw a niggah and his boys come out… I squeezed the trigger… **BOOM**!!! I missed the niggah I was shooting at because the impact from the blast made my gun jump in my hand and damn near ripped my thumb off. After that, my hand was bleedin' like crazy… it looked like my thumb was hangin' as niggahs emptied their shit at the Jamaicans.

A few days went by and my thumb needed stitches but I was on some self-heal shit. Niggahs was closin' spots down all week and they were outside talkin' shit, everybody was strapped as I came through greetin' cats. My manz ████, who ran the show, was there so now cats showed their true colors and started complainin'. "Yo, ████, what up with Shakim?" He asked "Why what's the science?" They explained the whole ordeal about how I gave ██████ a pass after he duffed me in my face and how I had cats stalkin' the spot and on post watchin' out for that niggah cause I said I was gonna kill him but I only smacked him up when I finally caught him. Niggahs was cryin' about how I gave him a pass and how I was walkin' around all carefree with no burner but I was the first to pull the trigger on some yardies (Jamaicans), who did nothin' but I gave a niggah who did something (stole on me) a pass and blah, blah, blah. My manz ██████, bein' old school, pondered over all the complaints and came back with some clown ass bullshit like "So you sayin' Sha is gettin' soft?" One cat says "I'm not sayin' that, I'm sayin'…" ██████ interrupted sayin' "Nah, Sha's gettin' soft and we can't have that shit! This is what we gonna do cause I don't have my boxing gloves with me. I'ma let y'all go in the elevator to go to the body with Sha Bio one by one but once the elevator goes up to the seventh floor and comes back down to the first floor **it's over**. Now Sha, you gotta go through these niggahs and then me, I'm last, so what's up?"

At this point, I was buggin', "What the fuck you talkin' about?" I scoffed. He repeats "You gotta go through these niggahs to show us that you are built for this shit!" I was like "Huh? I move more packs then all these niggahs, plus I can walk in any hood with my eyes closed, what da fuck you talkin' about?" As it all boiled down, I went body to body (trading strictly hard body punches) with like fifteen cats. We went in the elevator, pressed "7" and fought all the way up and back down. What's so funny about the shit was that out of fifteen dudes, I really only fought maybe four and that was the big niggahs who disliked me anyway, the rest faked it. When the elevator door closed and went up, we jumped up and down bangin' on the walls and yellin' then when the doors opened, I'd be against the wall "acting" like I was in so much pain and agony. In reality, I was really in pain from the first four fights, they were real. After all this shit, my manz, who came up with the idea for me to fight everybody still wanted his turn… in my mind, I was like "Damn!" As soon as me and ███████ got on the elevator, he started jumpin' up and down and the shakin' the elevator, tellin' me to yell, not knowin' that's what most of us already did. Until this day, ██████ thought niggahs whipped my ass on the elevator and niggahs thought he whipped mine, some funny shit right?

* * * * *

CHAPTER 11

Hip Hop was in full blast; music played a major role in the inner city hoods and was all over the radio, there was no escaping it. Emcees were no longer just harmonizing and doin' group routines, a lot of disco era jams were still bein' rocked crazily and break beats of these jams was bein' spun back and forth; these records were part of the elements of Hip Hop. Emcees were bein' more creative with the lyrics, bein' wordsmiths with witty metaphors and word play as well. There are too many emcees to name but in 1986 a couple dudes really changed the game such as DJ Eric B and his lyricist (The God) Rakim Allah, who came out with "Eric B is President" and "My Melody". A lot of cats were sampling break beats, mostly James Brown records but some cats were makin' beats from scratch. Break dancin' and poppin' wasn't on the fore-front like it once was when mainstream media was on the bandwagon, makin' movies like **"Flash Dance"**, **"Breaking"** and **"Beat Street"**. Now cats were doin' dances and makin' cuts about the dance steps like "The Peewee Herman", "The Wop", "The Happy Feet", and "The E.T." just to name a few cause there were so, so many.

Hip Hop was not only comin' out of New York, everybody was addin' on their version of it but I was still in a New York state of mind with thoughts of takin' over the planet. At that time, I saw no future in gettin' rich off of Hip Hop. I was too influenced by the fame, fortune and glamour of the fast life. Rappers was spittin' but they weren't showin' any signs of living good. The rapper "Just-Ice", who was from Hammels PJ's was doin' his thing but to me, all he had to show for it was a big Gucci Rasta Hat and a mouth full of gold teeth that were flooded with diamonds, rubies and other stones. Sheeet, I had all that and I didn't have a record out so what da fuck?

There was another emcee from Hammels, way back in the day named "MC Count". He was a short, brown-skinned little version of the Chief Rocker Busy Bee but he looked like he had little fangs and favored Count Dracula from Sesame Street. "Count" came out with a record in the early 80's, a response to the club /disco jam "Somebody Else's Guy", which was an ill jam by Jocelyn Brown, singin' about lovin' another woman's man. "Count" responded by sayin' he was that guy and why he was playin' both females. The record got heavy radio spins on N.Y.'s rap radio programs like Mr. Magic's Rap Attack and I used to see "Count" rockin' sweatshirts with "MC Count" ironed on the front. He was a good brother and later on in like 85'-86' when we were cuttin' records and makin' around the way tapes, "Count" would come through, sit with me and try to show me how to format a song. He was fuckin' with keyboards around this time too but after that one jam he had, niggahs seen him as a "nobody", a "One hit wonder" cause new records was comin' out every other day. "Count" was still in the P.J.'s and workin' a regular job but I respected him, he took time out to try and direct us to stay with music.

From travelin' throughout the boroughs of N.Y.C. goin' to school, battling rappers and just hangin' out, I started to notice that every borough had their own little anthem thing goin' and not just on the rap side of things but music in general. I was playin' clubs like The Underground (Union Square), Latin Quarters in Midtown, SNS Uptown, "371" in the Bronx and of course I was playin' the Queens and Brooklyn club scenes. Manhattan, really Uptown a.k.a. Harlem was rockin' the old Jackson Five joints like "ABC" and Marvin Gaye Classics. It was nothin' to be uptown and see cars and jeeps pullin' up, rockin' some ol' shit. They were sellin' tapes with these old school joints everywhere, we could be in a club and these old school classics would come on and you would know by the people's reaction that "Yeah, that's some uptown people right there". Old School cats was doin' the famous "2 step" with their hands in the air when the jam "Love is the Message" by MFSB came on. No matter where you were from, that song made you forget about your worries enough to party for a sec. Queens' anthem was Kenny Burke's "Rising to the Top"… that joint right there had niggahs open. Everybody from Queens who rapped, spit to that break beat; that song been sampled so many times but I still love it. Disco, Jazz, Blues and Rock N Roll were all being sampled or the bass was lifted or some element was used to make a Hip Hop joint, even Reggae records were bein' used.

The younger generation was steppin' their game up too, dem young niggahs was holdin' and movin' packages in the P.J.'s and when it came down to it, they was bussin' their guns too. Hammels Projects had little niggahs gettin' on and tryna shut shit down. The bullies of the 70's and 80's, who were nasty with their hands were all cracked the fuck out and gettin' smacked up by the young cats; crack changed the game dramatically. Little niggahs like Reggie (Hakim), his brother Rock, Myron, Ralo, Boo, Shannon, Kendu (Shabazz), Gregg, Young God and others were wildin' the fuck out, pushin' packages and shootin' shit up. Ol' School cats like "Money Mike" and "Dollar Bill", both of whom were respected for their hand skills in fights, were now hidin' from these little niggahs. A fella like me had been through a lot of shit already, like I said, I can't speak on a millionth of the shit I done been in. I'm just tryna give you a little insight on my growin' up in an era where a lot of niggahs couldn't even breath hard meanwhile, I wasn't even seventeen years old and I was "doin' me" somethin' vicious.

We were runnin' around shootin' up the boardwalk parties thrown by outsiders that had other outsiders comin' in the beach area, we was takin' their shit too, guns and all. Around this time, I was supposed to be goin' to Jamaica High for summer school but I would just go to show face and show off. My manz "Just" from Far Rock drove me to school on his motorcycle every day. A lot of Far Rockaway cats was barred from Jamaica High School over beef with some Edgemere p.j.'s cats and a cat named ████ from Rochdale Village in Jamaica. My manz from Edgemere knocked dude out so he had his crew stoppin' the buses lookin' for anyone from Far Rock. "Just" even started missin' days from school, I was going to school but I never went to class and as always, I kept a heater on me. One day, we rolled up to school and mad Rochdale

Village cats surrounded us, ready to fuck shit up. A lot of cats recognized me and had love for me bein' that I used to go to August Martin High School back in 1985 plus I ran with mad cats from Rochdale, who knew I was very thorough so I was told I was "good".

One weekend summer night, mad cats was loadin' up their hammers and shit because there was a beach party on the boardwalk and they were goin' up there to scope shit out, rob and shoot shit up. I came through after supplying my spots with work and made sure everything was everything. Once I touched the boardwalk, it was blocks and blocks of people but I couldn't find my Hammel PJ niggahs so I kept it movin'. I was laced up, rockin' a big cable, had rings on every finger and I saw mad Edgemere and Ocean Village cats plus cats I grew up with from the sixties so it was all love. Shorties was everywhere, sounds was blastin' and I finally found my niggahs, they were walkin' around scopin' shit out, schemin' on niggahs who had on big jewels if they didn't look familiar. Shit was crazy cause we did this shit every week and these outsiders still came out there every week to throw parties. I just don't get it! Niggahs was pullin' up in cars, parkin' in the lots; these parties attracted a lot of fuckin' people. This was the first boardwalk party I saw that was that packed with like, three or four blocks of niggahs and shorties. My manz is talkin' to a real cute shorty and once he got her phone number, he came and told us "Yo these niggahs from Jamaica, Queens is out here throwin' a party and a party is also bein' thrown for some Brooklyn peeps, that's why it's so thick out there, it's two parties that turned into one." Cats was takin' money to go to the store to get forty ounces of beer and you know I was with that! Next thing you know, I got me an ice cold "40 Dog" and I moved toward the deejay equipment cause that's where all the females seemed to be.

Once I got to the deejay area, I saw a crowd around the deejay as he entertained the crowd with his skills, cuttin' up records, scratchin' breaks of the latest jams. **Son was doing it**! I was stuck on stupid as son was cuttin' behind his back and the crowd was screamin' their asses off. I stood there drinkin' my forty, watchin' the show, I be on shit like that. Out of nowhere, Born C a.k.a. "Thunder Cuts" and Rasheem Supreme came up and stood by me. "Peace Shakim Bio!!" "Peace God!" As we stood there watchin' the deejay display his skills, Rasheem Supreme screams "Ah, that aint nothin', I can get him (the deejay)!!" He walked up to the deejay, stood in his face just watchin' him, the deejay saw Rasheem standing in front of him and shrugs his shoulders, as if askin' "what's up?" The crowd went bananas! The music stopped, a kid grabbed the mic and announced "Yo, anybody who thinks they can see my deejay, make sure you bring money with you because **we are takin' all bets**! "The crowd will be the judge!" Again, the crowd went bananas. Rasheem went in his pockets and pulled out some loose bills then turns to me "let me get some dough" so me and a few others handed him some bills, might have been a hundred dollars but Rasheem put it on the deejay table. The deejay said "Yo money that shit aint nothin' but chump change! I'ma let you go first I just hope you know how to mix and don't fuck my shit up, it costs more than that hundred dollars you put on the table". The deejay's boys matched the hundred dollars so now there was two hundred dollars on the table.

Rasheem put on the headphones and said "First up, I'm a MC reppin' Far Rock but I'ma show you how nice I am and how nasty I gets with these shits". As "Ra" started cuttin' the breaks the crowd cheered him on and Born C stood there watchin' his "deejay student". "Ra was doin' his thing but the needle kept jumpin' off cue, he sounded alright... he tried and he was above average, **no doubt**! The kid on the mic tried to talk shit askin' "Man, that's all Far Rock has to offer, what the fuck is that bullshit? Yo, show these nondescripts how we do it in Brooklyn!" The deejay got on and cut a record in as the breaks came in, he was cuttin', scratchin' and doin' hand movements, spinnin' the record, catchin' it, mixin' behind his back, doin' stunts and the needle never went off cue once. He hollered "Next!" as he snatched the two hundred dollars from the table. We started screamin' "Thunder Cuts! Thunder Cuts! Thunder Cuts!" then everyone from the sixties, 71-15 and O.V. started yellin' it. The kid on the mic asked "Who and what the fuck is a Thunder Cuts? Put a hundred dollars up to my equipment niggah!" **What?** That niggah just put his whole equipment up, speakers, record crates and all up against a measly hundred dollars. Born C was lookin' at son like he was crazy then dude on the mic asks "What Thunder Cuts, you aint go no money? Y'all broke out here in Far Rock too?" People started laughin', I say fuck it and slide Rasheem five twenty dollar bills, I had confidence in Born C, son was like that.

As the dough was put up, the deejay was like "I'ma let you go first" and Born C looked through the deejay's record crates and took out records he was familiar with. He looked at duke's mixer and smiled "I got this shit!" Born C got on and started warming up as Rasheem got the mic and excited the crowd, thrilling them with his ill rap skills. I was gettin' thirsty and wanted to touch the mic too, females was screamin' their asses off and niggahs was amazed by Born's skills. Without a doubt, the needle was jumpin' off cue but Born mastered that, did what he could then he started Riff-Raffing the breaks. Riff-Raffing is when you show how fast you are by constantly and consistently catchin' the break so fast that it sounds like you have the record talkin'. On the break "Good Times" by Chic, Born had the records goin' "Good, Good, Good, Good, Good", one turntable on "Good" then the second turntable on "Good", he was Riff-Raffing and the crowd was goin' crazy! Then, Born changed the records and started doin' his famous "Thunder cutting", which sounded like thunder. He showed his lightening fast skills and everyone was amazed even though the needle kept skippin'.

The crowd cheered and clapped as Born C got off, Rasheem Supreme gave Far Rockaway the ultimate shout out and screamed out "Peace to the God Shakim Bio-Chemical, he is in here!" Niggahs was barkin'! Duke, this Brooklyn deejay got back on and started cuttin' up the breaks… now remember, Born did amaze niggahs but this deejay had stunts and tricks. He was doin' all this spinnin' around, mixin' behind his back, cuttin' records while turnin' his hat backwards then he took the headphones off and was catchin' the break without listenin' to the cue. Then he started Riff -Raffing on "Good Times", he had one turntable sayin'

"Good" and the other sayin' "Times". The crowd went crazy, then he freaked it and had the turntables sayin' "Times" and "Good"; shit was sayin' "Times- Good" then he did somethin' I never saw before. Duke sped up the records to a hundred rotations per minute so it sounded like some Mickey Mouse, cartoon shit and he was cuttin' up the records and Riff- Raffing... then he slowed it down so slow, shit was crazy. I knew this kid had to be ill to put his whole mixing equipment, records, speakers and all against a hundred dollars, the crowd was goin' crazy; he won without a doubt but he came and shook Born C's hand though and said "Yo, you are nice, you are better than any deejay I battled and you handled my shit like you owned it but I keep that trick for cats like you!" We were talkin' but we never got the deejay's name because a fight broke out on the boardwalk.

Edgemere cats was swingin' on some kid from Rochdale, who they was beefin' with in Jamaica High Summer School; he was out there all jeweled up like Far Rock was sweet, niggahs was fuckin' dude up too. Then a golf club came into play and niggahs beat him in the head, his big chain and four finger ring came off as cats beat the blood out of him; next thing... automatic gun fire erupted. Bitches was screamin' and runnin', it was a frenzy out there and everyone started jumpin' off the boardwalk into the sand on the beach. It sounded like a million shots went off as everyone who had a gun started shootin'. Far Rock crooks was snatchin' chains, earrings and more shit. Niggahs was droppin' guns out there and what's so ill is the music was still on but the deejay was gone... All you heard was Bloc, Bloc, Bloc, Bloc, Bloc Bloc, Bloc, Bloc, Bloc, Bloc, Bloc then Blocka, Blocka, Blocka, Blocka, Blocka, Blocka, Blocka. Blaaaaat! Blaaaat! Blaaaat! Shit was serious. I made it out of there and came off with a chain but some real shit was mad cats was tryna hit me to get my jewelry. No matter where I went, cats was comin' in my direction until I pulled out, then they was like "Yo, he got a gun!" and runnin' in the other direction bussin'. I was just tryna get the fuck outta there, that's all. I stumbled on a "vic (victim)" with a semi-nice chain and piece on it, he gave it up quickly and I ran off toward the projects... another crazy night.

One day, I was outside doin' my thing and I heard there was a big talent show goin' down at Beach Channel High School later that night. Hammels P.J.'s was only fourteen blocks away from Beach Channel so everybody was gonna be there. While I was debatin' to myself whether I was gonna go or not, my manz "B.I. Self Allah" came out the building. "B.I. Self" was the rapper's rapper back in the 80's. He was part of the Funky A-Team but in reality, he WAS the "A Team". He was nice with the "verbals", and "Just Ice", who was makin' records like "Latoya", "That Girl is a Slut" and "Goin' Way Back" with KRS-One, was his half brother. Just Ice was also down with "Mantronix", he was doin' his thing. I always knew him as "Karate Just" because he practiced Karate / Kung Fu and wore sweat pants. I never knew son could rap though, I mean, I knew but it was all about my manz "B.I." "Just" started screamin' that he was from the Boogie Down Bronx when I knew son was from Queens. I have photos of me, him and Big Yang hangin' up in the Coliseum on Jamaica Avenue but again, I would see son ("Just") uptown and all that.

Back to B.I. Self though! Back in the 80's, "B.I." was always the first in the P.J.'s to have certain things like designer frames, gold teeth, big gold ropes and all that. He was a ladies man, fly cat, who was nice with words on the rap tip; I remember hearin' his name before I ever met him. I remember when he became God Body, he was settin' trends in Far Rockaway back then and everyone from Father MC to MC Serch took notes from B.I. Self. His name was floatin' around Far Rock and his name stayed in Just Ice's records. B.I. was also a part of our hustling team in Hammels but he was too fly to hustle. All he did was rent limos, ride around drinkin' bottle after bottle of Moet and livin' like he was a signed, famous rapper. He also had a mouth full of gold and was a well-known hood celebrity. I had a collection of tapes of his performances, guest appearances on tapes and early Just Ice joints where B.I. did the lead and Just was the background hype man. When B.I. rapped, the crowd sung along with him, this nigga had anthems! Anyway, "B.I." came out of the building and greeted me, "Sha Bio, Peace God! What's the science Lord?" I returned greetings "Peace B.I., nothing much, just out here gettin' this money!" He said "Look, I'm goin' up to the Talent Show at Beach Channel High School, I got a limo comin' and all, you rollin' with me?" "What do you think" I said? "Motherfuckin' right!!" I had mad respect for B.I., one time he stopped me from catchin' a body. I was drunk and lettin' my emotions override my intelligence, I got into a fight and pulled out to blast this kid in front of a building full of people and housing police had just went in. B.I. saved me that night, word!

Anyway, I put the work up and went to B.I.'s crib; he was in his room with outfits spread out all over his bed. He had about twenty pair of designer frames on the dresser and one of his demo tapes was blastin'. Son was gettin' ready for a high school talent show like it was a paid concert, **HIS** paid concert at that. See, the deal was DJ Polo, from the rap group Kool G Rap and Polo, was gonna be at this talent show. "Polo" had a baby mother who was originally from Corona, Queens but she and her family moved to Hammels P.J.'s and somehow, some shorties from the P.J.'s, who were in the talent show had convinced Polo's daughter's mom to invite him. Word spread fast so now everybody from Far Rockaway was goin'. Kool G Rap and Polo were part of Mr. Magic's "Juice Crew", they just released "Cause I'm Fly" and "It's a Demo", which was makin' crazy noise in N.Y.C. at that time. B.I. Self hung out with Just ice and rapper Biz Markie, who was also a member of the "Juice Crew". "B.I." was on his own dick crazily, he had photos and big blown up posters of himself with "Biz" and "Just" all over his walls. "Yo Sha, you always rockin' the new ill kicks but I'ma have to still rock my Bally's. You wearin' too much jewelry too, just rock the big rope with the piece on it, you can leave all that other shit here and oh yeah, I got some Ralph Lauren Polo frames for you unless you want the Gucci's."

Yeah, B.I. always gave me frames, like I said, I always got the "hand me down" designer frames from my manz but B.I. always beat him out. He stayed gettin' the flyest shit first and by the time I got the frames I'd still be the first to rock them in my little squad at school. Shit was kinda bugged out to me… I was like sixteen years old, B.I. was like six years older than me and he was gettin' all geared up to go to a high school talent show. I snatched up the Gucci's, back then, I had a flat top, not no tall boy shit though, it was barely a flat top and I rocked a half moon part cut in it; my shit stayed fresh. "Yo who's gonna carry the burner?" asked B.I. I said "Me of course!" as I showed him my 9mm. He saw my shit and said "Nah God, leave that here, I got a small .380 special that can fit right in your pocket. We goin' in a high school God and the 100th Precinct is right there. Take this .380… I'ma take the 2-5 (.25)." Yeah, regardless of anything, it was gonna be mad niggahs from all Far Rock's P.J.'s up at the talent show and P.J.'s was beefin' with other P.J.'s so we went strapped. B.I. was known in every project more than I was, it was an era that crack took over, everybody wanted to be a drug dealer so there was mad stick up kids plus B.I. got robbed in his own building a few months earlier by "Razz", so he was stayin' on point cause chick niggahs can turn brave-hearted at any minute.

We went down stairs, I was rockin' the ill leather front, Gucci frames, a big rope, brand new kicks, my gold teeth were shinin' and my pockets were swole and B.I. was lookin' like a famous emcee as we jumped in a limo that pulled up in the horseshoe (B.I. lived in the Horse Shoe Building of the Projects), everybody was wavin' at him. We had an hour to kill before the talent show so we rode around Far Rockaway drinkin' and smokin' blunts and this niggah even brought a tape of his exclusives and had it blastin'. "Yo, we not lettin' no one get in! No bitches, no niggahs, Nobody, Nothin'!" B.I. declared. "I got some pussy lined up for us after the show!" This niggah had the driver drivin' up on the main streets; he opened the sun roof and stood up so everybody saw him with his bottle in hand. Everybody was wavin' at this niggah like he was the fuckin' president or some shit… everyone loved B.I. Self Allah. We rode around all the main strips and by every project, I was still smokin', still drinkin' and listenin' to B.I.'s exclusives as they blasted through the speakers. I wondered why he never got signed or cut a record. I asked him "Yo B, why you aint come out yet?" He said "I'm shoppin' my demos now. I don't wanna be on the same label as "Just (Ice)" and I aint screamin' "BDP", I'm tryna get on with the label that kid "LL" came out on or I may become a Juice Crew All Star. Biz been lettin' niggahs hear my shit and I got this tape I'ma slide to DJ Polo **but I don't want G Rap to steal my shit!"**

As we rode by Beach Channel High School, it was mad crowded on both sides of the streets, we pulled up in the gas station (store directly across the street from the school) where everybody hangs out. Everyone looked at the limo, probably thinkin' DJ Polo was in it. B.I. got out holdin' a bottle of Moet and his sounds blasting, I got out with him, niggahs was crowdin' the limo, askin' questions and sayin' shit like "Yo B.I. what's up God, you rhymin' in the show tonight?" "Yo Father MC is supposed to come through". We heard it all as I mingled and talked small talk with cats I knew. Then I saw Born Supreme, Born Unique and Big Knowledge with the rest of the Hammels P.J.'s crew like twenty deep and lookin' devious. I greeted my manz Born Supreme "Peace Born!" He said "Don't tell me you up here with the project superstar B.I. Self!" All the P.J. cats started laughin'. "Sha, I know you aint up here fakin' with this niggah, wishin' he had a record contract when he's supposed to be workin' the package in the projects!" Everybody was laughin'. We went in that piece (Beach Channel H.S.) and it was packed. Born C "Thunder Cuts" was on the stage hookin' up his equipment. "Yo they got Petey and them from Edgemere dancin' in the show" I saw Petey do his thing in mad talent shows and different competitions, McDonald's talent shows and all, that niggah could really dance like a mothafucka. As I said before, he became a dancer for EPMD and appeared in all of their videos. It was rumored that he was fuckin' "Monie Love" when she first came out with a record. I knew son for a while, they called him "Fendi", he was always a dancin' niggah and he was at the talent show that night and we were up there.

.

As the show started, Born C was doin' his thing, Petey and his crew blew the other dance crews out of the water. What's so ill is the girl dance crew was from Hammels P.J.'s and they were the ones who were supposed to have DJ Polo there. Niggahs claimed to see him and all that but I didn't see shit. The emcees in the show were okay but nothin' to talk about. Word to my mother, a few people in the audience chanted "B.I.! B.I.! B.I.! B.I.!" and before you knew it the whole crowd was screamin' it out. B.I. was sittin' next to me smilin' from ear to ear, he stood up and raised his hands like he was a superstar and the crowd went wild. He was just standin' there with his arms spread out like wings and his hands just above his head while everyone was screamin' like he was Michael Jackson or some shit. I had to tap B.I. "Yo G, sit the fuck down!" Everyone was still chantin' and screamin' for this niggah as I saw mad Hammel cats in the back gathering up. It looked like they were about to move on somethin' in the back so you know I had to go back there, I was strapped with the .380 so you already know. When I got back there, I saw my student "Master Supreme Cee Allah" from the sixties, where I'm originally from after my family left Brooklyn. We greeted each other with a pound handshake and embrace. "Peace God!" "Sha Bio, if I would have known you come to shit like this, I would have beeped you. My manz, I was tellin' you about is up here and he wants to meet you". I asked "Who, DJ Polo?" we started laughin'… "Nah my niggah Al Monday" he said.

Before this, I kept hearin' about this Al Monday kid and not just from my manz "Preme" but from other cats. I had a shorty in Laurelton and I was shootin' through Jamaica, Queens regularly, my manz Hassan, who I met through my manz Sha Prince, used to come through and talk to us about this Al Monday kid. I used to wonder who the fuck this niggah was, he was from Farmers Boulevard but he went to Beach Channel and how he wanted to meet me… for what? I asked Supreme "Yeah? Where he at now?" I looked up and saw Hammels niggahs surrounding us, "Yo Born, What's up?" He said "My manz says he's beefin' with this cat from Jamaica, Queens and he is with the kid you're talkin' to now". "Yeah?" I looked at Preme "Preme, what's up?" Preme told me about a beef Monday had months ago with a cat from Hammels and how it was over nothin', they even fought and now that niggahs were so deep, the shit was brought back up. "Hold on Preme", I pulled Born to the side and explained how Preme was my peoples and Monday was too. I looked Born in his eyes and told him "It can't go down like that!" Born was my peoples and he controlled them Hammels wolves, he was their leader, he hugged me and said "I got that Shakim cause you're my **peoples**!" I called Preme over there and told him in front of Born Supreme that it was all good, there was no beef. I pulled Preme over to the side and told him I was strapped so it was all love. I ask him "Yo, where ya manz at?" He replied "I don't' know, he is around here somewhere." We didn't know this niggah Monday was roundin' up cats just in case these niggahs from Hammels tried to move on him. He rounded up some back up, not knowin' that them Hammel cats was strapped with the big guns, they were on their own turf and I already squashed shit.

The talent show ended and everyone was goin' out the doors, I went with the Hammel P.J. niggahs and it was crazy packed outside. I saw cats standin' around lookin' ill. I saw my student "Supreme" posted up with a Spanish lookin', Burt Reynolds lookin' cat and some other cats. Born Supreme got my attention "Yo, what's all that about over there?" I looked and me and the Spanish lookin' cat made eye contact so I walked in their direction thinkin' to myself, "I know this face from somewhere. I stopped at Preme and said "What's up?!" Preme introduced us... "Sha, this is Monday, Monday this is Sha Bio", we looked at each other and I told Preme "Yo, go straight to ya crib right now! No stopping' no where, I'ma be over there in one hour". B.I. and the limo pulled up, I looked at Born Supreme and said "Yo shit is deaded God, be easy! Peace!" I told B.I. I was stayin' up there, he asked why and reminded me he had some pussy lined up but lookin' toward the crowd, I told him I had to make sure my peoples was okay. He said "Aaah man, you stay up in some shit, just don't body nothin' young God, beep me in the morning". I was like "Peace!!"

* * * * *

"Drug dealers drivin' around, lookin' hard / knowin' their sendin' their brothers and sisters to the graveyard"

"Streets of New York"

Kool G. Rap

CHAPTER 12

This niggah Al Monday had an old ass, light green, mint colored Dart. He even had a name for it... somethin' like the "Blues Brother's mobile". The car had the wrong plates, no registration, no insurance and it was a blessing if it even started on any given day. Yo, check out how my manz had the car lookin'... on all four doors, he spray painted the windows black to look like it was real tint. He had the Mercedes Benz emblem spray painted on the back trunk by the key hole, it was positioned where the real emblem would be on a Benz and he had the Benz emblem spray painted on all four hubcaps; shit was serious! He aint have no car radio so he had a box radio with a cassette player so he could rock tapes. He had all the ill exclusive LL Cool J tapes that he kept blastin' also Grand Master Vic mixtapes. I got hip to DJ Grandmaster Vic when I went to August Martin High School in 1985.

Another ill thing about Al's "Blues Brother's Mobile" was once you got inside there were empty Old English 800 beer bottles, empty Calvin Cooler bottles plus forty ounces and quarts all in the back. He (Al) drove back and forth from Jamaica, Queens to Far Roc every day to go to school. The car was on the verge of breakin' down at any moment and the ill shit is we used to go to Brooklyn, Hempstead, Long Island, all over Queens, Uptown Manhattan, and the Bronx, we went everywhere in that bucket. Word on everything duke, one day the car wouldn't start up, we ran out of gas... Monday turned the ignition and the engine wouldn't turn all the way over. We laughed our asses off, Al was sittin' there with his quart of Calvin Cooler and I was in the back drinkin' my forty. Al said to me, "Yo Sha, let me see your forty" I was like "For what? You got your quart, you good". He said "Nah, for real, I'ma show you a trick but I need your forty. I said "What?" We're stuck with no gas and you want to take my brew, is you nuts?" Monday persisted "Nah, I'ma show you somethin', we will get more forties." I passed him my forty still in the bag and all, he stepped out the car smirkin' like crazy, opened the gas tank, took a swig of beer then he put the bottle in the gas tank. I hollered at my manz "Yo Preme, what is he doin'?" Preme replied "Chill G, he got this, he does this all the time". I asked "what is he crazy? He's gonna fuck up the engine!" This niggah poured my whole brand new forty ounce of **BEER**, into his gas tank and told Preme to lift up the hood. From there, he put a cap full of beef in the engine's carburator.

Monday got back in the car smilin' and shit, he stepped on the gas petal for a minute then he was fuckin' with the box radio while he just sat there. "Well?" I asked sarcastically. He turned the key in the ignition and said "Chill Sha" the car started like before but then it wasn't turnin' over... Sun, word to my seeds, the car started. I was sittin' there with my head fucked up as Monday looked at me, "You see why I don't fuck with Ole English". As we pulled of, I was still buggin' behind that beer in the gas tank shit; we stopped at the store and I bought two more forties. When I got back in the car, this niggah was playin' crazy games, drivin' passed gas stations and laughin'. "Yo, there go a gas station over there Al", I yell. He's like "So!" and we'd all start laughin'. We passed like six or seven stations before he pulled over and filled the tank because we had to let that forty burn a bit before we put actual gas in the line. Monday had a smirk on his grill that really had him lookin' like Burt Reynolds and shit.

We made a lot of moves in that bucket, pullin' crazy robberies and takin' long trips to Jone's Beach in Long Island, etc. When we got pulled over by police, they couldn't stop laughin' at his car with the spray painted windows and Mercedes Benz emblem on the hubcaps and trunk. We were pullin' up to schools in Mondays' ride so I could battle niggahs and all that. We went to house parties and movies, we came through in that whip and you couldn't tell us nothin'. We would be all the way in Brooklyn, pushin' Al's whip, blastin' the box radio, listenin' to Mr. Magic's rap attack as DJ Marley Marl spun the wax… we would even touch Coney Island's Amusement Park and all up in the Bronx at "Club 371", we were little niggahs makin' moves.

I used to live in crack spots, that shit is mad funny when I think about it now. I would open up a crack spot, clean out the back bedroom, hook it up with TV, VCR, stereo shit, mad tapes, tinted lights, fresh bed spreads and curtains and I'd have a thousand sneaker boxes with fresh kicks in them. I had to padlock and chain the back room every time I left, even just to go to the bathroom to take a piss. Shit was serious "B" word life, anything could come up missin' just that quick. I had the back room laced up so ill you'd forget you was in a crack spot although, the door was knocked on all day and night until I'd go to the back room and lock in. I lived in spots that made twenty-five hundred to three thousand a day. I would pack up my shit and move to another building or just up or downstairs every month or so until the apartment cooled down then, I might just use it as a packing den or cook up spot, wasn't no tellin'.

I was runnin' like three or four spots for my manz and livin' in them pieces like "What!" From time to time I went back to my mom's crib but never for long. Her husband was on some pure, straight up bullshit and had mom flippin' on ME, her only son. Mom wasn't havin' much of anything I was doin' and I remember comin' home to find my bedroom lock forced open, all my gear, sneakers, VCR, tapes, stereo, turntables, leather coats and shit in garbage bags by the door. Mom used to scream "I didn't buy you any of that shit so I don't want it in my house! Get it out of here or get out with it!" I had all kinds of ill shit in my room at mom's house. She found guns and all kinds of shit; my step pops was behind all of her protests. I remember she found my money stash and she wouldn't give it to me, then I faked her out by packin' my shit sayin' "I don't wanna be here when Domonic asks for his money, those Italians don't play!" It was so funny how fast she gave that money back after I said that… she believed black people were bein' used and couldn't have anything. We didn't have the planes to bring the drugs to the U.S., we were just pawns.

In 2001 when my mom's came to Cali to visit me in the Feds, we shared a good laugh about how I said "I don't wanna be here when Domonick asks for his money, those Italians don't play!" we laughed so hard on that visit. Mom always told me that she felt since I was a little one I would grow up to be a hell of a comedian or a lawyer because I was a "chatter box", always talkin' so when I started rhymin', she knew that was my thing. I used to be in my room watchin' tapes, with Supreme, Monday, Daymond or whoever. We'd be in my room watchin' DJ battles on VCR tapes. I used to copy and study those tapes, the DJ battles was ill. I had a tape of Grandmaster Vic from Jamaica, Queens, he used to put on handcuffs and tear shit up; shit was amazing. We used to watch those DJ battles, go to parties up at Five Towns Trade School, Far Rock's PAL or I.S. 8 in Jamaica; I still had to climb out my window at my mom's crib. By the time I came home from sneakin' out, bags full of all my shit would be by the door again so I would just move it all to my crack spots or to my manz crib. I was gettin' tapes from Monday that featured deejays I never knew existed around that time. Everybody was doin' the "Transformer" cuts and scratches, which was created by Philly's DJ Jazzy Jeff (The Fresh Prince's deejay, who was crowned the "Son of Flash"). The Transformer was a cuttin' and scratchin' technique that sounded like the robot noises from the classic cartoon and current popular "Transformers" movie series, there were all kinds of ways to transform on the turntables. I could mix on sideways cross faders or up and down mixers but a simple way to transform was / is to move the record back and forth slowly while you move the cross fader real fast like you're flickin' it. Some cats was using switches or convertin' their mixers to make this transformer mix. I even went to the "Underground (Union Square)" with Monday, Supreme and others and while cats was sweatin' the honies havin' fun, I was studyin' DJ Jazzy Jeff and how he did that Transformer shit, shit was ill.

Around the time when Monday was slidin' me tapes, deejays was doin' moves on Technic 1200 turntables. The 1200's had start/stop buttons and you could adjust the speed of the record by a control adjuster lever. Cats was comin' up with ill shit, like hittin' the stop button to make the record stop, causing that ill sound of music and words quickly slowin' to a stop. Deejays was usin' that effect to their advantage or they would back spin the record to the point that you could hear it like how Jamaican deejays do it, they called it "Reee-wiiinnnd". The noise effects and the cuttin' and scratchin' was some ill shit.

Then niggahs came up with some ill shit where they were playin' records backwards on the break beat instrumental parts at the same speed, it would have spun if you were playin' it regularly. Deejays was makin' tapes like that, rockin' a lot of "Public Enemy" beats like that. Blends was already in action too; this technique works when you take two different records / songs and make them sound like one. Usually, you take an a'capella R&B song and get a Hip Hop instrumental, blending them to make it seem like the R&B song was made on that Hip Hop beat. My tape collection was expandin' with early L.L. Cool J tapes and live taped park battles, it was a lot poppin' off and cats was very creative back then. Hip Hop was everywhere and everybody had records out or it seemed like it. Cats was rhymin' to the point where back in my school days, it might be like three or four real emcees and now it was twenty-five to thirty emcees and ten or more deejays in each school. Rap ruled the radio airwaves on all levels.

Time passed and I was runnin' around with Monday more than ever. I was fuckin' wit cats from his area and meetin' some real live niggahs and expanding my hustles. I linked up with some good cats like Harold "Hype" Williams, the whole Farmers Boulevard from 109th to 118th ave, Daymond John and the whole crew. We did mad shit and although I won't put our dirt out there like that, we did have fun hangin' out though. On a few occasions, I got locked up while buggin' out with them. Once out in Coney Island, another time we were on the Duece (42nd street in Midtown). Shit is mad funny as I think about that shit now cause they were all some squeaky clean lookin' cats from good family upbringings but they did mad dirt just like everyone else... they just didn't get caught. I even brought these niggahs to the P.J.'s I was hustling in. These niggahs was amazed by that shit I went through on a daily basis.

Monday used to come through and get me every day, sometimes he came through just to hang out with me in the trifling P.J.'s, where it was obvious that some of them cats from Hammels didn't really like me but when I came around they showed me all thirty-two teeth like I was a dentist or some shit. I held shit down accordingly and been through some shit in them projects over Monday comin' down but overall, he was still able to come through and niggahs had to respect that. Son (Monday) was comin' through in stolen whips and we would drive around Midtown Manhattan, schemin' and scopin' on the stick up tip. We were goin' out of state, frontin' and flossin' amongst other shit. Around that time, Monday was graduatin' from Beach Channel High and his pops gave him a brand new Jetta so now son was really doin' it. We went everywhere in that car and we kept it immaculately clean, touchin' every borough in N.Y.C. Monday was goin' through his ups and downs at home as well so he moved out, stole his own car and started livin' from place to place before movin' in with his girl and her family in Far Rockaway.

Me and Monday ran the streets crazily, makin' moves, tryna get that paper and we still played all the happening spots. We stayed geared up and all that and by then, the system was in the car with rims, tints and all. Monday was still comin' through in the ill stolen whips and dipped motorcycles as we did our dirt. What's ill is that one thing Monday didn't like about me was too many cats knew me no matter where we went. I knew mad cats, we could be in Long Island gettin' ready to stick up the whole corner and as soon as we surfaced on the corner, ten cats was shakin' my hand sayin' "what's up?", "Peace Sha" or some shit.

No bullshit, me and Monday went through mad shit together. I recall one night we parked a few blocks up in Queens as we went on a rampage stickin' up everything. We came back with mad goods and the car was gone. Shit was crazy, we kept circlin' the block lookin' for where we left the car until we seen some ill shit. Mondays' pop's truck was parked in the neighborhood, which meant he saw the car, parked his truck and took the Jetta, knowin' when we came back and saw the car gone and his truck parked up we would know what's what (he took it); shit was crazy but it didn't stop nothin'. We were gettin' stolen rentals from the airport because we had a manz who worked there and when people brought the rental cars back, he left two or three with the keys inside so we could take them. We were getting' into wild chases uptown with Po-Po, flippin' cars over, leavin' them on their hoods as we climbed out of the windows to get away. We were comin' through in stolen Ninja 1000's, ridin' around in rain storms all plottin' and schemin', shit was serious and got iller... Then this nigga Monday started rhymin' and "Phat Eon" was his next door neighbor, who had studio / deejay equipment so once again... music was available to me everywhere I went, I just couldn't escape it...but I was on the move and out of state on the regular.

* * * * *

CHAPTER 13

My life was crazy! I was movin' in different female's cribs, stayin' in so many cribs that after runnin' wild, me and Monday would either go to one of my shorty's cribs or his girl's crib to shower and get geared up. We were sleepin' in stolen cars at night cause we were on the "J.O.B." We stayed eatin' chicken wings and fried rice from Chinese takeout spots. I drank mad forty ounces and held my spots down, supplyin' the workers and fuckin' up the money... shit was illmatic. "Preme" entered the Navy and left us to wild out even more, then I moved on to turn shit up hustling out of state. I was still collectin' Hip Hop & Jamaican Dancehall tapes so out of town, I was rockin' Gill Bailey and Clive Hudson tapes that I recorded from their shows in N.Y. Ohio niggahs didn't even know what "Cuiff (song by Shelly Thunder)" was. I introduced them to Sister Nancy, Sister Carol, Ninjaman, "Eek a mouse" tapes. That's how I met my first son's mother, I was blastin' a yardie mixtape back in 1988, the kid (ME) was ill with it.

I remember how niggahs from Farmers Boulevard was happy that L.L. was gonna be on the Soul Train Music Awards. "B", niggahs taped that shit and everyone had that shit, not the whole Music Awards show, just certain parts like when Dionne Warwick introduced "L" and he came out spittin' about the Soul Train Awards over the beat to his song "I'm Bad". Then later in the show, he won some awards, came up on stage mobb deep and was wildin' the fuck out with dance steps and ill moves, jumpin' up and down, shit was serious. I can't even count how many times we would drink, smoke and watch that same tape, everyone had copies, I even took a copy with me to Ohio; "L" put Farmers on the map music-wise.

For as long as I can remember, Monday was very active promoting parties and artists. When I met him, he was promotin' house parties. That was the kind of niggah he was, always puttin' shit out there, tryna flip money. Since 1984, I had been playin' Hip

Hop clubs like "Latin Quarters" shows in Midtown, "The Underground (Union Square)", Empire Skating Rink in Brooklyn and other spots. I was doin' everything from bein' involved in talent show performances to bein' a fan in the crowd witnessing shit. Queens had a few spots that was rockin' too. We had Lacie's Skating Rink poppin' off crazily, a spot called "Encore" that changed its name so many times over the course of time and there were a few spots in the late eighties that niggahs could go to. Monday was promotin' house parties and even free park jams at P.S. 118 and O'Connor Park just off of Murdock Avenue so it wasn't surprising when he started promotin' parties and artists in the clubs. There was a spot on Archer Ave. called "The Q Club" that opened up in the eighties, well, it became known to us cats around that time. Now it's a Jamaican hang out spot that plays Hip Hop and mostly Dance Hall but in the eighties it was just Hip Hop. Al Monday was makin' serious moves… when he saw that The Q Club was available for rent, he was gettin' with cats, they'd put their dough together to rent the spot. Next thing you knew, flyers were made and passed around at every High School and in every hood. Monday was very associated with rapper L.L. Cool J (Todd), who knows Monday by the name "Al Krak (his graffiti handle)" and Monday did artwork on Todd's basement bedroom walls back in the days.

Because of his history with "L", Monday was puttin' L.L. Cool J's name on flyers to attract crowds, knowin' all he had to do is convince L.L. to show up. Once "L" showed up, you know he was gonna rock the mic, that's just the type of cat he was; **Back then, niggahs looked out for their niggahs!** The Politics of goin' through managers, companies, agents and all that didn't matter back then, if a rapper or his entourage was your manz and dem then **moves was made on the strength** of that friend or family bond. So Monday was makin' minor moves that turned out to be big events, even if he couldn't use L.L. Cool J's name because Todd's name was Def Jam's property, he would put "Birthday Party Jam for E-Love" because everybody knew "E" was L.L.'s man and crew member at the time. "E" also happened to live directly across the street from Al Monday. Any rational thinking party-goers would think that if there was a B-Day party for "E-Love", L.L. and other surprise guests would be there.

Within time, Monday was gettin' acts like DJ Irv and Jamaica, Queens favorite Hollis Crew MC Romeo to perform. Irv and Romeo were very well known on the underground scene and "Club Fantasies", which was another Queens Hip Hop spot. Back in dem days, it was easy to give a rapper or group anywhere from five hundred to two thousand dollars to show up and rock the mic. Bein' a signed emcee was enough and makin' yourself available for local appearances was ill. Niggahs was rockin' material that nobody ever heard before, tryin' their new shit or just rappin' their hit songs. There were rap groups that was fallin' off like Super Lover C and Casanova Rudd, who were Queens reps and very available to Monday through DJ Irv so C and Rudd were willing to make appearances too.

Even if a lot of money wasn't being generated, Monday's name was buzzin' on the strength of the parties so just rentin' the spot for one night was ill. The club always made money for real because they had security and made all the money from the bar areas, sellin' drinks and shit. Monday just attracted the crowd and got a percentage of the door fee but still, a couple extra hundreds as profit and havin' your name out there was enough for a neighborhood niggah movin' up through word of mouth and street grindin'. Next thing you knew, niggahs was makin' moves, throwin' parties, connectin' and pollying with the deejays at uptown underground spots. We were up in spots like "The Octagon" or the "Red Zone" and "Wetlands", where Funk Master Flex was spinnin' but he wasn't a big famous deejay yet, he was just a known underground deejay; DJ Ron G, who spun at Club Savoy in the Bronx on Thursday nights and DJ kid Capri were doin' their thing too. Monday and his team of Irv and Roe were connectin' with niggahs to get them to show up to little club events, just gettin' these niggahs names on flyers was attractin' big crowds and these deejays were killin' shit back then. "SNS" uptown closed down and the "Roof Top" wasn't really poppin' like that anymore. During the summers of "89-92", boat ride parties became a big event... Boat rides parties are jams thrown on big vessels as they cruise the river.

A ship could usually hold close to two thousand people and with a deejay, his equipment and drinks being served, shit was all that. Those were definitely the shits (place to be), everybody loved the boat ride jams that were hosted by DJ Ron G, Kid Capri or maybe some upcomin' underground deejay. All the females would be on the boats, dressed in their summer wear and all the hustlers, money getters, hood celebrities, Hip Hop lovers and party-goers would enjoy the music and the ride. The boat rides would usually only be a four hour thing but they were definitely "like that", especially at the pier, were all the action was at. All the honies and all the players would pull up in their ill whips tryna be seen. Monday was collaborating with other heads around the way to get dough up to put the boat rides together. Everyone was doin' it but in Jamaica, Queens, only one niggah was known for it and that was "Al Monday". Even other niggahs who were throwin' parties and other shit would put Al Monday's name on their flyers to attract heads. You know it will always be a dirty side of the game (you know). Al was gettin' with Daymond John to get dough to promote parties before Daymond established FUBU. Shit came a long, long way; they started with promotin' parties, then park jams, then Rochdale Community Centers, then came roller skating rinks, small clubs and boat rides. This was all the work of street niggahs who really crime about it / rhyme about it, niggahs couldn't be told Nathan!

Although the music ventures was jumpin' off, it wasn't a major thing to us. Monday was still doin' his street dirt with cats and he still had his street niggahs out there grindin'; niggahs had to eat no matter what. When you saw Monday, you saw Sha Bio, niggahs knew who I was, I was either sittin' in the passenger seat of a car Monday was pushin' or I was close by. I wasn't a part of every element of the ventures but I knew all about shit because I was Monday's arms and legs. Every crumb that got sold was through me, I always knew what was goin' down at all times. Even back in our small spree robbing days, no matter what, if we ran with you and your clique on a number, me and Monday thought alike. Even after we split all the moneys and broke out in our different directions, me and Monday always met back up cause we "dipped" and stashed the "dipped" money. "Dipped" is when you pocket or stash money that was part of the lick, you just didn't let other niggahs know. We may have run in your spot, search the shit, find fifty gees but we'd only bring thirty gees out cause we dipped twenty. We'd catch mad cats for their jewelry and go pawn shit but we'd keep certain pieces, get them fixed and cleaned and then we'd rock shit. When cats ask for their cut, we gave them what we wanted to give them. Niggahs was happy cause Monday made it happen, if it wasn't for him, they wouldn't have shit, he had a grimy side to him but he was my peeps.

One of the biggest shows Monday promoted was in Baltimore, Maryland back in 1991. Irv, Daymond and whoever else may still be talkin' about this particular party, you'll be talking about it too when I'm through speaking on it (LOL). This was a time when we wasn't doin' too good, a lot of bad luck was fallin' on us. We just lost a lot of paper and the feds was chasin' us for nothin' so we was on the move. Monday just got shot and I was makin' all the street moves with fucked up people around me. We were living in hotels, back street, rundown roach motels and all kinds of shit. Niggahs went from 750I's and M5's to squeezin' in Monday's mom's Datsun 210 or whatever number it was, moves was still bein' made without an end though.

One time, Monday rented a spot in Baltimore called "The Palladium", which was off of Reisterstown Road. The spot held like three thousand people, maybe more plus it had a bar and we made a lot of moves to pull this one off. Money went to gettin' professional flyers on cardboard paper made, posters and radio commercials. Monday really did it on this one, as much as we stayed in the malls shoppin' for gear, shit was real cause loot was needed, we even bought clippers to cut our own hair. We were grindin' and everybody played their part. Irv (Gotti) was the in-house deejay for a second, it was "Big Sincere" (Monday's Alias) or some crazy name like that and Roe Dog Productions featuring

"Black Sheep", "Ed O.G. and the Bulldogs", "Main Source" performing and "Father MC" was headlinin' the show with Jodeci. What was ill was even though Jodeci was on the flyer, they weren't gonna be there. This was right when Jodeci came out with "Forever My Lady" and females everywhere was goin' crazy. We knew everybody and their momma would come out to that event and we were the only ones who knew Jodeci wasn't gonna be there but Monday knew what he was doin' so fuck it! Monday had Kid Capri deejay and Ed Lover from "Dr. Dre and Ed Lover" host the event. Daymond John drove the groups from New York to Baltimore in his van, these groups showed a lot of love for niggahs, they knew niggahs was grindin' crazily and some of them performed for dirt cheap out of love and on the strength. It was a lot of inside politics involved for real, shit I don't really want to speak on. Just knowin' the right people, knowin' what chick could do this or that or knew this or that niggah.

The fact that we portrayed and blew up our "street cred" more than it was at that time played a big, big part in makin' this event come together. Monday was an ill thinker and we were surprised, shit... he might have surprised himself when he pulled this event off. He rented the whole floor of the Ramada on Security Boulevard, while Daymond drove the groups back and forth, shit was crazy. We had Father MC, who is my manz from way back, his dancer "Tricksy" and his security / main manz "Big Dad". Paul (Large Professor) from Main Source came through with his two deejays and his entourage, "Akinyele" was one of them. Akinyele got crazy drunk, showed out at the hotel and smacked one of the chicks that was down with us. Shit almost got out of hand right there, "AK" is lucky he aint get bodied that night too, it was that serious. Everybody from Farmers was there and Baltimore had a really good time as all of the groups did their thing, that shit was big to Al Monday.

I was back in N.Y.C., holdin' dem blocks down and gettin' ready to travel down south to get shit movin' accordingly. **The game don't stop and the show must go on**!! I was makin' my moves, pushin' weight and doin' robberies with my manz from Far

Rock, we got over the hump and were back on top again. I was between Baltimore and S.C. (South Carolina) gettin' it poppin', tryna make little moves. One of the chicks I was messin' with in S.C. was originally from Brooklyn, she had a cool sister whose manz was from "40" Projects in Jamaica, Queens; his name was Tone ("Half"), he owned a club down in Columbia, SC. With me bein' from Queens and very familiar with 40 pj's, Tone and I linked up and connected on many aspects and street shit. One thing led to another and I was tryna make moves. Father MC, Mary J Blige and Jodeci were on tour and I had their tour schedule so I was puttin' together an after party jam for after their concert when they hit the area. I was usin' the strength that me and Tim (Father MC) went to Far Rock High School together, we used to rhyme together and I used to hold him down when he was workin' in Kentucky Fried Chicken in Far Rock. They transferred him to KFC across the street from Hammels pj's, where I was scramblin' and guess who was holdin' him down, that's right, Sha Bio.

Back in 1987 – 88, son (Tim a.k.a. Father MC) used to give me free chicken every day he worked in that piece and I used to make sure no one fucked with him. I remember one night he was on the "Hank Love Radio Show" on WHBI (now WNWK) and he was bein' interviewed and shoutin' out his peeps and shit. I was on the block listenin'… when I didn't hear him shout me out, I called the station like twenty times. When I finally got through, I screamed "Put Tim on the Phone!" He got on the phone and asked "Who's this?" I said "Shakim Bio-Chemical niggah!" "Yo Sha what's up?" "You aint shout me out or Hammels either niggah, you know you gotta be here tomorrow!" Yo Father MC shouted me out and damn near everybody he could think of from Hammels P.J.'s. I'm talkin' about Lucky, Spade, Chiz, Chase, Born U, Born Supreme, Nanfu, B.I. Self, Lord Imperial; he did us right. I remember when Shateek Shamel from "40's" was his deejay and it used to be me and him plus "Agnus" cuttin' classes, smokin' weed, drinkin' forties and I was the only one who kept dough. I remember this Chinese jewelry store in Far Rock that took photos in the back… Father MC would go in there to take photos wearin' their jewelry, fakin' for the cameras like the jewels were his.

I remember when Father's teeth was fucked up, over-riding each other on the top of his gums. We used to cut school, go to Flea Port in Five Towns and he'd buy a ten dollar gold finger nail, go home and bend it over his front tooth. What the fuck you talking about? I remember I had to beat up his hype man "Nathaniel", had son scared to leave school. Father MC had already blown up but how could he not show love and come to my after party, I'm Sha Bio!! I was thinkin' if he came maybe Mary J or dem Jodeci cats might show face too. I had shit already mapped out plus another one of my chick's sisters used to mess with Father and had his phone numbers. I was cool with her whole clique and I loved most of them. Shorty played a big part of gettin' Father to do that show for Monday. I didn't need Father to perform, I just needed him to come on stage, tell everybody to come to the after party and say the name of the club. That's all he had to do and everything was set. I had the ill promotion comin' from Father MC himself.

Columbia, S.C. had two big colleges, Benedict and Allen, which were both Black Colleges and they were across the street from each other so mad honies were goin' to both schools. I used to be up there for hours, messin' with dem college chicks. I had a shorty from N.Y. named Lashaun (Pinky) from Pink Houses (Projects) in East New York, Brooklyn. She went to one of them schools (I can't remember which one) and I knew mad college heads was goin' to the concert so as far as my after party went, I had shit in the smash, lined up and ready to go. Monday was smilin'; proud of his ill niggah Sha bio but then the ultimate bullshit happened... **the concert got cancelled**! I was pissed like shit but I was still makin' moves regardless. I linked up with the owners of "The Heart of The City", me and Monday came through and they let me kick a rap over the "Check the Rhyme" beat by Tribe Called Quest (another group from Queens) and they were impressed. Monday was impressed by the size of the spot so we talked about rentin' it or bringin' artists down there to perform.

Makin' my street moves in Baltimore, I was touchin' up the clubs down there by just hangin' out. I also got in mad drama out there and ended up with a hundred and ten stitches in my head piece. I was meetin' a lot of chicks while chillin' in Hammerjacks, Paradox and a few other spots. I started messin' with this bad shorty named Tanya, who was definitely "like that", she had big singin' skills too. Tanya and her sister were featured on a big Baltimore City, Club Music smash called "Yo Yo Where's your Boyfriend At?" Tanya and some cats sang and Tanya's sister rapped, the song was big in B-More. Through Tanya, I met DJ Mike Crosby, DJ Reggie Reg and a few others, these deejays were big on Club, Go-Go and house music all in one type shit. Me and Mike Crosby used to bowl against each other every week at a bowling alley in West Baltimore.

Every weekend, the bowling alley would close at 10:30 p.m. while a deejay hooked up his equipment then they'd re-open at 12 midnight until 4 a.m. for "Rock –N- Bowl", which is where I met Tanya… the shit would be jam packed Friday and Saturday nights; parkin' lots and all. The spot would be jumpin' crazily, shorties were everywhere and they had like twenty-five lanes on one side and another twenty-five on the other side with twenty Arcade games in the middle. They also had mini-Blimpies and Dunkin Donuts concession stands, it was bananas! The music blasted and deejays played that ill shit while people partied and bowled at the same time. I was cool with the deejays cause they worked at Mondoman Mall in the record shop where I used to cop records to mix on my equipment that I kept at my son's mom's crib in West Baltimore. This "Rock-N-Bowl" event had a talent show on Friday and Saturday nights so me and my manz Shameek from Hollis used to go check out the talent. Shameek convinced me to sign up for the talent show so I did and I won like three weeks in a row. As I said, I used to bowl against the deejays so I was cool with them even though me and Reggie Reg didn't really like one another. I used to pick the record I wanted to rhyme to, way before-hand so I would get a hype crowd reaction and always had the upper hand in any competition.

One night, there was one cat who was super nice, he gave me a run for my money cause he had special made, premeditated rhymes he wrote just to battle me. This was in like 1992-93 and my rap handle was "The Motha Fuckin' Emperor" I had "I be Killin' Mothafuckas" and "I even Kill kids" on a smash and didn't let no one in B-More hear those except my barbers from Mondamon Mall, who I used to bug out and sometimes bowl with. On this particular night, this emcee gave me the bizness, called my name out and all that. What was so ill was that I wasn't even gonna sign up until I heard him call my name out. I was pushin' up on this chick and I heard someone callin' out "The Motha Fuckin' Emperor". Even though they didn't sell alcohol in "Rock-N-Bowl" I was already drunk because I snuck my bottle in, bought sodas from the concession stands and used the cup to disguise the liquor. Anyway, when I heard that I was bein' called out to battle, I made my way up to the deejay and he asked me why I didn't sign up. I signed up right then and went through his record crates lookin' for a ill beat to rap on, I found a "Heather B" joint, I can't recall the name of it though. When it was my turn to battle, I spit some shit and had everybody open then I did the ill shit... I pulled out like eight hundred dollars, put it on the deejay table and said "That's for anyone who feels they can beat me!" "Super MC" came up and stood there, he was the only one that moved so we were like face to face, the deejay dropped the beat, I pointed son out and spit half of "I Be Killin' Motha Fuckaz" then mixed in "I Even Kill Kids" within five minutes the whole crowd was standin' there with their mouths open. When the music stopped, Shameek was in the crowd, jumpin' up and down, clappin' crazily. The deejay was like **"Damn, did you hear what he said? He said I even kill kids, toss bitches like garbage lids / his whole life is about gettin' money and doin' ill jail bids...God Damn!"**

Some white people came up front and whispered in the deejays ear then the deejay got on the mic and said "talent show is over! There is no winner this week!!" he put the music back on and my mic got cut off. I asked son what happened, he said "Yo, they heard those lyrics you spit, saw how you look and they think you're serious. They don't want you to win anymore; that's it! That name you got "The Motha Fuckin' Emperor?" is the nicest name I ever heard, **you are nice**! When I left the bowling alley that night, there were crazy police outside. I never signed up for the talent show again but I was the first to bring Mic Geronimo's "Shit is Real" to the deejay. He played it and the crowd reaction was lovely. I was tryna get it rotatin' around so niggahs would know who Mic Geronimo was… meanwhile I didn't even know who that niggah was… other than the fact that he was Irv's new act and Monday had a hundred records at his disposal so I passed some out.

Another time, I was ridin' around Baltimore with my manz "Mahdi" from Brooklyn. We were in his Mahdi's Range Rover and we heard that Kid Capri was gonna be at Hammerjacks that night so I went to take care of my street biz then me and Mahdi met back up, this time he was pushing his Q45. I had two copies of Mic Geronimo's record with me so I made a couple of calls on the cell phone and I got us in the club for free. Once inside, we were minglin' and conversin' with chicks and cats I knew, security wouldn't let me get passed to see DJ Kid Capri, who was upstairs in the deejay booth / stage section. It made no sense tryna call him over cause he wouldn't hear me over all that music blastin' so I kept it movin' until the opportunity presented itself. Kid Capri got the crowd **hype**! He had some tall, Spanish hype man with him talkin' over the mic, hypin' up the crowd as Kid Capri spoke with his hands and kept the records spinning. Me and Mahdi were makin' moves, baggin' chicks, drinkin' up the bar then I walked towards where we were sittin', looked up and saw the Spanish cat in the deejay booth, he was lookin' down. We made eye contact and he nodded his head at me, I returned a nod. Then I thought quickly, he was screamin' "Uptown!" on the mic, even though we were in Baltimore. I looked back up at him and held up one finger as if to say "1" then I held up five fingers twice signifying "5", "5" meaning "155th st" in Uptown. He saw me do that and pointed up in the air meaning "Uptown" I nodded my head "yes". That nigga ran downstairs and got me and Mahdi upstairs to the deejay booth, got us all access stickers and drinks at the VIP bar. He was so happy that he introduced us to Kid Capri and I said "What's up David Love (Kid Capri's government name)" then I kicked some names he was familiar with. He took the two Mic Geronimo singles and said he would play them in a minute. The Spanish cat then came to me with another drink "Yo Shakim, where on 155th you from, Polo Grounds?" I said "Nah son, I'm from 155th in Queens!" You should have seen the look on his face when I said that, Kid Capri was dyin' laughin' but the cat was still happy to be around some N.Y.C. heads plus I knew mad cats uptown.

We started kickin' it and before you knew it, a blunt was sparked, Mic Geronimo's joint came on, we started talkin' again and I told him about a few rappers I was associated with like Father MC, even though by then, he had kinda fell off. I mentioned L.L.'s name, next thing you know, son had me at the deejay booth like I was frontin' about how I could spit. So I spit to the "Hemmin' Headz" instrumental, I only spit like ten bars and had the crowd screamin'. I always wondered if Kid Capri taped his shows, if he did, he got my rhymes on his tapes. While the Spanish cat got on the mic to big me up, DJ Frank Ski and Ms. Tony wanted the mic so they could make some announcements about some boat ride they had poppin' off the following week. Ms. Tony was a short, fat, black, Biggie Smalls lookin' niggah (yeah he's a male with the name Ms. Tony), who wore skirts and stockings. The faggot or whatever he was had a big song out in Baltimore called "Throw Ya Guns Up!" and that shit was killin' it in B-More. Ms. Tony made that house/go-go/techno shit in Baltimore heads love so much and DJ Frank Ski made that song Doo-Doo Brown. I didn't give a fuck about what they was tryna say so as the Spanish cat was passin' the mic to "Ms. Tony", I snatched it from him... her... or... whatever the fuck IT was and I let the crowd know my name and where I was from. "Ms. Tony" was tryna take the mic from me but I wasn't havin' it. Fuck I look like lettin' a niggah rockin' a skirt and stockings get shine like that. The Spanish cat was laughin' crazily as Ms. Tony cried to Kid Capri, who told me to give the faggot the mic (Kid aint use the word faggot though). The Spanish cat was callin' me as I stepped off and touched the bar. By then, Mahdi had shorties on stand-by, ready to ride out with us for the night. We bounced and from that time on, every time Ms. Tony saw me, the monster always gritted. I can't front though, I saw his performance before and when "IT" sang that "Throw Ya Guns Up" joint, the spot went bananas! The crowd went into a frenzy, screamin' and reppin' their hoods and screamin' "Blaow!"

* * * * *

CHAPTER 14

About a month later, Morgan State College had a Homecoming Party poppin' off. I came through with my manz and them from Hollis, Sharief and Roger. We enjoyed the scenery with crazy chicks everywhere as Kid Capri did his thing on the ones and twos. Niggahs bum-rushed the door, the party was packed beyond its capacity and the shit was off the meat rack. Kid Capri took the crowd back to the early 1980's with some disco shit and all that. When he brought shit back to the up to date shit, he put on Mic Geronimo's "Shit is Real". I was smilin' like shit, knowin' I gave him those records the first time he played them. By then, the cut, which used a sample of Denise William's classic joint "Free", had a buzz in NYC's underground. The next day I was in the mall with my two chicks that I club and run around B-More with when I got a page. I checked my pager, saw the triple six code (666), it was my niggah Monday, I called him back in ten minutes.

ME: "Yo!"

Monday: "Where you at?"

ME: "In the mall doin' what I do"

Monday: "Who you with?"

ME: "███████ and ███████████, why what's up?"

Monday: "Get rid of them and meet me by our stash crib".

ME: "Be there in an hour"

Monday: "One!"

By the time I got rid of the shorties, I got geared up in the new shit I just copped even though I was already geared up to begin with. My phone rang again…

ME: "Yo"

Monday: "Yo come outside, let's be out".

ME: "I'm on my way!"

I went outside and locked up the crib, this niggah Monday was outside sittin' on the hood of a metallic, sky blue 1993 850i with blue tints, sittin' on chrome rims. I was like "Yo how you pull that one off?" I recognized the whip; it belonged to "Kelly Blue", a street associate of ours who also threw parties up town. Son (Kelly) had a music production company called "Blue Diamonds Entertainment" amongst other ventures. He had crazy whips and he switched up regularly. Kelly Blue had a team that got down the way we did, one time, he took his whole team to Cali to attend the 1993 Soul Train Music Awards, son had connects in various aspects and all angles of the game; music, street and what not. He had an associate named "Miguel" (R.I.P.), who was from Flatbush, Brooklyn but he was known uptown for designin' clothes. Miguel specialized in all kinds of ill wear; velour, Leathers, silk with the sequined shit, whatever. He was known for his gear and fashion shows at Kelly Blues parties, where celebrities came through rockin' his designs.

Kelly Blue was rubbin' shoulders with Puff Daddy before Puff started "Bad Boy". Niggahs remember when he was down with "Butt Naked Entertainment" but that's another story. Miguel even laced up Blue's team when they attended the Soul Train Music Awards. Anyways, I got in the passenger seat, shit was all white leather interior and plushed the fuck out…

ME: "Shit is ill son"

Monday: "Yo the rims run close to 10 Gee's!"

ME: "Get the fuck outta here!"

Monday: "Here's the deal, He is comin' out there tonight mad deep, he got an after party at a club out here after the Morgan State joint tonight so we gonna touch that and chill. Go get the LS Lexus and push that, we all gonna be pushin' and showin' our true colors tonight to let B-More know **WE HERE!**"

ME: "I'm with that let's go get the Lexus"

Monday: "First we gotta spark this "L" niggah" (Monday pulls out a phat blunt)

ME: "We gonna puff in here?"

Monday: "Hit the window down and stop askin' stupid questions"

We pulled off and went to go get the other car. Again, Monday was drivin' the 850i and I followed in a white LS 400 Lexus. We drove into Baltimore's Harbor and went to one of my everyday hangouts, a seafood restaurant called "Moe's Fisherman's Wharf", which was an expensive spot but it was a spot where the money getters went to eat and drink on a much higher level. We got put on to the spot by MC Romeo a.k.a. Roe Dog, who became a bartender at the restaurant for a few months after movin' with his wife and kids to Baltimore from Hollis, Queens. Once we pulled in the parkin' lot, there were two more LS 400's and a Lex SC400 coupe, all sittin' on expensive rims and lookin' pretty. No doubt, Kelly Blue and company were already there.

The line to go in the restaurant was all the way around the corner, the spot was regularly busy like that but that this night was bananas for some reason. My pager went off repeatedly... it was Kelly Blue himself, pagin' me from his cell phone. I approached the line and saw him decked out in gators and an expensive leather coat with his whole crew in tow. We shook hands, embraced and I shook hands with his crew. Kelly said to me "Yo what's up Gangsta, I was just pagin' you. This line is crazy, they say it will be at least an hour or two wait for a table and I don't play no bar tables either." I wasn't wettin' that, I was like "I got this" as I went to the front of the line. I played this spot every day, sometimes two or three times a day and I discussed business with various cats up in that piece. This was one of my known hang outs! I was crazy cool with the owner and waiters, bartenders, even the dish room people. Waiters dropped what they were doin' to serve me because I tipped crazily and I am a man of supreme action. Once upon a time, I accidentally fired a gun in their bathroom. It was a mistake and a whole other story but the incident shook them up (smile) but anyway, as soon as I made it to the door and the waiter ██████ saw me rushed over to me and said "Shakieme" (all whites and others call me that like they can't pronounce "Sha-Kim" properly). I asked him "How's it going ████, yo where's ████████ at?" ████ said "I will get him and tell him you are here Shakieme, do you want your usual drink?" I said "yeah, get that for me but make it a double-double!" ██████ quickly said "Coming right up!"

You gotta understand how I had juice in this spot. I could send you, your peoples, family… whoever in there, give you the names of my personal waiters, tell you to tell them **Shakim** sent you and that they should take care of you and they would serve you like a king and put everything on my tab. Yeah niggah, Shit was serious like that! When I would go in there they would run up to me lettin' me know they took special care of my people and inquire whether I was told of the special treatment they got. They knew I tipped lovely, don't get it twisted, these waiters was doin' it too. One of my favorite waiters named ██████ was pushin' a black Nissan 300ZX, some up to date shit sittin' on expensive rims with triple black, Special Edition Benz, chrome rims on it. These Italian cats was doin' it! ██████████ even introduced me to other money getters and plugged me with connects and fly, gorgeous, Spanish shorties. I would walk in there one day and ██████ would have ten cellular phones for sale or he'd be tellin' me a bottle of Moet or Dom was being sent to my table from someone who wanted to meet me because he had told them about me.

Now tell me, was I frontin' or what? When I came in there, you would think I had money invested in that establishment duke! Back to the story though, we're in the restaurant and my favorite waiter ████████ came to me in a hurry. "Shakieme, Shakieme, Shakieme, my main man, how are you?" he asked while handin' me my drink. He said "This one's on me, it is four shots of Hennessey, your favorite". I said "██████████, what's going on? I got my peoples out here from New York, they said they've been outside waitin' for a table and they told you they were my peoples. What's going on? You got me looking bad". He said "I'm sorry Shakieme, it's so busy in here tonight and I couldn't move the people sitting in your area. I know you refuse to go upstairs but would you sit up there today?" "No", I replied. He said "I'm sorry, what if I call our restaurant the Wharf in Towson and have them take care of you or if I get you around the corner? Everything will be on me, do it for me please Mr. Shakieme!" I was like "Give me a minute, let me check with my peoples first." I turned around and walked to the door with a drink in my hand. Monday was talkin' to Kelly and company when I approached, they saw I brought the drink outside with me, Monday was like "Damn Sha, you sure you don't own this spot?" everybody laughed. I explained the situation and everyone agreed to go to another spot called "Pargoos" on Woodlawn. I went and told my waiter I will see him tomorrow.

I really wanted to stay and eat where we were because there were so many females geared up and lookin' beautiful in there. As I made it back outside, Kelly said "Yo Monday, I got ███████ and dem comin' up in the Land Cruiser, they're supposed to meet us here. Is Pargoos in this area, can they find it if we give them directions over the phone? This is y'all town, we y'all guests tonight!" Monday winked at me and told him "Don't worry Shakim got you!" We kept movin', Monday rode with Kelly and everybody followed me in the Lexus. I called Roe on my cell phone cause I wanted him to roll with me plus, knowin' I was gonna be crazy drunk, I wanted him to drive. Unfortunately, Roe couldn't roll because he was with his kids and he had to be at work later that night. Anyway, we went to Pargoos and got right on drinks, the Land Cruiser came through with my manz ██████ drivin' and two more cats in tow. "Yo ██████ and dem is comin' tonight too, they're in Bowie". I was like "O.k. O.k". We rode up to Morgan State and parked outside by the crowd and bugged out with the shorties and onlookers as everyone passed by and saw the 1993 850i lookin' crazy ill with a SC400, three LS400's and a Land Cruiser all parked up together, shit was serious!! We didn't even go in... for what? All the chicks was outside sweatin' us, WE were the show.

We were buggin' out, drivin' around the block, hittin' the liquor store, buyin' up bottles of Moet White Star and Hennessey. Me and Monday snuck off and puffed an "L", more of Kelly's people met up with us, they were pushin' a Mitsubishi Diamante. We drove around flossin', hearin' "ooooh's" and "aaaaaahs" from the crowd. Shit was lovely but I was laughin' because the whole time we were at Morgan State, the niggah Kelly's hand stayed glued to his cellular phone, he was yappin' crazily.

Around 2 a.m., Kelly shouted, "Yo, y'all ready, Miguel said shit is poppin'." I didn't know Miguel was in the mix too. Someone asked me, "Yo, you know where club ███████ is at?" I answered "Nah" and by then Monday was drivin' the Lex and I was in the passenger seat. He said, "Yo Sha, I hope you aint too drunk cause you're drivin'". I hopped in the driver's seat and Monday ran to drive the 850i so I followed him. I could see Kelly Blue's head with the phone still glued to his ear and as we pulled up to club ██████, the line was ridiculous. People were everywhere, across the street, in front of the club... in the parkin' lot around the corner... shit was crazy. Chicks were all over and they looked delicious. We parked directly across the street from the club when Miguel, who was a short jazzy dressin', Spanish cat with Spanish hair, took about six bad ass bitches over to the 850i. Everybody greeted each other with daps (handshakes) and followed Miguel across the street to the club. "Yo, it's about time, the after party is crazy and DJ Kid Capri was just warming up." "Okay, let's do this!"

As I came up on the sidewalk, observing the honies, I heard someone callin' my name "Yo Shakim! Yo Shakim! Yo Sha from Queens!" I looked to see who the fuck was callin' my name like that. It was Kid Capri's hype man, the tall Spanish cat I met at Hammerjacks, approachin' me with his hand extended. "Yo Shakim from Queens, what's up dog? I see you're doin' it, comin' through mad deep!" He pointed to the white LS400 and said "Damn, that's you?" Nonchalantly, I was like "Yeah son". He continued "Yo, I didn't know you rolled with Miguel." If you remember, I gassed this dude by tellin' him I was from 155th street

(Uptown) so I could get up to the Kid Capri's deejay booth so I could get Kid to play Mic Geronimo's new single, now he was seein' me geared up with my little ill jewels and jumpin' out of an ill whip with cats who were all pushin' ill shit. Dude continued "Yo Miguel was tellin' us that people from Queens was on their way and that it's y'all who throwin' the party. Damn niggah, I should have known it was you!" He followed me to the front, once we got there, Miguel pointed at me, lettin' security know I was "Good". I didn't get searched or anything, people on the line were staring. Son (Spanish cat) really thought I had shit in the smash for real. Sha Bio (I) was a good fronter, he brought me over to the deejay booth where Kid Capri was on the wheels of steel doin' his thing. "Yo, you remember Shakim from Queens?" Kid Capri shook my hand, I could tell he kinda remembered me but he was tryna put my name and face together. Kid Capri is a niggah who meets niggahs all day, everyday. He said "The one from 155th!" We all started laughin'. His man said "Yo, he's in here with Miguel!" Capri's eyebrows went up "Word?" I nodded my head in agreement and made my way back to the crowd lookin' for Monday and crew. Later we were buggin' out with the chicks, Kelly and Miguel had chicks everywhere, drinks flowin', Kid Capri was screamin' out "Blue Diamond Entertainment!" The music was "like that" too, shit was lovely. I didn't even know Miguel that well to begin with. I met him on a few occasions but never said much to him, I just knew he designed gear. I didn't know he was "like that". This niggah had bitches everywhere sweatin' him like he was some superstar niggah. He had the party all put together, had Kid Capri spinning, he had the spot packed and he was from "Now-Why (New York)". I was regularly bouncin' back and forth between NY, B-More and S.C. for years and I never heard nothin' about no after party? **Shit was serious!**

The party was ill! I was drinkin' crazy bottles of Dom and conversin' with my manz █████, who came through with the Land Cruiser. I'd known son for a while and never saw him very often. Kelly Blue had him under wraps but back in 1986 – 87', I gave son his first package. Out of nowhere, the music wemt down and some crazy stage lights came on. These niggahs had some show shit about to pop off, Miguel introduced some singin' quartet cats who came on singin' some slow jam shit but I didn't know who or what these cats were…Silk? A fake "Boyz II Men"? I didn't know. I did know that Blue Diamond Entertainment had a Philly group called "Live and Direct" but I didn't hear the announcement (too busy choppin' it up with my manz) so I didn't know if this was them or not. Females was screamin' and goin' crazy for these singin' niggahs. They wasn't tryna hear nothin' the kid (ME) had to say now. I was like "Yo ███, what the fuck is this shit?" My manz was like "I don't know Sha Boogie, they got some H-Town lookin' niggahs takin' over". I was hatin' "Man fuck that!" ███ was like "Yo you act like you gonna go take the mic and change all that HA! Look at how these chicks is goin' crazy over these cats, Miguel done out did himself this time!" Still hatin', "Man fuck that bullshit!" I replied. He was like "What, you want me to bum rush the show? If you go set it, I got you Sha, crew come first you know that!" I don't know what came over me but it musta been the liquor was takin' over. I took off my Coogie sweater cause I was rockin' the blue Police Issued, bulletproof vest underneath and why did I walk up front with a full bottle of Dom with my manz ███ following me? My manz was like 6'1" – 6'2" and about two hundred and fifty pounds solid. I went up to these singin' ass niggahs and snatched the mic on some "ODB" at the Grammies / Kanye West at the MTV Video Music Awards type shit; only difference is, I did this shit in 1993 (R.I.P. Ol' Dirty Bastard). I snatched the mic and said "Man fuck all this singin' bullshit, we aint come here for all that!" I screamed in the mic as all the fellas started shoutin' "Yeah!!"My manz snatched a mic from another cat and as if right on cue, DJ Kid Capri started cuttin' a record, I got witnesses to this shit. Kid dropped a beat and I kicked a rhyme while niggahs cheered me on, chicks was lookin' mad and shit as the singin' group just stood there lookin' stupid. I was wavin' my bottle, spittin' my lyrics and my manz started sayin'…

"You know you like the way it feels! You like the way it's goin' down! You know you like the way it feels! You know you like the way it's goin' down!!!"

I guess that was our hook… Miguel had the ill look on his face because I just fucked up his show. I was sweatin' crazily, Kelly Blue and company was laughin' hysterically, niggahs was cheerin' me on and shorties was cursin' me out. I looked up and saw Kid Capri's hype man, the Spanish cat, smilin' his ass off.

"You know you like the way it feels! You know you like the way it's goin' down!"

I rocked the spot!!! Miguel never spoke to me again after that, **I fucked his show up!**

The next day at about 1 p.m., the phone rang about twelve times…

ME: "Yooooo!"

█████: "Shakim, what's up, you still sleepin' huh?"

ME: "Yo who dis?"

█████: Damn, how many bitches got your phone number?"

I turned over in the bed to look at my caller ID.

ME: "Damn ████████ I knew it was you. I'm just wakin' up and I got a vicious hangover".

█████: "I bet, after all that drinkin' you did last night".

ME: "Huh?"

█████: "Yeah, I saw you last night in the club, showin' your ass on stage, you were drinkin', all up in bitches' faces and throwin' your money all over the place!"

ME: "yeah, so why didn't you come over and holla at a fella?"

█████: "Nah, you walked by me twenty times last night, I didn't want you to embarrass me in front of your friends or mine."

ME: "What?"

████████: "You heard me Shakim! Plus, I know you wanted to fuck somethin' else, you were in too many bitches faces last night, you sure I didn't interrupt anything right now?"

ME: "Stop playin'!"

████████: "Plus you ruined the party, you messed up that group's show and they were doin' their thing. You just ran up there and messed everything up. I didn't want nobody to know I know you."

ME: "What? Fuck you bitch! I rocked the spot, you seen my work! If you aint fuckin' or suckin' don't call me, hit me back, I'm sleep!"

-Dial Tone

Later that evening, me and my man hit "The Wharf", Kelly Blue was there, eatin' upstairs with a shorty and Miguel was up there too. I never ate upstairs… I just never wanted to go up there to eat. If I wasn't sittin' downstairs, I wasn't eatin'. I had heard stories of how cats got kidnapped out of The Wharf while they were sittin' upstairs so I kept my burner on me and ate downstairs. Miguel looked at me then he looked out the window. I nodded, acknowledging Kelly, who smiled and nodded back. Later that night we all linked up (minus Miguel) and touched another club called "Marco's". Miguel eventually showed up mackin' with two shorties, one under each arm and we all hit Baltimore street downtown by "Eldorado's" strip bar and "Crazy John's", where everybody drives by flossing'their shit, you know a Sunday night hang out. I can't really get into what happened that night cause all this other shit was said in my federal trial. Yeah, I got indicted in the top five on Kelly Blue's indictment, niggahs testified about a lot of shit while I sat there in court, watchin' these cats implicate me in what popped off that night in B-More (they told about the whole weekend, I'm surprised they left the "He fucked up Miguel's party too" out of it). I never saw Miguel again after that night, I got locked up December 21st, which was two and a half months later. During the summer of 96', they found Miguel slumped on his office table with slugs in his head (R.I.P.). I guess someone messed up his party again but this time it was **permanent**.

* * * * *

CHAPTER 15

THE MAKING OF "BELLY"; THE REAL DEAL

NOTE: This chapter is a very touchy chapter! Many of the people mentioned may catch feelings about what you are about to read. I am speakin' on how I feel and how I saw / see things. **REAL IS REAL!** Just because I feel what I'm sayin' is **right,** doesn't necessarily mean that it is accurate to others. The facts are **correct** but everybody has their **right** to different opinions and views.

Yo, when I tell you that Al Monday was my manz, believe me when I say so. I went all out for son and felt he would do the same for me. We had a lot in common, we did mad shit and was tryna make history together. I used to put everything on back burners to hold my manz down on moves and we were makin' a lot of moves both **minor and major**. If you were my manz and you and Monday was beefin', I'd flip and beef with you too. Monday had a vivid imagination and ideas to get us there from crime, rhymes, wantin' to make and produce records, movies, even aiming to own our own companies. We were tryna do big shit, layin' out the format to make everything happen even when shit was in shambles and niggahs was doin' dirt ball bad… Monday made ways to come up and front makin' everybody on the outside think shit was all good. When niggahs said they were makin' a movie about our situation and DMX was playin' Monday's character, a lot of eyebrows were raised on that note, especially mine and Monday's. We were both locked up and communicating regularly. At one point in time, we were flowin' about this movie "Belly" on an everyday basis. Roe was Hype's little birdie, who really tried to describe what he saw or thought he knew. Al Monday was looked at as a real move maker in the eyes of numerous industry cats like Daymond John, who is the founder of FUBU, Irv from Murder Inc, Hype Williams and others.

Before Monday got knocked in 1995, he was out there makin' moves, rhymin' with numerous cats and tryna pop off. I been incarcerated since December 1993, Monday was lettin' go of the drug game and focusing on music since then. He was writin' scripts with Roe and Hype, who was his childhood friend and was poppin' off as a music video director. There had been some talk of penning and producin' a street banger movie for some time. Monday was also runnin' with Irv, who got a deal with Blunt Records after which he signed his artists "Mic Geronimo" and the Original Queens "Cash Money Clique". He was with their entourage makin' moves but he would still go back to stealin' cars to make a few bucks. He was rhymin' with a cat from Jamaica, Queens named "B-1", who ended up on Kool G Rap's "4,5,6" album. "B-1" had a partner named "B-2", who was nasty too. Monday was rollin' with Irv and his artists, doin' shows and makin' connections to blow, I was in touch every now and then and kept bein' told "**Yo, we about to get this dough and come get you out!**" He told me about this movie script that was being written and how he and Roe was gonna have Hype present it because he could get a big budget. That's all he was talkin' about, Irv was doin' the soundtrack and Daymond was poppin' off his FUBU clothing line.

I tried makin' a few other moves before I came in (got locked up). I had my manz Vic from Hammels p.j.'s who I knew from way back, me and son used to rhyme together. I knew Vic was thorough because I ran the streets with him and he held me down while I was out there on the run in many angles; he caught a case dealin' with me and a few others. We ran up in this crack spot, tied up some Jamaicans and cleaned the spot out, we were on a little spree that night until police ran up on us, everyone got away except Vic but son held his water when the Feds questioned him about a fella (me). I used to bring tapes of Irv's beats so me and Vic could write and record, tryna pop off. Vic was my manz, we would write shit about our struggles, he was one of my rhyme partners outside of Me and Monday's circle.

In 1993 Monday had a lot of pressed up records of Irv's underground banger called "Shit is Real" featuring his artist "Mic Geronimo". Every time I touched a club in B-More, I passed the record to the deejay, sometimes it got played, sometimes it didn't even make it into the record crates. I was just scramblin' on the strength, there was no obligation, I didn't even know Mic Geronimo. I was just doin' my job as a street cat on the strength of Monday and Irv, knowin' once shit popped off, it "popped for all of us"… Lookin' back, I see that I had the wrong perception of certain cats I was dealin' with. I respected Irv's handle because he made sure beats was handy for me even though I never did anything with them other than listen to them and let other cats hear the shit. Like I said previously, I even went out of my way and pollied with L.L. about Irv's beats when "L" didn't even know who Irv was. Monday had this vision and used to say **"Shakim, when it comes to music and movies, we gonna be the illest... we can't lose! Trust me Sha, you don't need this drug shit, I'ma make sure we all get rich the right way!"**

(Recorded Voice) "This is a collect call from a county jail, the cost of this call is two dollars for the first minute and thirty-five cents for each additional minute. This call is from…" (my voice) "Shakim!" (Recorded voice) "To accept this call press zero now, to refuse this call press three! Thank you for using T.N.T. You may now speak"

ME: "Yo!"

Roe: "Sha, what's up my niggah, what's the deal baby?"

ME: "Yo Slow motion but I'm holdin' it down."

Roe: "Aint nobody takin' your shit is they? Ha, ha, ha, ha!"

ME: "(Laughin' hysterically) Ha, ha, ha, ha"

Roe: "Let me find out they took your gold fronts and they're feedin' you cold sandwiches and dirty water! Ha, ha!"

ME: "Nah, Roe, you know I run shit everywhere I go niggah, I would have you washin' my drawls!"

We fell out laughin'.

Roe: "Yo, what are they talkin' about doin' to you? I need you out here! I miss goin' in your closet, takin' your clothes, kicks and shit… You're my family!"

ME: "Yo, the Feds got me so I don't know what's what but it don't look good. They gave me some rinky dink ass lawyer and shit."

Roe: "Damn my niggah, shit is crazy, we need you out here!"

ME: What's up wit niggahs?"

Roe: "Yo, Irv got this new niggah named Jay-z; Big Jazz from Original Flava's manz. I've known dude for a minute, he can spit a little somethin' but he can't fuck wit Roe Dog though. Anyway, Irv is grindin' with him and he got Mic Geronimo but he aint getting' the push he needs to put him out there. Black from Cash Money Clique is in trouble, niggah in jail too."

ME: "Yeah? Who the fuck is dem niggahs anyway?"

Roe: "Dem niggahs aint nobody, you know I'm out here workin' my ass off tryna keep the kids well fed and a roof over our heads. I wish you were out here, you was sweeter than Santa Claus! You sure dem rough niggahs aint takin' your shit niggah?"

We laughed again.

Roe: You aint got that Glock now, ha ha! I know you miss that Moet and Henney!"

ME: "Shut the fuck up! Yo, what's good wit Hype?"

Roe: "Yo, we wrote up the scripts and everything, I'ma put you and Bunz (Monday) in the movie, it's about y'all niggahs. I'ma blow up on that shit! Irv is fuckin' wit dem niggahs who aint gonna blow, aint no one iller than Roe Dog wit this MC shit yo, check out this new shit I wrote niggah!"

Roe hit me with a quick sixteen bars.

Roe: "What you think?"

ME: "Shit was ill Roe, why Irv aint fuckin' wit you on shit? I thought he would put you out first or after Mic Geronimo."

Roe: My manz aint even sign a niggah. I'm out here watchin' him make moves while I follow Hype like a flunky. Ya boy Daymond is makin' big moves with his FUBU shit and I'm parkin' cars at a fuckin' hotel, writin' this script and all that. Yo, you gotta help me with a few missin' pieces though niggah cause **this is for us**. When I get dough, you get dough, I aint no Chicken George niggah either niggah!"

ME: "Yeah, yeah, right now I'm tryna think of ways to keep makin' moves while I'm in here, **the game don't stop**!

Roe: "You spoke to Bunz? He wit Mic Geronimo and dem now. I seen him wit Dean… Dean got the new drop 325i, the phat candy red shit. Bunz makin' sure you good my niggah?"

* * * * *

"A Thug Changes.... And Love Changes... and Best Friends become strangers"

"The Message" – Nas

CHAPTER 16

It's hard for me to speak on December 21 1993, which is the day I got locked up for the charges I'm currently doin' time for to this day (18 years later). I made a lot of mistakes on December 21, 1993 as I didn't follow my instincts. I wasn't even gonna go outside that day, I was supposed to be in court in Baltimore for a shooting case I made bond on so I decided to stay inside all day and lay back. **Yeah right**…. I was all the way in Columbia, South Carolina, still on some loose cannon shit. I'm not gonna point fingers, won't blame no one but **myself**, I take full responsibility because I was supposed to be layin' low that day. I had pussy in the hotel laid up with me and more pussy lined up for later that day, later that night and I had money in the streets but **NO**, I had to be greedy, it's a long story so I'll leave it alone for now. When I got knocked, like always, I thought I would be able to maneuver my way out of shit with the fake I.D. joints and make bond before my prints came back no matter how much my bond was but this time it didn't go down like that. A fella had to lay it down for a minute, I was stuck in Richland County Jail in Columbia, S.C.

I had been through the S.C. Prison System on a little vacation before so it was cool but my prints came back, my identity was blown so I was stuck like Chuck. I had warrants in a few states so a fella wasn't goin' nowhere but I was still makin' moves regardless, doin' what I had to do to maintain in the facility, **you know… The Game Don't Stop**, well, it didn't stop for Shakim Bio just yet. I did what I could and I had my dogs out there still doin' what they do so a niggah was still "living". I stayed in that spot thirteen months and **kept shit gully** without an end. I was still killin' the phones every day, the doors was bein' kicked in as shorties came to see me and I can't remember ever missin' a store day or visit. A fella like me was "living". I kept my voice on them streets as I communicated with Monday and others, niggahs kept me in tune and on beat. Monday was on some next shit though; son was always on that "**out of sight, out of mind shit**" anyway. I know him too well and I know how he rocks, he never refused my calls and I always knew where to find him but son aint have it in him no more as far as street activities was concerned. Shit wasn't goin' right since I was gone as far as street moves plus some shit popped off and my manz Takim (**R.I.P.**) got shot and killed in front of peeps.

Monday was focusin' on some next shit, tryna get his life right, he was now in the Nation Of Islam (he was **always** interested in viewing Farrakhan tapes, goin' to Mosques etc., etc.) I was hearin' son had the bow tie jump off and was sellin' bean pies and shit. He had a son now and he was fuckin' with that music shit hard, runnin' around with Irv and his artist **Mic Geronimo**, the **Queens Cash Money Clique** as well as doin' shit with Hype Williams. Every time I spoke to Monday, all son said was "**I'ma send you some books Sha, get focused cause we gonna be on some next shit now. This music shit is "ours" son! I'm puttin' these movie screen plays in motion and makin' some ill moves. We gonna get you some ill lawyers and get you out but you gotta be focused cause we gonna make history in this entertainment shit!!**" This niggah was killin' me with this shit but I was stuck in jail and shit was gettin' ugly for me, no lawyers was comin' through, I didn't get the books Monday promised to send, son wasn't even really checkin' for me and this was my "main manz" so I had to keep my moves movin'. I stayed in close contact with Monday regardless of the false promises, this was my manz.

Every time I called Ro, all this niggah talked about was movie scripts, how I should be writin' some shit cause Hype was "gonna open doors for us", "Irv is gon' be that niggah' and blah, blah, blah. I didn't see it cause it was such slow motion but the pieces was fallin' into place though. As shit was bein' built for the better, elsewhere, things was bein' destroyed. The DEA was buildin' an ill case on some cats from Corona, Queens and somehow, me and Monday was named in the indictment. Shit was crazy "B"! I got caught up and was put on the top five of the next niggah's indictment. As I was wildin' out bein' the ill jail niggah, shit was gettin' serious! In January 1995, the Feds came up in Richland County and kidnapped a fella, took me to Atlanta U.S.P. Then I was transported to Norfolk, Virginia and hit with a fourteen count indictment... my head still hurts from that shit, **OUCH!** What's so ill about the ordeal was that I wasn't part of that conspiracy and I really didn't rock wit dem cats like that, I was loosely associated with a few of 'em so while I'm in jail bein' "Me" and Monday was on some music shit, the Feds built their case and these niggahs ended up flippin' and oiling me up, placin' me in their shit. When the Feds brought me to Virginia, I was still in touch with my street cats and me and Monday always spoke whenever we could but it wasn't as much as it used to be... the love was definitely still there though.

I was in a county jail in Virgina with most of the cats from Corona and Flushing, Queens, who were also on that indictment. I was tryna figure out how I got placed in that picture while the Feds was still out there roundin' up more niggahs. I trusted that Monday was slick enough to remain out there because we ducked the Feds for years but after fourteen or fifteen months of me jailing, Monday got hemmed up on a "Hum Bug". They caught him doin' what he did best, "**stealing cars**" so "**Al Monday the downtown Car Thief**" was behind bars. When I got word that Monday got knocked, I didn't believe it so I called around the way and niggahs was talkin'; I was callin' the same cats he was callin' so communications was intact. It took a few weeks before he was brought to the same jail I was bein' held in but they had him on a different block, on another floor and at first, it was a little tension cause niggahs was tryna get in my ear about my manz. You know how that goes, I was in for a little over a year and he wasn't holdin' me down or playin' his part like he should have so niggahs tried to come between us but I wanted to see him and talk face to face. A few niggahs was "aggie" with him over some next shit but Monday didn't have no real obligations to dem niggahs like he was supposed to have for me.

As I went back and forth to court, I finally got to see Monday, sit down and build with son. He was tellin' me about some movie scripts / screenplays that he and others was workin' on, music and some next shit too. I was sittin' there lookin' this niggah in his face, thinkin' "**I been sittin' in jail over a year, I'm lookin' at ten to life in the Feds, facin' numerous life sentences elsewhere, this niggah aint been holdin' me down and here he is talkin' about some entertainment shit?**" I couldn't see or understand how he could talk about this shit, my loyalty to this niggah is above comprehension and I had / have sincere, ultimate love for this niggah, he was my true comrade but I also had the urge to swing on this niggah and beat his ass for shittin' on his dog Shakim Bio… **shit was too real**.

Me and Monday sat and kicked it every chance we got. We would be in the corner of the courthouse bull pen, talkin' or choppin' it up when we were bein' transported in the vans. We was on two different floors back at the county jail so I was tryna move to his floor or get him moved to mine and he was tryna do the same but it never happened. We was even callin' the same peeps, leavin' messages for each other to try and make moves. He kept on and on and on and on about these moves concernin' a movie script that was written, how Hype was gon' get us right and about Irv's music and shit; he said "it was just a matter of time". Monday got acquitted of all Federal charges and that surprised everyone on our ordeal, even him. It was definitely a blessing from the higher being but son was also caught up on another state ordeal with me in Ohio. When he got extradited to Ohio and I went through the Federal System and began servin' my federal sentence, we still kept in touch.

I got indicted again on some homicides and drug charges and was brought back to Ohio for trial… I sat down there for thirteen and a half months (96' – 97'). Monday and I stayed in touch on issues concernin' **freedom** and of course he kept me abreast of the activities of our niggahs Hype, Daymond and Irv; out there doin' it in the Entertainment Industry.

Hype was already a **BIG** factor in the music video game, Irv was at Def Jam, Fubu was nationwide and I was regularly in touch with Daymond John (Fubu) and Roe. I brought Monday back from his facility but it was really to kick it with him and use his advice on my trial strategy. It was good seeing him and the rest of my "Co-dees" (on that ordeal) again. Monday still let me know that it was on and poppin' with the entertainment shit and he left me with Irv, Hype and a few other phone numbers. A few months went by and Monday got on some next, next shit in his scribes to me concerning that movie shit. It seemed a monkey wrench was tossed in somewhere and niggahs was goin' about shit their way. Monday's attitude changed up and he was talkin' differently. Around this time, me and Roe was speakin' regularly, sometimes I would call Roe two or three times a day. Roe was questionin' me about little details that happened in certain street episodes and I wasn't really fillin' him in cause the shit was better left "**unsaid**". Monday was against niggahs doin' a movie on our street activities and I never knew what the flick was supposed to be based on but somewhere along the line, Ro flipped the concept, did the script and Hype and them added and subtracted from it. I was thinkin' it was based on the struggles, ups and downs of niggahs comin' up in the streets while tryna get on in the entertainment industry. I don't know what caused these cats to flip the shit into a drug story in which the characters were based on us, depicting scenarios closely similar to events that took place in our real lives… but they did. I still don't know what kind of screenplay was originally written by Monday or whoever. I didn't know how shit got turned into what it turned into, I just know one day when I called Roe, he was excited and from then on, whenever I read Monday's scribes, his whole attitude changed up, he wasn't feelin' niggahs no more.

Recorded voice "…. **Thank you for using Ohio Sprint… your call is connected!"**

Roe: "Sha, what's up baby boy?"

ME: "Same shit, different toilet, the God is still standin'."

Roe: "C'mon Sha, I'm family. You can tell me anything son, I heard what happened, fucked up how they did you. Dem Feds found you guilty, gave you all that time; had me cryin' behind that shit. How did Bunz (Monday) get acquitted like that my niggah?"

ME: "That's the way the dice was rolled, I can't understand it either. I'm on my direct appeal now. I got railroaded, I just don't know where, can't pin point it but it went down like that, you know?"

Roe: "Yea Sha, I know."

ME: "What's up wit you doe?"

Roe: "Right now, we're in the works of havin' some big wigs look at the scripts. I really put in work but I need to make a few adjustments, you aint really tellin' me how certain "eps" went down, like that ep when you sicked Ive on Bunz".

ME: "Nah son, it aint rock like that. I never sent Ive to get at my manz. I love Monday even though son is grimey on a lot of aspects of shit. I didn't send Ive at him."

Roe: "Yo, Bunz came to me with tears in his eyes, he told me **you** was tryna dead him Shakim... **he told me everything**; how y'all was a team and you thought he was shittin' on you so you put Ive on a mission to lay him down. Bunz asked me to never cross him like that, you really had him shooked."

ME: "Roe, **word life sun... on everything**!!! I never sent Ive at him... that was a big misunderstanding. I built with son, he knows... plus that was a long time ago, Ive is dead now. Alfred knows I wouldn't do him like that, we did too much together. I stopped Ive from gettin' at him but that's between us, its dead now."

Roe: "Yo Bunz will never forget that shit. I know you Sha, been around you for the longest. **You can be dirty too**, you know you sent Ive to murk Bunz, Ha! Ha! Just don't send noone to kill me my niggah. I'm tryna do this movie!

ME: "Quit playin', I never did that."

Roe: "Well I put it in the movie, I got you sendin' Ivan to kill Bunz. The same way I heard the story but I twisted it... plus I put Takim gettin' murked in there too."

ME: "Nah son, don't do that, leave all that shit out of it!"

Roe: "Y'all was some ill niggahs, I had to do it Sha! Man, fuck all that. What's up wit you bein' in Ohio? Why they got you out there now?"

ME: "They came and took me from the Fed pen I was in, I got indicted on those bodies again, they tryna make it where I never get out, you know?"

Roe: "**Why? You aint got nothin' to do with that shit**! Damn Sha, they tryna kill you for real, I wish I could put that in the movie script. I got you in there I just left out how you drank all the time Ha! Ha! Ha! I want to put that y'all got framed but still show how you was the ill cat."

ME: "Leave all that shit alone, don't go there!"

Roe: "Yo, that niggah Hype is schoolin' me; he really looked out for me. I been on mad video sets, you seen me in Nas' Street Dreams video? I'm in Vegas by the tables... I'm chillin' in that joint."

ME: "I seen it, I peeped you."

Roe: "ill aint it? I gotta send you some flicks of that, the R. Kelly video we did, that Busta shit... I'm in the making, just think, last year I was parkin' cars at a hotel and teachin' tennis to rich crackers, now I'm writin' scripts and doin' videos! What I don't understand is, Hype is tryna put his name down on my shit as a writer too, what you think? Fuck that! I'ma send you mad flicks. How you look on the money side, you got dough on your account, you good?"

ME: "I got twenty dollars on my shit."

Roe: **What**? Sha… Daymond is killin' 'em with that FUBU shit, his shit is in every store, everywhere. Dem niggahs aint send you no dough? What da fuck is up wit dat niggah?"

SHA" "I'm good!"

Roe: "Twenty dollars? Get the fuck outta here! Irv aint hit you off? Twenty dollars? No, they can't do you like that baby boy! I'm sendin' you some money today, give me your address."

I gave him the address.

Roe: "Call me whenever you need money, anytime son. That's fucked up how niggahs aint flood your account crazily. **Twenty dollars**? You gotta be lyin' niggah!"

ME: "I got twenty dollars on my shit."

Roe: "Dem bitch ass niggahs! I will never do you like that when I get that dough from this movie. I'ma get Johnny Cochran to get you and Bunz out, y'all my niggahs. I'ma get you out Sha, **on my seeds niggah**. They killed my brother Abby but I still have you and Bunz. You my brother too and I love you kid. I'ma get Johnny Cochran and his team. I know y'all aint do that shit, he can beat it easily, he did it for O.J. and that niggah was **guilty**! I need my niggahs out here livin' it up like they're supposed to. When I get big money, you get big money niggah but for now, I'ma send you some little shit cause twenty dollars is ridiculous. I'ma mail it out tonight…. With the flicks. Yo, listen to this new rhyme I got niggah… listen!"

Roe kicks an ill rhyme.

Roe: "How that sound?"

ME: "Shit was ill, I like it."

Roe: Yo, keep callin' me yo and start writin'. Write some shit so we can do a movie or somethin'. You got skills son, start writin' some shit, shit you see, shit you be goin' through, shit that happens around you. We gonna make shit happen, hold on, my daughter wanna say hi to you, hold on."

I spoke to his daughter.

Roe: "Yo, call me next week, we startin' on this movie shit. We gonna blow my niggah! Fuck that niggah Irv, that's why Mic Geronimo can't sell a record now and Jigga is gonna fall off. He shoulda fucked with Big ROE DOG!! Listen, I love you kid, you always my son I forgot to raise, call me next week. I'm mailin' that out to you tonight... **ONE**!!!"

ME: "Ahite Roe... **ONE!**"
                              -click.

                    * * * * *

"Full of larceny, who wants parts of me? I'm vicious, mad malicious cause shits real on these roads to riches"

-"Rather Unique"

AZ The Visualizer

CHAPTER 17

July 1997
Calling from the United States Penitentiary in Terre Haute, Indiana.

Phone ringing… a male answers.

"Hello?"

"Yo can I speak to Irving?"

"This is him, who this?"

"Shakim"

Irv: "Shakim? Shakim! Yo, what's up niggah? Oh shit, what da fuck is up Sha?"

ME: "Nothin' much Irving, a niggah still standin', you know?"

Irv: "Yo, I know man, I can't believe I'm talking to you. I miss my niggahs! Are you alright Sha? What's up? Speak to me."

ME: "I just came back from that Ohio trial shit, they slayed me down there son, shit is crazy!"

Irv: "Yeah, Al told me about it. He said you got bigger too. Shit aint the same without y'all. I got y'all though. I'ma be that niggah in a minute and I'ma make it happen, get y'all out of there. I got a few things in motion."

ME: "Yeah I heard. I'm hearin' you're livin' out there son, I'm hearin' real good things."

Irv: "Yeah, I'm about to blow! Yo, you know "Green Eye Born" is home? He did nine years before they found out he was innocent. It takes money and I'ma be straight in a minute, just be patient baby."

ME: "Yeah I know "Green Eye". I was in the Four Building on the Island with son back in 88', he worked in the gym, he's home now... that's good"

Irv: "Yeah, I'ma be able to give niggahs jobs, I'm not at Blunt Records any more, I'm A&R at Def Jam. Big niggah up there Sha, I'm about to run shit!!"

ME: "Yeah?"

Irv: I got some things in motion, I'm the merger between Def Jam and Roc-a-Fella. I'm working on this new niggah who is about to shut the game down. Niggah from Yonkers named DMX."

ME: "I think I heard of son"

Irv: "Yeah and I got my little manz from my group Cash Money Clique I'm about to push. I'm at work developing him now Sha, in a minute I'ma have my own label!"

ME: "What's up with Mic Geronimo?"

Irv: "He still doin' things at Blunt. I couldn't take him with me but we still fam. Yo! Give me your name, number and address so I can get at you, send you shit, can you get boxes, sneakers and music?"

ME: "Nah, I'm in the Feds, I can't get shit."

Irv: "I be lacing Al up wit shit, let me know what's up"

I gave Irv my government name, register number and address, he read it back to me. I heard a little kid in the background.

ME: "Who's that?"
Irv: "I got a son now Sha

ME: "Yeah? Get outta here niggah!"

Irv: "Hold on! Say hello to my niggah Sha, say Peace Shakim!"

Little fella said "Peace" and tried to say my name.

Irv: "Sha, if shit works out Russ gonna let me do my own label, unless I negotiate a deal elsewhere but Russ is my niggah and I'ma show him that **I am the streets**. But when I get correct money-wise, you, Al and all my niggahs are gonna be **super straight**. I got my manz Black up north too. Yo, Sha, I'm going to give your address to my girl Jazz, they call her "Big Jazz", her name is Jazz Young and she works at Def Jam too. She loves writing and sending out shit to jail niggahs. She calls them her "Little Boyfriends", she is good peeps and she'll take care of a niggah."

ME: "Yeah do that, that's cool son."

Irv: "Yo my manz ███████ be doing a lot of shit for me too, I'ma give him your shit right now, hold on let me call ███████ ."

ME: "Yo! Yo! Yo! Nah, no three way calls, you'll get me in trouble son."

Irv: "Aight but I'ma call ███████ , that's my niggah, he got some flicks and all that. I'ma have him get at you as soon as I hang up with you, he just left the Feds.

ME: "Yeah, yeah!"

Irv: "But don't forget, never hesitate to get at me and ask me for anything, the world is going to be mine in a minute Sha!"

I could hear Irv's son shoutin' in the background.

Irv: "That's my little heart right there Sha! Yo, I can't send you no music?"

ME: "Nah son, you can't send me shit but dough, flicks and mags."

Irv: "I got you, I'ma have Big Jazz bless you and my manz ▮▮▮▮▮▮ gonna get at you. This niggah knows mad cats and got juice in every state we touch."

ME: "Yeah, I know ▮▮▮▮▮▮▮, tell him I said Peace!"

Irv: "Yo, take down my address, write me niggah."

I took down his address and repeated it back to him.

ME: "What's up wit Roe, when you gonna put him out?"

Irv: "Man, Roe is bullshitting but he is wit big Hype dog, we gonna be straight and get y'all niggahs out. They working on getting that movie project done, that shit is gonna be real big, it's about y'all niggahs!!"

ME: "Yeah, I heard, I heard."

Irv: "I got you Sha, if you ever need anything, music… if you got anyone trying to get on wit music, get at me, call me anytime. I'ma be big in a minute and take care of my niggahs. Jay-z is the hottest thing out there, I'm about to have DMX shut shit down. If things work out, I'ma be doin' the soundtrack to Hype's movie (Belly) about y'all."

ME: "Just don't forget me niggah!"

Irv: "I got you. Yo, let me go, I'ma call ▮▮▮▮▮▮ right now so he can get something at you. Call me anytime Sha."

ME: "No doubt, I'ma get at you every two weeks or so."

Irv" Do that my niggah, keep your head up. We got you out here, we gonna get y'all niggahs out, **I'm serious**!"

ME: "I believe you son, I'ma call you in two weeks."

Irv: "Hold on… (he tells his little boy) say bye to Sha!"

Little man screams "Bye Sha!"

Irv: Sha, take it easy, get at me, let me know my manz ▮▮▮▮▮ got at you. Big Jazz is gonna love you, she loves street, thug cats like you. Send me some pictures so I can show off my ill crew to niggahs at Def Jam!"

ME: "I'ma shoot some to you this week!"

Irv: Bet, get at me Sha, I'ma be that niggah and you will be too."

ME: "Game don't stop son, one!"

Irv: "Love!"

-click.

Another phone conversation:

"Hello?"

ME: "Roe, what's up son? Did you get my scribe and those documents I sent you?"

Roe: "Yeah, yeah, that shit was ill, those murder reports on Ivan. They even pulled an old slug out of his butt cheeks.. Ha! Ha! Ha! Damn, no wonder he never wanted to sit down. I wrote him into the movie too, some ill shit. We tryna get Method Man to play

"Ive". This shit is gonna be the illest movie ever. I changed all y'all names but it's all good."

ME: "Yeah? Y'all budget big like that?"

Roe: "We just waitin' on the green light from Artisan (Film Company). Hype was gonna do the Fat Albert movie but our shit is first, we just waitin' on the production budget. Once we get the green light, it's on my niggah. You speak to that niggah Irv yet? You know he's really livin'. He put DMX and Jay-z on... he shitted on me but I'm about to blow regardless, you speak to that niggah yet?"

ME: "Yeah, I called and spoke to him a few times. He says he's gonna be gettin' at me soon."

Roe: "Soon? That fat niggah got cake to get at you now! How can he forget his niggahs like that, is he blessin' Bunz (Monday)?"

ME: "I don't know, I aint really wettin' (sweatin') all that shit cause niggahs is gon' see the Sha Illest again, I'm back in trainin' now."

Roe: "Just don't send no niggahs like "Ive" at me!"

* * * * *

Early one morning while I was in Terre Haute U.S.P. tv room with my manz and dem watchin' videos on B.E.T, I got up out of my seat and went towards the phones. I was about to call "Roe", that was still my niggah even though he was always lyin' about how he was gonna to mail me some flicks, this money order and this that and the third. He came through maybe once or twice but he did a lot of lyin' but anyway I called and Roe's wife Shonda picked up the phone and recognized my voice (Why not? I called all the time even when I was on bricks). Me and her was cool, she was excited and told me some good news "**Tony (Roe) and them got the green light for the movie!!**" She broke the news to me before Roe could, she was so happy and I could hear it in her voice. Roe jumped on the phone and told me "**it's on!**" He was talkin' all this crazy millionaire shit for real now and how he was gonna get me and Bunz (Monday) out. The name "**Bunz**" was a private joke between me and Roe but I really came up with the name. Monday was always on some serious shit, niggahs would go to Monday with their issues and son would be on some "**NO!**" shit so they would come at me complainin' then I'd go back to Monday on some sit down, real shit tellin' him he can't be shittin' on niggahs we fuck with. Niggahs was lookin' up to him and he was "Shit Master", he would shit on you quick if he wasn't feelin' you or your reasons. So cats was small time complainin' when I came through with Roe, I sat there listenin' and laughin' at the shit cause I was rollin' with Monday regardless, he never shitted on me (yet).

Roe started complainin' too though… on some "**Who the fuck Alfred think he is? Niggah can't do Roe Dog like that, I'm a Hollis Ave Vet! Sha, you go sit down and talk to this niggah, he will listen to you!**" (Sounds familiar don't it?) I'd say "Damn sun, what you sayin', my manz is hard on y'all but soft on me?" Roe kept on "He listens to you Sha, that's our niggah but he listens to you more than anybody." I was like "Damn sun, you sayin' the niggah is really Al Bunz?" That niggah Roe fell out laughin' at that shit and we been usin' the code name Al Bunz as a joke ever since, even when Monday was around us. It took him a minute to catch on then one day he asked "**Who the fuck is "Bunz? Why y'all keep whisperin' about this niggah Bunz**?" Roe would fall out laughin'. Monday realized and said "Yo, I'm tellin' you niggahs stop fuckin' playin' wit me! My name aint no Bunz!"

We were still laughin'.

"Think I'm soft, just try me!"

We was like "Okay Bunz"

I remember Monday got real serious on me when I called the crib one morning and a shorty picked up the phone...

"Hello?"

"Yo!"

"Sha what's up boo, where you at, you in town?"

"Yeah, yeah… yo, my manz there?"

"Yeah Sha, what's up?"

"Put Bunz on the horn, let me speak wit Bunz!"

"Bunz? Who the fuck is Bunz?"

"You know, that niggah Al Monday"

Shorty mentioned that "Bunz" shit to Monday and all shit hit the fan, son got on the phone cursin' me out, threatenin' me, sellin' me death and he hung up on me. I aint see Monday for over a week behind that shit but when we finally saw each other again, shit was back to normal. Whenever we got blunted, I slipped the name "Bunz" in every now and then and he would say "Y'all niggahs aint gonna stop playin'?" I'd tell him "Get off that bullshit!" He warned "Okay but as soon as someone calls me Bunz I'ma make an example". You know me, I'd say "Yea Bunz".

How the fuck did I know Roe was gonna name the main character "Bunz" in the movie Belly?

Ever since that niggah Roe told me they got the green light to start castin' and shootin' the movie, I couldn't catch up with son for nothin' in the world, not even on his cell phone. Then, one day while I was watching MTV videos, the news came on… MTV News that is and the reporter said "**Music video Director Hype Williams is preparing to shoot his debut film about two childhood friends from Queens. The film's cast includes numerous Hip Hop Artists, a Jamaican Dancehall Artist and R&B Artists. We'll keep you posted on the film's title and developments.**" I was like "**Oh shit, it's on for real!!!**"

Then, on BET's "Rap City" the film was brought up again but not really in specifics. The rapper DMX started doin' feature appearances on a few posse cuts like L.L.'s "4,3,2,1" and the Lox's "Money, Power and Respect". He had a single called "Get At Me Dog" that was bangin' crazily with a video that was shot in "The Tunnel" Night Club in New York City. DMX did an interview on BET one day and they asked him if he was acting in an upcoming movie and he answered **"Yeah, I'm Hype Williams main man in a movie called Belly. I play a character named Bunz, who happens to be a real life, good friend of Hype's so I'm honored to play a part in Hype's first movie**." Then, word of the casting of the movie got quiet for a second and I couldn't catch Roe on the phone at all, so I said fuck it! I was busy workin' on my appeals on my Federal and State cases so I focused on that.

On March 1st, 1998, I was comin' from the yard back to the housing unit. As I mingled and talked shit with the fellas, a C.O. came out with the mail bag and yelled "Mail Call". Niggahs crowded around waitin' for their name to be called. You know I was also in the midst as I caught mail regularly and this day was no different. My name was called numerous times and as I got each letter, I noticed one with no return address. I turned the letter over and on the back it said "Tony Rome". I'm like "Who the fuck is Tony Rome?" I opened the letter by removin' the staple (way before I got my mail, it was opened by the prison's mail room so they could check it for contraband, then they stapled it back shut). The letter was from Roe, who started the letter by sayin' "Aint no sunshine when it's **ON**! Aint nothin' change but your address sun!" He got to kickin' it about he knows he been duckin' me and lyin' to me but he still got mega love for me and blah, blah, blah. Then he brought up the movie he wrote and how he was with Hype, helpin' him shoot it. He told me the movie was called "**Belly**" and he gave me a rundown of the cast, which included Nas, DMX, Method Man, Taral Hicks, T- Boz from TLC and others. Roe claimed the film was off the hook and he was gonna take some flicks and send them to me. He said I should stop stressin' because I'm supposed to be God and blah, blah, blah. He said we were gonna be millionaires and I should lay back, it was on and he was gonna make shit happen. Then he told me his wife was pregnant with their fifth child, a boy. He stressed me, told me to start writin' and keep writin', said I was his brother from another mother and it was **ON**! He said "**I get down for my dogs baby boy! You know I would not just fuck you out of nothin'!**" I was sittin' up re-readin' the scribe in it, as if he could see my face as I read, Roe asked me...

"Yo Sha, what's up Sun? Why you showin' off the diamonds in your grill?"

Shit is **ON** Sun, niggahs is shootin'that flick "**Belly**" and comin' to get you out!"

I sat there smilin' and continued reading.

Irv: "Hello?"

ME: "Yo! What's the deal niggah?"

Irv: "Shakim, what's up my niggah?"

ME: "Same shit but I keeps it thorough."

Irv: "No doubt my niggah. Yo, did you get anything in the mail from my peoples? I gave your numbers to ███████ and Jazz."

ME: "Nah son, I aint get shit from nobody at all, **especially not your peoples**."

Irv: "Yeah? Yo, I'ma call ███████ again and give him your name and address. I told him you was my manz and he should get at you and make sure you were right. It just be that he be mad busy runnin' around for me but I'ma get it done right away"

ME: "Yeah, I hear you. What's goin' on otherwise son?"

Irv: "Shit is crazy out here in N.Y. They (Police) got a gang patrol unit out here cause this blood shit is crazy out here. These little niggahs is rippin' old ladies in the face out here Sha!"

ME: "It's like that out there?"

Irv: "Yeah, I can see you bodying one of these kids out here, that shit is crazy. Police be picking up niggahs who got anything red on and they're taking them to the precinct to take photos for their books. They are labeling niggahs now sun."

ME: "Yeah, shit sounds crazy."

Irv: Yo ███████ started a photo thing that showcases "around the way" model chicks and shit, kinda like "Jet Beauty of the week" shit. He got some ill shorties in there and he's trying to hit up all the jails wit flicks. You know he been in as far as State and Feds. This niggah ███████ is a legend and he is down with the team. I'ma get him to send you some of these flicks. Shit is called **"Picture Perfect."** We trying to start businesses out here and give back to the community Sha. Niggahs is switching up, doing right, we trying to get this money, get right and get our peoples out. I want to give jobs and shit to niggahs who come home from jail to keep them in line and out of trouble, you know?"

ME: "That's right son, that's the move right there."

Irv: "Yeah, wait 'til you see these pictures, shit is ill Sha! Yo, I'ma get some other joints to you also and some loot… I know you need some."

ME: "Yeah, yeah that's what's up."

Irv: "That movie project is underway too… Al just sent me some photos of him; I got your shit too. I got y'all joints in my office at Def Jam, everybody sees y'all flicks **and they know who y'all are**! I'ma get at Jazz, see why she aint get at you yet. She gotta put you on."

ME: "Yo, listen, I been listenin' to some of these niggahs spit in here. Some of these niggahs is crazy nice, I'm still tryna make moves, I got yardie spitters and all."

Irv: "Listen Sha, anything you want me to hear, send it to me at Def Jam in care of **Irv Gotti**. Yeah, they call me Gotti now, that niggah Jay-z gave me that handle. I run shit at Def Jam Sha, send me whatever you want me to hear, I'll listen to it."

ME: "You got that!"

Irv: "Send mail to me at my crib, don't have no one send me no demo joints to the house though."

ME: "I got you son, I got you."

Irv: "Yo Sha, you my niggah. I'ma call ███████ now and get him on that now. I gave him your hook up. He be so busy but I'ma put some dough in the mail for you, you should get it by Friday. Call me next week, I'm about to bounce out now."

ME: "Ahite Duke."

Irv: "Watch Rap City next week, I'ma be on there with **DMX**."

ME: "Got that, I'ma have the whole prison watchin' that, you know I still run shit. **One!**"

Irv: "One my niggah, I'ma get at you."

-click.

* * * * *

I remember readin' every review, every story, anything out on the movie "**Belly**"... I read it. I was thinkin' "**Yeah, my niggahs did that shit, niggahs about to get mega rich and come get me and Monday**". I was lookin' at the big line-up of **DMX, Nas, Method Man, Taral Hicks, T-Boz** with appearances from A.Z. and others, they even had a Jamaican artist in the line-up. The movie was advertised and promoted in every Hip Hop and music magazine there was, they even had a special on MTV and I was **OPEN!** Publicists went as far as sayin' that Belly might be the biggest thing since "**Beat Street**" because of the big Hip Hip Cast. They said it would be bigger than "**Krush Groove**" and "**Who's The Man**" plus it was a street flick so huge results were expected. Hype Williams was already ranked in the top three music video directors, he changed the music video game with the Fisheye Lens, ill concepts and he was doing everybody's shit from Hip Hop Icons like L.L. Cool J to Biggie Smalls; he was killin' 'em. He was directing R&B shit for R. Kelly, Blackstreet and Usher, nobody could see sun and this was one of my menz from the late eighties. So the music world and media, knowin' Hype Williams produced a movie with a star studded cast of Hip Hop and R&B singers meant all eyes on him (Hype). Shit was bein' talked about in every magazine, on MTV News, BET's Rap City and Def Jam was doin' the soundtrack that was expected to be huge as well, I was open crazily… then the bullshit came in from all angles.

I couldn't reach Roe on the phone no more, his cell was disconnected and letters I flew to Hype's "Big Dog Film" offices in Manhattan's Greenwich Village section, were comin' back stamped "Return to Sender!" I started callin' Roe's wife Shonda as well as Irv's crib, speakin' to Irv's wife Debbie. Everything seemed cool at first then out of no where, Irv's number got disconnected. Letters I sent to Shonda to hit Roe with went unanswered so I knew niggahs was switchin' up. The numbers I had for Hype suddenly needed an access code to go to his voice box, office or any form of contact with him. **Shit**! I had the niggah's number but no access codes, what type of shit was that? I still don't know… Every magazine had an advertisement for Belly in it and every now and then I saw commercials for the film's release date, **shit was real**. Niggahs was about to blast off but I couldn't get up with niggahs, all lines of communication got deaded. I didn't know what was goin' on.

I was seein' all the articles, previews, interviews and hype over the movie but niggahs wasn't barkin' at me. Then, more bullshit came into the picture... Magic Johnson! Yeah, purple and gold, number thirty two (#32), **Earvin Johnson**… that niggah started shittin' on niggahs. Mr. Johnson started investing his money in buildin' his own nationwide Multiplex Cinemas. He owned Theaters in New York and Los Angeles and he began speakin' out against my people's movie, pointin' out the negative messages the film's content was givin' our youth. He said our people need more positivity in our communities and since **Belly** depicted violence, drugs and profanity, he wasn't gonna show the movie in his theaters. He was tryna get others to back him up like he was boycottin' the flick.

I started hatin' that niggah Magic Johnson after his protests. Here was a basketball star, straight up legend, Magic Johnson, stoppin' other niggahs from tryna eat. Same niggah who said he came from the hood, same niggah who got on national t.v. live, in front of cameras to say that he was **HIV Positive**. Every program on t.v. was interrupted for this niggah to come on and say that shit. Niggah was cheatin' on his wife, fucked all kinds of chicks and caught **HIV** but don't know where he contacted the disease. All the crackers started backin' off son, they shut down their endorsement deals and abandoned him cause he got that "**Nigger / Homosexual disease**". Nobody wanted anything to do with him but **US** as black people stood by him regardless and supported him. He ended up playing Olympic Basketball in 1992 as part of the "**Dream Team**" and niggahs cheered him on even when crackers and others (some niggahs too) was sayin' negative shit about him, tryna get him banned from playin' because he had the disease. We (Black folks) still supported him and gave him a chance, just think of all the basketball players who played ball with him out of love despite of his disease. This niggah was **HIV Positive** and they still accepted him and showed him mega love… so what he made some mistakes in life? He was still our brother!

Eventually America changed their views and jumped back on Magic's infected dick, he retired a basketball legend and became a spokesman for HIV and of course, he became a businessman, investing in all kinds of ventures from entertainment to food chains. He was doin' the damn thing so why the fuck was he shittin' on the movie **Belly**? He wouldn't show our shit in his theaters and son had mad pull, this slowed shit up for a minute and caused others, who jumped on his bandwagon, to start speakin' out against the movie too.

After some thought, I began to see Magic Johnson's protests as a blessing in a way because Hype and Roe was on some real funny shit before Magic started protesting. Just think how they would have acted if shit was all lovey dovey; Hype ended up shittin' on Roe anyway. Roe only got "Co-writer" credits for the movie and he aint get no money. The movie budget was in the millions and it grossed in the multi-millions, not even speakin' on the soundtrack on Def Jam, which was bananas. Roe aint get NO DOUGH… only "Co-writer" credits. Then to kill shit even worse, Hype had writin' credits. Ro claims he wrote the flick himself but Hype put his name there as well as bein' the director. It was Hype's debut film plus **on his strength**, he got the production budget deal and backers so Roe had to roll with it. Then to make shit iller, **Nas** got "Co-writer" credits too. So think… everybody knew who **Hype Williams** and **Nas** was but who the fuck is **Anthony Bodden** (Roe's government name)? Who ever heard of him? He was a "**NOBODY**" so son got jerked by a niggah he knew for the longest. So while Roe thought shit was sweet, thought he could jerk us… he got jerked.

At the time I didn't know that it would be years before I would get to view Belly, the only thing I was goin' off of was what I was readin' in my music mags and the street news when I was vibin' on the phones. Roe never gave me a full rundown of exactly what the movie was about, I just knew that in November 1998, shit was gonna show in theaters and everybody and they momma was talkin' about goin' to see it. Even through the motion when niggahs started gettin' real funny styled by changing their numbers and not respondin' to my scribes, I still thought cats was gonna keep shit real. Roe kept tellin' me that he was gonna help us; we were "gonna blast off, blah, blah, blah". I wrote him a few fucked up scribes too cause I seen the cross comin'. I called his crib and his wife Shonda was real upset at me, she had read one of the letters I sent to Roe… she said "Sha, that's my Tony and the father of my children, I read what you said you will do to him; you supposed to be our friend." I explained to her that's just how we talk to each other and she shouldn't take it serious. I assured her there was love there.

One day I came up with an idea to reserve me and Monday's position so we could come up off of this movie the same way niggahs was tryna come up and capitalize off of us. I was gonna write Vibe, XXL, Source, Rolling Stone and Spin magazines and explain to them who I am, tell them my situation and tell them about me and Monday's characters bein' portrayed in Belly. I shared this idea with Roe, who immediately begged me to **Chill**. "Nah son, don't do that shit, chill the fuck out. **We got you!** We aint gonna do no bullshit, we wanna blow. We can't let it out that the movie is actually about y'all niggahs cause of the shit y'all in jail for and you in the Feds. Let us do this our way, get the money and get y'all out. Remember, it's gonna take money to get you out. **Please Sha, don't fuck this up! Please**!" I thought about it and kicked it with a few of my close convict comrades, who all said "Word Sun, you might mess shit up with that idea, magazines gonna run to interview y'all, dig up your backgrounds and see how ill y'all was and they will shit on that movie." So I chilled... in hindsight, I should of went with my first mind and made that move.

Hype had some real big power houses backing **Belly,** on some **Artisan Entertianment** presents a "**Street Life Production**" shit; a partnership between Hype's "**Big Dog Films**" and Larry Meistrich's "**The Shoot Gallery inc.**" The film was produced by Bob Salerno and Ron Rotholz, who were big wigs. James Bigwood was an Exectutive Producer, who had credits as Associate Producer on "**New Jack City**", "**Juice**" and "**Posse**" amongst other films. James was also the production manager on "Waiting to Exhale" as well as other production roles in films. Larry Meistrich (also Executive Producer of Belly) was the company Chairman and Chief Executive Officer of "The Shooting Gallery Inc." and has played an intregal part in some one hundred films, commercials and music videos. Malik Hassan Sayeed (Director of Photography) was involved and he had an extensive body of work in theatrical productions, features, music videos and commercials and had worked with Hype on a number of music videos. He also lensed Spike Lee's basketball drama "**He Got**

Game", which was his third collaboration with Spike Lee following "**Clockers**" and "**Girl 6**". His additional credits at the time included Ice Cube's "Player's Club". **David Leonard** (editor), who done work with some of Hollywood's top filmmakers, was a real professional and had too many credits to name. **Regan Jackson** (production designer), who designed extravagant and surreally distorted sets for many of Hype's videos, also designed commercial sets most notably a Shaquille O'neal spot for **Miller Lite**, **Nike**, **Sony Playstation** and **Pepsi** amongst other works.I say all that to say… this niggah Hype had some "power" backin' him on his debut film **Belly**. **Shit was real Duke**! A niggah couldn't tell us **nothin'** and Roe was in a position where he was definitely makin' moves and he was even startin' to act like he was "**too important**".

The flick had a financial powerhouse behind it and a hell of a cast of music and entertainment stars. They even had a real actress named Taral Hicks, who was in movies like "**A Bronx Tale**", "**The Preacher's Wife**" and "**Just Cause**". She was on tv with "**Educating Matt Waters**" and an episode of HBO's "**Sax Cantor Riff**", she even guest starred in several music videos. So it wasn't like… this shit was some low budget flick with small names or no names. **Shit was some real shit**. Hype even had actor **Frank Vincent**, who played roles in movies like "**Raging Bull**", "**Goodfellas**" and "**Casino**". Hype met him in 1997 and hooked up through a mutual friend, **Tommy Matola**, who was the head of **Sony Music** at the time. So it was some real money bein' thrown around and some real major figures playin' their part infront of the cameras as well as behind the scenes. The movie budget was said to be around eight to ten million dollars, maybe more. Hype even had to use some of his personal money so a lot of scenes was cut out. As all of this was takin' place, I was in the Feds, strugglin' with my appeals and gettin' caught up in prison politics; tryna eat and live. I really believed in my niggahs and I thought once shit fell into place, shit was gonna be love-love. Then the letters started comin' through and niggahs who saw the movie was askin' me mad questions. Now they wanted to know if certain scenes and epps were true, "Was niggahs really gettin' it like that?" "Who was who and how did Nas escape to Africa, who is he?" "Did we still have someone out there?" "What's the deal with"Bunz" role? Cause in the flick he was workin' with the Feds."

I hadn't seen the film yet so I was on the phone asking their opinions on the movie, hearing how much it blew up or how "it was ahite" and how ill it was. "Yo Sha, which one was you, Nas, Method Man or that kid Knowledge?" Then my manz told me he got the joint on tape and how him and his wifey studied it. "Yo, Sha, that niggah Knowledge is **YOU!**" Then Roe confirmed it. My manz gave me a rundown of the movie, told me what it is and put me up on the slammin' soundtrack, which had a song called "**Dogs 4 Life**" featuring Nas, DMX, Method Man and Ja Rule. The beat was some shit N.W.A. sampled on one of their early albums and the video for the song was shot by Hype Williams. D'Angelo had an ill cut on there called "Devil's Pie" with a ill beat produced by DJ Premier. N.O.R.E, Raekwon and Mya were on the soundtrack too, shit was definitely off the meat rack. Belly even got a "Source Award", Them niggahs aint even acknowledge us niggahs though, it wasn't long before Roe claimed Hype left him for dead... so he say.

The way I finally got to peep **Belly** was crazy; I had to use my Supreme Charisma. The deal was, I just got transferred to this next Fed Pen and a few guys I was acquainted with was enrolled in an Anger Management Program, which was a six to eight week class. I had already completed that same class but in another penitentiary and usually, when you complete a class, the counselor brought in a movie from the streets as a treat. Everybody was votin' to see "**The Cell**" starring **Jennifer Lopez** or "**Belly**". My manz told me that they was gonna see one or the other, he didn't know which one though so I convinced him to invite me so I could peep whatever movie. He said he didn't know if he could pull it off so I asked him who was the counselor in charge of the class and once he told me, I went to work on a move. I pulled out the preliminary and preproduction notes to the movie **Belly,** the ones Roe sent me on one of the few times he came through on his word. I also pulled the photos of the makin' of the film and some old scribes he hit me with while they were still filmin' the shit. I took all that shit to the counselor's office one afternoon and went at him like "listen, I know y'all don't owe me shit and I'm not in your Anger Management class but I heard you was thinkin' about showin' a movie called Belly…" I ran down a short summary of how my peoples wrote and directed the movie, showed him the flicks, letters and preproduction notes and told him "Look, I been in for a minute and I got a very, very long time to go, I may never ever get a chance to see this movie." He said to let him think about it because he decided to bring the movie "**The Cell**" in bein' that everybody wanted to see Jennifer Lopez' ass. As he kept lookin' at the flicks and scanning the notes I brought in he asked "You know these guys?" I said "Yeah, they my peoples!" He looked at the computer and saw Roe was on my visitors list and said "Let me think it over." I don't let inmates watch movies if they are not enrolled in my class, watchin' the films is a treat for the guys who enroll and complete the course so let me think it over". He handed me back my shit I said "Okay" and I left.

Two days later my manz told me that the counselor inquired about me, wantin' to know if I was a thorough dude. My manz told me he vouched for me, askin' the counselor "What? Do you know who that is? Check your files, he's very solid!" A few days after that, I saw the counselor. He asked me where I worked and after I told him he said he would call my job and get me pulled so I could go watch the movie. He said "nobody knows you're not in my class so you know what that means, right?" I was like "Yeah, I can't say shit". The counselor kept his word but what he didn't know was that I was makin' moves too. A few cats from N.Y., who was in the class had set up the seats where we were gonna be in the front rows controllin' the tv and VCR. We had popcorn, zoom zoom and wham wham jump offs jumping off.

On the day the Anger Management Class would watch the "Belly", I got pulled from work and was told to report to the chapel, once I got there, everything was set up. I got put on to see the flick and moves was made where we had locked shit down. **Word "B"**, I sat right in the front of the tv, with peeps surroundin' me to watch the flick. I studied the joint and rewound certain parts as I finally got to watch the movie I had been hearin' about for six years before it was actually made. I absorbed every bit of the flick, my high wore off from the weed I hit earlier, I was overwhelmed and my emotions were mixed. I was mad, excited, open and very disappointed all at the same time. After the movie, niggahs and even the counselor was askin' me mad questions about certain epps, scenarios, who played who's character, did this or that really go down or happen the way it was depicted in the movie and was this a true story. I sat there mad than a motherfucker, thinkin' to myself **"This is the shit that got niggahs switchin' up and on some "Self" shit? Got niggahs on some bullshit?"** A lot of shit in the story and certain scenarios in the film wasn't right, **"Niggahs did us like that and still wasn't showin' no love? We still in here with no lawyers, stuck in the "Belly" of the beast."**

There's a big difference between how a niggah is actually livin' and how he looks like he he's livin'. **Let me explain**… you might have seen me out there geared up, jeweled up, pushin' a phat whip and always flauntin' but the reality of it was, I could have really been "hurtin'", livin' day by day and barely getting' by but to you it looks like I'm doin' big things. I don't know exactly how cats was seein' Monday but what was depicted in the movie **"Belly"** was far from reality; it was blown out of proportion crazily. Don't get shit twisted, niggahs was doin' our thing and makin' moves but overall we were strugglin' and strivin'. They never showed our struggle as black youths tryna turn bad situations and choices into positive results. Cats was tryna pop off, remember, I started out as an emcee then I got caught up in the spider web of my environment. I don't want my negatives to be glorified, nah, look at my positives. I did wrong but I tried to do it for the right reasons. I'm not tryna justify my thugness but I want you to also know a fella has potentials to be productive and constructive. I am a **"builder"** not just a **"destroyer"**. People may only remember me for negative or destructive moves I made but that's because they wasn't around me "like that" to know or understand ME.

From the beginning of "**BELLY**" they had niggahs on some ill shit, robbin' clubs and shootin' shit up, then the lifestyles was ill like, niggahs was caked up a little somethin'. I don't understand if that was what Roe and them was tryna project in the viewer's minds or if that's how they saw things from their stand point but Roe had been around us so much that he knew shit was definitely real with us. He was around when niggahs was hurtin', schemin' and plottin' on how to come up… he'd been behind the steering wheel, when we was hungry and he saw when niggahs was barely maintainin' but had to put up a front like we were "poppin' off" . Roe knew the real, he wasn't hip to everything because he was left outside as far as exactly how the drug moves was goin' down but he knew that we were ill niggahs tryna make it and we was "semi" gettin' it. Sure we had more than the average cats but sometimes shit wasn't rockin' like that. I can take ten gees and make it look like a million just from the way I was spendin' and livin'.

Belly had a lot of funny situations that I aint even gonna speak on. Some funny shit was the scene where I ("Knowledge") was supposed to have called from jail and spoke to Bunz (DMX) tellin' him that "Black" was a snake. Another scene I got a chuckle out of was when Bunz pulled a gun on "Black" in the basement and was shootin' at his feet orderin' him to strip butt naked in front of everybody; I got a real good laugh out of that shit. I laughed at the part when "Black" came for some "get back" and came across the street while Nas (Sincere) and A.Z. was talkin' in front of the barbershop and when A.Z. saw Black comin', he got ghost on Nas without tellin' him Black was comin'. Then there was parts I wasn't feelin' at all... I didn't dig how they portrayed "Knowledge". I've built with Roe a thousand times since I been in the Federal System to get a clear understanding of why he did what he did with the characters in the movie and who was to portray who. He kept the spin game goin' cause he knew certain shit was supposed to stay as it was and not put out there. First of all, Nas character didn't exist… the name "Sincere" was another name Monday used; bein' around me, he learned basic mathematics and alphabets, which are lessons studied by members of the 5% Nation or Nation of Gods and Earths so Monday took "Sincere" as his God Body Attribute. Nas' character was more of Roe just tellin' the story as Nas' character narrated it in the film. It was like Roe bein' around us, witnessing certain things and his stand point where he didn't want to seem like an outsider so he created that character but at the same time, certain elements was put together and somehow Nas ended up addin' his input and becomin' a co-writer of the film.

Now as far as the move of puttin' the "food" in the car's bumper... that was supposed to be left out of the script. If they never brought that out, I would have never mentioned in this novel, the story of Irv gettin' shit taken from the bumpers of the car before he drove it out of town. In the beginning, niggahs was rockin' the bumper move until Irv told someone, who ended up snakin' him and robbin' him. "Knowledge's" character was allegedly supposed to be based on me in real life.

"Knowledge" was the one who made shit happen, he was really "Bunz" arms and legs. He was the one who handled everything and put "Bunz" on to the Nebraska move. "Knowledge" was also the ill jail niggah, when he wasn't out there "living" he was in jail "jailing". They had "Knowledge" livin' it up, rockin' rolexes in jail and no matter where you was, "Knowledge" was able to find you no matter what. You could be on the run, hidin' and your phone would ring... and boom, it was "Knowledge" callin' from jail. That's some personal shit cause to this day, I still pop up and call cats and they wonder how the fuck I be gettin' their numbers. I stay on the phones and can reach out to anyone but "Knowledge" character wasn't what it was and I could never agree to that bein' my character no matter how much Roe assured me.

Now that scene where "Knowledge" allegedly sent "Shameek" (Method Man) to kill Bunz is very, very touchy. "Shameek" was my manz ██ (R.I.P.). He was a good, thorough comrade who loved to put in work. His guns barked crazily with no ifs, ands or buts about it. A lot of events can not be spoken on because the federal ordeal I'm on now, holds me accountable for a drug related shooting that ██ did out of town while I was in the county jail. The Fed records reflect that ███ allegedly came from N.Y.C. to visit me and while out there, he allegedly shot up a rival street cat. All things that I don't speak on can't be proven so it's a street rumor that I left in the streets. It is better left "unsaid", to remain a mystery of whether I did or even could call hits from behind bars. The mystery added to my street and jail credibility and who my manz ███ is, holds a lot of weight for they claim he is responsible for over fifteen murders. There was somethin' in the air about me beefin' with "Bunz" for him shittin' on me in the past. So I supposedly sent ███ at him, the streets put that in the air. Me and Monday mingled with the same people and before ███ met Monday, it was a "███ and me thing" for a minute but ███ had heard a lot about Monday from the streets.

Me and Monday was never at odds with each other, Roe kept askin' about it but me and Monday sat and built about the situation. It was a lot of he say / she say, animosity built up and niggahs was whisperin' in both of our ears but we cleared that shit up, we linked back up and became dem ill niggahs again. This was between 1989 – 91, son (Monday) showed me how much love he had for me when he sold his Acura to bail me out of jail but whatever he shared with Roe before that when shit was in the air, Roe tried to put drama in the air in the movie. I'm always an ill niggah and I try to live it up to the best of my ability on streets or in jail but I wasn't rockin' no rolexes in jail, a fella made moves when I could, I even bailed niggahs out of jail from my prison money account while I was in jail. Niggahs can front now if they want to cause ███ is dead but all dem niggahs was shook of Sun, **ALL DEM NIGGAHS**.

Big up to all Yard Mon Massive fa sho! Yush!!! Without an end I will always have love for my Jamaican people. Both of my parents are from the island of Jamaica and I grew up in a Jamaican household, listening to the Reggae sounds of Bob Marley and The Wailers, Jimmy Cliff, Gregory Isaacs, Dennis Brown, John Holt and others including Dancehall Music from the early Yellow man, Eek-A-Mouse, Ninjaman, Nicademus, Sista Nancy, Sista Carol, Shelly Thunder… it's too many to name. I BEEN rockin' and tapin' joints from the early eighties when Gil Bailey and Clive Houston was on WHBI 105.9 Fm. I still fucks with Dancehall Artists like Buju Banton, Mega Bonton, Super Cat, Junior Cat, Beenie Man, Capelton, Bounty Killa, Spragga Benz, Vybze Cartel, Mr. Lexxus, Wayne Wonder, I can't sit here and name everyone but you get the picture. I like the rudebwoy, soundbwoy clash type ting, massive gun shots pon di champion sounds.

I played Jamaican parties and all when I was a free man so when they said that a Dancehall Artist was playin' a part in **"Belly"**, I knew where niggahs was tryna go with that, they was gettin' too personal. There was a Jamaican named ███████ that Monday was dealin' with on the car tip. ███████ was a brown skinned, heavyset, well paid older cat, who had spaced out teeth, scars on his face and he kept phat whips. He was a real good, sincere dude so Monday started dealin' with him on other moves, not just cars. Nobody really knew dude like that, other than seeing him in nice, expensive cars and casually dressed with jewels on. It took a minute before I met him but when we met, we clicked immediately and what strengthened our bond was how he looked at me and saw I was Jamaican blooded (somehow Jamaicans can spot that in me) so he started tellin' cats that he was my **"uncle"**.

███████ was tryna train me to be a business man and turn me away from the street oriented shit. He schooled me to a lot of different shit, we used to hit the malls, go shoppin' and hit the clubs too. He was a money cat who liked to play the background and bag females on the strength of apartments, cars and jewelry. He kept me laughin' with that cause while I was pushin' up on females, goin' through the conversation he would cut in and ask them "wha ya want, how much is it gwaan cost? Wha eva yu need mi hav it to give ya!" and before you knew it, he had that shorty on his team. We played out of town and all that, makin' moves and gettin' money. I used to owe him big money and I'd pay him when I felt like it, meaning, I'd flip the money before I hit him with what was his, he understood the game but he was tryna school me so I could retire early and not make it to where I am now, prison or even worse, the graveyard but I didn't listen, I rebelled.

A few cats got to be around ██████████ if they were around Monday enough. Hype was just gettin' into the music videos and he used to ask Monday to borrow ████████ cars for certain videos because ████████ kept all the phat joints; Porshes, Benzes, BMW's, Volvo's, the new Acura at the time, you name it, he had it. He kept them kitted up wit phat rims, sounds systems and all that, his hoopties was even hooked up; I remember when Monday bought a seven series from him. Roe was around Monday sometimes so he met ████████, dude would come around on his own cause he recognized real street cats. ████████ had me by at least fourteen or fifteen years in age but we used to drive around and chill out, hit the clubs and meet chicks then it was back to our business. Niggahs could only assume what his potential was and what role my "Uncle" played. Yeah, after a while he got loose and dealt with certan cats on street aspects so it wasn't hard for Hype and Roe to ask certain cats what was up. ████████ was also ill cause I saw him get gangsta on niggahs too and I mean, he really put pressure down with gun in hand, accent on blast "mi gwaan ask yu once, where is mi loot?" I seen niggahs sweatin' and shakin' as I stood there lookin' serious, watchin' "Unc" put the "timmy" down. Later on we'd be crackin' up, cryin'-laughin' and drinkin' and he'd keep askin' me **"Yu seen how eye & eye had dat Yankee Yout**?!!" **Him piss inna him pants!"** That was my manz, he let me get away with a lot of slick shit that niggahs would get murdered over. He would cut me off for a while only to come back in a month or two and put me back on but only because of the Jamaican blood in my veins.

One day in early 1998, while in Terre Haute U.S.P., I was in the chow hall, pollyin' with my Yardie breddren "Smiley", of the notorious "Poison Clan" and he told me that he got word of the hush-hush casting of **"Belly"** concerning the Jamaican Artist. He told me a few Yardies tried out but the part was given to Louie Ranks a.k.a. Louie Rankin. I was familiar with Shabba Ranks (I used to mess with Yardie, a female from his management entourage) and familiar with Cutty Ranks a.k.a. "Cutty Rankin". Louie Ranks / Louie Rankin is a respected Dancehall Artist with underground hits, he had a tune about a gun called "The Typewriter". In an article I read, he spoke on back in Yard (Jamaica), where Rudebwoys shoot out with police. He told a story of how police ran up with their big guns, shootin' it out and a Rudebwoy started shootin' his massive gun and it had police runnin' for cover because of the rapid automatic gunfire. The police was like "**Wha di blood clot is dat di mon have**?" and the reply was "**Typewriter**!!" because the gun sounded like a professional secretary typin' like seventy-five to eighty words per minute.

So Louie Ranks got the part, he had the strong Jamaican accent and credibility but I don't understand how they had him portrayin' my manz ███████ like that. It was real interesting but some scenes was so outrageous that I was like "Hell No!! Get The Fuck Outta Here!" I wasn't understanding Roe's storyline, he had ███████ as the "Original Rudebwoy" but the move with him havin' "Bunz" travel to Jamaica to murder his rival was way too out there. I wasn't understanding where that part came from; how ███████ was sonnin' my manz like that… I know Roe and nobody else saw my manz goin' out like that. They wasn't put on to any kind of ill moves that was made, Monday wasn't the type to talk about shit and he definitely wasn't bein' sonned. Then there was the "Scarface" scene, where they came to get the "Original Don Dada", the shootout scene and then a female snuck up behind him and slit his throat? Get real with that bullshit, they killed my manz part crazily but that's Hollywood for a niggah I guess; in reality, he's still out there livin' it up. ███████ was involved in part ownership of a few clubs, businesses and was quietly exiting the game and the street shit. I know if he ever read this novel, he will know it's him I'm shoutin' out and he'll make ways to link up wit him Yardie Nephew to mek sure everyting wit eye & eye is crisp. Where you at Unc?

"Tommy Brown" was as alias used by one of my associates who was affiliated with us but at times he wasn't with us. We always had a competition thing goin' on with son nevertheless, he was my manz too. We got money together on many occasions and at one point, son was holdin' me down. Him and "Bunz" stayed at odds so it was funny that they had "Tommy Brown" and "Bunz" the names of the character played by **DMX** in "Belly". "Knowledge" was played by **Oli Grant a.k.a**. "**Power**", who served as an executive producer for Hip Hop group the Wu-Tang Clan. "Power" also served as the CEO of "American Cream Team" that founded "Wu- Wear Inc." in 1997. **Method Man a.k.a** "**Shaquan**" played "Shameek". Method Man is also part of Wu-Tang and he's had some successful solo releases. Both him and "Power" are from Staten Island, one of the five boroughs of N.Y.C. "**Method Man**" and "**Power**" **are both God Bodies / 5%ers**, I don't know "Meth", who is also known as "Shaquan" personally but I know him through a mutual friend, **Clifton "Panty Raider Ruckus" Fuller** from Park Hill Projects in Staten Island, who was bidding with me in Richland County Jail, South Carolina. I told "Ruckus" about Irv and Hype back in 1994, Ruck is my peeps and we still keep in touch. Method Man was his peeps who flooded him with money and flicks in '94 while we were biddin' in the County, waitin' to come to the Federal System. I'm not sure if "Meth" or "Power" knew or understood that the movie was based on our real life situations and scenarios or if they was even aware of our existence. Same with Nas, I don't know if he was filled in on the sciences of our existence, for all they knew, they were just playin' their part in the movie, **who knows**?

Another touchy issue in "Belly" was the murder of shorty young buck in the Atl when "Bunz" started them two young bucks arguin' at the table in "Justins" restaurant and shorty got his brains blown out; Roe tried to describe what happened to our little manz Takim (R.I.P.) in that scene. Takim was my little manz from Farmers Boulevard, a young gun, who aint take no shorts. A lot of heads around the way was partially blamin' me for his murder even though I was in jail when he got killed. They claim that I had him under the wing, drinkin' all the time and son would wild out when he was drunk. He also happened to be drunk and wildin' out the night he got murdered. I don't really know the whole story on that epp, all I know is that when I got knocked in S.C., different divisions of police and Feds went down there to I.D. and interview me so I called and told niggahs to bounce cause "**The heat was on**!"

Takim said he was goin' to the ATL with "Bunz". Before I came in the system, I told shorty to be careful and on point cause because he was bussin' his gun crazily; a loose bullet ready to kill but he gave me his word that he was gonna chill out. I had him on "Alcohol Punishment" but he could drink all the beer he wanted. Takim was my little manz and he held me down on many occasions. Before he left, he assured me that everything was alright and he would hold me down, he even dropped me some bread and some brand new Jordans.

As soon as I got the Jordans, I got on the phone to holla at some peeps. It was Monday morning, I was at the phones rockin' the new Jordans Takim sent me and first thing I heard was on the phone was "Yo Sha, you aint gonna beleive this shit, Takim got murked out in Atl over the weekend, "Bunz" stayed with his body until the cops came and they locked him up." That's the same way it went down in "**Belly**" but the scenario was switched up. It is a very touchy issue and me and Monday never really got to fully build on it but it changed Monday's life for real. After that, I knew **shit was real** cause he left the "Food Department" and was on some "Nation Of Islam" shit for real, I just don't understand why Roe had "Bunz" in the movie makin' a deal with the FBI to work and kill shit. That shit raised a few eyebrows because Monday was surprisingly acquitted in my Fed ordeal. It was like Roe was tryna put a bone on my manz but niggahs know Monday didn't rock like that. Shit was just a movie with certain situations and scenarios that niggahs been through, wasn't nobody on the team fuckin' wit Po-Po **Oh No!!**

* * * * *

I've always been a fella with a mind that produced a billion thoughts per second so you know I kept strivin' to put together moves to come up and generate money; I went at numerous cats with numerous ideas. See, there's one thing people do and that is sleep on people in prison but I understand the hustle from the street perspective so I'm forever happy that my dogs made it and are in positions to live comfortable but at the same time, they lost their grasp on the streets to know what the streets want. You gotta know how to keep the consumer's interest. You can't do that from behind an oversized desk on the eightieth floor of some Midtown Skyscraper. You gotta keep your ears and eyes in those streets so I'm never tryna say that niggahs get rich, switch and forget where they came from , well some do... okay... most of them do but what I'm gettin' at is... some lose focus, some don't want that connection to the streets no more. I'm about "**maintaining the focus**". While you are sittin' behind that big desk, always on the move, jumpin' from meeting to meeting, speed ballin' to get this or that done, I'm in here "**Thinking**", comin' up with mega ideas. I'm the type of cat to bring ideas to the table so we can put things in motion, manifest results and live off of the rewards. I am not about comin' at anyone with my hand out, beggin'... nah, I don't rock like that. I know and understand the struggles and hard work my niggahs put in to get where they at today. I'm strivin' to add on with ideas, projects and moves. I done went at niggahs with all kinds of shit; music, books, movies, clothing designs, **you name it**.

Before the thought of penning this novel, I had ideas that I went at certain heads with. I got a thugged out, ghetto love story titled "**Loyalty**", shit is bananas! I went at Ro and Daymond, sendin' them a synopsis of the story. I had moves put together, like web pages on the internet. One was a lawyer trust fund to help me obtain a lawyer to represent me on my cases. Another idea I had was some entertainment type shit like a F.E.D.S. / Don Diva Street Magazine but on the net, dealin' with prison life, prison politics and prison celebrities. I wanted to start a publishing company and a few other projects that all should be in motion by the time this book is published. **The Game Don't Stop**! I had cats I was networkin' and pollyin' with on streets, puttin' together beats and rap demos. Cats in the Penal System, who got peeps on the streets, I was connectin' with them tryna make somethin' pop off. Irv always stressed if I had any music and or artists I wanted him to listen to, I should get it to him and believe me Duke, I was gettin' some ill spitters and beat makers at him but of course… I got **no feed back from Irv**. Then I started networking with R&B songwriters on the streets and inside prison who were still tryna make moves and pop off. Monday started his "**Black House Entertainment**" record label from inside prison and I got one of my comrades featured on the "Black House State Blues" compilation cd.

I was still networking over the phone so my manz from bricks (out in the world) gave me a scoop about Irv havin' a hard time marketing his female rapper "**Vita**". She wasn't pennin' her own lyrics at the time so I got on that A.S.A.P. by steppin' to my manz from Cali, he had a baby mom who was part of Snoop's female rap group "**Doggy's Angels**". My manz name was "**Pay Dog**", he was from Long Beach. I gave him the task of showin' his pennin' skills cuz he was a talented spitter. So son wrote an ill joint, even though I sent him back to the lab more than ten times to re-do certain parts because he was usin' West Coast slang. After he perfected it and spitted it in front of cats, niggahs was open. We named it "**Murder Murderess**", we typed it up in manuscript form and I priority mailed it to Irv at his Murder Inc. offices. I gave him that ill joint for free to show him I still got shit in the smash. Son never barked back at me and the shit was so hot I was waitin' for Vita to surface with that piece or dare spit it as a free style on "Rap City". Shit was ill, believe me and I came at Irv from all angles, I guess son wasn't feelin' a fella now that I was behind all this concrete and steel, I don't know. I had this cat spit over all Irv's beats on a demo and everything, son aint bark back but gave me a shout out on the album insert credits of his year 2000 L.P. "**Irv Gotti Presents... The Murderers**".

I was also drillin' Roe on some moves, gettin' at Daymond and I started branchin' out and touchin' other avenues too, I stay pollyin' and networking, **always building and findin' new ways to elevate self and create opportunities for others to eat and live**. It's like niggahs aint takin' jail cats serious but **trustfully**, when I pop off and blow on one of my own moves without them, how will it look? Especially knowin' they had the opportunity to make shit happen with me? NIggahs was still on that **SELF** shit. My manz told me way back that niggahs would shit on a fella on some get rich and switch shit. **Damn**, **sun aint lie** but at the same time, the niggah who told me that shit was actually the one who was doin' a lot of the shitting. What really had me thinkin' was that from the beginning of the whole movie process, throughout all the false hope and promises niggahs was feedin' us, I never actually heard Hype promise niggahs shit and he never said he was out to help us. Even after the smoke cleared I didn't hear from son. I can only go off what I was bein' told by Roe on the phones or what Monday wrote in his letters, I never hear nothin' directly from Hype's mouth. Even after the big hype factor that led up to the movie's release, Belly hit theaters, shit didn't do what they thought it would and Roe started cryin' that Hype jerked him.

Monday got at me in 1999 with another story, he had people makin' three-way calls to catch up with Hype cause Hype was on some real bullshit, feelin' that he was at a point in his career where he couldn't associate or be linked to niggahs like "us". The movie aint do what he thought it would and furthermore, he allegedly had a vendetta against Monday after Monday got locked in ATL and needed money to bail out quick. He allegedly called Hype, who was blowin' up in the world of music videos. Hype sent the money but after Monday bonded out, instead of money, Monday gave Hype an Infinity M30 but never got a chance to give him the paperwork and title to the car. So later on down the line, Hype got pulled over in the car, went through some harassment from police and the car got impounded bein' that he didn't have any documents to prove the whip was his. He kept gettin' at "Bunz (Monday)" to get the paperwork so he could get the car out of impound but when "Bunz" hollered at the dude (our niggah) whose name the car was under, son allegedly snaked "Bunz" and "Hype" by gettin' the car out of impound and sellin' it because the car was registered to him, which technically made it his car.

So Hype was under the impression that Monday played him in the same manner he played him many times growin' up. Hype saw this as his chance to get "Bunz" back. He allegedly shitted on us as far as helpin' us with money in order to get lawyers and private investigators on our Ohio ordeal, which we are really innocent on... but son turned his back on niggahs. That's the story I got and I never got to speak to Hype personally, after that, his address and numbers changed. We got shitted on and then Roe claimed that he was left in the cold with no proceeds from the film, only co-writing credentials. So we was back to square one, **Ground Zero**. Then Monday's baby mom wasn't feelin' how in the movie, they had her in the movie callin' Police to trap "Bunz" off, I wasn't feelin' that either. Nor was I feelin' how they flipped the joint where she killed my manz "Shameek" when it didn't go down like that but it's all Hollywood and in Hollywood anything goes... but we in real life and the reality of shit was, **them niggahs wasn't bein' real**.

Shit been illiotic for the kid, I was sittin' in prison watchin' niggahs blow up and live comfortable; the same cats who used to fuck wit a fella like me. That's how life be, its funny like that sometimes. I still had to keep it movin' regardless, I am never mad or hatin' on the next man. They made their moves and paid their dues even if they were usin' our situations or tryna use us as chess pieces to advance their game to do so. **Do You!** I still have major love for my dogs. I just learned throughout the whole ordeal to never rely on niggahs no matter who they are. "**I lost all my faith in mankind**". **Nobody will hold you down the way you hold them down if the positions was switched up**.

I would still see articles in various magazines, interviews by certain niggahs, **frontin'**. One example is from like a March or April 2002 issue of XXL Magazine with Suge Knight and his Death Row crew on the cover. There's an article with a niggah screamin' how he was in Ohio with "his crew" and how shit got crazy and the Feds came in shuttin' niggahs down. Mad convicts came showin' me the mag and how a niggah was screamin' about how ill "his crew was" but niggahs is in prison fucked up with football numbers while he out there **fakin'**. I just don't get it, same niggah makes the cover of the "Source" screamin' Al Monday out. He was all in "Felon" magazine, same way, same shit while Monday's in prison with a life sentence, stugglin' but still comin' up with ill ideas to come up and generate money to obtain lawyers and investigators to work our issues.

A lot of political moves and networking of "who knows who" went on where professors became very interested in our Ohio ordeal; one being a professor named David Protess, who researches cases where people have been wrongfully convicted of murder and rape and is one of the nations top law professors with a very good track record of provin' the innocence of people convicted of crimes they didn't do. Professor Protess had a journalism class of students, who take on cases as projects where they researched every element of cases, interviewed witnesses and examined evidence, documents and crime scenes thoroughly. The students would turn over stories where files were kept from people that would free men or shift the weight off of them. They attacked our ordeal and saw that we had been framed. The nations top investigator, Paul Ciolino, also bares witness to this fact and states that he's "seen thousands of cases but this (our case) takes the cake, they (we) were definitely framed."

FUBU made moves and got our Ohio ordeal featured in F.E.D.S. magazine in the spring of 2002. Meanwhile, these law students were on top of the case, producin' witnesses and obtainin' affidavits, showin' that we were framed for a double homicide. They also saw our association / affiliation with certain Entertainment Industry cats, they interviewed one, who instead of helpin' us and our cause, allegedly bragged about how **ill his niggahs was** and how the movie "Belly" **was about his niggahs**. These students must have went and viewed the movie because they mysteriously abandoned our case, I assume, after seein' similarities in situations and scenarios. I was like **"Damn"**, how doggie gonna do that when these student's objective was to help us get back in court with evidence that proves we are actually innocent? What kind of shit was son on? Yeah, we ill niggahs but Monday was / is already and I will eventually be sittin' in prison for some shit I aint do or have a part in. The students was already investigating and diggin' backwards, seein' niggahs was street cats who made ill moves but **we are innocent** of the double homicide we were charged for. Why would he brag about the movie? That aint help our situation… we aint live off the movie, we aint eat off of it at all. Nobody gave me a **red cent**. I can't understand how niggahs scream they "got love" but aint showin' no love. **Where's the love at**?

You've read this chapter and you've probably seen the movie, you decide for **yourself**. Everybody has their views and opinions as to what transpired. In an interview with "Street Prospective" Magazine, Roe said the objectives of the movie "Belly" was to get his niggahs out of jail but a lot of shady business came out of certain cats and shit aint pop off so his niggahs is still sittin' in prison. **How real is shit**? Nevertheless, Shakim Bio-Chemical / The Omega Jon Christ still got mega love and keeps it thorough. I'm still floatin' around in the Federal System, makin' moves and stayin' on top of my case issues and projects **"The Game Don't Stop!!!"** I'm still the **Illest**!

* * * * *

**Note:

THE FOLLOWING BONUS CHAPTERS ARE FREE OF CHARGE

CHAPTER 18

JAY-Z vs. NAS, NAS vs. JAY-Z, YOU vs. ME, ME vs. YOU

NOTE: It is not my intention to compare these lyrical cats; both are wordsmith assassins with witty wordplay, metaphors, curveballs and precious jewels buried in their lyrics, both emcees are gifted and can be considered "Before their time".

Jay-Z a.k.a. "Jay Hova", "Jigga", "Young Veto", "Hov" amongst other aliases, is labeled "**The God MC**". **NAS** a.k.a. "Nasty Nas", "Esco", "Nas Escobar", "Nastradamus", and "The General", calls his self "**God's Son**".

You make the decision! Is one of these cats the God MC? Is the other cat God's Son? Sounds crazy, don't it? Both these gifted men have the ability to guide the youth; not just lyrically but by setting trends, spittin' fashion statements and revealin' our ghetto stories. These cats are our Ghetto news reporters, our messengers who kicked the everyday politics in a language we understand so well and the whole world is graspin' for "**Hip Hop**".

In the following chapters, you will see how these two dudes' lyrical skills not only affected the outside world but they also affected us cats in prison. A lot of shit is actual, I had to adjust a few things because it was said by convicts, who voiced their opinions and told their opinions and views because they know both emcees by association, affiliation or whatever. A lot is said and meant, a lot means nothing. I kept it as real as possible and held no punches, **Nas gets it and Jay-Z gets it**. I trust I will open eyes to the reality of this shit and not to get people in their feelings... well, you know how I feel about other people feelings: **I wipe my ass with your feelings**! Read and Enjoy... - The Omega Jon Christ

The ill Brooklyn niggah from Queens (**You know who!**) made his way off the weight section of the recreation yard after an extensive workout, a fella like me just got through doin' pull-ups, dips and push-ups. The count on the reps was crazy, we talkin' about five sets of twenty reps of pull-ups with twenty dips and thirty pushups. Five more sets of fifteens with fifteen dips and thirty push-ups then five sets of twelve with twelve dips, thirty push-ups and five sets of ten pull – ups with ten dips and thirty push-ups. All behind the back pull-ups then I ended with five sets of chest on the universal flat bench. A fella was feelin' type ill and brolic but in reality I was a slim but solid185 lbs with a 5'10" frame with crazy diesel seventeen "inches and a push" arms but no legs. I looked like I belonged out there in Cali, that's the Cali look, big up top but the legs look like string beans. I'd been in California for like sixteen months at this point, the Federal Prison System is illiotic; they had a N.Y. Cat like me way out there in Lompoc, California. Before I got there, I never even heard of Lompoc but I found out it's like two or two and a half hours from Los Angeles. Lompoc is a Maximum Security Federal Penitentiary, I was sent there after about a five month stint in Marion Super-max in Illinois, where they had John Gotti and Howard "Pappy" Mason at. Yea, I went there and repped. All live cats at that spot know my name as I met some real live and deep brothers on that end. Marion was an ill experience!

I had been in Terre Haute U.S.P. for five years and I had like eight and a half years in the Federal System altogether by the time I got to Lompoc, which was my third spot in the Feds. Shit is crazy how they had a fella traveling the world through the Fed Pens!!!Anyway, I had just worked out as I said before and I was standin' by the gate in Lompoc, drinkin' some cold, cold water from my water jug and conversatin' with my manz "Y-Born", a God Body from Kentucky. Y-Born was my work out partner on the pull-ups. I was in Terre Haute U.S.P. with him, son was a live wire and repped to the fullest.

"Yo, Shakim, what's the science God?"

"Nothin' Y-Born… that was a good work out Son, what you think?"

"Sha, you gotta slow down. What are you provin' by doin' high numbers on pull-ups like that? You are burnt out doin' twenty sets, then chest".

"It was only five sets of chest G, I rather sweat makin' preperations then sweat at time of war" (**D.C. "Lil' Man" I know you like that one!!**)

"Cut that shit out Sha, you know when it's time for war, I got ya back. I'ma be right there wit you, pushin' that knife, you know how I get down".

The God was correct, I knew him well, he beat his co-defendant in the head with a 2 by 4 and one time in the chow hall in Terre Haute U.S.P. (The Hut), I had to stop him from beatin' a man to death with a heavy duty, iron can opener. Y-Born don't be playin' no games, he was a slim and trim, cut up, defined brown-skinned brother. You would never believe that he was almost forty years old with his cornrow braids and massive tattoos but when he smiled, you knew somethin'. The God had no teeth in his mouth, they all got pulled out. Back in 1995 - 97', when we were together in "The Hut", Y-Born had massive gold teeth, ten on top and ten on the bottom, now he had none, NO TEETH AT ALL. He got a thirty year sentence for drug conspiracy and I think he got an extra five years for beatin' his "Co-dee" down like that too. Y-Born was a real cat and made sure I was "livin'" and wasn't in need; he was a real good brother.

"Yo, what you up to anyway "Y"?"

"I'm waitin' for them to call this recreation move so I can go in, take my shower and get my seat in the t.v. room. They got some shit bout dem niggahs Jay-Z and Nas comin' on t.v."

"Word? What station?"

"Sha, you know I don't know all that shit. I just know it's comin' on. It's only like two… maybe three stations it could be on, B.E.T., MTV or VH1. Someone in your unit knows, believe me, niggahs gonna watch that. I'm surprised of all people you didn't know about that!"

"Nah G, I didn't hear about it".

"Cut the jokes Sha, you in the middle of that shit. Stop actin' like I don't know you rollin' with Nas, you from QB too? C'mon!"

"Nah, I'm from Queens Borough, not no Queensbridge!"

"Same shit to me Sha, I'm from Kentucky!!!

We both laughed as we stood by the gate, waitin' for the recreation move (Rec move). Recreation move is when the prison opens up for movement so we could go from one activity to another, whether it was the yard, hobby craft shops, gym, store, movies or wherever. It's a ten minute move but for real, it seems like a five minute move that only happened at ten minutes to every hour so wherever you go, you are stuck there for an hour when the next move is called. The Rec Yard in Lompoc is real big. It had four or five pull-up bars with the dip bars and Roman Chair around the track. There was a section with numerous universal weights benches and tables like some picnic shit was set up around the track. There was Handball, Tennis, Bachie ball, a full and two mini half court basketball courts, a mini golf course, a horseshoe field and they even had a card table section under a shed, where niggahs played cards and gambled. On the yard, under the shed there was a color t.v. that stayed tuned to B.E.T. and niggahs stayed watchin' videos. The t.v. was supposed to be tuned to sports but videos and sports rule in the Feds. You couldn't escape the shit, the young generation was on music hard (still is), especially Hip Hop. By now, Hip Hop was on another level, shit was more than a culture, it was life itself. Niggahs watchin' videos? Turn from B.E.T. and you might get killed, no matter what Fed Pen you're in. **B.E.T. Ruled**!!!

"Yo Shackkim, Com air breddren, me waan ollar at yu!!"

I turned and saw the "Yardie Dreads" sittin' down on the benches, throwin' bread crumbs to feed the birds. I fucks with the dreads, I've mentioned that my whole family is Jamaicans. I tell Y-Born...

"Yo, I'ma be right back!"

"Yo make sure you make this move Sha and don't start talkin' with your Jamaican folks and stay out, I'm goin' in!"

"Ahite G! Ahite!"

I started walkin' straight thru where da birds dem was eatin'.

"C'mon ya man! Shackkimm, yu always walk straight in where da birds dem eat! Yu done scare off dem birds Star!" Shouted Huey.

As I walked in and kicked the bread crumbs I said...

"Fuck them birds, they gotta get it how we get it, we in Jail".

The dreads laughed as I gave dap handshakes. It was about six Jamaicans outside by the benches, four were seated, two were standing. As I shook Huey's hand, he said...

"Wha gwaan Jamerican Rude Yout?"

Huey was a brown-skinned, chubby Yardie with a short, Cesar hair cut. He used to live in Cali and N.Y. He'd been in Prison over twelve years and was on Delroy Edwards a.k.a. "Uzi Delroy" case (Uzi Delroy is a notorious dread, who terrorized Brooklyn in the 1980's). Huey always called me "Jamerican" because both my parents are natives of Jamaica but I was born in N.Y., makin' me an American so add Jamaica and American and you get "Jamerican" cause I'm Jamaican blooded but I got Yankee ways; I'm N.Y. to the core! Huey was still stuck in fashion; he wore different designer glasses everyday. He would switch up from Gucci, Cartier, Chanel, Armani, Prada, Versace, you name it, Huey had it. He was like thirty-nine years old and he would come out to feed the birds everyday and the birds would come out of nowhere. Huey was sittin' on the bench, rippin' up bread and throwin' it.

"Cha, move it mi throw dem birds its lunch, Star!"

Also, standin' up by the benches, was "Lizard" and believe me, they didn't call him "Lizard" for nothin'. Lizard was from the Bronx but born in Jamaica, he could chat dance hall lyrics and all. He was on some pure entertainer type shit and he had a life sentence. "Twin", a yardie from Brooklyn, was also sittin' on the benches. He had a twin brother who was also in the Fed System, he was the "good" twin while his brother was the "bad" twin, known to stab and chop up cats in the system.
"Yo Shack (what Twin called me for short), wha yu av fi di lungs?"

"I aint doin' nothin' Twin"

"C'mon Shack, yu are di Fubu bwoy, everybody done know yu di man!"

"Yea right"

Salah, who had short dreads that only hung to his ears, was standin' up next to Lizard...

"Mi a look fi di corn now, mi air it pon di wess end, Shack, look inna it fi I, si who av it, zeen?"

"No doubt" I answered back.

Shawnie was a brownskin yardie with dreads down his back. His face was scarred up viciously from a razor attack allegedly demonstrated by the "bad" twin when they were together in another Fed Institution. How could he look the "bad" twin's identical twin in the face everyday, knowin' his brother did that to him? I don't know and I never asked him either. Shawnie still thought that he was God's gift to the earth, they called him

"Fashion Dread", he was just in it for the looks, his accent was even gettin' "Americanized" but believe me, he's 100% Jamaican. He asked me...

"Yo, you gonna watch that Jay-Z, Nas shit?"

Shawnie was from Brooklyn and loved to keep that controversy shit in the air.

"Yea, I'ma check it".

"Mi gwaan see it too, yu know I gotta rep Brooklyn!"

I was about to say somethin' when Twin interrupted...

"Yo, mi gwaan go in and check it too, mi a Brooklyn dude but mi roll wit Nas Escobar!"

"Cha!! Mi don waan air no rap tings, mi tryin' feed mi birds!" snapped Huey.

"Solo" was also there, he was a dread with long locks down his back, four dreads caked up in the front that shot up in the air (no matter what, his front dreads was always stickin' up on some unicorn type shit) and long mini dreads in his beard. He jumped up and while walkin' away toward the gate he said with his heavy Jamaican accent...

"Man com inna prison to feed birds? Den im say im nah waan air no talk pon rap? Wha wrong wit im blood clot?!!"

All the dreads was laughin'.

"Move ya rass clot, si wha yu started Jamerican? Di man wak pon where dem birds eat and dem fly away!"

Everybody was laughin' as a voice on the intercom shouted "**This is a movement back to the housing area from recreation. I repeat... a one way move!!! Incoming Only**!!"

Twin and Lizard looked around...

"Yo, mi eddin' inside yu know? Mi affi catch dis Jay-Z ting! Salah, yu stayin' out?"

"Yea, mi gwaan keep Huey company".

"Yo, mi see yu tommorow, LIGHTS!!"

Twin and Lizard walked towards the front rec yard gate that leads to the inside hallways of the prison. Everything was on the insides, the units, chow hall, rec center and the gym, the only thing outside was the rec yard and the Uni-core factories. Huey was still throwin' breadcrumbs on the ground when he said...

"Yo, Jamerican, mi affi si yu, we mus sit down to chat and reason bout tings, mi soon touch and mi waan keep in touch wit mi breddens still so mi talk to yu likkle more, zeen?"

"Yea Sun, I'ma go in. Yo Salah, I'ma look into that for you too".

"Okay, likkle more (See you later)!"

As I walked towards the gate, Y-Born was slow walkin' waitin' on me. During the rec move from off the yard, goin' back inside would be so crowded… then you had to go through a long hallway that was dark with three to four blind spots where you could attack and tear a niggah up. We talkin' about eight hundred to a thousand or more convicts comin' in from the rec yard, walkin' in the hallways. We went through the metal detectors that lined up like toll booths, four side by side with tables and Correction Officers standin' there, checkin' our belongings. Me and Y-Born was walkin' as I said "what's up" to different convicts who were walkin' in on movements themselves. It was handshakes and

"What's up" and keep it movin'. To put you more on point about the Federal System, it's very geographical; everything is based on where you're from. Fed Prisons contain people from all over the world, who allegedly violated Federal Laws of the United States of America so just think... people from all over the world, from the fifty states and from different countries, all locked up behind the concrete and steel walls of the Federal Prison System. In the Feds (and prison in general) a lot of things are based on race, religion, gang set, east coast, west coast, south, mid-west, you name it, it's all a divide and conquer type of thing when we all locked the fuck up.

Lompoc Federal Correction Complex is in California and home of the Crips and the Bloods so we talkin' about five hundred different Crips from different sets and about two hundred and fifty bloods from different sets. My numbers may be wrong, the count could've been more but then you had the Mexicans, who over populated the whole prison. There were Mexicans everywhere and they were on some divide and conquer shit amongst themselves. They had sets like the Northerns, Sorenoe's (South), the Border Brothers, it's just too many to name and identify but they be beefin' and warring amongst each other; not to mention every other day they were beefin' with blacks. Then you had the whites... the Arian Brotherhood (AB), the Dirty White Boys (DWB), Bikers, all kinds of shit. When I tell you it's geographical, believe me, it's **GEOGRAPHICAL!!!** Every state, gang, set and race have a section they either sit at whether it's in the t.v. rooms, chow hall, gym, pull-up bars or rec yard, everything is geographical in the Feds. How shit is set up in the Feds is every section is considered or called "Cars". So you got the N.Y.Car, which consists of N.Y. heads, The D.C. Car, which consists of D.C. (District of Columbia) heads and so on and so on. Because we were on the west coast, we were the East Coast Car, which consisted of all the eastern seaboard states but different cars in the East coast convoy. You will understand it more as the story's plot thickens.

"Yo Sha, you straight in your block? You don't need nothin'?"

"Yea, I'm good Y-Born, I don't need anything".

"No food or anything? You know I own stores in every unit, what you need, stamps?"

"I'm straight sun, I don't need nothin'!!"

"You got Oreos down there? I know you love dem Oreos!"

"Yeah I got like twenty packs or so"

"Good, bring me two packs!"

Y-Born always did that shit, he'd ask me what I need then tell me to bring him shit but that was my niggah right there; he was a real cat. We walked the hallways, heading towards our housing units. Lompoc had twelve housing units named by Alphabet letters and there was a west end and an east end. I lived in "F" unit on the west end, Y-Born was in "D" unit, which was the code program and dorm on the west end. As we passed the movie theater, we look at the posted movie billboard which read "Romeo Must Die".

"Yo Sha, you know we gotta see that shit twice! I gotta see my baby Aaliyah!"

"No question, we gonna see that!"

Lompoc had a real theater that was just like the theaters on the streets… seats and all. It was dark in there and they even stepped up the game with dvd's jumpin' off on the movie projection screen. They showed all the up to date movies and changed them twice a week. Shit looked like a real theater on the streets and they had a soda machine but you had to bring your own popcorn, zoom zooms and wham wham jump offs and shit. They had a metal detector in that piece but you know that aint stop nothing. As me and "Y" kept walking, the hallways were crowded.

C.O.'s were standin' outside the unit's doors as convicts waited for the "Out Going" movement.

"Yo G, I'ma holla at you tomorrow cause I'm stayin' in tonight... I got mad letters to pen and a few phone calls to make"

"Ahite but come to breakfast in the morning and don't have me waitin' like last time Shakim, come out, I wanna holla at you!"

"No doubt" I said, as I made it to the front of my unit. I hit Y-Born with a pound handshake and embrace. Y-Born gave me his toothless smile and said...

"Make sure you bring my Oreos too... two packs!"

"I got you, I got you, PEACE!"

As soon as I walked in the unit and through the metal detector, my manz Woody, a blood from Los Angeles came up to me...

"Yo, Sha-Forty, you know they got our relatives comin' on the t.v. tube, you know we got the seats posted up. We gotta "B (See)" the relative from "QB!"

Woody a.k.a. "Woody L" was six feet tall, about a hundred and ninety-five pounds, brown skinned; a husky cat with that long permed hair, Cali look. He was "Blooded out", it was a big thing poppin' off where the West Coast Bloods had mad love for the N.Y. car and now that N.Y.C. was "Blooded out" crazily back on the East Coast, it was even more love and a lot of East Coast rappers like Ja Rule, Capone & Noreaga, Tragedy, Cam'ron and his Dipset let their Blood affilation and association be known; It was even speculated that L.L. Cool J, The Lox, DMX and many others were "Blood related". Nas was on that list too, niggahs had him "Blood Affilated" to the point that niggahs was pointin' him out bein' "Flamed up", rockin' a lot of red colored clothing and throwin' so called hand signals in videos. It was even said he was sendin' "Blood" messages in his lyrics.

I don't know... I had been in prison for a minute by this time... I try not to let a lot of shit go over my head but some things may seem obvious and some shit is just in niggahs heads and imaginations. Nas holds Queensbridge p.j.'s down and screams "**Q. B**.!!" which is the biggest Housing Project in the United States, sittin' right there in the borough of Queens, in N.Y.C. Rappers like Mobb Deep, Cormega, Capone, Littles, Big Noyd, Lake, Screw Ball, Marley Marl and MC Shan and Roxanne Shante... yo, its just too many emcees / rappers comin' out of Queensbridge to name. Nas kicked in "Got Yourself a Gun" that "Q.B. don't stand for no Quarter Back". When he said this in the video for the song, he threw up the "B" and niggahs in Lompoc went crazy! So "Q.B." was now "**Queens Bloods**".

Farmer's Boulevard is really what the "**F.B.**" in **FUBU** meant, for that is where all four of the FUBU cats is from. Believe me son, I know so just go with it... niggahs on the street flipped the "F.B." concept to "Farmers Bloods". The Bloods were all over N.Y.C. but the Crips were too. A lot of rappers was affiliated with the Crips and word on streets said Jay-Z was one of them. Niggahs is ill how they speculate and assume and a lot of the time, their hunches turns out to be actual facts. You gotta be swift and changeable and catch the lyrics these rappers kick, the clothes they rock and the way they throw their hands. Hip Hop is way more than a music thing, it's a big culture, no... it's a fuckin' way of life. I'm a Queens cat, I have affiliation with Bloods and Crips, how is that? At this point, I'd been in the system for eight years or so and I met cats from everywhere. Then out of nowhere, N.Y. got caught up in that ganglife shit. Everybody got "Bloody" or "Loc'd up". I been a Five Percenter since the late seventies and now Blood Five Percenters, who called themselves "50-50", were emerging and the rap group "Wu-Tang Clan" was rumored to be involved in that.

Anyway, since I'd been in Cali, I became a gang specialist type niggah because gangs was all that was around me. I could meet you, hear where you were from and I'd know what set you claim, rep and all that other shit. I'm cool with Bloods and Crips but I'm just an ill cat, even though the Bloods fuck with me real, real hard. All my dogs in N.Y.C. is "blooded" and I get flicks of them "flamed up" with mail full of the lingo and I stay on the phones so I was always up on shit. My affiliation with the Bloods is ill but I'm an ill Queens cat; born in Brooklyn, God Body Blooded, not Blooded Godbody but its still all "hood", feel me? I fucked with the dog Woody L, I even had a seat in the Blood section of the t.v. room and could sit in the movies and chow hall with them. There were a few East Coast Bloods in Lompoc, one was my peeps so niggahs knew what it was, Blooded or not, I hold my East Coast niggahs down. Anyway, as I hurried to my one man cell, I told Woody...

"Yo, let me jump in the shower real quick and make me some oatmeal and raisins!"

He said...

"Yo relative, make sure you bring some Oreos to the t.v. Room!"

On the way back to my cell from the showers, I bumped into my manz from N.Y.C., there were like twenty-five to thirty New Yorkers out there in Lompoc... well, twenty-five to thirty GO HARD NEW YORKERS in Lompoc, maybe more but I'm talkin' about niggahs who you could "**see in their walk and in their lean**" that they were from N.Y.C. There were five N. Y'ers in my unit, one named Saekwon, who was a brownskinned, chinky eyed, stocky built, wanna be pretty boy thug from the Bed-Stuy section of Brooklyn; son had been in the Fed System for over ten years by the time I met him, he looked and acted like a Brooklyn niggah too. The N.Y. car was splitted in two cars, Saekwon ran one of them; he said...

"Yo Sha, what's the deal Sun? You know your soft ass manz from Queens is about to come on t.v., that's a soft ass cat... my manz from the "Stuy" bout to be on too and he gon' expose that niggah".

"Yeah?"

"Yeah, you know Brooklyn niggahs run Queens as well as the rest of N.Y."

As I entered my cell, I said...

"Yeah, I know Brooklyn niggahs like runnin' their fuckin' mouths"

"Damn Sha, you from BK, why you screamin' Queens for?" Saekwon asked on his way to the t.v. room.

Me and Saekwon had heated debates based on that Queens - Brooklyn shit; I fucks with him though, for he knows how I carry shit, I'm a Brooklyn born niggah from Queens and I go hard too but bein' from Queens, I had to go extra hard to let cats know aint nothin' sweet. "Q.B." don't stand for Queensbridge to me, to me it stands for Queens Borough and I'm lettin' niggahs know Queens is a thorough borough, we don't take shorts, not even on a Newport (some Riker's Island shit), fuck that rap shit. Them rappers talk it, I LIVE IT! Anyway, I got dressed and all that shit, made me some oatmeal and raisins, snatched up my red drinkin' jug and a few packs of Oreos and made my way downstairs to the microwave. In my unit, there was like seven Bloods, about a hundred Crips, five New Yorkers, maybe six or seven white boys and all the rest were Mexicans so N.Y. niggahs had to go hard and put our work and mark down, knowin' that we was out of our zone way out on the West Coast... N.Y. niggahs make it anywhere we at, we at home.

"Sha-Bio whats up homie?"
I said "Blood up Son!" as I passed a few Bloods on my tier and put my oatmeal in the microwave. My other manz "Pay Dog" came over to me.

"My main man Shakim from Queens, what's crackalackin'? You know Nas and Jigga comin' on tv in like five minutes"

"Yeah, I know" I said, as I gave him a pound and with that smirk on his face he asked…

"Yo, you sittin' with us or you with your Blood crew?"

Pay Dog was six feet two inches, weighed like two hundred and twenty-five out of shape, chubby pounds with brown skin and curly long braids. Pay Dog's baby's mother was a member of Snoop Dogg's "Doggie's Angels" female rap group that came out slightly before or a little after the year 2000 ball dropped. Pay Dog was from Long Beach, Cali, where Snoop Dogg is from and he repped the Rolling 20's Crip set. Pay Dog crip walked and all that good shit. He taught me that in that "Crip Walk" dance, they be spellin' out their hood, their set and they also be disrespectin' other hoods and sets. He was a Crip that was open-minded and would conversate with other niggahs who wasn't in that gang life; he was also a talented rapper. He was in the Federal System for drugs with a fifteen year piece. I fucked with him cause of his genuine realness.

"Yo Pay Dizzle, you know I aint on no set trippin' time, I'm good in every hood, you know?"

"Yeah, that's right Sha".

"Yeah but Woody held me a seat in the Bloody section, I'ma come holla at you every commercial break to show you I got love for the L.B.C. though".

"I like y'all Queens niggahs, you are very charismatic"
Pay Dogg slapped me a pound and said…

"See you in the t.v. room homie".

The t.v. room was just about packed like a fuckin' basketball or football game was on or somethin'. The Cali cats in Lompoc was ill, when a Lakers game came on, these niggahs had posters of Kobe Bryant, Shaq and the cover of Shaq's book on top of the tv, pictures up on the wall and the whole nine yards. They'd take them down after the game but they praised Kobe like he was "Jesus". If you talked about the Lakers you better have a knife on you cause Cali niggahs had major love for the Lakers and the Oakland Raiders too. Ah shit, you couldn't tell these niggahs nathan and no nathan wasn't out there but if he was he remembered the last time he jumped out there (curve ball). Cali niggahs would be in their feelings (upset) if the Lakers or the Raiders lost but as I was sayin', the t.v. room was packed like the O.J. Simpson verdict was about to be announced.

Stink breath Veto, yelled "Yo what time does the shit come on? With all these fuckin' commercials MTV be showin', damn!"

Veto was a Harlem cat, who would always side with one niggah then he'd switch up to side with the other, it was a question mark of whether he was even from N.Y. He was sittin' with "Infinite", another BK representer from Linden Plaza in East New York. Infinite or "Inf" was one of those scientific God Bodies, who spoke in a very circumlocutory way, he could never just say some shit, he would over talk shit and use too many words tryna sound intelligent. Even when he was wrong, he made himself sound correct but he was my peoples regardless. He said…

"The science of the situation is currency pays for shows and they get their currency from showin' all these false advertisements of illusionary products"

Just as Infinite got into his so called "explanation mode", Saekwon interrupted sayin'…

"We not tryna hear all that bullshit, we tryna see Jigga!!"

Saekwon kept smart, slick remarks slippin' out his mouth and for some reason he didn't dig Infinite too tough.

The finally program came and "Sway" from "Sway & Tec" mix show was on the screen sayin'…

"We're here to bring you details of the ongoing lyrical battle between two of Hip Hop's greatest lyricists, Brooklyn's Jay-Z and Queens' Nasty Nas"

The program's host, Sway Calloway, went through both spitters careers from their beginnings to the peak of the battle, where the beef was believed to begin to where it escalated to the back and forth curveball lyrics both emcees threw at each other and to the eventual call out. They even did a thorough reference check on both of the insulting lyrics to see which one held more truth and weight. MTV went to the extreme of puttin' lyrics on the screen and searchin' for facts, givin' points to the emcee who held more weight with each offense. The program was good but not acceptable to a real cat like me, who also stood in the park jams in the late seventies, early eighties and indulged in the Hip Hop movement and culture. It was good for t.v. and was a good promotional stunt to advertise both emcee's albums, which were comin' out one behind the other. Jay-Z was releasing the "Blueprint", which got a five mic rating in the Source Magazine; Nas would drop "Stillmatic", which also got a five mic rating.

Nas also got a five mic rating on the "Illmatic" L.P. but seemed to change his lyrical direction after the success of that album. He went from Nasty Nas to Nas Escobar, Nas Esco to Nastradamus. He went from the ultimate street storyteller to the drug lord spittin' mafia shit and was enlightening the world with political lyrics then he'd go back to street shit. The argument was... Jay-Z defined himself as a "Hustler" and claimed that Nas watched the Hustler's activities from his project window then made songs about what he saw. B.E.T.'s show "Hits" even went as far as huntin' people down in both Brooklyn's Marcy projects and Queensbridge projects in Queens to hunt people down for verification on these cats street credibility. Adding fuel to their differences, every magazine jumped on the bandwagon, promotin' a battle between the emcees.

Just like the streets be talkin'... The prisons do too!!!

The critically acclaimed lyricist "Nasty Nas" was exposed to the rap game by rapper / music producer "Large Professor" and while watchin' and listenin' at the jams in the parks Nas was influenced by Hip Hop since the 1980's. Large Professor, who was part of the group "Main Source", gave young Nas his debut in form of a verse on "**Live at the BBQ**", which was an all-star posse cut on Main Source's first album in 1991. On his guest appearance with Main Source, Nas stood out when he spit lyrics like:

"**Street Disciple / my raps are trifle / I shoot slugs from my brain just like a rifle / Stampede the stage / I leave the microphone split / play Mr. Tuffy while I'm on some Pretty Tone shit / Verbal assassin / my architect pleases / when I was twelve / I went to hell for snuffin' Jesus / Nasty Nas is rebel to America / Police murderer / I'm causin' hysteria**"

Everybody was like "**Who the fuck was that**?" The young cat's lyrics stood out on a four man song, with lyrics like:
"**Kidnap the President's wife without a plan / and hangin' niggahs like the Ku Klux Klan**" and "**Slammin' emcees on cement / cause lyrically / I'm iller than an A.I.D.S Patient**".

Nas had niggahs everywhere, OPEN. I still remember the first time I heard "Live at the BBQ". I was in Lorain, Ohio bubblin', when my manz from "Up top" jumped in the car with Main Source's "Breaking Atoms" tape and he took control of the sound system while I drove. When he went to that song (BBQ), I kept rewindin' Nas' part.

"**When I was twelve / I went to hell for snuffin' Jesus**"

I was like "**This niggah is ill!!!**"

After Nas went shoppin' his demo in an attempt to get a deal and was even turned down by Russel Simmons, who claimed he "Sound too much like Kool G Rap", Nas hooked up with former 3rd Bass rapper **MC Serch**, who included Nas on another posse cut called "**Back to the Grill**" where Nas again outshined his peers with lyrics like:

"**This is Nas kid you know how it runs / I'm wavin' automatic guns at Nuns / I'm stickin' up the preachers in the church cause I'm a stone crook / serial killa / who works by the phonebook**"

In 1992, Nas ended up releasing his own song called "**Halftime**", which was featured on the "**Zebra Head**" soundtrack. This was the cut that landed him a record deal with Columbia, Records; Son killed it with lines like…

"**I set it off with my own rhymes / cause I'm as ill as a convict who kills for phone time**".

I bought the single for the tape deck in my car and on vinyl for the mixing equipment we had… the beat, the bassline and all that was slammin' as Nas' ill lyrics grabbed listeners...

"**I used to hustle / now all I do is relax and strive / when I was young / I was a fan of the Jackson 5 / I drop jewels, wear jewels hope to never run it / with more kicks than a baby in a mother's stomach / Nasty Nas has to rise cause I'm wise / this is exercised 'til the microphone dies / back in eighty three I was an emcee sparkin' / but I was too scared to grab the mics in the parks and / kick my little raps cause I thought niggahs wouldn't understand / and now at every jam I'm the fuckin' man / I rap in front of more niggahs than in the slave ships / I used to watch "C.H.I.P.S." / now I load Glock clips / I gotta have it / I miss Mr. Magic / versatile / my style switches like a faggot**"

Nas let it be known that his name was "**well known like the number man**". Real Hip Hop heads like me was checkin' for him. Son was crazy nice with his (**Still is**). This was at a time when New York wasn't really holdin' it down on the rap scene like we were known to do. The East wasn't a beast on the Hip Hop set no more, the West Coast's "Death Row Records" held that number one spot. It wasn't until 1994 when Nas debut album "Illmatic" and Biggie's "Ready to Die" dropped that the East took the title back. I somehow ended up with a copy of about fifteen or twenty of Nas' songs before Illmatic came out. I also got locked up before the album came out but when it dropped, only ten of the twenty Nas cuts I had on the tape actually made the album. Hip Hop Magazines was crowning Nasty Nas as **"The Second Coming"**, **"The New Rakim"** and **"The Prophet"**. Right then and there before the album, Nas dropped the "Nasty" and was just goin' by Nas. "Illmatic" was an instant Hip Hop Classic but it wasn't until his second L.P. "It was Written" in 1996 that Nas got his commercial success. Nas then flipped his name to many aliases and he put together a rap team called **"The Firm"** which consisted of him, **A.Z. Foxy Brown** and **Cormega**, then "Mega" was later replaced by **"Nature"**. In my opinion, this was when the whole Nas vs Jay-Z thing started brewin' because these two lyrical cats had a big conflict of interest and were tryna outshine each other.

   The Conflict: Ms. Foxy Brown, who was part of Nas' group "The Firm" but was Jay-Z's "Bonnie" and Jay-Z, her "Clyde". Jay-Z and Foxy had a formula together where they rapped on each other's albums. Jay's first big hit was "Aint No Niggah", which featured Foxy, who was already known to the Hip Hop world, kinda put Jay-Z in the forefront even though he was known "underground - wise". His single "Aint No Niggah" was on the "Nutty Professor" soundtrack and had a video for visual affect. Another song Foxy came out with was **"I'll Be"**, which featured Jay-Z on the hook. At the time, Foxy was considered the **female version of Jay-Z**, she was poppin' as his "Bonnie" but was part of Nas' supergroup while she continued featuring Jay on her solo albums **"Ill Na Na"** and **"China Doll"** and in return, she would guest appear on Jay's **"Reasonable Doubt"** and his **"Vol 1"** L.P.

In This Corner....

   Shawn Corey Carter, also said to be known as "MC Shawnie D", then "Jazzy" before settling with the name "Jay-Z", hails from the Marcy Houses, located in the Bedford-Stuyvesant section of the borough of Brooklyn. Jay-Z started rappin' in the mid "80's" while attending Westinghouse High School with the late **Christopher Wallace a.k.a. the Notorious B.I.G.** a.k.a. **Biggie Smalls** and rapper "**Busta Rhymes**". **Jay-Z** allegedly defeated **Busta** in a lyrical battle and started his rap career as "Big Jazz's" hype man. Big Jazz was a part of the rap group "**Original Flava**" and eventually came out with a few songs that was rotating in N.Y.C. to which he did shows with Jay-Z as his hype man. Jazz, along with rapper **Big Daddy Kane**, who at that time was at the peak of eloquence with his rap career, made a house tape which featured Jay-Z rappin'. At this point, Jay was also "**Hustling**", makin' moves and livin' the "**street life**".

In 1989, Big Jazz, along with Jay, came out with a single called "**Hawaiian Sophie**" but Jazz wasn't really poppin' off as much as other popular cats on the rap scene. Jay then disappeared and got caught up in his street ventures, goin' back and forth out of town. Somewhere in 1991, **DJ Clark Kent** convinced Jay to come back to N.Y. to pursue his rap career. Jay returned and upon his arrival back, started networking and tryna make things happen once again. In 1993, Jay was introduced to Harlem Native **Damon Dash**, who was promoting parties and managin' different groups and it so happened that "Original Flava" (group Jazz was in) was one of those groups. Tired of bein' turned down by record execs, Jay decided to start his own record label and with **Dash** and silent partner **Kareem "Biggs" Burke**, "**Roc-A-Fella Records**" was born with no financial or promotional backing. Jay attacked; bein' featured on a cut called "**Show & Prove**" along with **Big Daddy Kane, ODB (Ol' Dirty Bastard of Wu-Tang Clan), Shyheim the Rugged Child** and **Big Scoob**. He was also featured on a posse cut on Mic Geronimo's first L.P., another posse cut called "**8 is enough**" on rapper Big L's first album "**Lifestyles of the Poor & Dangerous**" and on an **Original Flava** single called "**Can I get you Open**?"

In 1995, Jay came out with a single called "**In My Lifetime**" that had a B-Side called "**Can't get with that**" which also featured a video where Jay was rhymin' with a fast **Das Efx stiggity style**. Jay-Z was known in N.Y.C.'s **Underground** and was one of the last men standin' in a famous battle where he and rapper **DMX** went head to head in a lyrical battle that started with many but ended with just X and J; the battle got so heated that guns was pulled out. Jay had a street buzz, burnin' up in N.Y.C. This Bed-Stuy, Brooklyn, retired Hustler with a braggadocious style, rhymin' about drivin' the illest whips with tv's in the headrest. Former A&R of Def Jam, DJ Irv (Irv Gotti) can vouch for the fact that Jay was actually livin' this life before he got famous.

In 1996, Jay-Z dropped the double sided single "**Dead Presidents / Aint No Niggah** (ft. Foxy Brown)", whiched marked the end of Jay spittin' with that Das Efx stiggity style; he was now killin' em with a slow flow and was ridin' the beat soundin' like he was actually talkin'. The Dead Presidents beat had a sample of Nas voice from his cut "The World is yours" off his 1994 Illmatic L.P. The sample of Nas' voice repeated in the chorus of Jay's song…

"Presidents to represent me (Get Money!!) I'm out for Presidents to represent me (Get Money!!) I'm out for dead fuckin' Presidents to represent me!!"

Jay followed with lyrics like:

"The Soviet, the unified steady flow, you already know, you light, I'm heavy roll, heavy dough / Mic machetied your flow, your paper falls slow / like confetti, mines a steady grow, bet he glow / pay for, dead it from blow, better believe I have eleven sixty to show / my doe flip like Tae-Kwon, Jay-Z the Icon, baby you like Dom, maybe this Cristal's to change your life, huh, roll with the winners / heavy spenders like hit records: Roc-A-fella / Don't get it corrected this shit is perfected / from chips to chicks just drivin' a lexus / make it without your gun / we takin' everything you brung / we cake and you niggahs is fake and we gettin' it done / Crime family / well connected Jay-Z / and you fake thugs is unplugged like MTV / I empty three,

take your treasure / my pleasure Dead Presidentials, politics as usual Bla-oow!!!"

The song "Aint No Niggah" was followed by a video for "**Dead Presidents pt. 1**" and "**Aint No Niggah**" with **Foxy**, a star was born. Rap "**King of N.Y.**" **Biggie Smalls** was even givin' interviews in magazines, speakin' about the lyrical flow of upcomin' Jay-Z, sayin' Jay was his favorite emcee and the next hot thing out there besides "Biggie" himself. All heads was checkin' for this emcee, who was gettin' big props from Biggie Smalls. **Biggie** claimed he would kick his rhymes to Jay before he laid it because Jay was so nice and Biggie valued his opinion, he said Jay did the same with him. BIG even admits to goin' back to the lab to re-do his lyrics to match up to his manz Jay-Z's standards. All this and **BIG** was already a commercial success and no one really knew who the fuck this Jay-Z guy was but before long, everybody was checkin' for this Jay-Z niggah. 96' was the year Jay released "**Reasonable Doubt**" and he had a cut on the album called "**Brooklyn's Finest**", featuring the **Notorious B.I.G**. / **Biggie Smalls**. **Jay and BIG** went back and forth with the lyrics, tryna outshine each other with their braggadocious lyrics. Shit was Bananas!! Check it…

(Jay-Z) **Jiggaaa Biggaaaa....**
Niggah, how you figure...
Peep the style and the way the cops sweat us / the number one question is can the Feds get us / I got vendettas in dice games with ass betters / and niggahs who pump wheels and drive jettas

take that witchya....

(Notorious B.I.G.)
... Hit ya, back split ya / fuck fist fights and lame scuffles / pillow case to your face make the shell muffle / shoot your daughter in the calf muscle / fuck a tussle, nickel plated / sprinkle coke on the floor, make it look drug related most hated...

(Jay-Z)
...**Can't fade it while y'all pump willie / I run up in stunts silly scared, so you sent your little manz to come kill me/ but on the contrilli / I packs the mack-milli / squeezed off on him / left them paramedics breathin' soft on him / what's your name**?

(Biggie)
Who shot ya? / Mob ties like Sinatra / Peruvians tried to do me in / I aint paid them yet / Tryna push 700's they aint made them yet / Rolex and bracelets is frost bit, rings too / niggahs round the way call me Igloo / Stick Who? Motherfuckers!!

(Jay and BIG)
Jay-Z and Biggie Smalls / niggah shit ya drawls
(where you from?) Brooklyn goin' out for all
Marcy-that's right - You don't stop
Bed-Stuy - You won't stop Niggah
Shit couldn't get no iller than that... two Brooklyn Heavyweights shinin' together? Biggie with a niggah named Jay-Z a.k.a. "**Jigga**" goin' rhyme for rhyme with him. Niggahs all over was goin' **CRAZY!!!** Jay-Z's attack on N.Y. was now known everywhere as he kicked some of the slickest shit in his lyrics, like in his single "**Can I Live?**"

"**While I'm watchin' every niggah watchin' me closely / my shit is butter for the bread they wanna toast me / I keep my head, both of them where they supposed to be / Hoes'll get you sidetracked then clapped from close feet**"

Jay was killin' them with just one L.P. One thing about Jay-Z... from the time he emerged and for eight summers straight, he monopolized the rap game by always havin' a hot song in rotation, a street banger, a club banger and a video in rotation. He was **still the "Hustler"**; from the **Crack game** he took this strategy to **the Rap Game and milked it.**

In 1997, **Irv Gotti** brought **Jay-Z, Dash** and **Burke** to **Def Jam**, where they negotiated a venture / deal, **Roc-A-Fella** was now with **Def Jam,** which gave them the marketing and promotion needed to make Jay-Z even larger than life and Irv Gotti was the reason for the merger. For ten years straight startin' in 1996, Jay-Z dropped an album every year, Roc-A-Fella did big things like signing artists like a **young Memphis Bleek**, who was put on by Jay and also hails from Marcy P.J.'s. Later Roc-A-Fella signed Philly's Beanie Sigel, Jay was on the rise and so was Roc-A-Fella Records.

The Set Up

DJ Irv was definitely on the rise as well. After leavin' **Blunt Records**, he became an A&R at Def Jam Records. He brought **DMX** to Def Jam, got him signed and was the merger between Roc-A-Fella and Def Jam. Irv also helped **Ruff Riders** negotiate a deal with **Interscope**, in return, Def Jam gave him a chance to start up his **Murder Inc**. label with Def Jam. The original "Murder Inc." was supposed to be DMX, Jay-Z and two newcomers, one was Ja Rule from the Queens Cash Money Clique but with DMX and Jay-Z both being risin' stars, there were creative differences and the project didn't fall into place. Irv moved on with Ja Rule and put together a roster for Murder Inc. Jay-Z's Roc-A-Fella Records was makin' crazy noise and Jay, the Co-CEO of the label and the top artist, released **"In my lifetime, Vol. 1"** in 1997.

* * * * *

Early March of 1997 marked the murder of Notorious B.I.G. / Biggie Smalls, which left the **"King Of N.Y."** slot open. As I mentioned earlier, Jay put together a roster for his label, signing Memphis Bleek, who had that fire in him and was out to prove to his new mentor that he could hold shit down. The young Bleek came out with an album called **"Coming of Age"**, which went gold. Young Bleek, for some reason, always threw lyrical curveballs at Nas that only real Hip Hop heads caught onto. In return, Nas would answer back with curveball assaults in his lyrics too and there was a back and forth thing goin' on. Somethin' was in the air between Nas and Bleek but it was evident that the young Bleek was nowhere near lyrically ready for "Nasty Nas". Why was Bleek gunnin' at Nas? Where did this hatred come from? Young Bleek screamed…

"Play your position / your whole lifestyle was written". (Ironically, Nas' second L.P. was titled "**It was Written**").

At this time, after Nas' super-group "The Firm" and their "The Firm" L.P. didn't reach the heights it was expected, Nas was doin' a lot of guest appearances with his fellow **Queensbridge** comrades"**Mobb Deep**" and Staten Islnad's "**Wu-Tang Clan**", using aliases "**Nas Escobar**" and talkin' that street life guns, drugs, money and hoes type shit. Back in the early 90's, while on tour with Original Flava and Main Source, Big Jazz had his protege' Jay-Z travelin' with him, while Main Source had "Nasty Nas" with them because both Jay and Nas had potentials of bein' the next up and coming ill spitter in Hip Hop. Rumor has it that while at a club somewhere on the tour schedule out of state, there were technical difficulties with the electricity and sound equipment; the mic and music kept shutting off, messin' up the performances, leavin' club goers hyped and vexed (mad).

The technical problems at the venue that night got so bad that they couldn't be overlooked and both camps were disappointed by the sound failures that sabotaged their performances. On top of that, they had a very rowdy crowd to face. Shit got so ill that it was agreed that it would be in everybody's best interest to bounce but the N.Y. crews were trapped off in the club and had a hard time gettin' to the tour bus they all shared. Out of nowhere, Jazz's hype man Jay-Z brandished a tech-nine semi auto and let the crowd know shit was real in the field. Both camps made it to the tour bus safely and got out of there. This was an experience both camps truly remember and it was spoken on by Main Sources lead man "**Large Professor**" in a 2003 issue of **XXL rap magazine**. Later on, Young Nas kicked lyrics about guns and Jay-Z rejected Nas' deposit stating that he showed Nas his first Tech, he said Nas knows nothing about guns and remembers Jay's actions from that early 90's club episode. Jay maintained that Nas was faking with the gun stories and faking with the warlord and kingpin stories too, He (Nas) was just a gifted emcee who made up tales of things he heard about or saw but was never a part of.

Then it was the conflict of interest, both emcees was very associated with **Foxy Brown**. To outshine one another, it was rumored that Jay-Z was ghostwriting for Foxy while she was his "**Bonnie**", while Nas penned for her while she was part of "**The Firm**" and it was evident whose lyrics was better. Hmmmmm.... all this while Foxy was allegedly goin' back and forth with stories, gossip and whatever on both emcees, well you know how it goes... **You doin' you** and **I'm doin' me** but we don't fuck wit each other like that. **You shinin', I'm shinin'** and we in competition tryna **outshine** each other while we both happen to mess with the same group of shorties. So when she's with you she speaks about things concernin' me and my clique, when she with me she speaks on you and yours so we both try to give her somethin' more to brag about to let the other know **its real over here**. Who knows, it probably didn't go like that. Foxy's part was probably nothin'. **Hmmm**... and to set it off, Jay-Z made a single called "**The City Is Mine**", claimin' the "**King of N.Y.**" Slot. Nas released his third L.P. with a single called "**We Will Survive**", where he tributes both **2Pac and Biggie**. In his lyrics dedicated to **B.I.G.**

Nas spit…

"**Since you been gone there's a lot of fake wanna be King of New Yorkers tryna claim your spot**".

In his song "**Where I'm From**", Jay-Z spits…

"**I'm from where niggahs pull your card / and argue all day about / who's the best emcee Biggie, Jay-Z or Nas…**"

Again, the question Jay's lyrics asked was "Who's the best emcee, Biggie, Jay-Z or Nas? And it's so very ironic that Nas answered that question with the title of his third L.P. titled "**I AM**". Now you tell me if that was a hell of a curveball that went over your head... or was that a fastball? Nas told that niggah Jay-Z "**I AM**"... tell me that shit wasn't **ILL**!!! Stop lookin' stuck on stupid and keep readin'. Nas claimed that for some odd reason, Jay-Z been obsessed with him and his style for the longest time. He said ever since they met, Jay was tryna connect and exchange thoughts and that it got to the point where Jay was callin' Nas' crib when Nas never even gave Jay his number to begin with. Nas claimed that Jay went out of his way to get his number.

In a late 2001 interview, Nas says he saw Jay at an album release party and Jay sat down with him to squash any differences between himself and young Bleek. Nas claims that Jay allegedly said that Bleek was a big fan of Nas even though he was out of Nas league in his attempts to throw curveball assaults at the lyrical genius. Nas claimed that Jay said..

"Memphis Bleek could never be a Jay-Z or a Nas and due to his failure to grow, Beanie Sigel, who was also signed to the "ROC" would never pass his "Gold" sales status.

Even if this was said, Nas was never supposed to put it out there like that. Jay came to him to smooth out differences and in return, Nas gave magazines somethin' to run with. Nas claimed that Jay came out with that Das EFX, fast stiggity shit then out of nowhere, he slowed his shit down tryna sound like Nas and Jay kept his name in his music one way or another; tell me he wasn't influenced by Nas rhyme style. Then, **Mobb Deep** started goin' back and forth lyrically with Jay, who was at the top of the rap game.

The Call Out:

At the 2001 HOT 97 Summer Jam, Jay-Z got at **Mobb Deep's "Prodigy"** with a hell of a performance that included a giant photo of a young **"Prodigy"**, wearin' a some type of ballerina outfit and Sparkling "Michael Jackson" jacket. Jay embarrassed Mobb Deep with this low blow and said **"You guys don't want it with Hov', ask Nas, he don't want it with Hov', Nooooo!!!"** From right there, it was ON!! Nas then addressed shit in a single called **"Stillmatic"** but it didn't cut the cake and Jay jumped out there and answered back with **"The Takeover"**, addressing **Nas** and **Mobb Deep** and he really got in their business. I'ma let you decide who was better, Jay-Z or Nas... As we go to convicts, confined in The Lompoc, California Federal Prison, the New York car was takin' this shit very seriously, some real **borough vs. borough shit** with other states, cities, towns, gang sets, races and all that takin' sides. Cats even spit these niggahs lyrics line for line, **I'm talkin' bout niggahs with twenty, thirty, forty, fifty and sixty years, even life sentences, meaning, they are never goin'** HOME in this lifetime and they knew Jay and Nas rhymes better than they could spit their own cases or case cites that could get them back in court or possibly **HOME**. Some cats would talk good, some would talk bad; it was some real **Wendy Williams** shit goin' on. Look what these two niggahs started... tighten your boots kitko, cause even **YOU** could get it!!!

Story moves on:

Next day, early morning, 6:05 a.m., Saekwon was in his kitchen whites in the chow hall where he worked in food service. He worked the 4:30 to 12p.m. shift, makin' sure the different juices and sodas in the Beverages Bar were stocked full as well as the Hot Bar, where he made sure the side dishes such as potatoes, rice and whatever vegetables on the menu was full during Mainline; Mainline was when the prison population came in to eat. It was about one hundred and eighty to two hundred tables, broken off in sections all throughout the chow hall. The table had a seat on each side, meaning, four seats to a table. It was usually a sit down, eat, finish, get up for the next man to sit and eat but shit didn't always happen that way.

The Chow Hall is where everybody sat down to gossip and talk shit about everything from news, sports, prison news, gossip and whatever. You might not see your manz because he was housed in a different unit on the other side of the prison but if you sit in the mess hall and wait for his unit to come to chow, you would catch him and could sit down to conversate on all kinds of shit. So the chow hall was more of a meeting center to talk even if the menu was fucked up for the day, niggahs still went down to the chow hall to link up with comrades or whatever. The seating situation was also very geographical, every set, every race etc, had their seating arrangement.

The N.Y. Car's spot was in the middle, where we could see both doors of convicts comin' in and goin' out. Bein' East Coast niggahs all the way out on the West Coast, we sat and ate with Baltimore, Philly and a few Jersey heads that was there. We had six tables locked down so that was seatin' for twenty-four convicts, even though we were way deeper than that. So the sit down, eat and leave was in effect except for a few, who were known gossipers and talk shit niggahs.

After Saekwon set up the hot bar, fillin' it with pans of oatmeal and raisins and making sure he had enough pans on deck, he went over to the beverage section where Dread Shawnie was helpin' out, makin' sure it was set up with cold milk cause the doors opened from 6:15 a.m. to 6:50 a.m. As long as everything was set up and on point, everything went smooth. There were two lines on both sides of the wall and a NO PORK sign in the middle of the chow hall. Once everything was set, "Sae" went to the tables with Shawnie followin' him. They were waitin' on those doors to open so niggahs could come in with the early morning gossip. Big Eastwood from the Bronx came out of the kitchen's dish room. Eastwood was brown-skinned, 5'11", about 220 pounds with long dreads. He ran the dish room until 12 p.m. and was a Bronx N.Y'er for real. As he approached the tables with his waterproof apron over his starched kitchen whites, he asked...

"Yo what's good Sun?"

"Nothin', just got shit ready so these greedy ass niggahs can come and get it and get the fuck out" Saekwon answered nonchalantly as he sat down and kicked his feet up in an empty chair. Big Eastwood said...
"Shawnie, what's up bro?"

"Nothin' man, same ole ting" said Shawnie as he sat down, joining Saekwon. Eastwood took a seat too and asked...

"Yo, you peep that MTV bullshit on the Jay-Z - Nas thing?"
"Man I thought they were gonna be on the show or at least battle, that shit was some pure bullshit for real. I thought Jay was gonna at least kick a few bars to that bitch-ass Queens niggah" Snapped Sae.

Eastwood then exclaimed...

"Who Nas... is you crazy Sun? Jay aint fuckin' wit Nas, my shortie uptown played me that "**Ether**" shit over the phone and Nas is lettin' Jay-Z have it! He all up in that niggah's ass, Jay can't get in his business"

Saekwon snapped back...

"You mothafuckin' crazy "Wood", that niggah Nas is a bitch, you frontin'!"

"Sae, you really got Nas fucked up Son... so what son is from Queens, he is the illest. You know that for yourself and you know Queens niggahs is holdin' shit down crazily. They were cushion back in the early eighties but dem niggahs went on a rampage Son, now they got **Rap** on lock!!!"

"That's all they got is some rappers" Shawnie added.

"Y'all niggahs is lookin' at where Son is from and overlookin' his skills, Queens aint soft Son. You aint goin' out there wit that bullshit. I know you and Shakim be goin' through it crazily down there in the Unit!"

Eastwood started crackin' up.

"Yeah, he talks that Queens bullshit but Sha knows Queens aint shit plus he don't count **He a Brooklyn niggah**!"

Saekwon made sure Eastwood heard that part as the doors opened and convicts started comin' in, hittin' the three lines leading to the front where the food was served on trays.

"Yo, Sae, I'm gone kid, I gotta run my dishroom and stay on top of my cup man before shit gets hectic but you know we gotta finish this at seven o'clock cause you got Queens fucked up Son. You heard all that shit Mobb Deep be kickin'!"

"Dem cats aint fuckin' wit Jay, they bitch ass niggahs for real"

Sae started laughin' and Shawnie went over to keep an eye on the milk at the beverage bar.

Ten minutes later

Saekwon walked from the hot bar back to the tables to find Veto, Infinite and Jimmy Fingers, a Hip Hopped out Jamaican who despises Jamaicans. Physically, "Fingers" was all cut up, dark skinned with the Shabba Ranks look. He was from Brooklyn's "Poison Clan" and was a vicious killer with more "L's (Life Sentences)" than L.L. (Cool J). They called him "Fingers" because on his right hand he was shot with a ten guage shotgun that blew off his thumb and half of his index finger and he still had pellets in his remaining fingers. Even with this damage, Son was far from a handicap, he had more bodies than a body shop.

Also sittin' at the table was another Brooklynite named Jimmy, who was a light skinned, cut up cat with curly hair that he kept in cornrow braids. Son had the whole top row of his mouthpiece shinin' wit diamond gold fronts. Jimmy was a young cat and it showed in his conversation, ways and actions. "Little Black" was sittin' at the next table; he was black as tar with an ill scar goin' from the left side of his face to the back of his neck. Black was also L'd the fuck up (hit with many life sentences), he was another Brooklynite. Big Sha-Prince from Boston was there, Big Sha was a big, yellow, two hundred and fifty-five pound cat who was so New Yorked out that it was hard to believe he was from Boston. Sittin' at the table next to Sha -Prince's table was me and Y-Born and as we was talkin' about some money moves, Y-Bron was tryna convince me to open up a store in my unit.

"I'm tellin' you Y-Born, there is like four or more stores in my unit already Sun, that shit aint gonna work".

"Sha, so what if there are TEN stores, people still gonna spend at your store, everybody fucks wit you. I know you can hold down a store in that unit, just think about it. You act like you aint really with that other thing all the time so this is more legit".

Y-Born tried to throw me a curveball, I said...

"Look Sun, to be truthful, I don't have enough patience to keep up with cats who owe. I can't wait to get paid or be dealin' with that credit shit and check-ins. I seen it all just by watchin' the headaches the other four store men get. It looks like they lose more than they gain for real, for real, **you know**?"

"You shoulda just said all that instead of tryna spin me with how many stores is in your unit, God. I'm tryna help you stay out of trouble."

"I'm GOOD G, word! Stop sayin' "So you can stay out of trouble too"... I be layin' back on my style".

I saw Big Nose Mark at the milk machine, fillin' up two cups and approachin' the tables. Mark was six feet tall, brown skinned with a big assed nose. Sun was from Bed-Stuy, Brooklyn and at the time, was down twelve years or so. He kept mega controversy goin' all day and night, kept the jokes crackin', started all the bullshit and was very, very geographical, basically he was full of shit. I was surprised aint no one send him home in a pine box yet. Don't get me wrong, Mark could be cool but most of the time, he kept the bullshit goin' to the point that niggahs was ready to go to war with each other, never him though. Even if niggahs got in a fight, win, lose or draw, whatever, Mark was always talkin' that shoulda, coulda, woulda shit. What should have been done, etc. etc. There wasn't one thing that this niggah didn't comment on, he was so worried about everybody except for himself; he counted **P. Diddy's** money, **Master P's** money and everybody else money. He knew who was doin' what, who was capable of this, that and the third but I never saw him put no work in at all plus I was in Terre Haute U.S.P. with him, he was all mouth and talked a good one at that. He was Mike Tyson with the talk for real. He approached the tables lookin' for a place to sit and he screamed...

"Damn! A niggah can't even sit and eat cause you got all these non-Brooklyn niggahs at the table talkin' about nothin', shit!!"

He sat with Black and Sha-Prince and the mood changed as soon as he sat down. Y-Born looked at me and said...

"Sun, I'm gone, this big kid got one time to disrespect me and I'ma show him".

"Chill Sun, chill" I told him as I looked at Mark.

"Yo Mark, its too early in the morning for the bullshit niggah!"

Saekwon chuckled.

"You know how it goes, **if you're not from BK, you're a farmer**, you know that Sae... Philly, Baltimore and dem Jersey niggahs need to sit over there with D.C.".

As he said this, Mark pointed to the other side of the chow hall, he wasn't eatin' just toyin' with his milk while everyone was laughin'. Mark then directed a comment to me.

"Yo, QB's Son, what's good? You wanna come back to Brooklyn or you still reppin' soft ass Queens?"

All eyes went on me because everyone knew it was about to be some shit.
"Come on Duke, I aint tryna hear all that bullshit, it aint even seven o'clock in the morning yet. You screamin' all this B.K. shit but you act like you on Cali time you backwards ass niggah. You know where I'm from, you seen my work, you was in the "Hut" wit me. You know how I carry it Slim."

Mark sat back... it showed on his face that he was amazed by my remark.

"That's what I'm talkin' about, you a Brooklyn niggah, you need to send word to dem Queens softies on how to carry shit Sun".

"Fuck all this back and forth shit! There's a lot of you Brooklyn softies in the Fed System and I don't know if you fit that description yourself".

After I snapped back, everyone started laughin'.

"Ah niggah, you know what it is, Brooklyn runs everything, when you ever heard of a Queens, Harlem or any other niggah for that matter, dictate to Brooklyn cats, huh? Okay then!"

Everybody shook their heads in agreement, Veto was lookin' stupid. He pled...

"Come on Mark, Harlem aint got nothin' to do with this shit."

I knocked on the table and said...

"Yo, Y-God, I'm gone!"

I left my tray and all… Y-Born picked up his tray, looked around then picked up my tray.

"Saekwon, Peace, I'ma holla at you later."
        Y-Born walked toward the dish room slot where the dirty trays, cups and garbage was put and I waited for him at the door. Mark said with a smile on his face...

"Sha needs to find somewhere for his Kentucky peoples to sit at, this aint the God Body section".

Fingers and Jimmy started laughin', Big Sha-Prince didn't like that comment.

"Yo fuck all that bullshit! I'm sittin' where I want! You go find somewhere else to sit!"

"Calm down Sha, you know you're under B.K.'s wing".

Niggahs was crackin' up again. Infinite stepped in sayin'...

"Yo Mark, but the Gods sit where we want!"

"Yo, we aint even gotta go through all this" barked "Black".

"I'm just sayin'...." said "Inf".

"Kill all that, we know we got the tables, Mark is just talkin'".

"Yeah well he needs to know that or make that shit known" said an annoyed Sha-Prince.

"Chill with the bullshit y'all, y'all back and forth over a section in the chow hall? Come on man" argued Veto from Harlem.

"First of all, it's a big question mark of where the hell you should sit at, you square from Delaware ass niggah. Where da fuck is you from anyway?" Marked asked Veto as everyone from the tables started laughin' along with Veto, who fought back while chokin' over his milk.

"Fuck you Mark!!!"

"Nah, fuck wit me and you fuck wit **Brooklyn**!" Mark said as he got up leaving his tray with everyone picking up their trays, heading to the dish slot then going out the door. Saekwon was still there crackin' up... he loved that early in the morning bullshit. He looked at his watch and wondered why most of the N.Y.er's didn't come for breakfast but he knew one thing, it was fried chicken wings for lunch and niggahs wasn't missin' that shit for nothin'.

Lunch Time

"Black" made sure he took two pans of chicken wings off of the "Officer's Menu" count to make sure his N.Why homies and affiliates had extra even though niggahs was gettin' back in line two and three times anyway. Black secured a job in the C.O.'s diner hall, which was connected to the convict's chow hall. It was a nice payin' slot plus he got to be familiarized with a lot of C.O.'s and who was who. He would give us that info cause them C.O.'s be gossipin' like a mothaphucka too. Niggahs was fuckin' wit Black tough cause he stayed wearin' his kitchen whites with his new smellin', starched smock on. Niggahs had jokes though, sayin' Black be tap dancin' back there on some "Yes sir masser, no sir masser" type shit. They joked on him to death but turned around and always ask for extras, which came off the C.O.'s food cart so in actuality, they joked on Black but then buttered him up to get that food like today, there was extra chicken wings and pineapple upside down cake courtesy of Black, cats had to take ten extra wings and leave some for the next unit to come through with more

N. Why cats. Again, niggahs was hittin' the line two and three times anyway, chicken is a big thing in prison, especially fried chicken. You can't tell niggahs **NOTHING** on chicken days. Everybody had the ill greasy fingers from stuffin' their faces, suckin' the meat off the bone type shit and talkin' while Saekwon was in the middle of shit.

"Yo, that Jay-Z shit was kinda weak, they tried to play my manz goin' back to where Son was speed rhymin' and shit, showin' Son with the Hawaiian Suits" said Jimmy.

"Niggah, you aint even old enough to remember when Hawaiian suits was the shit, you still got Similac on your breath" cracked "Fingers".

"Sheeeet, my brothers kept me laced up **always** so you don't know what you're talkin' about. Plus you was in Jamaica somewhere walkin' around barefooted niggah!"

Laughter irrupted and Fingers didn't like bein' reminded that he's Jamaican.

"But Jay was still killin' it then with that speed rap shit and even back then, Son was dipped with the phat rope with the anchor on it."

"Yeah but still… they tried to expose my manz like he slowed his shit down cause of that Nas cat."

"Yo!!! screamed Eastwood, "What I don't understand is why cats is sleepin' on that cat Nas. Son is crazy nice! His first album was classic shit, I know all you niggahs felt that joint "One Love", when y'all heard that shit!"

Everybody was smilin' in agreement with Wood's comment. "One Love" was a classic, all jail niggahs felt that shit. It was a jail letter Nas wrote his manz in the form of a rhyme. Fingers, Black, Sae, Sha-Prince, Veto, Dex from Jersey, Mark,

Shawnie, Jimmy, no one could argue with Wood on that one, "One Love" touched a soft spot on niggahs. Sha-Prince sat back, dropped his chicken wings in his tray and said...

"Yo, I used to play that shit twenty-four-seven, Nas and Biggie's shit but that "One Love" was the truth."

Niggahs was touched by the thought of one of their people on bricks takin' the time to write them so when Nas put a song on his album that served as a scribe to his manz who was locked up, he was felt by real niggahs locked down everywhere... spittin' his letter to his mans was some ill shit...

Sha-Prince started reciting Nas lyrics...

"What up kid / I know shit is rough doin' your bid / when the cops came you should've slid to my crib / but fuck it Black / no time for lookin' back its done / plus congratulations you know you got a son / I heard he looks like ya / why don't ya lady write ya / told her she should visit that's when she got hyper/ flippin' / talkin' bout he acts too rough / he didn't listen he be riffin' when I'm tellin' him stuff / I was like "yeah" / shorty don't care / she a snake too / fuckin' wit dem niggahs from that fake crew that hate you / But yo guess who got shot in the dome piece / Jerome's niece / on her way home from Jones Beach / it's bugged plus little Rob is sellin' drugs on the dime / hangin' out wit young thugs that all carry nines / and night time is more trife than ever / what up wit Cormega did you see him are y'all together?/ If so, hold the fort down represent to the fullest/ say what's up to Herb, Ice and bullet / I left a half a hundred in your commissary / you was my niggah when push came to shove / one what?"

Altogether, everybody at the tables said in unison...

"One Love!!!"

"Yo Fam, that niggah Nas is like that!" said Eastwood. "I was in Lewisburg when my manz played that shit over the phone and tears was comin' out my eyes duke, word!"

"What?"

"You sensitive ass niggah, cryin' off a lucky song by a niggah who lives in soft ass Queens because he got ran out of Brooklyn in his childhood".

Mark just had to fuck things up and get on some straight bullshit. More N.Y.er's was comin' in the chow hall as niggahs held the tables down until they came with their trays of food, then niggahs started raisin' up.

"Yo, Eastwood, come straight to the yard when you get off. We gonna be outside kickin' the "Willie Bo-Bo, **you know**?"

As Mark was headin' out, Sincere and myself came to the tables with our trays. Serious Wisdom, who was from Portsmouth, Virginia and had multiple life sentences, shouted... "Peace Saekwon!" The God Serious Wisdom was very swift and changeable with lessons and caught up in raps crazily. It was like the kid didn't have a "L", he carried it like he was goin' home any day. "Sincere" was a little "Puff Daddy" lookin' cat with curly hair, he kept the 360 waves spinnin' and big gold front with rubies on his front tooth. Sin might have weighed one hundred-forty pounds, soaken wet; he'd been "in" since 1991' and got caught up in all kinds of shit since he was down. He went from FCI mediums to Marion Super-max to U.S.P.'s. and at this time was three or four years short to go home. I had mega love for Sin, he was from Hollis, Queens and the closest New Yorker to me, knowin' we knew the same people and I was very familiar with his hood. That was my little manz, he crowned himself "**The Hollis Don**".

"Yo Sha, I got chicken wings that Black sent up front for you, go ahead and do whatever cause mad niggahs already came in".

Saekwon showed me the pans of chicken in the chair on the table next to where I was sittin'.

"Ahite, Sun… Sin, Serious… y'all tryna go or what?"

Everybody dug their hands in and grabbed some chicken wings.

"Yo Sha, what you thought of that Jay-Z - Nas program last night?" asked Serious.

"It was acceptable on some t.v. shit, you know? But I don't know G, I fucks wit Jay on certain levels and I fucks wit Nas' shit on certain levels. I was checkin' for Nas shit when I was out there and my manz Irv was doin' music for Big Jazz back in 92'-93', that's Jay's manz and shit."

"What you mean you fuck wit Jay on certain levels?" asked Sin.

Sin liked hearin' my insights on shit cause I speak from doin' the knowledge or from knowin'.

"Nah, when Jay talk that street shit, you know that hustler shit, slick shit, I fucks with him but now Son got all commercial and screams clothing brands and this that and the third and I aint really feelin' how he be screamin' shit for companies but that's how Son gets his dough. He's changin' the game cause Son always got bangers for the clubs plus one or two street joints."

"But Nas be in that same direction too Sha" Serious added in.

"Yeah and they came out around the same time, Nas had a head start on Son. Jay is crazy consistent with his shit" Sincere added. "Both of them niggahs is like that!!"

"Word!"

We all agreed as "Unique" from Harlem approached the tables with his tray.

"Sha-Bio! Peace Sun, Peace Sin, Serious!"

"Peace, "U", what's good?"
"That chicken Sun, where da stash at?"

Unique was another Jamaican cat who disguised his accent. He was a slim semi-cut up, built, dark brother with shoulder length dreads from Harlem, N.Y. Harlem is in uptown, Manhattan and is the Mecca of New York City. Unique was a good dude but was caught up on bein' "World Famous" in the Penitentiary. He was the average Harlem dude, who always wanted to be seen and known as the first one to set a fashion trend in the prison with his tailor made (altered) zip down sweat suit jackets and exotic pockets on his sweatpants, knowin' damn well that it was considered "Contraband" when the police caught up with it. Unique wanted to put that image out there that he was still holdin' digits as far as money went but in reality, he was only holdin' crazy digits on the time side, he had elbows (life sentences). I was very familiar with his ordeal for I too was also caught up in a big drug conspiracy and convicted in Norfolk, VA, the same place Unique was convicted.

Like myself, Unique was caught up in a big, high profile case and what made it so ill, the government alleged that every once in a while, both of our conspiracies at one time, linked up to help each other out on the drug side of things. They even had witnesses from Unique's case that testified at my trial and what's so ill is I never sold a crumb in VA. So me and Unique's case was related, we were close and could relate on certain issues even though he kept the millionaire stories on blast about his past activities. He owned a club in Harlem called "Mecca 2000"in the late 1980's and early 90's and he had a lot of celebrities in there. The club was a well known hustler's den, where rappers got to mix with the drug dealers. Unique had thousands of photos of his club ventures and every Don Diva magazine that featured his club.

Unique was like a lot of us convicted cats who were caught up in the Fed System, we get so caught up in our past lives, we can't let go and focus on the future. We still think we got shit in a smash, not knowin' that once we was gone, we was replaced by the next up comin' "Don" but as long as the streets kept our names alive and showed love, we couldn't be told **NOTHIN'**!! We gotta learn to get together and get on our case ordeals so we can get back in court and give back these alphabet letters and football numerals that these crackers be dishin' out like free cheese. He stayed on his case and kept it in his mind that he would soon return to those streets, he had a lot of connections in the music industry and a few others as do I. It wasn't nothin' to bump into a convict who mingled, raised, was a mentor or something to someone in the entertainment world. We were / are the niggahs the entertainers wanted to be like but look who is getting paid lovely and look who is doin' all the fuckin' time.

Anyway, as I hitted Unique with the chicken stash...

"Yo Sha-Bio, we gotta find someone who got chicken wings for sale in the unit so we have some for later on tonight fam."

Me and Unique was in the same unit with Saekwon, Veto, Black and Infinite. It was six of us but really only five because Veto was claimin' one spot even though he had a N.Y. registration number. First he had family in N.Y., then he was from N.Y., then another story but he knew Unique from the streets. Veto's life sentence had him fucked up in the head, he knew Harlem and the Bronx like the back of his hand but he claimed Delaware. Movin' along... Serious still wanted to hear some shit so he brought the Nas and Jay convo back up to full blast.

"I like Nas better than Jay, I can relate to Nas better".

"How? First Son is a street cat, then he's a kingpin / warlord, then he's political, then he is conscious... so what Nas is you talkin' about?"

Unique was already in the convo that quick as he started mixin' his rice with his corn and puttin' hot sauce on the wings.

"Yo, I don't give a fuck about either of dem cats Sha-Bio, I'ma tell you some shit, I tried to get Damon Dash to bring a few of his acts to my club... Me and Dame go way back but Son faked on me. He was promotin' a lot of parties uptown, I am uptown, "You know?" he's a real fake dude. I knew him when he was broke and had to come around me and my clique that fake ass niggah and if Jay fuckin' wit him that means he fake too. As for Nas, I like his shit but he can't make up his mind about who he is. He aint keepin' it gully. Check his verse in "Oochie Wally", the beat is crazy bananas but he let his lil' brother, body guard and some new niggah kill him on that song. Nas dumbed his style down; Jay would never do that but fuck dem niggahs. They both know and heard of Mecca 2000 Sun! Dem cats know who you is too Sha Bio... Nas was in "**Belly**", he knows who you is Sun!"

Unique proceeded to devour the chicken and rice. I noticed the chow hall was really crowded as all three lines stretched damn near out to the hallway. Niggahs was comin' for that chicken, Saekwon came back over to the tables...

"Yo Sha, you good on chicken?"

"I'm straight!" Sin and Serious agreed with me, Unique looked up ...

"Yo, Sae, bring some more so I can hit my manz wit some!"

Saekwon looked at Unique like he was crazy, then he looked at me.

"What's up wit ya manz Sha? Don't he know if he want somethin' he gotta spend some of those fake millions?" asked Saekwon, as he walked in the other direction, leavin' us at the tables. It was about twenty wings left. I looked for Y-Born, I had to get him right with some chicken wings, even though I knew he was probably already good but that was my manz.

"Yo, Sae,"

I called for Saekwon. Me and Sae had an understanding too, even though we went through it regularly on some borough - borough shit and his mouth was slick but other-wise, he was a real good dude. He looked at cats differently, it wasn't about what you WERE doin' or drivin' or how much money you held out there, we were in prison now. With Sae it was all about what you're doin' **now**.

"Yo, Sha, what's up?"

Sae asked as he came over to the tables lookin' at his watch.

"Yo, ten more minutes and my shift is over!"

"Yo, Sae, I don't know if Y-Born came in yet and I'm about to bounce out to the rec yard, hit him with these wings if you can Sun."

"If he aint in here by twelve, twelve fifteen, he dead then" Sae answered.

"Ahite then, come out to the yard, we gonna start pull-ups at one maybe two o'clock".

"Yeah, Mark and dem is out there so I'm goin' straight out with Eastwood".

"Ahite, **ONE!**"

I got up with Sin, Serious and Unique, who was stuffin' his face with cake and drinkin' water at the same time...

"Yo, Sha" Unique said while wipin' his mouth, still chewin'...

"I don't know why you let these cats come into prison thinkin'
they shot callin' or runnin' somethin' when on the streets, they
wasn't even in our league or on our level, you know Sun?"

Unique was referrin' to Saekwon and that comment he made at the
tables regarding extra chicken wings. Unique and "Sae" wasn't
feelin' each other too tough.

"It aint nothin' Unique, you just gotta know how to carry shit.
Niggahs in these spots don't owe us shit! But Sae is my manz, we
will have wings in that unit tonight".

As we made it out the kitchen doors with Sin and Serious behind
us, Sincere said...

"Lets go hit the yard!"

We all agreed and headed in the direction of the yard.

The Yard

We was walkin' the yard for at least fifteen minutes,
stoppin' every now and then to small talk with fellow convicts,
when they called the incoming move and half the rec yard went in,
leavin' us as we kept spinnin' the yard.

"Yo, look at Mark and dem over there conductin' a seminar by the
big basketball court. Everytime we spin by, he seems like the only
one runnin' his mouth" Unique said as we spun by them again.

"Yo, Sin, come here Son and bring QB's finest with you, we gotta
straighten this shit out Son".

Eastwood, Sae, Shawnie and Black came on the out-
coming move from the chow hall so it was now Sha-Prince, Mark,
Fingers, Jimmy, Veto, Infinite and about ten other N. Why heads

along with several other Cali heads and a couple Baltimore cats present.

"Yo, Sin, these niggahs Sae and Mark got Queens fucked up! Let them know Nas is the **King of N.Y**!!"
Sin was grinnin' ear to ear. I found a seat on the court benches next to Mark.

"Yo, Nas is ill, y'all know that!" Sin said.

"True, True but Jay is **Nasty**!" Jimmy answered back.

"Jay holds B.K. down without a doubt" chimed Infinite.

"Lets settle this shit for once and for all. I know like a hundred Jay-Z joints. I'ma spit his shit and show you that aint nobody seein' Sun". Fingers shouted as everyone gathered around to hear this shit. Fingers said...

"Check this shit from **Reservoir Dogs**, how Jay killed it, Son said...

"I know pop, you can't stand us / cause we cock them hammers / run in your crib, no prisoners, pop your grandma / locked in the slammer? / Nope! Popped up in Atlanta / crossed up in a drop, I popped the antenna / Whoa... watch your manners / when my veins pop like scanners, like rain drops you hear the thunder when I cock the cannon / Big thang, big chains / aint shit changed / get brained in the four dot six Range / shit mane, switch lanes / every town I hit, switch planes / bitch flipped big caine, flow wit no cut, you take it in vain / vein to the brain / muh fucka's is noddin' and throwin' up, you know that, you don't wanna owe that man / he'll hit ya, get the picture, kodak man? / Got a love for war / I don't floss no more/ I just sit on my money 'til I'm above the law / how the fuck you gonna stop us with your measly asses / we don't stop at tolls we got EZ passes / niggah, multiple cars and divas with D Classes /

Iceberg sweat with I.B. on the elastic / shit/ Beyotch!! What the fuck? Ya heard me? Put some more beat on that joint!"

Niggahs rolled with laughter when Jimmy said…

"Aww shit niggah, we got the Jamaican version of Jay-Z in Lompoc with us!"

"yeah Sun, I told you Jay was nice. I'ma hit you wit another one to let you know for sure. Let you know it's Brooklyn. I gotta let you know where I'm from".

"Staar, wi from Yard, di dutty rock, **Cha**! Wha gwaan sayin' yu from Brooklyn? Lizard said as he came over.

Fingers said…

"Fuck all that Shabba Ranks shit, I'm from Brooklyn!! Check it...

"I'm from where the hammers rung / News cameras never come / You and you man hung in every verse in your rhyme/ where the grams was slung / niggahs vanish every summer / where the blue vans would come / we throw the work in the can and runnn!! / Where the plan was to get funds and skate off the set / to achieve this goal quicker, sold all my weight wet / faced with immeasurable odds still I get straight bets / so I felt some more somethin' and you nothin' check! / I'm from the other side, where other guys don't walk too much / and girls in the projects won't fuck us said we talk too much / so they ran up to Tompkins and sought them dudes to trust / I don't know what the fuck they thought them dudes is foul just like us / I'm from where beef is inevitable / summertime's unforgettable / boosters in abundance buy a half priced sweater new / your word was everything so everything you said, you did it / couldn't talk about it if you aint live it / I'm from where niggahs pull your card / and argue all day about who's the best emcee Biggie, Jay-Z or Nas / where the drug Czars evolve and the thugs are at odds / and at each other's throats for the love

of foreign cars / where cats catch cases hopin' the judge R&R's / but most times find themselves locked up behind bars / That all / I'm from where they ball and breed rhyme stars / I'm from Brooklyn Son (Fingers took "Marcy" out) just thought I'd remind y'all /Cough up a lung, where I'm from? Brooklyn Son, aint nothin' nice!!!"

The sun made Jimmy's diamond fronts shine as he said...

"Yeah, that's what I'm talkin' about! Jay got B.K. on full blast and rap on smash Son! Nas can't fuck wit son!!"

"Sha-Bio... you a Brooklyn niggah, where you at Sun?" Fingers asked me and Sincere stated.

"Get the fuck outta here, Sha is holdin' Queens down, we from the other side of things, we aint no **Queensbridge niggahs** but to set the record straight I gotta let you know Nas is the truth".

Everyone gathered around Sincere, who spit some Nas' shit.

"That niggah Nas said...

"**Fake Thug / no love you get the slug / CB4 Gusto / your luck no / I didn't know 'til I was drunk though / you freak niggahs, played out / get fucked then ate out / prostitute turned bitch, I got the gauge out / 96 ways I made out Montana way / the good F.E.L.L.A. verbal A.K. spray / dipped attaché'/ jumped out the Range emptied out the ashtray / a glass of Zay make a man Cassius Clay / red dot plots, murder schemes 32 shot guns / regulate with my Dunns / 17 rocks gleam from one ring / you let me let y'all niggahs know one thing / there's one life / one love / so there can only be one king / The highlights of livin' / Vegas style roll dice in Linen / antera's spinnin' on Milleniums / 20 Gee bets I'm winnin' 'em / threats I'm sendin' 'em / Lex with tv sets the minimum / ill sex adrenaline / party with villains / A case of demi sec to chase the Henney / wet any clique with the semi tech who want it? / Diamonds I flaunt em /**

chicken heads flock I lace 'em / fried, boiled, amaze 'em / taste 'em / crack they legs way out of formation / it's horizontal how I have 'em / fuckin' me in the Benz wagon / can it be vanity from Last Dragon / Grab gun it's on though, shit is grimey / real niggahs buck in broad day light with the broke mac / it won't spray right / don't give a fuck what they hit / as long as the drama's lit / Yo, overnight thugs bug because they aint promised shit / hungry ass hooligans stay on that Parana shit"

On that note, Mark of all people, asked...

"Damn Son, that shit was ill, when did Nas say that shit?"

"That's "The Message" off of "It Was Written" answered Sha-Prince.

"I told y'all niggahs Nas is "like that" lyrically!" Screamed Eastwood and the small crowd agreed with him.

"But the question is… is he fuckin' wit Jay!!"

Nobody could answer that question without an argument.

"Sin, finish that joint Sun" screamed Sha-Prince.

"Fuck all that shit Sin, we aint got no time to be recitin' other niggahs shit, spit some of your shit, let 'em know why you the "Hollis Don".

I put the battery in his back and he smiled from ear to ear.

"Nah, we good for now, I want to hear some Jay-Z shit and put a Nas joint up to every Jay joint."

"You aint tryna go there Son, Jay got mad shit and Nas aint seein' Son" Fingers shot back "We can go line for line Sin".

Everyone watched and waited to see what was good and who would say what.

Eastwood said "Fuck that, Nas is the truth, Son said in "New York State of Mind"

"Rappers I monkey flip 'em with the funky rhythm I be kickin' / musician / inflict the composition / of pain I'm like Scarface sniffin' cocaine / holdin' a M-16 see with the pen I'm extreme!!"

Mark fronted...

"That shit aint all that hot, Jigga says better slick shit than that in his wack songs".
"Sun, Nas said some shit on "Memory Lane"

"I hung around the older crews while they sling smack the ding bats / they spoke of Fat Cat / that niggahs name made bells ring black / some fiends scream about Supreme Team / a Jamaica, Queens thing"

"Let me find out you want to be from Queens now" Marked said to Eastwood.

"Nah Pa, I'm B.X. to the heart, you know that, I just feel Son's (Nas') shit, I feel Jay's shit too though".

"What kills me is how Nas screamed a hot ass rat ass niggah's name like bitch ass Fat Cat. What part of the game is that? I give the "Preme Team" their props, Prince was holdin' it down when he was here but how you gonna scream Fat Cat? That niggah was super **HOT**!!!" vented Mark.

"Shiiiiiit! What about Jay and dem screamin' shouts to AZ and Alpo? Dem niggahs is hot too!!! They even talkin' about makin' a movie about them rat ass cats" countered Sin.

"Nah, that's Damon Dash" said Sae.

What's the difference? Jay or Dash, they still the "ROC", it's gonna be a Roc-A-Fella film, right?"

"Yo, I remember Dame goin' to the F.E.D.S. magazine, talkin' about Fat Leon from Uptown, Harlem is so fuckin' hot and how much of a snitch he was but he turns around and "Big Up" Alpo and Dem. Jay even got a record out about hot niggahs called "A Week Ago" but a week later he jump on some hot niggah's nuts who told on mad uptown niggahs and the whole D.C."

Veto stepped in "I remember Dame throwin' parties uptown on some "Final 4, The Best Out or some shit like that, tryna be around the real hustling niggahs. How he gonna call Fat Leon hot when he used to come to "142nd to be under niggahs like "Murder Lou Simms"? Fat Leon ran the "142nd Street Lynch Mob" and had Dame and dem on leery stats out there. I know Son, I was there, I got fam on 142nd."

"And Delaware too" shot back Mark as everyone started laughin' again. Unique stood up to talk; everyone knew he was one of Uptown's finest.

"Dame and his clique wanted to be in a lot of uptown niggah's shadows, just like how Irv wanted to be under Sha-Bio and his manz Monday's wing, right Sha?"

"Irv is ahite, that's my manz Monday's people, he was cool" I shot back.

"Nah niggah, that's Preme from the "Preme Team's" manz, he aint gettin' at y'all like he supposed to" Said Sae, who swore he knew so much. To that I said…

"Don't worry about who gettin' at me Duke, worry about you!"

"Man fuck all that bullshit! Let's get a game of B-Ball or somethin'. Better yet, lets go do some pull-ups 'til the yard closes".

Everyone agreed with Fingers and started walkin' towards the pull-up and dip bars by the N.Y. spot we claimed.

Movin' in packs, we finally made it to the pull-up bar, that's my thing right there, pull-ups! One by one each man made his way to the bar, doin' correct, complete pull-ups then goin' to the dip bar; some did push-ups and stomach reps on the Roman chair. Everybody was workin' out, tryna outshine each other then you had some niggahs that was purely in the way, like "Infinite", doin' half assed pull-ups, kickin' his feet like he was doin' the "Electric Boogaloo".

"Look at that fake Monopoly money the God is givin' up" said Black.

"Shit, it's hard liftin' up two hundred and thirty solid pounds" said Infinite, as he dropped from the bar and walked to the dip bar to do some half assed dips and everyone started laughin'.

"I didn't know there was real Monopoly money to begin with"

"What's the deal wit dem dips "two hundred thirty pound God"? Saekwon asked.

"I can only do me, that's what y'all should be doin', **YOU**, I'm two-thirty SOLID!!"

Laughter was everywhere.
"Leave the God alone" said Sincere, as he did fifteen pull-ups behind his back no problem, followed by Unique, who did the same.

"Yo, I got some ill shit that's gonna kill y'all, check this Nas shit out!" said Sha-Prince as he climbed up on the bar…

"I woke up early on my Born Day / I'm twenty it's a blessin' / the essence of adolescence leaves my body now I'm fresh in / my physical frame is celebrated cause I made it / a quarter through life some Godly like thing created / got rhymes / 365 days annual plus some / load up the mic and bust one / cuss while I puff from / my skull cause it's pain in my brain vein money maintain don't go against the grain simple and plain / when I was young at this I used to do my thing hard / robbin' foreigners take their wallets their jewels and rip their green cards / dip to the projects flashin' my quick cash and / got my first piece of ass smokin' blunts wit hash / now it's all about cash in abundance / niggahs I used to run with / is rich or doin' years in the hundreds / I switch my motto / instead of sayin' "fuck tomorrow" that buck that bought a bottle coulda struck the lotto / I once / stood on the block wit loose cracks produced stacks / cook and cut (Sha-Prince fucked the lyrics up but we all do that sometimes) to get my loot back / times is illmatic / keep static like wool fabric / Pack a four matic / and crack your whole cabbage!"

Everybody started singin' the hook.

"Life's a bitch and then you die / that's why we get high cause you never know when you're gonna go / life's a bitch and then you die / that's why we puff lye / cause you never know when you're gonna go!!!"

"Now that shit was ill and some classic shit, I give it to that niggah, he do have some ill shit! Out of a hundred joints, ten is ill" said Sae.
"What?" asked Eastwood, who only did five pull-ups.

"The God is nice, I give him that. He just be wailing (Lying) too much" said Sae.

Inf was like… "Show and prove!"

"First he's ill, a killa, he knows he saw his first tech when Jigga showed it to him. He aint been in no real shit, the illest niggahs in his clique was "Ill Will", who got slumped, Cormega, who aint fuckin' wit him cause he knows Nas is fake and Lakey the kid, who doesn't fuck wit Nas like that either."

"But if it wasn't for Nas, you would have never heard of Cormega or Lakey the kid, if it wasn't for "Life's A Bitch", you would have never even heard of A.Z. the Visualizer".

I jumped in and did twenty easy behind the back pull-ups with everyone watchin'.

Sin said "A.Z. is a Brooklyn niggah at that too and he is nice".

Black, who has two life sentences for the same hardcore shit these rappers brag about, murder, drugs and mayhem, said…

 "Nas is just a vivid story teller, how many niggahs you know who spit shit they really did? Real gangsters don't do that".

Black is livin' proof that niggahs is just story tellin' and "Fingers" is another example of realness as he went up on the bar and matched my twenty pull-ups. He said...

"Yeah, you aint the only one who could do twenty either Shakim Bio-Chemical, I do twenty sets of twenty!"

"I can't see you on that Sun" I replied. Twenty sets of twenties is a lot and Fingers physique showed that he worked out tremendously. "Yo, y'all check this next Jay shit, to show you he is iller than Nas". Said Fingers as he took off his shirt to show his cut up body and gun shot wounds. "Cut up" meaning, super on point arms, chest, shoulders and stomach. He started spittin' Jay lyrics...

"A lot of speculation on the monies I've made / honies I've slayed / how is he for real? Is that niggah really paid? / Hustlers I've met or dealt with direct / is it true he stay in beef

and slept wit a tech / what's the position you hold?/ can you really match a triple platinum artist buck by buck wit only a single goin' gold? / If Roc-A-Fella should fold / and you're left out in the cold / is it true you back to chargin' mothafuckas eleven for an "O"?/ for the millionth time, askin' me / Questions like Wendy Williams, harrassin' me / then get upset when I catch feelings / Can I get a minute to breathe? / and in that minute you leave / while I'm lookin' at my Roley Ice drippin' on my sleeve / uh, nice watch / do you really have a spot? / like you said in Friend or Foe and if so… what block? / what you doin' in L.A. wit Phillipinos and Eses? / Latinos and Cheve's / down by Pico with Frederico? / I'll answer all your questions but then y'all got to go / now the question I wanna ask is how bad you want to know? BLAOW!!!"

"That's right!!!" screamed Mark as Fingers started spittin' another verse from that song.

"**Know my style... motherfuckers can't rhyme no more / bout crime no more/ 'til I'm no more / cause I'm so raw / my flow expose holes that they find in yours / wasn't for me / niggahs'll still be dyin' for whores / but I hate when a niggah sit back, admirin' yours / young blood you better get that, we fryin' baccars / niggahs don't wanna be confined to ridin' the iron horse (N.Y. Subway) / and don't listen to them rappers man they're dyin' to floss / I used to be O.T. (Out of Town) / applyin' the force / shoot up the whole block then the iron I toss / come back with the click playin' Diana Ross / I'm the Boss and this is how it's gon' be / burnt the turnpike, wild miles on the "V"/ I got mouths to feed, till they put flowers on me / and kiss my cold cheek, chicks cryin' like I was Cochise / Tombstone read "He was holdin', no leaks"/ started from the crack game and then so sweet / freaked it to the rap game, Jigga the O.G. / On MTV, tellin' how I sold "D" / and used to back work up out of apartment 4B / Me and my homie / started out Co-D's / picked the mailbox lock cause I aint have no key / had the chain with the anchor when Jazz made**

"Sophie" / then I went low key but now I'm back, it's on Mothafuckers"

YEAH!!!!

"Don't get me wrong Sun, Jay is nice as a mothafucka, I fucks wit Sun when he gets grimey and talk that talk but he got rich then switched too".

"Yeah?"

Sin jumped up "**Fuck that**!" He started spittin' a next Nas joint, he was so hyped he spit the Chorus and everything…

(Chorus)
"Street Dreams are made of these / niggahs pushin' Beamers and 300 E's / a drug dealers Destiny is reachin' a key / everybody's lookin' for somethin' / Street Dreams are made of these / shorties on their knees for niggahs wit big gees / who am I to disagree? / Everybody's lookin' for somethin'"

(Verse)
"My man put me up on a share / one fourth of a square / headed for Delaware (Sin pointed at Veto) with one change of gear / nothin' on my mind but the dime sack we blazed / with the glaze in my eye, that we find when we crave / dollars and cents / a fugitive with two attempts / jakes had no trace of the face now they drew a print / though I'm innocent till proven guilty / I'm gonna try to get filthy / purchase a club and start up a realty / for real G, I'ma fullfill my dream / if I conceal my scheme/ then precisely I'll build my cream / the first trip without the clique / sent the bitch with the quarter brick / this is it / fresh face / N.Y. plates / got a crooked eye for the jakes / I want it all, armor all Benz and endless papes / for God sakes / what's a niggah gotta do to make a half a million / without the F.B.I. catchin' feelings?"

"That's right Sin!!!" said Sha-Prince, who started spittin' some next Nas.

"Yo my mind's seein' through your design like blind fury / I shine jewelry / sippin' on crushed grapes / we lust papes / and push cakes / inside the casket at Just's wake / it's sickening love just finished biddin' upstate / and now the projects / is talkin' that somebody gotta die shit / it's logic / as long as it's nobody that's in my clique / my man Smoke / know how to expand coke / and Mr. Coffee / Feds cost me /two mill to get the system off me / life's a bitch but god forbid that bitch divorce me / I'll be / flooded with ice so hellfire can't scorch me / Cuban cigars meetin' Foxy at Demars / Movin' cars / your top papi Senor Escobar"

Sun, that "Affirmative Action" was the shit! The beat and all" shouted Jimmy "That shit is ill! Nas do be comin' with some ill shit, he said "He be flooded with ice so hellfire can't scorch me!" Did you hear that shit Sae?"

Sin jumps back in "Fuck that bullshit, here's some classic Nas shit that inspired that niggah Pac to come out wit some shit".

"I seen some cold nights and bloody days / they grab me bullets spray / they use me wrong so I sing this song to this day / my body is cold steal for real/ I was made to kill / that's why they keep me concealed / under car seats, they sneak me in clubs / been in the hands of mad thugs / they feed me when they load me with mad slugs / seventeen precisely one in my head / they call me Desert Eagle / Semi-auto with lead / I'm seven inches four pounds / been through so many towns / Ohio to Little Rock to Canarsie / livin' harshly / beat up and battered / they pull me out / I watch as niggahs scatter / makin' me kill but what I feel it never mattered / when I'm empty I'm quiet / findin' myself fiendin' to be fired / broken safety niggahs place me on shelves / under beds / so I beg for my next owner to be a thoroughbred / keepin' me filled up with hollow heads"

(Chorus)
"How you like me know? I go Blaow! It's the shit that moves crowds / makin' every ghetto foul / I might have took your first child / scarred your life / crippled your style / I gave you power / I made you buck wild!!"

"Yeah, that's where Pac got the idea for his song **"Me and my girlfriend"**, after listening to Nas shit" Shouted Sha-Prince, who then went to the dip bar and did Twenty-five dips.

"I feel that cat Nas, word, he is like that. I gotta keep it Brooklyn but one thing's for sure, Nas is in the top three emcees with **Jay** and a tie between **Raekwon** and **L.L.**"

"L.L.?" asked Sae.

"Yeah, cause L.L. been around for so long and still keep it comin', still spit that ill shit".

"You just sensitive that's all young buck" responds Mark.

"I'm just here thinkin' how Sin just hit us with three back to back Nas verses like he's iller than my manz Jigga" kicked Fingers.

"So what you sayin'?" asked Black, knowin' he was puttin' a battery pack in Fingers back to start some more shit.

Fingers went in, spittin' Jay's Imaginary players"...
"I spit that other shit / that's a nice mothafucka shit / Fed time follow me around, deep cover shit niggah / you're beer money / I'm all year money / I'm poppin' you aint gotta count it it's all there money / I never change money cause niggahs got strange money / narked up, marked up, fucked up in the game money / I got ball money, double XL money / you got flash now but time will reveal money / I spit the hottest shit / you need it I got it shit / that down south Master P bout it bout it shit / I got blood money, straight up thug money / that brown paper bag under the mattress drug money / you got show dough, little to

no dough / sell a bunch of records and you still owe dough / I got 900 and 96 plus four more dough / you crazy? You fugazy I'm loco wit dough Pa'po!"

"That was ahite, it wasn't one of Jay's hottest"

"Hold up, I'ma hit you with the last verse then cause he's spittin' at Mase. He said...

"Groupies, I leave em, all fucked / awe struck / your single was 99 cents, mines was four bucks / last year when niggahs thought it was all luck / but this year I've done it again, Jiggaaa what the fuck / niggah stop whinin' / Jigga still shinin' / niggahs kept complainin' so I copped more diamonds / rock more Versace, aint nothin' sweet / I still throw Tree (3) in ya' body / fleein' the party / y'all can't go wit me / Nope / Flow wit me / bet 50 / not dollars either I brought some dough wit me / I flow like the five series / in various areas and blow holes in your weak niggah's theories / It's funny how one verse can fuck up the game / you bought a 4.0 you better get your change / Aint no platinum in those Cartiers, switch your frames / aint no manicure's on board / then switch your plane"

"Sun, aint nobody flossin' it crazily like that niggah Jigga so kill all that and Sun can get real gutter with the spill check it...

"Check 1, check 2, you know what to do / Primo, cold crush when I give it to you / Friend of foe Yo? State ya biz / you tend to dough? Ah, there it is / Me? I run the show, Oh and these kids? / Don't like nobody comin' around here fuckin' wit they doe for shit / you're enterprisin' though and I like you / but I fuck wit the big dogs so, I gotta bite you / look, its out of my hands / and you gettin' money round here... is not in the plans / so hop ya ass outta that van / head back to Kansas / I'm sendin' niggahs back up in campuses / chance is slimmer than that chick in Calvin Klien pantses / let me guess, they said it was money round here and the rest is me stoppin' you from gettin' it / correct? / sorry to hear that / my guess is you got work at

the hotel .. I'll take care of that / you'll see, now please... give me the room key / You're twitchin', don't ... do that! you're makin' me nervous / my crew? well, they do pack, them dudes is murderers / so would you, please put ya hand back in sight / they don't like to see me nervous, you can understand that, right? / You draw? better be Picasso, you know, the best / cause if this is not so, Ah, God Bless / you leave me no choice / I leave you no voice / believe me Son, I hate to do it just as bad as you hate to see it done / now calm your boys / cause I'm findin' it a little hard to concentrate with all the noise / get the point? I'll let you go / before you leave / I guess I ought to let you know / I need those keys / and promise you never / no matter the weather / don't ever ever ever ever ever ever ever ever ever come around here no mo!!!"

Everybody started crackin' up as Fingers put emphasis and looked at Sin pointin' his finger at him.

"Sin, don't you ever ever ever ever ever come around here wit dem Nas rhymes no mo'…

BROOKLYN!!!!!!"

"Fuck all that bullshit! Fuck Jay-Z, he a bitch anyway, he aint even stab "Un" but he took blame like a bitch ass niggah".
"Shorty, every time I see you, have a Nas joint on deck cause I'ma keep hittin' you with Jay's shit and drown your little ass".

Laughter!

3:15 Yard Recall

Everyone went back to their housing unit to get ready for the 4 p.m. stand up count, as soon as I hit the unit, niggahs in front of the t.v., watchin' videos as usual. Convicts had their walkman radios tuned into the t.v. channel cause there was no speakers in the t.v. The only way to hear shit was by tunin' in through your walkman, that way the C.O.'s could always hear shit, some shit they call "Noise Control" so you had niggahs walkin' around with headphones on, watchin' music videos.

"Yo, Sha-Forty, what "B" up Homie?" hollered Woody as he came over to me.

"You know our relative Nas repped on the tube last night, aint no one seein' him, **Oh, slash that, aint no one "Beeing" him**!!"

"That's right Woody-El" I said as I gave him a pound (handshake).

　　　　The C.O. opened his office door for mail call. In Lompoc, the police get the mail bag from the mail room and all the mail is already sorted and searched for contraband. Money orders were taken out and the receipts was left in the envelope with the mail plus the Feds scanned the incoming and outgoin' letters. When we mailed letters out, we couldn't seal the envelope, the Feds had to scan it first to make sure we wasn't tryna do criminal activity or whatever (yea right). The C.O. took the mail out of the mail bag and slid it through the slot alphabetically, according to first letters of last names. There were twenty-six slots for each letter in the alphabet, you lined up and once the line moved, you had to say your last name and the C.O. looked in that slot to see if you got mail. The line was long as hell as convicts lined up.
"Yo Sha-Forty, mail call!!!" said Woody as he went toward the line.

"Yagga, Yagga, Com forward and si I & I!"

　　　　That was my manz "Solo", the dread who had dreadlocks down his back with dreads caked up in the front that stuck up in the air like a unicorn. That was my manz right there, we sparked up crazily and made moves; he definitely kept a fella right. Solo was also from Brooklyn, well, when he came to the U.S. from Jamaica, he lived in Brooklyn. As I climbed up the stairs to the third floor to Solo's single cell, (all single cells was on the third floor) I said...

"Yo, Solo what's up Duke?"

"Yo, Yagga Yagga (That's what he called me), mi affi do a few tings to mek sure wi eat good and smoke good, zeen!? Mi av yu dis weekend on di corn, mi mekin' out a list fuh store now but go checc fuh I & I and si if mi mail reach!"

I said, "I got you!"

I goes back downstairs and the mail line was super long, you know I made my move and got in line skippin' cats, I got in front of Woody, who said "Go head Forty, you good!" When I made it to the C.O. Office I said "**Edwards**", he looked and gave me four letters and two magazines, he already knew I was regular with the mail flow, still am.

"Yo, C.O., look and see if "Bashford" has mail also", the C.O. checked the "B" slot and said "No", my man Solo didn't get mail, I was like "O.K."

"Yo Solo, it don't reach!" I holla'd up to him on the third floor from where I was standin' on the first floor.

"Wha yu mean it don't reach?"

"You aint got no mail, that's what I mean!" I holla'd back

"**NOOOOO**!!! Mi av mail, mi av mail" he said as he came down the steps. It looked crazy seein' a dread with dreads in his beard and dreads stickin' up in the air.

"Wha ya mean mi av no mail? Mi Mada say she send off mi tings and mi mada nuh lie". said Solo as he skipped the line and asked the C.O. to check the "B" slot for "Bashford". Convicts was gettin' vexed cause Solo skipped the line like that but they saw how upset and loud he was. The C.O. checked again and said "No, nothin' for Bashford!"

"Wha di bumba clot yu mean nuttin' fuh mi? **Mi av mail**!"

Niggahs was impatiently waitin' on line… once the C.O. checked and you either had mail or you didn't, once he handed you mail or… not, you kept it pushin'.

"Yo, Solo, get the fuck off the line, you know you aint got no mail!" Black shouted from the back of the line and everyone started laughin'.

"Mi av mail!!!"

"Aint nobody know you in America niggah get da fuck off the line!!!"

"**NOOO! Babylon dem try to play games pon we Yagga-Yagga, mi lekka dem reach**!"

"Come on Solo" other convicts said "We tryna get ours, you holdin' up the line!!"

"Mi av mail, mi kno it!"
I looked at Solo, "Yo, it aint come today, it probably come tomorrow"

"No, Mi mada nuh lie, she say she send it, it reach Yagga-Yagga! Today mi store day, it reach mi breddren, wi soon si, **zeen**!!"

"Get the fuck off the line!" screamed Sae as everyone started laughin' but for real, it really wasn't a laughin' matter because niggahs was gettin' vexed, Solo was holdin' up the line. I looked at Solo again...

 "I guess you can't go to the store today Solo".

The C.O. looked at Solo and said…

"Listen Bashford, I checked the slot twice, you have no mail so if you keep standing there, you're holding up the line. I say there's nothing for you, **LOOK**!" He put his hand in the "B" slot and said "It's empty, no one with the last name starting with "B" has mail O.K?"

Cats with last names that started with the letter B started gettin' off the line.

"No, Mi av mail"

Now the C.O. was gettin' vexed.

"Bashford, c'mon guy"

"Chek di bag den, mi av mail, **CHEK DI BAG**!!!"

"**NO, BASHFORD, NO**!!!" shouted the C.O.

Solo wouldn't move, niggahs was mad "Yo, C.O. shake the bag for this niggah so he sees there's no fuckin' mail in there!" shouted another anxious convict.
"You want me to stop what I'm doin' to check the mailbag for mail I know isn't there?"
"**Check the bag! Check the bag! Check the bag**!" everyone was shoutin' like they was singin' a fuckin' song.

"O.k., I'll show you and everybody else there is no mail in here".

He picked up the mailbag and started shakin' it. "See, there is no mail in there, **See, no mail**!" The C.O. kept shakin' the bag and out of nowhere, a small envelope fell out.

"Look at dat dere!!! shouted Solo.

The C.O. picked up the envelope and looked at it, it said "Carlton Bashford" on it.

Yo B, you may think I'm frontin', WORD IS BOND this shit really happened.

"Oh, there was one letter in there and it is yours" said the C.O., who was lookin' amazed himself.

Everyone was goin' crazy, nobody ever saw that shit happen before. Solo knew his letter was in that bag, he snatched his mail from the C.O.'s hand, turned, faced the crowd, waved the envelope in the air and said...

"See!!! Mi mail reach, mi av mail!! Everyone eyes was wide open, that was some ill shit.

"Man, fuck that! You put that shit in there, I aint goin' for that bullshit!" Shouted Black and everyone laughed.

"**Mi av mail, see it! Mi mada nuh lie, mi mada nuh lie**!!" He looked at Black and waved the letter in his face as he taunted "**Mi mada nuh lie**!" then he looked at me and said "**And no ice cream or nuttin' fuh yu Yagga-Yagga**!!! **MI MADA NUH LIE**!!!"
From that day on, every time convicts went to get their mail and learned that they had none, they asked the C.O. to "Please shake the mail bag" with hopes of a letter for them fallin' out like had happened in the Solo incident, only to get their feelings hurt and ego crushed. That shit never happened again, shit was like winnin' the Hundred Million Dollar Lotto.

"Mi mada nuh lie! If she say she send it, den it send, Jah know! Mi mada neva lie! **BO! BO! BO!**"

Solo celebrated as he walked back upstairs holdin' the letter high above his head. After everybody got their mail, the C.O. yelled...

"Count Time!! Everybody lock in!!! **It's Count Time**!!!"

* * * * *

"Just about... the best out any niggah realer than me?

…is in the mess hall...with his chest out"

"It's Alright"

Jay - Z featuring Memphis Bleek

(Memphis Bleek's verse)

CHAPTER 19

As the door closed to my "One Man" cell, I sat back on my bunk waitin' for the C.O. to call our range to stand up for count. We had to stand up for count at four o'clock p.m. everyday and the count usually lasted for thirty to forty-five minutes. We had to stay in our cells until the count was cleared in the whole institution. Shit was long but I didn't mind, it gave me a chance to be by myself and be "on the streets" while I read my mail. Havin' a "One Man" cell is a convict's blessing and my cell was plush, considering the livin' conditions and circumstances of bein' in prison. Other than Marion or A.D.X., Lompoc was the only penitentiary I'd been to or heard of in the entire Federal System where a niggah was privileged to have a single cell. In Lompoc, the third floor, which was the top floor / tier, was all single cells and to acquire single cell status, you had to have a year of clean conduct but shit was worth it. Bein' in a single man cell gave a niggah his space to move around and be on his own time, meaning, not havin' to share space and put up with the difficulties of havin' a cellmate. In a double bunk (cell shared with another inmate), you might be relaxin', readin' a book, writin' a letter or just sleepin' and you gotta get up cause your cellmate gotta take a shit. You might be sleep at night and he is up all night, so the light is on when you tryna sleep, then you up, he is sleep. It's just a lot of complications with havin' a cellmate.

There is good and bad to it but bein' in a single man cell **kills it all**, you don't have to worry about cleanin' up after no one but **yourself** and you can have your cell up to your own standards. I kept my cell immaculately clean, floor waxed, bed made and I didn't have to worry about havin' a celly and his company or anyone touchin' my shit. Put it like this Son, **a niggah was livin'**!!!

When you stepped up in my cell, you was comin' into my little universe, I kept the locker phat with food, under my bed was numerous pairs of fresh footwear, on my picture boards I had blown up photos of me on visits with my mom, my sons, shorties and photos of myself from the streets and when I was in different institutions. I had the flyest calendar with all the ill honies, I had shelves put in where I kept my clothes and I paid to get a desk with a stool attached to the wall. I had slidin' windows put in, I had an electrician come to put in an electrical outlet, had tv speakers hidden in the big light on the high ceiling wall area and a transformer in the wall with a radio that worked through a wired up switch. I had a homemade antenna hangin' out the window so I could catch the radio stations too; all this "luxury" was black market shit that was considered contraband in the prison but it was normal to see shit like that. Everyone who had a single cell had shit like this in their spot. Many times, when they would do random searches and cell shakedowns, a C.O. would overlook certain shit but if he wanted to be a hard ass, he could confiscate and write a niggah up for havin' certain shit in his possession but my little crib was ill, especially for a niggah in prison. I'd hit the switch and music would play from the unseen speakers like I was in an elevator type shit, I had an amp hooked up to my radio, some jail house radio cat made amps from radio parts and walkmans; **some ill shit**.

I kept my shit tuned to a Hip Hop / R&B station in either Bakersfield, California or Los Angeles and what was ill was I kept the radio in the wall but I had another walkman that I used for the tv's so I used my Koss headphones for that and kept them on and tuned to BET on the tv downstairs. I couldn't see the t.v. but I could hear it while I was locked in my cell so I was goin' back and forth between listenin' to the sound system in my cell and listenin' to the videos or t.v. all at the same time. This was how I did my thing, I kept the sounds low and kept the headphones on my head instead of my ears so I could hear the C.O.'s when they called my tier to stand up for count. You didn't want to be caught sittin' down on a stand up count when the C.O. reached your cell cause that could get you a write up and a write up meant you could lose your single cell. So movin' along with the story, I was sittin' on my bunk listenin' to the radio with my headphones on my head with only one on my ear, listenin' to videos on BET's "Rap City" and at the same time, I was lookin' at the four letters I got at mail call, seein' which one I was gonna read first before I glanced through my mags. One was a "Felon" magazine that had Nas on the cover, I also had a "Source" magazine with Jermaine Dupri on the cover so I glanced through the album reviews and saw that Nas "Stillmatic" got a 5 Mic, Classic review. Then I heard a C.O. holla **"E Range, Stand Up Count!"**

E Range was my range so I immediately stood up and while still goin' through my "Source" real quick. Nas "Got Yourself" came on the video station and that shit is bananas cause Nas spits ill on that "Sopranos" beat so I put my headphones on and pumped up the volume. Two C.O.'s walked by countin' as I sat back down this time snatchin' up the "Felon" mag. "Felon" magazine is like a spin off of "Don Diva" magazine, it's been said that some former Don Diva staff started it, I'm not really sure about that information but the joint is still official. I fucks wit Don Diva, F.E.D.S. and Felon mags, they all some real street mags dedicated to street, hood people and prison heads, giving them the honor of a chance to tell their stories. Sometimes these magazines glorify street stories too much though, speakin' on convicted kingpins and their lives, how they used to live and how they was "gettin' it" but overall, the mags kept heads abreast and on point with what was poppin' as far as music and trends.

In the issue of Felon magazine I had just got in the mail, I peeped that Nas had a tell-all interview so I said to myself, "I gotta read that shit later when I lock in for the night." then I threw both magazines on my desk. I turned the volume on my Walkman down to hear what was on the radio; they had a female and male arguin' about who was the hottest lyricist, Jay-Z or Nas. That shit was crazy because everywhere a niggah turned, that's all that was bein' talked about on the radio, in mags, videos, in the streets, in prison chow halls and yards; **Jay-Z and Nas**. Dude was talkin' about who was more realer, the female was talkin' about who was more sexier, who made the hottest songs and said the tightest shit. Between songs, people was callin' in with their opinions and they even promised a call-in vote later that week where they would feature two songs by Jay-Z and two songs by Nas. Jay-Z with his "**Takeover**", Nas' response "**Stillmatic**", Jay's comeback "**Super Ugly**" and Nas' "**Ether**".

All this talk of Nas and Jay shit goin' on everywhere, I listened in on my headphones and Big Tigger was on "Rap City" talkin' about the Jay-Z / Nas thing too. I took my walkman off and Jay-Z's "**Can't Knock The Hustle**" came on the radio; that's my joint so I turned that shit up, I fucks wit Jay when he talks that slick, street shit, especially before he found commercial success and shit. I liked Jay-Z the street cat, who spit that ill shit like he did on "**Reasonable Doubt**" but a street cat like me know life is all about growth and development so me bein' a niggah stuck on lyrics, I know a true emcee is supposed to grow on every album they come out with. I guess I wasn't acceptin' Jay-Z's growth… I was stuck on him spittin' that ill, street shit that I was so used to livin'. I aint really with that commercial shit so sometimes I wasn't really feelin' Nas or Jay but they always surprised me with some gutter shit. Both them niggahs was well rounded in both fields, commercial and street but Jay was more consistent and all over the radio, while Nas was laid back and not heard as much as Jay was.

One thing I truly respected about Jay's hustle was the fact that from the time he came out in 1996, he always stayed in radio rotation cause he kept comin' with more and more joints. He came in the music industry with a street hustler mentality / strategy. But "fuck all this Jay-Z and Nas shit", I picked up my envelopes to read my mail, The shorties "love me like cooked food". I also saw that my manz got at me, he was out there makin' ill beats and workin' the camera, he just got an internship at BET too, he was about to do big things. Damn! Guess what he was talkin' about... Nas shit was the hottest shit in N.Y. right now and that Nas was killin' Jay. **I just couldn't get away from that shit!**

* * * * *

Count cleared and the doors were opened thirty minutes later…

"H to the Izzo, V to the Izzay / for shizzle my Nizzle used to drizzle down in VA"

Convicts was in front of the Television that was located on the first floor flats. There were three t.v.'s on the flats, not includin' the t.v. room. The t.v. room on the far end was the movie t.v, where mostly the white boys or whoever, could watch movies that was aired on channels like TNT, CBS and ABC amongst others. The middle t.v. on the flats was the Spanish t.v. that the Mexicans ran; they stayed watchin' that channel and nobody better touch it. The first t.v. on the flats was the one that stayed on B.E.T. In the t.v. room, was the sports t.v, even though every now and then it was used to show other programed events. It wasn't no specific rule dealin' with the t.v.'s it was just a code of honor amongst convicts as far as how the t.v.'s were run.

You could be anywhere on the flats and tune your radio to any t.v, so you could be watchin' the Spanish station, lookin' at the females and at the same time, you could be tuned to the sports t.v. in the t.v. room, listenin' to the scores. You could see the t.v.'s on the flats from the second and third tier so it was nothin' to be in your cell and have your radio tuned to one of the t.v.'s and even if you couldn't see it, you heard it, that was how B.E.T. was.

"Yo they play this Jay-Z video all day, everyday. I'm tryna see my boy-boy Snoop Dogg and the East Siders!!" screamed one of the Crips as some of his comrades agreed.

"Word up Cuz!! I'm tired of watchin' all this East Coast rap shit! Jay-Z can't fuck wit Cube or Dub C!!"

"Yeah Cuz!!"

"Niggahs is all on Jay-Z nutsack but homie aint shit... The homie Jay-o Felony served that fool and Jay-Z aint respond back Cuz!"
"Jay-Z is supposed to be the Beast from the East Cuz!"

"They show this video all day, then Rap City, then 106 & Park... I'm tired of this bunk bullshit Cuz! Listen to what he is sayin', stealin' the Big Homie Snoop shit, them East Coast niggahs aint all that Cuz!!"

"Say Cuz, you seen his other video?"

"Nah Cuz, he got another one?"

"Yeah Cuz, they showed it on the new joint of the day on 106 & Park two days ago. Some shit called "Girls, Girls, Girls" and the homie got them phatties all in there Cuz!!"

"He still aint better than the big homie Snoop Cuz!"

That was what some of the conversation was like, especially amonst them niggahs from Cali. You had convicts who was really into sports hard, all in the tv room glued to ESPN. It was nothin' to see eighty convicts watchin' Sports News and tunin' their radios to BET on the flats, that way they were gettin' the best of both worlds, sports and music videos. As soon as they heard a song, they jumped up to go to the BET t.v. to catch the video. Niggahs was talkin' about this Jay-Z "Girls, Girls, Girls" video all day and was tryna catch it; it was talked about so much in only two days. "Infinite" was one who was also tryna catch Jay's new video, he was standin' in the t.v. room watchin' ESPN Sports because Cali time was three hours behind East Coast time so sometimes, the East Coast teams, like the Knicks, 76ers or Detroit games wasn't shown on Lompoc's stations, you had to go to ESPN for the Sports highlights and scores.

"**Recreation Move!!!**" shouted a C.O., as it also came over the loud speaker.

"**This is a one way move to recreation for all those not desiring to go to chow. The rec yard, Hobby Crafts, Gym, Library and Chapel are now open. Ten minute, one way move!!!**"

"Peace Shakim"

"Peace Infinite, what's good Son?"

"Shit, its real strange seein' you up in the sports t.v. room God, what's good?"

"I just came through to scream at Sae, that's all. You know I don't care about sports like that, feel me?"

"No doubt, no doubt! Yo Sha, you seen Jay's new video yet?"

"Yeah, I peeped it, it was decent."

"I'm tryna catch that"

"Yeah, no doubt. Yo, I'ma play the library after chow, I got this lawyer dude readin' the transcripts to my Ohio State Case and shit".

"Word? How shit lookin'?"

"He still readin' all the information and details, I'm just checkin' up on him and questionin' him along the way to make sure he is really on it and not just speed scannin' through my shit, you know? Can't have no one playin' with my case or my life, fuck around and I will body Scramz".

Laughter…

"Damn Sha, why dem millionaire niggahs you know out there aint payin' lawyers for your cases?"

"Fuck all that shit Inf, dem cats aint obligated to do nothin' for the kid. I stay good! Yo, I'ma scream back at you later, I'ma call the town and see what's good on that end"

I shook Infinite's hand and turned to leave, Infinite was standin'
there watchin' the scores bein' shown on the bottom of the screen,
he was tuned to the BET t.v. but was watchin' sports; Son was
definitely tryna keep up on both videos and sports.

"Yo, you think Iverson gonna score another fifty points tonight?"
asked Dave, who was another sports junky.

"Who the 76ers play tonight?"

"The Pistons… and they playin' in Philly".

"Nah, he aint gonna hit fifty but that score may go over a
hundred… or ninety, the Pistons got a nice squad."

"What's the points lookin' like on the ticket?"

"They givin' Detroit three points"

"I'ma take Philly in overtime" Infinite looked at Dave's ticket then
he walked up and asked A.D, the San Diego Blood.

"Yo, you goin' to chow A.D?"

"Yeah, why what's poppin'?"

"I'ma see who they got freestylin' in the booth then journey down
to the chow hall so I'ma leave my radio in your spot".

"It's all good Inf, who they got on Rap City anyway?"

"Philly's Most Wanted."

"Ah dem busters is bullshit! They had one hit and that's it!!"

"Yeah, you're right plus they got chicken patties for dinner, I'ma
run down there and come back to catch the scores and 106 & Park.
I'm tryna catch that Jay-Z shit."

"Manhattan keeps on makin' it, Brooklyn keeps on takin' it, Bronx keeps creatin' it and **Queens keep on fakin' it**!!" Mark sang, upon seein' Sincere walkin' towards him as he sat with Fingers, Jimmy, Eastwood and Veto on the rec yard benches by the tennis court. This was considered the N.Y. section, where N.Y.ers usually claim that particular Pull-up / Dip Bar. It was well after six-thirty p.m. and niggahs was just sittin' around enjoyin' the nice, Cali weather.

"Fuck you soft bitchass Brooklyn Niggahs!" responded Sincere as he made himself comfortable between Jimmy and Eastwood.

"Whoa! Whoa! Shorty watch your fuckin' mouth, you remember what happened back in dem days; Brooklyn was runnin' Queens. Pappy Mason was slavin' y'all niggahs" shot back Mark, as niggahs started crackin' up.

"I aint tryna hear no back in 1984 stories niggah, Pap aint run shit! He was takin' orders from Cat but that was then, **this is now**! Y'all niggahs aint all that!"

"Yo, y'all niggahs better leave little Sincere alone, shorty been in Marion before and will eat one of y'all if y'all keep playin'." Shot Eastwood, tryna Hype shit up in a jokin' manner.

"That niggah was in a F.C.I. and got caught up in the crack riot in 95', he didn't even do nothin'. He went to Marion for nothin', they found that niggah hidin' under his bunk cause he aint wanna get caught up in shit. They still whipped his little ass and sent him to Marion but he was quiet up there. He wasn't rappin' or none of that shit up there now was you Sin?" joked Mark.
"Y'all niggahs stay on joke time constantly, grown men with life sentences, wantin' to play all the time. Y'all don't take nothin' serious, Mark you big nose ass niggah, you got a crack case and was in a Pen and aint do nothin' you Unicor workin' ass niggah. Niggahs in F.C.I.'s went harder than niggahs in the pens, you probably checked in".

Everyone was laughin'.

"Yeah Son and the script changed up. It now goes "N.Y. niggahs got crazy game but out of state niggahs is all the same / Brooklyn get crazy loot cause when there's beef they aint scared to shoot / Harlem knows how to play / mack the 600's gettin' crazy paid / niggahs outta Queens got shit on lock / strapped with the Glock runnin' up in your spot"

Eastwood got up proudly and shouted...

"But if it wasn't for the Bronx, none of this Rap shit would be goin' on / so tell me where you from!"

"Son, y'all niggahs better recognize that shit. Hip Hop started in the BX son, **BX!!** Not Brooklyn or Queens... In the Boogie Down Bronx by a niggah named **D.J. Kool Herc** and son was a straight up Jamaican!"

Niggahs looked at Fingers and started laughin'.

"Man, git offa dat bullshit! I been reppin' BK for the longest Son so kill all that Jamaican shit... I mean, true I'm 100% Yardie and all that but you know where I'm from and how I carry shit... Mi ah Poison Clan Mon, zeen!?"

Fingers looked around with a smirk on his face... No one disputed or wanted to challenge him about that, Son was known to buss his guns. He barely escaped the death penalty when he was found guilty in Federal Court and his case is cited in full in the Federal Law Reporter for all to see. Son was a killin' monster!

"See, heads mus undastand that I was neva interested in foolish tings like bein' Rasta or this PNP or JLP ting or Sprangler bizness, Touchie or Shower Posse bizness. I was neva in no political type ting, dem all open prey to me. All I need is my Heckle and Koch or

Desert Eag. I'm a Brooklyn Niggah…That's that! From wen I come to this country, I leave all that other shit in Jamaica!"

"Damn that's ill, a Jamaican who aint tryna be Jamaican" kicked Eastwood.

"Nah Sun, I aint neva say that. I am what I am, feel me? Look at you, you a Yankee niggah from the BX wit dreads so to some, you tryna be Jamaican!"

Everyone laughed at that statement.

"I'm just not into that shit. I got away from that when I came to the U.S. I'm a Hip Hop niggah and I represent the struggle, zeen? A Yard Yout named "Herc" came to the U.S. and started the biggest culture in the world".

"I know what it is" Mark said and caught everyone's attention so we knew he was about to start some bullshit, he continued with his theory….

"Dem Jamaican niggahs is poor as shit out there, its fucked up on that little ass island".

Everyone was laughin' again.

"Your family was glad to get the fuck from outta there so you aint tryna remember none of that broke shit. You came to America and seen how easy shit was, shit that was hard in Jamaica is nothing' over here. We was takin' advantage of the shit that y'all was dreamin' about Son, you seen that shit and went crazy. Plus you was young back then and bein' around the real niggahs in the Borough of Brooklyn, you became a product of what was around you. You need to thank your mom for bringin' you to Brooklyn Son!"

Laughter erupted again.

"Yo Mark, don't be talkin' about my moms Son, we can Jokey Joke about anything but leave my moms out of shit".

"I wasn't talkin' about your mom in no negative way or nothin'".

"Son, just leave my mom outta your mouth".

"C'mon y'all leave that shit alone" Said Veto... "We just bullshittin' that's all".

"That's what I'm talkin' about" added Sincere. "Niggahs always on joke time when shit is serious. Life is serious but this niggah here wanna be comical all the fuckin' time. It's about a trillion years sittin' right here amongst us"… Sin looked around. "Veto, Eastwood and Fingers got L's. Jimmy, you are fortunate to see the light beyond the tunnel. I been in since 90', I'm lucky to touch down soon but a lot of niggahs may never touch. Mark, you been in since 91' and will be home within ten years or so. This shit is too serious, niggahs is dyin' in here...gettin' murked. We are the forgotten soldiers, these crackers aint playin' wit us at all but we wanna play wit each other when this **shit is real**. We bein' warehoused in these prisons, these are concentration spots. Niggahs is walkin' around with life sentences, we walkin' around here with the killer looks, killer walk and killer talk but actually, we aint doin' nothin' **but killin' time!**"

"Yo B, Sincere is sayin' some real shit, niggahs gotta wake up and know shit is real".

"Everyone already knows shit is real." barked Mark. "I aint tryna hear all that "reformed man" bullshit. Shorty is just like us...Some are thugs… Some is scared ass thugs."

Niggahs started gettin' up, walkin' away in different directions, leavin' Mark sittin' on the bench.

"Next thing y'all niggahs is gon' be screamin' lets go back to Africa shit!!"

"Yo Eastwood, Son, we need to be in the Law Library more regularly. Shit is gettin' ugly in these spots kid. Fuck all this bullshit, I'm tryna go home too."

"Yeah Fingers, shit aint no joke. I done seen cats come in, go home and come back in on new ones. It's like a repeated cycle Pa, I gotta get these elbows off me and get back out there to my family".

"When's the next time you goin' to the Law Library?"

"I go everyday at seven p.m. but I needed a little Sun in my life… Pa, you need to tell that niggah Mark to grow the fuck up; Son gonna get fucked up with that always playin' shit."

"Exactly!"

"Niggahs gotta think for themselves and work on bein' better human beings. Everything aint based on Hip Hop, fun and games. **Shit is too real**"...

(Meanwhile, back in F-Unit, inside the prison)

It was approximately twelve to fifteen convicts in the unit's t.v. room, watchin' ESPN to get the update on Sports. Saekwon was sittin' there in the first row, dead in front of the t.v.; sweatin' the basketball scores was a part of his daily ritual. Saekwon was part of a Black Market Gambling Ring that was secretly, openly rotatin' bettin' tickets on sports such as Basketball, Baseball, College and Professional Football and sometimes Hockey, all depending on the season. You could bet straight up or against odds with points teasers and all kinds of shit. From two games to how many games is bein' played that day or weekend. The prison bookies got their statistics from the sports section of the newspaper and other researchin' methods plus street connects. These odds and points were typed up on a paper slip called a "Ticket", tickets were passed around by "Runners", who took all bets, then took them to the bookie and associates who marked them in their books. You could bet anything from four stamps to four books, dependin' on the odds and points, you could hit the jackpot for twenty to thirty or more books of stamps.

These gamblin' pools also had name titles to their tickets such as "**Come and Get It**", "**Crunch Time**" and "**Black Gold**" just to name a few; this was big business in prison. It was rumored that Saekwon was part owner of the ticket he was a part of, then it was said he was a worker, then he was "part executive" then front man and main runner. No one really knew except Saekwon and the ones who were really behind the ticket, which was New York, Dominican convicts. All niggahs knew was that Saekwon kept hundreds and hundreds of books of stamps and if anyone on the west end hitted his ticket under the title Saekwon was part of, Saekwon was the one who made sure they got paid in full. I wasn't into sports in any form or fashion so I wasn't placin' any bets or anything. as I said before, I didn't follow sports like that and still don't. I mean, I may show up for a game every now and then but the only time you seen me sweatin' any sports was like the NBA All-Star or Championship Games, Super Bowl or Boxing, shit like that. I would occasionally watch the WNBA Games to see the honeys play cause there are some fine women in the WNBA. Either way, Saekwon made sure I was straight, even though I wasn't part of his gamblin' scheme, I still held him down win lose or draw. So it wasn't no sweat for him to throw me ten or twenty books of stamps on GP. I had my hands in all kinds of different activities as it was, I was always makin' moves doin' this or that and I kept a prison detail (job) while my hands were in the underground Black Market activities that went on within the facility.

Once a man is committed to the Federal System, he has to work a job detail; this enables that man to accrue money on his account even though family and friends can send money orders or wire transfers to his account. You still have to have a job detail of some sort and the jobs range from Food Service in the kitchen, where they have all types of jobs like dish washers, pots and pans, cooks and cats who clean the tables and floors. For every element of the kitchen, there is someone assigned to a job detail. There are Unit orderlies and orderlies in the hallway corridors, gymnasium and there are yard workers. There is someone assigned to every element of the prison and I mean **every element**, nothin' is left out. When I was in Lompoc, some jobs paid as low as twelve cents an hour... yeah, believe it or not, niggahs was earnin' twelve cents an hour and we got paid on a monthly basis. How much you made an hour depended on what position you held and you got grade pay. Grade 4 - twelve cents, grade 3-twenty cents, grade 2-twenty-five cents, grade 1 - up to thirty-five cents and you could get a recommendation for bonus pay so at the end of the month, you could earn up to fifteen to thirty dollars sometimes more, depending on how many hours you put in and how much of a hard worker you was and oh yeah, I must not forget… education played a big part in your pay rate because if you didn't have a High School Diploma or G.E.D., you couldn't pass Grade 4 pay. Then they had Unicor, which was / is a factory job and the highest payin' job in the prison's job detail. Unicor was / is some straight up modern day slavery shit in prison but cats had to do what they had to do to earn money.

Federal Prison Industries (F.P.I.) was created in 1934 by the U.S. Congress for the purpose of providin' federal inmates with opportunities to learn trades and acquire skills while incarcerated but in reality, they were trappin' us off in modern day slavery by warehousin' cats, knowin' they took away all money and property allegedly related to our federal offense. Judges, prosecutors and lawyers all had stocks and shares invested in this private FPI so it was in their best interest to send us to these concentration spots. FPI operated / operates under the trade name "**UNICOR**". These factory jobs was like some street jobs because we was doin' line work that actually was for the streets. We was makin' furniture, U.S. mail bags, electronic cables for the Air Force, Army clothes, towels, blankets, all kinds of shit and they also paid in grades. Grade 5 started out at twenty-five cents an hour and payday was also monthly so its like you're gettin' a welfare check at the beginnin' of each month in the Federal System. Everybody got their monthly pay and spent it in the store or whatever. You know when its pay day cause niggahs act brand new like how cats react on the streets each first of the month.

Lompoc's Unicor also had a printing factory and a sign factory; convicts made up to $400 a month over there and was on some "Big Willie" shit in prison. Some dudes was stackin' their money, others was makin' it only to turn around and spend it all right back at commissary. Some cats was payin' fines and restitutions that the courts imposed on them; shit is serious in the Federal Prison System but job details and Unicor aint the only means of gettin' money.

The system has all types of convicts from all walks of life. Niggahs stayed comin' up with ideas to make a dollar, if you could think of it, niggahs was doin' it; washin' clothes, ironing, cleanin' cells, cleanin' sneakers, cookin' food, sellin' anything you could think of, runnin' gambling pools, doin' law work, writin' letters, drawing, artwork, makin' leather accessories at the hobby shops, sellin' drugs, extortion, cuttin' hair... believe me when I tell you there was some of everything goin' on. You didn't even have to go to the prison's commissary, there were stores that was run by convicts that were open during hours when commissary was closed and they had everything commissary had. All this shit was illegal but it's prison life, the game don't stop cause a niggah lifestyle on the streets did. Prison is just another spot where real hustlers gotta know how to live and maneuver cause it's big money in the prison system. You got convicts who still make moves to eat and live in the penitentiary and you got some of the biggest drug kingpins and bank robbers workin' in Unicor. The Feds aint no joke, they take all your possessions, oil your ass up with crazy digits on the time side and put you in the Fed System broke than a mufucka. Even the most crookedest crook gotta break down and work at the Unicor factory.

Anyway, niggahs was sittin' in the t.v. room, sweatin' ESPN, watchin' the game scores as they flashed on the bottom of the screen and the host was talkin' some sports shit. You seen niggahs crumble their tickets up, once it blew up (meaning they lost). Shit was so serious that some cats skipped dinner to stay and watch the game or wait for the scores to scroll across the screen. They either go cook a meal, eat junk food, buy somethin' from the store man or cop somethin' when the food man came in with made sandwiches or soft tacos; shit was crazy how they even had a food man sellin' cooked foods. Saekwon sat in his seat smilin' as the scores appeared on the screen, he checked the books he had with him and was glad cause so far, nobody hit his ticket line with any wins. He was also smilin' because he played a ticket with his rival line "**Come and Get It**" and he won a straight bet. He only won ten books of stamps but it was a big thing to be a part of one line and play the rival line, tryna break them. Ten books wasn't nothin' but knowin' who the winner was, made shit look ridiculous. All other ticket lines was run by Cali cats so East Coast convicts was always tryna break the ticket line to bankruptcy just as the Cali Cats was tryna break the one and only East Coast Ticket in the prison.

"Ha!"

"What's up Sae?" asked Larry Love, a Compton Crip, who also ran a ticket line and would play the East Coast ticket.

"You know what's up niggah, check your books! I just hit y'all for ten books."
"Ten books aint nothin' Sae, I spend that to get my clothes washed and have my cell cleaned."

"You aint sayin' nothin', I'm used to the ten to hit my private barber." Sae said with a smile as he brushed his wavy short hair.

"It aint nothin' but a small thing to me" kicked Larry Love as he went in his pockets and counted six books. "I gotta give you the other four when I go to my cell."

"Nah, hold on to that cause I'ma put it on the next ticket y'all come out with, I'm tryna break y'all niggahs!"

"Shiiit homie, then you need to stop bettin' so small; bet ten or fifteen books then!"

They both started laughin'... Infinite came rushin' into the t.v. room.

"Yo Sae, you hitted Larry Love's ticket?"

"Damn niggah, why you worryin' about what the fuck I do and talkin' about my business? Suppose I didn't want niggahs, mainly niggahs like you, to know".

"Pardon me God, I didn't mean it like that".

"Yeah that niggah hit my shit" barked Larry Love.

"How much you hit for?" asked Inf.

"None of your fuckin' business! Yo, L.L. don't be tellin' niggahs shit, he should have picked the right teams then maybe he would hit too!" Barked Saekwon, while him and Larry shared another laugh.

"Yo Inf!!" Screamed Paydog, "Jay-Z's new video is on 106 & Park!"

"Damn!" shouted "Inf" as he rushed to finally catch the video, only to notice that he didn't have his walkman radio so he couldn't hear the t.v. "Shit! Yo Sae, let me hold your radio!"

Saekwon's facial expression answered Infinite's question and Inf knew not to ask L.L. (Larry Love) so he rushed to the flats. Seein' Jay-Z on screen, he started checkin' the chairs on the flats, lookin' for his radio or one he could use to see this video. After he couldn't find a radio to use in order to hear Jay-Z's song while he watched the video, Infinite got in his feelings and took shit to a whole new level, he shouted...

"Damn, which one of you crab ass niggahs took my radio!??"

The whole unit got quiet.

"Yo, who the fuck you talkin' to Cuz?"

"Yo, hold that word down Cuz!"

Usin' the word "**Crab**" was one thing a niggah didn't do unless he wanted war. Then again, if you didn't know, you didn't know but it wasn't hard to find out. Crips and Bloods had words they used to disrespect each other, **Crab** was taken as disrespect by Crips but the word had a whole different meaning on the East Coast, especially in N.Y., where "Crab" was a sheisty, dirty, low life type of person. The word had various meanings but those was words that was in that category. Callin' a Crip a "Crab" or usin' the abbreviation "CK", which stood for "Crip Killer", was very disrespectful to any Crip Gang Member. That was like talkin' about a niggah's mom or tellin' a niggah "suck my dick", which was the most disrespectful assault that could be said in any jail with results bein' war, beat down or even death. So Infinite, who used the word "Crab" in the East Coast context, offended these Crips, who looked at it as a curse word, disrespectin' their culture and gang life.

"Damn Cuz! You trippin' like that?" screamed Larry Love, who was a Compton Crip and held rank amongst his peers.

"L.L., I aint mean it like that, I meant it another way" reasoned Infinite.

"Damn Homie, you disrespectin' us Crips when you scream that shit Cuz!"

There was a few snickers and side remarks made by other convicts who wasn't Crips.

"Son, where I'm from, a niggah can say whatever out of his mouth as long as he aint directin' it to no one specific, it aint that much of a big deal L.L."

"That shit means a lot where we from. Just like how y'all use words and foremost niggah, I aint your "Son", I aint from N.Y." retorted "Big Bull", another Compton Crip, who was really not tryna hear no explanation.

"Yo Joe, the niggah already said he didn't know Joe, so leave that shit alone". Said "E" from D.C. D.C. cats was known to call niggahs "Joe", like how N.Y. Cats use "Yo" or "Son" and Crips use "Cuz". "Joe" was just a word, an expression.

Convicts was semi-gatherin' up to see what was up and what was goin' on.

"Yo, you good Inf cause this shit aint nothin'."

"Yeah, I'm always good, I'm from BK! shouted Infinite.

"Damn Inf, why you had to turn around and dis us Bloods now?"
        "BK" was the abbreviation for "Blood Killer" and the Crips sprayin' and tattooing that (BK) on their bodies. "BK" was the abbreviation for "Burger King", "British Knights" and of course it was the abbreviation for the borough of Brooklyn. But out there on the West Coast, it was what it was. Even them East Coast bangers understood the lingo and how we rocked and got down. You knew if it was used to be disrespectful, by who was usin' it and how it was bein' used but out there in Cali, this was how they lived; them niggahs was so serious that when Crips used letters, they dropped the "CK" in common words and replaced it with "CC". So instead of spellin' "Nutty Block Crip", they wrote "Nutty Blocc Crip" and that went for anything they wrote that ended with "CK" they spelled it with "CC" and was dead serious to the point that it was acceptable out there. The bloods, on the other hand, crossed out anything that started with the letter "C" so instead of saying "cigarettes" they called them "Bigarettes". The "C" was replaced

by a "B". Instead of sayin' "I'll see you later" it was said "I'll B you later" and the word "See" don't even have a letter "C" in it but it sounds like "C"... them niggahs was serious as a motherfucker out there, even the East Coast Bloods was rockin' like that but only amongst themselves.

"C'mon A.D., you know what I'm sayin', I know you aint trippin' Son!"

"Nah, I know you don't mean no harm homie, I know it aint no Blood Killers over here" A.D. said as he eyed a few Crips.

"Plus Homie, you trippin' over nothin'" as he handed Inf his walkman radio. "You left the shit in my cell, Yo slash that, in my "Bell", when they balled grub time dog".

"So this niggah was about to start a gang war over nothin'" Saekwon said as he walked towards the t.v. room.

"I fucked around and missed Jay-Z's video" said Infinite as he put on his headphones. "I gotta catch that shit!"
Entering the sports t.v. room with a devilish grin on his face, Saekwon, who always had a slick remark to say, said...

"Fuck around, Jay-Z gonna get you bodied out here in Cali!"

"Damn Homie, why your manz Saekwon trippin' like that?" asked A.D.

"Fuck that niggah, one day that mouth gonna get him fucked up!" replied Infinite as he stared at the sports t.v. entrance like he had the urge to go in that direction after Saekwon but some invisible energy force was holdin' him back.

* * * * *

It was 6:45 a.m. on Saturday morning, the Cali heat wasn't in full effect yet even though it was close to the winter season. In

Cali, the weather was always the same all year round, even on Christmas the sun blazed Hip Hop and R&B (Some NY Shit meaning it's hot as shit) like a muthafucka. The early birds was out on the rec yard, some runnin' the track, some on the universal weights, some playin' tennis or whatever it was that they did on the early weekend mornings. These was the days that the Crips and Bloods came out to play organized basketball against each other, which always led to an argument but rarely a fist fight. N.Y., Philly, N.J. and Baltimore usually ran ball against each other or against D.C. Some dudes just sat around and shot the breeze with each other, while watchin' the game. This was also when we New Yorkers, who worked out on the Pull-Up and Dip Bar came out to get that "muscle money". We came out on the 6:30 a.m. rec move, for all those who didn't desire coffee hour, which was breakfast but they only served coffee cake or cinnamon rolls with assorted cereal, milk and coffee. You could come out to the rec yard after the coffee hour or beat all that by skippin' the 6:30 move.

There was a rec move every hour until 9:30a.m., when it was yard recall to return to the housing units for the 10a.m. stand up count. I could tell there definitely was gonna be a lot of activity and movement goin' on this early morning. This was a day when the west end got the movie theater and "Romeo Must Die" featurin' the late Aaliyah, who had just died in an air plane crash a few months earlier; the movie also featured DMX and Jet Li. Convicts was out on the early grind, tryna locate who had the best weed for sale and the best wine cause niggahs was tryna get right for the first showin' of the movie, which was at 12:45p.m… moves had to be made now and deals had to go down, shit was serious.

"Peace Shakim!" shouted "Sincere" as me and Unique made our way to the Pull-Up and Dip Bar that the N.Y. car held down.

"Peace! What's the deal Sin?" I said as I embraced Sin with a pound and hug. That was my little manz right there. "Peace Serious!"

"Peace Sha, Peace Unique!"

We all dapped and embraced.

Also there and already gettin' their pull-ups in motion was Fingers and his sidekick Jimmy. Comin' from the track was Black, Eastwood, Sha-Prince and the God JaQuan, who I hadn't seen in three weeks. Last we saw this cat JaQuan was before he fooled a N.Y. newjack in the kitchen to come to the dish room to meet an "imaginary God", who wanted to meet him only to meet a single edged razor blade "Ox" to the face. JaQuan gave shorty a buck-fifty (stitches / scar), sayin' it was present from "Prince", who sent word from another institution that shorty was on his way to Lompoc with an unpaid debt he left. That debt was now paid in full... in blood.

JaQuan got snatched up on an investigation because he had a little bitty speck of blood on the sleeve of his shirt but he held tight and shorty, the victim, kept his mouth sealed so they let JaQuan out of the box after a three week vacation. JaQuan was six feet tall, around two hundred and ten pounds, brown-skinned with long dreads. Although he was of Haitian descent, both of his parents was natives from Haiti so he spoke fluent creole, JaQuan was a Brooklyn thoroughbred to the core. He was God Body but wasn't too sharp on his lessons but he was a real good cat, who represented N.Y. to the fullest, played the frontline at times of war and he was loyal. He always showed me and others love no matter what.

"Peace JaQuan!! Damn Sun, when you made bond niggah?" I said as we laughed and embraced.

"I came out yesterday after four o'clock count but I was layin' low to ease up on some loose ends, you feel me?"

"Loose ends? Niggah aint no loose ends left out here doggie, all you had to do is send a kyte out and niggahs was cleanin' up shop, smell me?"

"Yeah Shakim, I know you gonna make sure shit is good for the God"

We both smiled.

"Unique, what's up?"

"You."

JaQuan dapped up with everyone.

"Nah, I wanted to slide up on Saekwon, I heard the God was doin' good and was disrespectin' the God Infinite so I was gonna ease up and build with Son".

"Cut that shit out Jay, dem niggahs always be goin' through their little bullshit."

"Where Sae at anyway?"

"Niggah in that chow hall but he will be out by 7:30 rec move. You know that niggah works ten shifts in that kitchen!" shouted Black.

"Ah niggah, I heard you was still tap dancin' for them crackers too."

Niggahs was laughin' cause it was ever so true.

"Shakim you always protectin' that niggah… Fuck that niggah! He got a real slick ass mouth" shouted Black. "Someone needs to check that niggah Saekwon before his mouth gets the whole N.Y. car in some bullshit".

I paid no attention to that shit, I knew niggahs was up to some bullshit and Infinite had some input in that shit too; niggahs was conniving like that.

"Yo JaQuan, you been workin' out while you was in the box? You tryna get it on with these Pull-ups?" asked Sincere.

"What? Fuck liftin' weights, I lift light ass nickel plates!" screamed JaQuan, as niggahs started laughin'. "Sin, you know I aint wit all that workin' out shit. I'ma leave that to you tough ass niggahs... Me? I'm good... all I need is that "Thing Thing"" JaQuan spitted a razor out his mouth. "I stay good!"

"I know that's right!" I responded, watchin' "J" throw that shit back in his mouth. Son was very skillful with that razor, bein' able to keep it hidden in his mouth plus he was able to hold conversations while it was hidden in his mouth too. That shit was only good for sneak attacks though, plus we was out west, where them Cali cats wasn't on to how we move but back in N.Y.? …that shit was older than me. I seen cats on Riker's with they whole mouthpiece leakin' from gettin' hooked off on before they could spit (the razor) out but everything was love there regardless, JaQuan was a real god cat and went hard like he had a life sentence but in reality, he only had fifteen years, which was still a lot but not to some cats, who was too stretched out on the time side.

"Yo, let's get this paper".

Niggahs got on some non-stop, back to back pull-ups, dips and push ups work out.

"Yo Sha, you was listenin' to that Jay vs. Nas shit on the radio last night?" asked Fingers as he got off the pull-up bar. "I know you was listenin' Sun".

"Yeah, I was tunin' in to that shit off and on plus I read Nas' interview in the Felon Magazine."

"Let me peep that joint God" "Serious" was basically callin' "NEXT!" on my Felon mag.

"As soon as my squad in the unit done, you got it".

"Shit, God should be first" answered Serious.

"C'mon Sun, stop tryna run game on the illest niggah."

"Shakim, for real Sun, other than Nas, who out there you think is fuckin' wit Jay?" asked Sha-Prince.

"Me niggah... Sha-Bio! What?"

Niggahs laughed.

"Sun you aint nice like that no more, you aint fuckin' wit Jay!"

"Fuck dat niggah, you mean he aint fuckin' wit me! If Jay was on this pound, Duke would be my junior, feel me?"
"Nah Sun, on some real live shit"

Everyone started huddlin' around to listen to Sha-Prince as he was doin' sit-ups on the Roman Chair.

"There gotta be some niggahs other than Jay or Nas that's nice too, there's mad cats that can spit crazily!"

"Man, what the fuck is this? The fifty greatest emcees countdown and you a big light-skinned Tigga?" asked Fingers.

Cats was dyin' laughin' and chucklin'.

"Everybody so stuck on Jay-Z and Nas and not focusin' on other emcees in the Hip Hop World... Shit, we just did like fifteen sets, we got time to kill. I just wanna get my niggah's opinions that's all".

"Word, you're right God, I'm feelin' you on that."

What we on? Old School, New School or what?" asked Eastwood. "I'm an Ol' School cat so you gotta let me know exactly where we at".

"Lyrics, that's what we on, straight up lyrics. Niggahs who can spit and lyrics that got substance" answered Sha-Prince.

By then, a few cats from both Baltimore and Philly were comin' in our direction from the big court but only two stopped.

"Sha-Bio, what's up Ack!?" shouted Zafir, from West Philly, a dark-skinned Muslim with a full beard.

"Ack? I didn't know you was an "Ack" Sha" joked "Serious". I said...

"Quit the jokes"
I directed my attention to Zafir...

"Yo, Zafir, what's good fam?"

We gave each other a pound, Zafir was drenched with sweat from playin' ball and him walkin' from the court to where we was at only meant one thing, he lost and was comin' to talk shit.

"Yo, what's up Fingers, Jimmy, Eastwood, Sin, Serious?" Za asked as he threw his hands up to play box with Big Sha-Prince. That's one thing about them Philly cats, they all swear they're the nicest with the hands; Philly is known to breed boxers though.

"Yeah!! What's goin' on JaQuan? I see they finally let you out Ack! Za hollered as he faked a jab and spun off on Sha-Prince to greet JaQuan, who greeted him...

"What's up Zafir?"

The two exchanged pounds.

"Unique, what's up Ack?"

"What's up Za?"

"Man, I'm out here runnin' with these here young boys, we up by four points, why these young'ns can't shoot no ball Sha? They let them D.C. boys catch up and everything, we was up by four points! Young boys come up in here fresh off the streets and can't even run a full court game without runnin' out of breath, need to leave dem cigarettes alone!!!"

Zafir found him a seat, dug in his sock and pulled out a pack of Newports, niggahs started laughin'.

"Yo Cheese, what's good?"

"Nothin' much"

"Cheese", who was a bald headed, brown skinned, stocky cat, was Zafir's runnin' partner from East Baltimore; when you saw one, you saw the other unless Zafir was with his Muslim cats.

"Man Sha-Prince, don't play no ball with this niggah Zafir, he don't pass the ball, he take too many shots and he can't dribble. We was up and he turned the ball over twice, how D.C. even caught up to us" shouted Cheese.

Zafir laughed as he fumbled with his matches.

"What's up with y'all brothers anyway? You got JaQuan out here and young buck Jimmy? Shit, aint sweet when both of these brothers is together."

"Nah, we just kickin' it, just got through workin' out. Now we vibin' on other shit than Jay-Z and Nas, who got potentials and can really spit lyrically, you know?" Jimmy's gold and diamond teeth gleamed in the morning sun as he informed the newcomers.

"But knowin' I'm more of an Ol' School niggah, I wanted to know what era they speakin' on" Eastwood added.

East, Zafir and Cheese were all over thirty-six, they was in the same unit and hung out tough together.

"Well that should answer y'all question easier then" responded Zafir... "Old School is "The Fresh Prince" and new school is that young boy Beanie Sigel!"

"What?" asked Jimmy; disgustedly.

"C'mon, y'all know Zafir was gonna come with that Philly shit" Black giggled.

"Yeah and what? You know most of y'all grew up listenin' to the Fresh Prince so I know I aint lyin' and Beanie Mack is the best signed cat out of Philly, he is killin' cats that's signed to the ROC and lets not forget we got Evie-Eve who can spit just as good, shorty is like that!" shouted Zafir.

"You got a good point but that's your opinion Ack, first off, Beanie is nice but he aint all that, he just got ate by Jadakiss".

"Jadakiss? Man, I just left Lewisburg eighteen months ago, wasn't nobody talkin' about that shiny suit youngster Jadakiss, Beanie got Philly on lock Ack!" proclaimed Zafir.

"Yeah, he got Philly on lock, Philly, that's it!!!" shouted Black.

"Don't get it twisted, Beanie is "like that" and he's in the top ten of new school emcees but he aint seein' Jada, I heard the back and forth freestyle between dem two, that niggah Jada is the truth". Sincere hollered.

"We got another young boy under Beanie, named "Freeway", who spitted on "1-900 Hustler" he is nice too" stated Zafir.

"No doubt, no doubt!"

"We got another young boy that's rockin' mixtapes named Cassidy, he's like that" said Zafir.

"Never heard of him"

(Laughter)

"Well, you gonna hear about him soon"

A voice on the intercom barked across the prison's yard...

"Ten minute move from the housing area to the rec yard for the west end"

Aint no one budge, the conversation turned into a heated debate.

"Yo Za, is you even hip to Jadakiss?"

"Yeah, he one of dem shiny suit cats Puff was pimpin' from the Lox."

"Okay but Son can spit though!! Sheek and Styles P is nice too".

"Beanie could spit too!"

"Yo, this is what I'm gonna do Son, I"ma spit some shit from Jada" Jimmy kicked.

"Hold the hell up youngster, that aint fair cause I don't know none of Beanie's raps, I'm damn near forty years old".

Laughter exploded.

"I tell you what then cause I don't want you to get me wrong, I'm a fan of both niggahs, Beanz and Jada so I'ma kick a joint they both spitted on and it was on Jay-Z's shit"

"Reservoir Dogs niggah"

"Oh shit, I forgot dem niggahs both spitted some ill heat on dat joint" shouted Sha-Prince.

"Now I want you to pay close attention cause I'ma spit both their verses. Beanie first then Jada's O.k?"

"Spit it!"

"Dig the niggah Beans said...
"Yo, Pressure busts pipes… it's time to apply it now / pick out a quiet town and tie it down / make niggahs lock it down, y'all know where to buy it now / Beanie Mack I supply it now / my squad roll deep in foreign cars with two seats / couple of 5's, a 6, a few jeeps / bag enough coke to last a few weeks / in case niggahs wanna test / vest and a few heats / you really wanna test my name? and test my game? Until you have me test my aim?/ Y'all niggahs is nuts like testicles / hit you up in your apartment building vestibule/perhaps it's best for you to keep on walkin' / heat from the noggin' keep on sparkin'/ Platinum Prezzie, Bezzie, stay sparklin' / Copp off the lot, never see me at the auction / Pint of Bacardi darken /when it's hawkin' /out on the strip until I reach the margin' /not tryna meet the sergeant at the precinct / eatin' cheese sandwiches down for the weekend / locked up with dirty white boys and ricans"

"Now peep out Jada's verse... Son said..."

"Now if I kill you, I probably do ten in the box / come down on appeal then I'm killin' your pops / you feelin' the Lox, niggah why you grillin' the Lox? / if this rap shit don't work..niggahs still in the spot / you bring it to me, I gotta lose your family/ gangstas don't die... they get chubby and move to Miami / shit is deep now dog but it gets deeper / fuck it, the weather's nice and the price is much cheaper / I put it on tape, you gon' buy it, I put it in a bag / you gon' try it, y'all niggahs can't deny it /

Lotta cats still tryna study my last bounce / Tell you what, get a beat tape and a half ounce / they got me where I can't be without my large gat / Teflon long sleeve and my hard hat / don't matter if I'm openin' up or headline / doin' the speed limit or pushin' red lines / six months in the county or Fed time / I'ma be the "Kiss" niggah until its bedtime / anything I'm on..is a classic / any niggah ever had beef with son is a bastard / anytime I spit... I spit acid / L.O.X. Ruff Ryder you heard we got the game mastered!!"

"Ten minute move from the housing area to the rec yard, East end, the Chapel is now open" announced a voice over the intercom on the prison's yard.

"Yo Zafir, you can't front on that shit, Jada got busy on that shit!!" shouted Sha-Prince.

"Yeah, he is nice, I give him that" answered Zafir.

"Yo, Beanie got some gems he spitted on his first album Duke, like..."

"What's your life like, cause mine is real / everything signed and sealed"

I had to slip that one in as Jimmy agreed.

"Word life Sha, he got his nut off on that joint"

"Crackers got me locked in the can / got me fuckin' my hand / while my wife on land / fuckin' my man" shit was serious Sun!"

"Damn Shakim, you ridin' wit Beans?"

"Nah, I'm just lettin' it be known every time he step in the booth he brings the truth… but I'ma ride with Jada Sun, hands down Son is **rated next**".

"You heard Son spit on that "Knock Yourself Out" Joint?"

"Word! Especially the joint that comes on right after it in the video".

"Shit is illmatic Son".

"Beanie got mad heat too though."

"Both them niggahs is ill, feel me?"

"Who, Jay or Nas?" Big-nose Mark walked up followed by Saekwon. Mark was Sae's manz; they were both Bed-Stuy cats who stayed conspirin' that bullshit together.

"What's good Mark? Sae?" Sha-Prince greeted them as they both dapped and pounded everyone.

I shot a glance over to JaQuan, signaling him to be easy for right now. JaQuan acknowledged me with a sinister smile on his grill.

"JaQuan, Peace God, what's up Sun? When you came out?" asked Sae, lookin' real surprised.

"I came out yesterday"

"And only now I'm seein' you? Why you aint come to dinner or send me word you was back out on the pound?"

"Man, aint no one gotta tell you shit niggah! Who appointed you that niggah that niggahs gotta answer to?" asked Black.

Niggahs was laughin' but overall, this shit was serious as Saekwon turned to look at Black and said...

"Fuck you talkin' about little sucker ass niggah?"

"Niggahs don't owe you no explanation of this or that, you heard what the fuck I said niggah!"

"Well anyways" interrupted Jimmy... "We was on to somethin' before y'all came with this shit".

"Niggahs was on some rap / Hip Hop shit, we on that now so we aint tryna hear all that fake rah-rah shit right now" I kicked.

"Lets get back into this top lyricist shit" suggested "Fingers".

"Yo for real Son, there is so many cats to choose from... from the old school to new. Shit is crazy right now" Unique said while takin' a seat next to Sin and Cheese. "You got Beanie and Jadakiss but what about other niggahs who is ill like the God Raekwon?"

"Word!"

"Meth"

"Killa Priest"
"Gza and GhostFace both nice" kicked Sincere.

"Yo, that Purple Tape "Only Built 4 Cuban Linx" was a real classic Son!!"

"Word Life!"

"That white boy Eminem is crazy nice".

"I got some shit for y'all"

"What?"

"What y'all niggahs know about Grand Puba?" asked Unique.

"What? Grand Puba Maxwell, who was with the Masters of Ceremony before he got with Brand Nubian?"

"I forgot Sha-Bio is the Hip Hop specialist" Laughed Unique.

"Grand Puba was ill with the verbals, who is hip to Grand Daddy I.U.?"

"Yo, that niggah was ill too Sun!"

"What about Tracey Lee?" asked Zafir.

"He was nice too".

"Twista is ill and that cat Common is bananaz!"

"Word!"

"Keith Murray".

"Grandmaster Caz" Shouted Eastwood.

"Yo, that was a ill niggah from the Cold Crush, remember when they battled Dr. Rock and the Force M.C.'s?" I inquired, askin' no one in particular.

"Who?" asked Jimmy.

"Never mind, it was way before your time Son."

"A.Z. is on that lyricist list too."

"No fuckin' doubt, Son is serious."

"That niggah Big Pun was one of the illest cats ever too!"

"Yo, one ill cat who is definitely an ill lyricist is that niggah Black Thought from the Roots" I kicked.

"Yeah, Tareik is like that" responded Zafir.

"O.C."

"What!! Whatever happened to that niggah?"

"Most Def and Talib Kweli"

"Dem niggahs is crazy nice!"

"Black sheep, Dela Soul and EPMD."

"Blastmaster KRS One".

"No Question!!"

"Pudgee the Phat Bastard".

"Cam'ron is a monster".

"ODB"

"Kool G Rap".

"Yo that shit G Rap was spittin' in the eighties and nineties can still relate to shit cats spit today fam...

"When I die, scientist gonna preserve my brain / donate it to science to try and explain the unexplained / what's wrong when I inhale and exhale / I'll challenge the next female or the next male"

"Aw shit... a Kool G Rap fanatic."

"Don't forget about Big Daddy Kane, he is ill too. Him and G Rap tried to outshine each other on the symphony" kicked Saekwon.

"Yo, that shit was ridiculous, that's when cats was creative Sun".

"Yo, no need to recite on the mic... you need to get off / cause your a rip off / I'ma rip up / get rid of / cause you bit off / bite off / ate off / imitate off / to get paid off / so G Rap can get laid off".

"Damn Sha… you serious huh?"
"Suckers robbin' me blind for my rhymes you might as well say stick 'em up"

"Can't front on G Rap Son, word".

"That niggah Canibus is crazy ill".

"L.L. niggah."

"Yo, the God Rakim, hands down."

"Yo...imagine if Jay-Z had a G Rap or Rakim goin' at him in those days, would he even be standin'?"

"Jay wouldn't have no real shine especially if BIG was still here".

"Word!"

"I don't really know about that one Son."

"Yo... what y'all niggahs know about "Organized Confusion?"

"What's that? Some next Queens shit Sha?"

"Damn, y'all not onto dem cats?" asked Sin.

"Yo, one of dem made that "On No" with Most Def and Nate Dogg".

"Yeah, that Pharaoh Monh cat, Son is crazy nice."

"Yeah Son, Prince Po and Pharaoh Monch... O.C. used to spit wit them crazily too. They had "South Side" and a joint called "Fudge Pudge" back in 91'. I fucks wit C.N.N., Tragedy Khadafi and Mobb Deep too though".

"Damn Sha, you definitely know that Hip Hop Sun."
"Yeah, I'm stuck on lyrics, yo dig, I'ma tell you some ill shit". West Coast got a few ill spitters like dem Alcoholiks dudes is nice, Ice Cube, The Luniz is nice, Snoop is ill, Jay-O-Felony is nice but hands down the illest on the West Coast to me is Rass Kass".

"Son is amazing but he's crazy underestimated, his lyrics go above mad niggahs heads."

"Nah niggah, dat niggah Kurupt is the truth on the west!!"

"Fuck dat niggah!"

"I'ma tell you a cat who's ill but now son be on some other crazy shit."

"Who Son?"

"Redman?"

"Word... Son be buggin' out"

"Yo, Unique, you hip to Son's first L.P. "Whut?... The Album?"

"Nah Sha, I mean, I knew the joints that was bangin' in the clubs and all that cause I had an ill deejay in my club but I don't recall specifics of the album".

"What year it came out?"

"92'"

"Yo, dig fam, Red is crazy ill wit the verbals, we used to press rewind on his shit all the time. I went to see him at the Apollo in 92' at EPMD's last show before they broke up. Red was there, Das EFX, K-Solo with DJ Ron G, Scratch killed the show with his turntables. That niggah Red was ill. On "What? The Album" he got a joint called "Reggie Noble meets Redman" that shit is ill. "Tonight's the night", "Rated R", Yo listen to Son, he says...

"Do a drive-by? Fuck that, I walk by and spray shit and carve my name in your pavement / I was rated X but flexed, I beat up the devil wit a shovel so he dropped me a level". Then Son spits... "I grab my dick wit a tight grip / cause I might flip / Yo Red, kick that hype shit on who you had a fight wit / I had a fight wit Chuck / cause that Punk mothufuck tried to stab me in the gut / so I dazed him wit an uppercut".

Son says some off the wall shit like...

"Do dom dom di do dom ding / extremely wild like the hair on Don King / A nigga who rip you from your wrists to your armpits" this cat be sayin' some real ill shit."
"I feel that, I feel that. Yo... what's up wit that niggah Big L Son, you hip to him?"

"What? Son is extremely ill with his, I been hip to Son since the **"Yes you may"** remix".

"Remix?"

"Yeah yo, the **"Yes you may"** original joint had Lord Finesse, A.G. and Percy P".

"Yo Lord Finesse is ill too and A.G.... but Lord Finesse is like that!"

"Sha, what you know about Lord Finesse?"

"I used to rock his shit too dun, Lord Finesse? I been hip to son since back in the days, he was the one who took the title from Mikey D from Queens at the World Supremecy Freestyle Champ Title".

"Damn Sun, you a Hip Hop Head for real niggah!"

"Yo, back in the 80's, Lord Finesse had a legendary rhyme battle with Percy P".

"Who is that? I never heard of Son."

"What? Son spitted some of the illest, most ridiculous shit. Dig, on the "Yes You May" original, Son said…

Those I decompose / from nose to toes / and will dispose of all of those / who chose to go to my shows / you gotta hand it to me / you know I'm uno / so doin' no Judo / or sumo / can do damage to me".

"Damn Sha, I didn't know you was on lyrics like that!"

"Yeah, then on the remix, Big L came through...

"Everyplace I seem to go / niggahs know my fuckin' name / I'm floorin' niggahs and I only weigh a buck and change / I only roll wit originators / chicks stick to my dick like magnets on refrigerators".

Niggahs bust out laughin'.

"Yo Son was nice and had crazy punch lines".

"He was down with "Children of the Corn" a.k.a. "Children of the Corner", which was him (Big L), Herb McGruff, who was another nasty niggah, Killa Cam, Murder Mase and Bloodshed".

"Yo, L was nice, they say Jigga was gonna sign him to the ROC before he got murked".

"Yo L outshined Jay on a posse cut, L was nice Sun. He got a joint with G Rap, another joint with O.C. on the 8th Wonder break beat, he got some other shit wit Sam Spit and A.G. Son said...

Picture me walkin' around broke... no way pal / Big L's money more longer than the O.J. Trial".

More laughter.

"Yo, Killa Cam is killin' the mix tapes right about now Son, him and his Dip Set Clique".

"Yeah?"

"Word Life!"

"And he just signed with the ROC now too".

"Yeah, I read that somewhere."

"The ROC is about to be untouchable cause they about to get M.O.P.".

"M.O.P. is ill, especially if they get signed to the ROC, remember "4 Alarm Blaze?"

"With Jay-Z... is you kiddin'?"

"Black Rob is ill too, where he at?"

"Yo, believe me when I tell you that kid Lil' Wayne from Cash Money is a monster!" I said.

"Word, he is crazy, him and that kid Ludacris".

Everyone agreed.

"Yo, where is the Boot camp Click at?"

"Underground"

"Dem cats was nice too, Black Moon, Smith & Wesson, O.G.C., Helter Skelter."

"Yo, Smooth da Hustler and Trigger the Gambler, now known as the "Smith Brothers"

"Remember "Broken Language?"

"That shit was sick!" screamed Sha-Prince.

"I still mess with A Tribe Called Quest" said Zafir "Whatever happened to them or the greatest story teller Slick Rick?"

"Word".
"Mothafuckin' Scarface is the illest niggah".

"C.L. Smooth!"

"Big was ill on stories and Pac was too".

"Yo, who remembers the "Trends of Culture"? They had an ill joint called "Off and On", I used to blend that beat wit Mary J's "Real Love".

"Damn Sha, you was a deejay too?" asked Mark, on some funny shit.

"Yo, Sha-Bio, the fallen legend, what's up Niggah?" shouted Jam Dog, a Dominican New Yorker who stayed on the braggadocio and fly time. He was walkin' in our direction with Spanish, one-eyed Nelson from the Lower East Side (of Manhattan), seein' them two niggahs together meant somethin' big was jumpin' off.

"If it aint Bio-Chemical" we dapped up.

"Jam Dog, what's good Son, what's the deal Nelson?"

"You, you, that's what's up. Yo, Sae, Fingers, East, Za, Sha-Prince, Jimmy Jam, Uniqueness, all y'all niggahs What's up? I see you Cheese, JaQuan, welcome back niggah".

Daps and pounds went around.

Jam Dog was about 5' 10" and chubby but swore he was built and cut up, he stayed talkin' big shit with his Cartier glasses and Timb boots. Jam was from Washington Heights in Manhattan and he was gettin' dough in his days but was still thinkin' he was the shit and liked to shine on broke cats. Altogether, he was a real good dude and was on joke time but he talked big money cause he got big money, stayed on the visits and keeps the illest street footwear and best smoke; I fucked wit him.
"Yo Bio, we need to holla Sun!"

"Yeah, yeah, we need to, later on." I replied.

"What y'all niggahs up to?" Jam asked as he posted up, fixin' his Cartiers while Nelson jumped on the pull-up bar. Nelson was a go hard Spanish cat but he was also a Latin King, he held his down and fucked wit us regularly. The N.Y. Latin Kings semi branched themselves off from N.Y. a little somethin', not so much that they weren't considered N.Y. but enough for others to take notice and separate the N.Y.ers from the Latin Kings. Nelson was one of the ones who always came around and acknowledged niggahs no matter what; even when he was with his Latin King Comrades, son came around when N.Y. had beef too. Jam Dog only fucked with a select few N.Y. cats, he was a homie but was on Spanish / Dominican Power time then he'd be on money time. A lot of cats wasn't feelin' him cause they didn't really understand him, that was my manz cause he stayed real and got down grimey like I did too.

"We on some Hip Hop shit over here Jambino" answered Jimmy.

"You don't really know too much about that, you on that Salsa shit".

Niggahs was laughin'… Jam took offense to that.

"What? Niggah, I'm from Uptown! I used to be a deejay, they called me DJ Jamz niggah. I was out there rockin' way before you could even come outside niggah! Sha-Bio, school him, let Son know!"

"DJ Jamz?" Niggahs was cryin' laughin'.

"Yeah, I was known all through Wash Heights and the BX".

"Where in the BX?" asked Eastwood, tryna be funny.

"I was playin' Roxy's, Fun House, Rooftop, Latin Quarters, Union Square, T's Connection, Disco Fever, Tunnel back in 85', all that… All dem know me niggah!"

"Tunnel in 85'? Get the fuck outta here!!" screamed Mark.

"Yeah niggah, I was rockin' in the Tunnel in 1985 niggah, before most of y'all was even allowed to go outside! I was around Run-DMC and all dem rap cats, they used to come to V.I.P. to clock me niggah. Everybody in Washington Heights, Uptown and the BX know me, I'm the Original Pink Panther!"

"Who?"

Niggahs was really crackin' up after Jam said that.

"Who?" asked Zafir, who wasn't understanding what all of this was leadin' to.

"I'm the Original Pink Panther baby! I had the ill pink custom made Pumas and had the pink top Uptowns, that Cam'ron niggah is bitin' my shit. Ask any Old Head Uptown about the Pink Panther Jam Dog".

"Get the Fuck Outta Here!!!" yelled Fingers.

"Niggah" yelled Jam "You can't even name the first Hip Hop record and its not that "Rapper's Delight" shit... none of y'all young cats know the first joint."

All eyes was on me, the Hip Hop ill niggah.

"Yo Jam, I bet you I know!" I said confidently.

"Nah Sha, I know you better know niggah!"

"King Tim the Third and the Fatback Band" I said with certainty.

"O.K. O.K." Jam Dog responded.

"Yo, you gotta understand Son, I'm a Hip Hop Head for real. I'm stuck on lyrics and I'm a Break Beat Junky. I can go back in the crates to Spoony G and The Treacherous 3 when they were a rap group before Spoony went solo. I'll take you back to the Legendary Grandmaster Flash vs Grand Wizard Theodore. I could go to just about any break beat, do you remember "Catch a Beat" by Grand Groove?"

"Damn Sun, you goin' way back Sha."

"Yeah, we was vibin' on some lyricist shit. I remember when shorties was ill too, like Sparky D, MC Lyte, Salt & Pepa, when Lyte went at Antoinette, Dimples D... I seen all those shorties perform before B" I said as I took control of the conversation and held court.

"The Funky 4 Plus 1, who was "Sha Rock", when Angie B was rappin' before she was Angie Stone the singer, Roxanne Shante, the Real Roxanne, I can go on and on and on Son".

"Who you think is ill now Sun?"

"I don't know, you got Eve, Ms. Jade, Foxy, Da Brat, Kim, Trina, I fucks wit Rah Diggah crazily, a little Missy (Elliot), Lauryn Hill, Vita, That Bitch Remy Martin aint nothin' nice, I heard shorty spit on Pun's shit and on the "Ante Up" remix"

"Yo, where is Amil?"

"Who?"

"Amil from the ROC"

"Who?"

"Okay niggah, I get it".

"Yeah, I'm on beats too if you need 1-0-1 on that shit."

"Niggah name some niggahs then."

"What? Paul C, Pete Rock, Buckwild, Mr. Walt and the Beatminers, Showbiz..."

"Okay, okay!" shouted Jam Dog.

"Easy Moe Bee, Large Professor also known as Extra P, The Beatnuts, Eric Sermon, Sir Jinx, Sam Sneed, Battle Cat, RZA, Premiere, Dr. Dre, DJ Quick, Yogi from C.R.U., The Hitmen, Q-Tip, Public Enemy's Bomb Squad" I listed.

"Damn niggah you ill."

"Lord Finesse, Dr. Butcher, DJ Scratch, Mobb Deep's Havoc and that new white niggah Alchemist, L.E.S., Daz, Mellman and I'm just goin' off the head right now niggah."

"Yeah, don't test the God" shouted Unique.

"Niggah, name ten real niggahs on the pound" shouted Mark.

"Shit, we know you aint one of 'em!" yelled Sincere.

Laughter...

"C'mon now Sin, Queens cats aint all that. Steve Stoute from Queens and he let a niggah like Puffy beat him down" shouted Mark.

"Yeah, its whatever Mark, Brooklyn niggahs aint all what it appears to be, it's live wires everywhere, from up north, mid-west, to down south and the west coast. Stop puttin' BK on a pedestal like y'all cats can't get it too. Anybody can get it Son, no one is immune includin' myself." I had to get that off my chest. "See, Queens cats aint ridin' nobody nuts! Niggahs you idolize, idolize me niggah! I'm from Far Rockaway niggah, I aint gotta do no name droppin'. Just ask niggahs from your town in the Stuy, like Ali White, all the way to Cypress to that niggah King Tut, stop actin' like everything is based in Brooklyn. Everywhere busses their gun. I'm a known niggah out there too shorty, in N.Y.C., all five boroughs and out of town niggah, fuck you sayin'?"

"Yo Sha, let him know God!" smiled JaQuan.

"Yo, on the low, that niggah Mark is thrilled to be around me Son, I'm tellin' you".

Niggahs was laughin'…

"Yo Sha-Bio"
"What's up Jambino?"

"Niggah, name the whole D.I.T.C. crew then, I know you can't name all dem niggahs!"

"Shit... put some money up then!"

"I put up what I got for you... I bought you a little somethin' - somethin'. I'll give you that plus what I had for later niggah."

"Bet! The Diggin' In The Crates Crew, Lord Finesse, DJ Mike Smooth, Andre the Giant, Showbiz, Percy P, Big L, Buckwild, O.C., Diamond D, Deshawn and that niggah Fat Joe the Gangsta!"

"Damn niggah! I thought you didn't know about Fat Joe niggah!"

"Ha, ha niggah, this is it - whut! Louchini fallin' from the sky, let's get lit whut!"

Jam slapped me dap and slipped me a small package.

"Son I been fuckin' wit Joe since 92' shit".

"Joe is ill Son, he is well known in N.Y. to put it down niggah".

"Fuck outta here!" screamed Black.

"Shit, y'all niggahs sleepin' on Son, crazy heads Uptown and the Bronx who know Joe, know son aint no joke or to be played with. He ran shit wit some ill cats like Tony Montana, who is dead now and Big Frank, who's in the Fed System."

"Fuck does that mean niggah? Everybody was somebody and ran wit ill niggahs" responded Fingers.

"Son, just peep the niggah Fat Joe's gangsta niggah. Pun and the Terror Squad was performin' somewhere up top and Jay-Z and his clique bought out the whole bar, V.I.P., the front and the back bars. When Terror Squad hit the bar and seen shit was bought out and they couldn't cop drinks that shit bruised their egos and pride. "TS" confronted Jay and them and words between both crews were exchanged and Pun allegedly put his hand in Jay's face, mushed or pushed him and niggahs from both sides was ready to set it right there but Jay told his team to chill. Next day a package got Fed-Exed to Terror Squad, Fat Joe and others. Jay sent Rolexes courtesy of Roc-A-Fella, lettin' "TS" know it was no beef and money aint a thing to a niggah named Jay-Z."

"That's right!"

"Anyway, not seein' the hidden meaning, Joe and dem took that shit as a weakness and ran with it. It was some things said on Hot 97 with Angie Martinez, who rolls with TS but fucks with Jay and them. Assaults on minor soldiers from both sides transpired and allegedly Fat Joe said "Fuck that!" and called Jay out on the radio sayin' "You know who I am and where I'm at, we could settle this shit now, however, wherever!"... no reply niggah."

"Hold the fuck up Sun, you aint spittin' the whole story niggah, I'm from Uptown... what happened after that bullshit was there was a game at the Rucker, cars is lined up, TS came through and bullets blazed as niggahs popped off on dem niggahs. TS whips was riddled the fuck up. Word Uptown was they were on Dame Dash's turf and he got Harlem on lock so wasn't no such thing as fuckin' wit Jay or the ROC. It was on but not no major shit. Both teams don't fuck wit each other but they respect each other's gangster. Fat Joe got a lot of street credibility and all that, he's a real niggah".

"That's what I was sayin' niggah, y'all cats is sleepin' on that niggah Joe. He keeps it gully out there, Son about to get his shine on. He is steppin' up his lyrical skills and he's one of the real niggahs from the streets."

"Shit, DMX is a real niggah, Son so ill and real that he spit for Def Jam's Lyor Cohen through his teeth cause his jaw was wired. Son spit with a broken jaw. He used to go through mad hoods doin' bullshit, he battled Jay and them. Sha, your manz Irv was behind that shit. He put dough up and Dame put dough up. Niggahs was uptown at a pool hall, DMX and them battled. It was Jay-Z, Sauce Money, Original Flavor, which was Jazz, Original and Harlem Nights. Shit was big and legendary cause niggahs was spittin' crazily. The battle ended with Jay on one side and DMX on the other, they were the last two standin', goin' at each other line for line. At the end, guns was pulled out by niggahs from both sides, that's some real shit" kicked Unique.

I said "Yo I'ma tell you some real shit, some real shit is that niggah Puff. Son put his whole team from Howard University in D.C. on. Everybody he threw parties with, he put all dem niggahs on the map from Amen-Ra, D-Dot, Harve Pierre, Chucky Thompson, Stevie J, Nasheim Myrick, that cat Mark Pitts and Don Pooh. Son put his whole team on and I really respect Son's handle for that shit cause most cats forget niggahs once they get on, believe me Son, I know".

One by one, I looked and everyone was listening...

"Puff put dem cats on, they are now beat makers, A&R's, Producers, music label executives and upcomin' CEO's and they all owe their careers to that niggah Puff. He remembered his niggahs and that's some real shit there."

"I feel you on that shit Sha" kicked Fingers. "That's some real shit and I didn't know that faggot niggah Puff did real shit like that".

Fingers got up, niggahs was stretchin' their limbs.

"Yo, y'all comin' back after count?"

"Yeah, for a minute, we got moves to make, we got movies today. I'ma shoot down there at 12:45 and at 6p.m."

"Word!"

"Yo, Sha-Bio, take a walk with me" Stressed Jam Dog, as we took off towards the track to walk a couple spins and conversate.

"Yo Sha-Prince, who you feelin' on the freestyle mixtape shit?"

"Shit, it's hard for me to catch my little brother so he could let me hear shit."

"Yo, I'm feelin' Joe Budden, Son is killin' the mixtapes!"

"DJ Clue had Fabolous killin' shit but now Son got singles out, I'ma see if he just as hot".

"They got this cat from Long Island named Bumpy Jaxxon, he's killin' shit too".

"Cam'ron and Dipset got mixtapes out uptown" added Unique.

"Dipset is killin' it Uptown Son."

"Yo Son, that niggah Cam'ron is crazy witty wit the wordplay. Son been killin' shit since "Confessions of Fire" and "Sex, Drugs & Entertainment".

"There's this cat named "Streetlife" who fucks with the Wu, Sun is crazy official and that dude Bathgate is ill too."

"Yo, right now the hottest shit in Queens is 50 Cent and his G Unit niggahs, Tony Yayo, Bang 'em Smurf and Lloyd Banks, dem cats is ill" spitted Sin.

"Yo aint that the same kid who made "How to Rob?"
"Yeah, Son got shot up like a year ago, niggahs ran up and aired Son the fuck out in front of his grandmother's crib."

"Yo, my manz Ramel from Cypress told me about that kid 50, they used to call him "Boo-Boo". Yeah, Ra went to August Martin High School in Queens and said he took a pistol from that Boo-Boo / 50 cent niggah. Ra got thirty pieces in the Feds now, I heard Ja Rule and dem Murder Inc. cats spazzed out on Son (50) too."

"Believe me Son, that niggah gonna get on and blow crazily, 50 Cent is the truth".

"Yeah, you hip to da niggah Saigon?"

"Nah, what's up?"

"Son is crazy nice too, straight up jail slash street cat. He crazy gully wit the lyrics."

"Yeah? Whatever happened to that niggah Cormega?"

"Niggah probably fell off or back in jail or some shit, like dem cats B1 and B2."

A rumble of laughter filled the air…

"Yo, Mobb Deep got a new cat named "Big Noyd", who's bananas!"

"Yeah, I been heard of Son, he been hit up like ten times too; he killed Mobb's new song "Burn" with Vita on the hook."

"Yo, that's vicious!"

"Noyd been out, he spitted on "Give up the goods" that was on the Infamous, had the best verse on the track."

"Dem Mobb Deep niggahs is ill Son, Havoc is bananas wit the tracks."

"Yo, my manz let me hear a joint by Noyd called "Shoot 'em up", it's out on mixtapes, Son is bananas!"

"Yo, they got a cat from Queens named "Graph"… he's killin' the mixtape game right now."

"There's so many ill niggahs out there killin' the mixtapes".

"Word, that 106 & Park freestyle shit aint nothin', yo I heard a Styles P freestyle that's ill too."

"Yo, Jay-Z manz Jaz-O got a joint out on mixtapes gettin' at Hov called "Ova".

"Word?"

"Word life!"

"Niggahs aint seein' Hova Son, that niggah got the game on lock right now."said Fingers. "Son is killin' the game in at least five or six different categories, the tightest and best flow, most consistent, most charisma, the realest stories and he sets the most trends."

"And Son is from Brooklyn!" shouted Mark, proudly.

Fingers continued...

"Yeah, that too and he got two ill cats Just Blaze and Kanye West doin' the ill tracks."

When I finished spinnin' the track with Jam Dog, I went back over to the group and saw Jimmy, Mark, Sae, Fingers, Black and Sha-Prince was back at it with Sincere while everybody else was sittin' back trippin' on these niggahs and Spanish Nelson was still workin' out on the pull-up bar. I said to my self, "These niggahs still on that Hip Hop debate and that borough vs. borough shit, Brooklyn this, Bronx that, fuck that! Queens this and Queens that niggah!"

"Yo, what's on the agenda for today fellas? You know the west end got the movies today".

"Aint nothin' really poppin' Son, niggahs is gon' do the usual, talk shit, smoke, drink, whatever." spitted Fingers.

"Yo, we got like forty-five minutes to kill before yard recall. Lets go over and see what's jumpin' at the big court" kicked Saekwon.

We traveled to the big court, where the Crips was bein' crushed by the D.C. team. Convicts was at the sideline talkin' big shit as D.C. kept the niggahs in amazement with their team effort, passin' the ball around and scorin'. That's one thing about the D.C. team, they played real organized ball and had no problem what so ever bein' aggressive. "E" was the head coach, he screamed for everyone to stay on their man. "E" was in my unit, "Big 6" was out there too. He was like 6'8" or some shit, big goofy niggah like Shaq and was a dominant force for the team. Warren, Rob and Troy were their superstars. The D.C. team won every championship from the summer to winter seasons. The Crip team was down by fifteen points, we was watchin' it and still debatin', this time about female celebs.

"Yo, Eve is lookin' good nowadays, I'm tellin' you, she is doin' it, that niggah Stevie J can't handle that ass."

"Yo, Mya is lookin' lovely too" spitted Eastwood.

"Beyonce is killin' it right about now" kicked Saekwon.

"Y'all seen that new chick Ashanti? Shorty is lookin' proper." said Jimmy.
"I'm feelin' that shorty Alicia Keys, shorty is lookin' right!"

"Shorty is mad hood, I'm feelin' that" kicked Fingers.

"Man, dem bitches wouldn't fuck wit no niggahs in prison, especially a niggah lookin' like Fingers!" shouted Mark.

"Yo, big nose bitch ass niggah!" shouted Fingers. "You was payin' crack-heads out there in the world. You wasn't gettin' no bitches at all, Big ant-eating nose ass niggah!"

The whole crowd watchin' the game started laughin', which shut Mark the fuck up.

"Yard Recall.... Yard Recall!!!!!!

* * * * *

On the way from the yard, JaQuan called me so I waited for him to catch up.

"Yo Sha, word life God, I was layin' back bein' easy on the strength of you but I'm waitin' on Sae to jump out there so I can expose that niggah."

"I hear you Son but it aint nothin'… leave shit alone".

"Only for now but I'm waiting... Peace!!!" As we dapped up and embraced, I made my way toward the west end. I saw Black and Unique waitin' for me, I thought to myself…

"Shit's about to get ugly."

Right after the ten a.m. Stand-up Count, we locked out (doors opened) thirty minutes later. I made my way to the second tier to go to Black's cell… I wanted to build with the God to get an insight on what was goin' on. Me and Black was real cool and we were both cool with Saekwon and JaQuan. Inside the unit Black was around Sae and outside the unit, he is with JaQuan plus he didn't look too surprised at seein' JaQuan, like me and others was so he knew he was out the box and what was on JaQuan's mind, that niggah knew what's up. As I made it to his cell, I heard them call a rec move to the yard for those not desiring "Brunch".

"Yo, Black what's good?"

"Peace Sha, what's the deal wit you Sun?"

"You! Yo, what's the deal with JaQuan and Sae?"

"Sun, ya manz Sae aint playin' fair wit cats so there's animosity and larceny in the air but other than that, Sae got a real slick mouth and be comin' out his face towards niggahs and cats aint really feelin' that."

"Yeah? So how come JaQuan feels he's the one that gotta scream at Son?"

"Infinite, even though I aint really wit it… Infinite is puttin' shit in the God's ear."

"Damn Sun".

"Man, fuck all that shit Sha, Saekwon needs to stop doin' all that bullshit."

Right on cue, Saekwon came in from the count from chow hall. He made it back to the unit on the rec move and was comin' up the stairs to the second tier to Black's cell. Unknown to both of us, Sae was at the door…

"Saekwon needs to stop doin' what?" asked Sae, lookin' at me, then at Black.

"Hold up Black, what's good Sae?" I asked as I made it to the door of the tier.

"Yo, I'm not feelin' ya manz Infinite right now, Mark told me some bullshit in the kitchen at work this morning about somethin' supposed to be in the air between me and that bird ass niggah Inf. Yesterday he jumped out there and said some bullshit and dem Crip niggahs felt disrespected by it. Shit wasn't really nothin' but it still coulda escalated into somethin'."

"Yeah, I heard somethin' about that shit" I answered.

Black interrupted, stating...

"Yeah and Sae wasn't holdin' "Inf" down, that Blood niggah A.D. came to his rescue."

"What you mean? Niggah said some bullshit that he wasn't supposed to say" argued Sae.

"Fuck you mean? Niggah, we from N-Why, how da fuck niggahs gonna tell you what to say or not to say? You aint hold him down so he let da home team know how he felt".

"That's some real broad shit right there, he shoulda spoke to me if he had a problem with the way shit transpired."

"This shit is some real bullshit Son, you supposed to hold niggahs down, right, wrong, whatever Sae" I said.

"This shit is over some leavin' his radio somewhere, chasin' a Jay-Z video then disrespectin' the Crips by callin' niggahs "Crabs". I can't hold a niggah hand or control what comes out his mouth."

"But you can still control or help control a situation if it's needed" answered Black.

By now, Infinite was comin' down the stairs on his way to the flats from the third tier, Sae called him…

"**Yo Inf!!!**" Shouted Sae... "**Yo, Inf!!**"

"Yo, what the fuck you screamin' my name like that for?" barked Infinite.

"Inf, Peace God!" I responded. "Yo, what was the deal with what happened yesterday?"

"What you mean?" asked Inf.

"How my name get in that bullshit?" asked Sae.

"Your name? I don't fuck wit you to be puttin' your name in shit." responded Inf.

By then, we had moved back into Black's cell but Black went out the cell, leavin' me, Sae and Inf in a cell that was too small to hold three niggahs.

"Niggah, you almost got yourself in some bullshit yesterday and like a bitch you ran and told niggahs like you need a father figure." said Saekwon with a finger in Inf's face.

"Hold the fuck up! First of all, don't be pointin' your finger in my face and secondly, who you callin' a bitch? Bitch!" shouted Infinite.

I stepped between them cause they were too close for comfort and shit looked like it was gonna be real ugly. Black was at the door along with Solo the dread.

"Fuck that shit Sha, move the fuck outta the way and let dem niggahs do dem!" shouted Black. "You peacemakin' motherfucka!" How you gonna come from Marion Super-max to a pen, wavin' a white flag? Get outta the way!" shouted Black angrily.

"Move Yagga - Yagga! Move ya bloodclot!! shouted Solo.

Them niggahs was dyin' to see a fight, then Saekwon reached over me to point at Inf and said...

"I called you a bitch! You lucky dem niggahs aint beat your ass yesterday!"

"Aint like you was gonna hold me down, soft ass niggah!!" shouted Inf as I pushed him to toward the back of the cell and I pushed Sae toward the door like a referee in a boxing match.

"And I'ma tell you one more time Saekwon, stop pointin' your finger in my face!!"

"Or what bitch?!!"

Them niggahs was makin' too much noise and attractin' attention.

"Yagga-Yagga, move ya bumbaclot, let dem clash!!!" screamed Solo while Black had that Sinister grin on his grill and was motionin' with his hands for me to get out the way.

I was comin' to the conclusion of movin' out of the way but I pushed Inf back, I hate to see God fight God. I was stuck on morals and principles (still am) and I felt shit wasn't that serious but Sae and Inf had some hate for each other or built up tension stemming from somethin'. Sae came with that finger in Inf's face and just as I was movin', Inf pushed me into Sae and followed with a three piece over my head in Sae's direction but only one punch grazed Sae's face. I threw my hands up towards Inf and barked…

"Yo, what the fuck?!!"

Inf's eyes got wide and he was lookin' at me, Saekwon was tryna charge Inf but I pushed him back. Black was at the door smilin' his ass off as Sae pointed at Inf.

"You coward ass niggah, you just fucked up, get ready to ride out".

Sae spun out the cell to go get a joint (Weapon); we all knew Sae went to get strapped up with a knife.

"Damn, Inf... what the fuck you swung with me in the middle for?" I shouted.

"Pardon self Sha but I told that niggah not to put his hands in my face."

"Yo, y'all niggahs gotta get out my cell, I don't want no blood in my shit and I get locked up under investigation!" screamed Black with that smile on his face.

Inf left the cell, hurryin' to the back of the second tier to retrieve a weapon from someone.

"Yo, Sha, you shoulda moved and let dem niggahs go at it!" declared Black.

"Man, shut the fuck up!" I barked exiting the cell.

Niggahs on the flats was lookin' up and cats on the third tier was lookin' down. Shit!!! It was about to be some shit.

* * * * *

As I climbed the steps to go to the third tier to find Saekwon and stop him from comin' back with a knife, Veto was comin' down.

"Yo Sha, what's up Sun? What the fuck is goin' on? Inf just ran up in my joint lookin' crazy, askin' me for a jump off... screamin' he got drama wit Saekwon."

"Some bullshit popped off and he went at Sae in Black's cell, where Inf at now?"

"Damn, word? He went at Sae?" Veto asked with a surprised look.

"Yo, he went somewhere, I'm lookin' for him now. He might of went to "E" for a bikkie, he is somewhere in here lookin' for a joint."

"Damn… yo go find him and hold him down. Build wit him, talk some sense into that niggah. I'ma go find Sae and do the same. Home team can't go at Home Team like that Son."

"I feel you" said Veto in agreement.

"Yo, I'm goin' at Sae's spot now, I got this".

"I'ma holla at Inf".

"Yo Veto, brush your fuckin' teeth before you do any talkin'." I joked.

"Fuck you Sha" Veto replied as we took off on our missions to calm the situation before it got any more out of hand than it already was.

* * * * *

From the time I made it to chow and sat down at the tables, niggahs wanted details of what transpired between Sae and Inf. Askin' shit like, "Did Inf really hook off on Saekwon and Sae aint fight back?" Black already spreaded the word of that little epp he witnessed, it was crazy. That shit was all niggahs wanted to talk about at the N.Y. tables so I made it to the yard with Sincere, Serious and Unique in tow, they kept on wantin' to know what popped off. I kept it movin'…

"Yo, Shakim!!" hollered JaQuan, who was with Sha-Prince, Jimmy and Fingers. JaQuan already had that funny grin on his face so I knew he already heard the news.

"What's good Gods?" I asked.

"Peace!" shouted Sincere, as we all dapped up.

"Yo, little shit stain ass niggah" Fingers said lookin' at Sincere.

"Niggah, I feel like tearin' your head off wit a Jay-Z joint. I told you keep one on deck, little Puffy lookin' ass niggah."

"Man, fuck you, banana boat ass niggah."

Niggahs started laughin'.

"Alright dig, I'ma hit one and you hit one, cool?" asked Fingers.

"Spit!" snapped Sincere.

"Alright!" Shouted Jimmy as niggahs came close to hear what Jay-Z rhymes Fingers was gettin' ready to hit us with. There were cats comin' over just to listen.

Fingers began... "Yo Dig...

"I love bitches / thug bitches / shy bitches / rough bitches / don't matter you my bitches / gold diggers / witchya eyes on my riches / can't knock ya hustle for real, exotic bitches / I'm game tight / see it all through the platinum French frames wit the French name in the same night / pull your little tight friend / lift your little dress like light wind / hah.... then I slide right in / ... you know the whole repertoire / U.S. ... to the U.S.S.R. / sexin' in a Lexus car / match wits with the best of y'all / the rest of y'all's like vege - tables in my presence / check it / reminiscin' on nothin' you ever heard / Ice Berg... / Slim baby ride rims through the suburbs / funds come in lump sums, never ends deferred / get money like I'm down south Wednesday the third / It's on!!"

Convicts started singin' the chorus...

"Dough to get / more shows to rip / I suggest you all roll wit the clique/ who you wit?
Frozen wrists and flows is sick / more O's than you know exist bitch / who you wit?"

"Can't scheme on em / Roc-A-Fella got a team on em / chicks dream on him / trick cream on him / lose it when dudes think its just music / lean on em / flash green on em and diamond rings on em / sexy 'round the way girls down to "Miras"/ I'm somethin' every girl gotta have like Levi's Chiquita... me got more / see I brawl / you can love me or hate me / either or.../ I'ma stay winnin' / rock the custom drop Bentley's / never eat at Denny's and party like little Penny / Can he live? / Trick on main chick but if she leave just as quick indian give / Ha Ha ... / Now what I look like givin' a chick half my trap ? / Like she wrote half my raps / yeah I'm havin' that / You'll be the same chick as when you came / leave the bankbook and the credit cards and take everything you came wit".

The Convict choir sang again...

"Dough to get / more shows to rip / I suggest you all roll wit the clique/ who you wit?
Frozen wrists and flows is sick / more O's than you know exist bitch / who you wit?"

"Damn Sin, I don't know if you can top that one" shouted Jimmy.
"Fuck that bullshit, check this joint out!" Sin wiped his mouth and spit some Nas shit.

"Ayo, a young wild beautiful love child / you like them thug style / link rockin' / mink coppin' / hit you on the sink/ hundred dollar drink poppin'/ the head make him take you shoppin' / a foul doctrine / reminiscent of my first time up in a chick / you was innocent but now you rent a dick / wear the tightest shit / Chanel lookin' real / airbrushed nails / hit the gym / hit the scales / heaven sent but negligent / to see a prophesy / your ebony tone is lockin' me / the way you moan make me day dream of you on top of me / wishin' I could be the one man / but you juggle way too many willies all in one hand / you wanna run up in clubs / gettin' rubbed on / niggahs pull ya hair / shake your phat rear / get your fuck on / followin' week you back there but what you stuck on /weed, clowns and cars /

puffin' wit some little niggah / husband not knowin' but you believe she mother Earth of the Seas / niggahs thirst you / but you just let em hurt you and leave / what up ma? ? frontin' like you naive/ push ya man's whip / call police when you flip can't understand it / yo, it should be a throne for us / but for now that's a whole different zone for us"

Sha-Prince took over the chorus as the crowd sung along.

"Diamonds all shinin' / lookin' all fine / pretty little face / get a little high / young girl's strugglin' tryna survive / Mother of the Earth / she made you and I / Just tired of playin' the same old games / messin' wit my mind emotional things/ and there goes a black girl lost"

"Yo like Isis / she got you heartbroken and felt lifeless / grow up girl, you said you want revenge so now you act the nicest / to whoever gettin' down the trifest / to get his mind all you do is give him somethin' priceless / cause in time / he'll realize the thighs is all he needs / more than weed / then you hit him off with lies and greed / there you go again / startin' wars / makin' me more yours / seem to get a kick outta keepin' me on all fours / face glitterin' I'm addicted to you / original wisdom body got me picturin' you / igloos of ice, trickin' on you / you never listen to this niggah spendin' Franklins on tennis anklets / must of had a bad deal in the past though/ can't even keep it real wit a niggah wit cash flow / say men are all the same / what we need to do is break these chains / you got your job part time and school is your night thing / wit dreams without a doubt it aint far from now / you gettin' interviewed / but your boss is into gettin' screwed / typical day that the black girl sees / comin' home wantin' more from a college degree"

"Yo, Yo Son, that shit right there is some serious ass heat, Jay aint fuckin' wit Nas on that joint!" shouted Sha-Prince.

"Yo son, that shit was serious" agreed JaQuan.

"Son, don't get me wrong, Nas is crazy nice but he aint fuckin' wit Jay on any level be it flow, flossin', money, business-mind... shit, whatever. Jay so ill Son, that niggah got an album comin' out with R. Kelly. A whole joint with that niggah called "The Best of Both Worlds", feel me? Meaning the best niggah in R&B right now and the best spitter in Hip Hop" announced Fingers.

"That's some real shit right there!" proclaimed Jimmy.

"Yo, that's gonna be ill to see those niggahs collaboratin' like that. I heard Nas and R. Kelly on some joints but a whole L.P. wit Hov and Kells, shit is serious."

"Yo, watch your mouth shorty shit stain". Fingers said as he fixed the du-rag on his head.

"Yo, I'ma spit this next joint to show you that Jay even got a joint directed to dem rat ass niggahs. He got joints for everybody, street cats, club, business heads, broads, rats, whatever, ya dig? Check it! Son said...

"Growin' up in the hood / just my dog and me / we used to hustle in the hood for all to see / Problems ... I called him / he called on me / we wasn't quite partners I hit him off wit a P / let him unlock doors, off my keys / yea we spoke, much more than cordially / Man, he broke bread with me / my business spreads wit me / the Feds came to get me / we both fled quickly / wasn't quick enough to jump over the hedges wit me / got caught / and that's when our relationship strayed / used to call me from the joint till he ran out of change / and when he called collect and I heard his name / I quickly accepted / but when I reached the phone he's talkin' reckless / I can sense deceit in his tone / I said "Damn, dawg, what? Nine weeks and you're home?" / I just sat, spat no more speech in the phone / the crackers up there bleachin' your dome / you're reachin' / I said "the world don't stop, I've gotta keep, keep on" / from there I sensed the beef was on / I ran to the spot, store to add some features to my phone / to see if I had bugs and leeches on my

phone / can't be too safe / cause niggahs is two faced / and they show the other side when they catch a new case / it's on"

(chorus)
"It's cool when you had hella weed to smoke / and you bought a new home where you could keep ya folks / I don't see how this side of you could be provoked / uh-huh, uh-huh / it was all good just a week ago.

Funny what seven days can change / a stand up niggah now you sit down to aim / used to have a firm grip now you droppin' names / uh-huh, uh-huh... it was all good just a week ago"

A hyped Fingers said... "Check the second verse Son…"

"Like I put the toast to your head and made you sell / we both came in this game blind as hell / I did a little better, had more clientelle / told you put away some cheddar now your cryin' for bail / seventeen and I'm holdin' on to around a mill / I could bail out, blow trial and come around on appeal / had niggahs thinkin' I was from uptown for real / I had so much hustle plus I was down to ill / like a brooklyn niggah, straight out of Brownsville / down and dirty / down to fight to round thirty / freezin' on them corners still holdin' my cracks / lookin' up and down the block / fuck is the dough at? / came from flat broke to lettin' the dough stack / you tell them Feds I said I'm never goin' back / I'm from Brooklyn and Brooklyn don't raise no rats (Fingers is from BK but not from Marcy so he said Brooklyn instead) / you know the consequences of your acts / you can't be serious"

Fingers, Jimmy, Sincere, Serious, JaQuan and even I sang the chorus, that was some real shit right there… so serious that even rat niggahs put their heads down or stayed away cause feelings was touched.

"Yo Son, that shit was the truth!"

"Word life! Yo Son, listen, I aint about to fuck wit y'all on this rap shit... I got moves to make and a movie to catch" I said as I dapped niggahs up.

* * * * *

The yard was crowded as a lot of activities was goin' on at the same time. Unique came by and was smilin', givin' me the cue that everything was good. I hit Fingers with a handshake at the same time, slippin' a small package in his hand.

"Yo, Jam showed me a little love wit some Purple so I'ma bless you all wit a lil' somethin'-somethin' to blaze wit Jimmy and JaQuan, feel me?"

"Good lookin' Fam", Fingers said as he embraced me.

There was a crowd under the shed watchin' Soul Train on the t.v. "Yo, Uniqueness, what's good God?" I shouted as I walked towards Unique. We dapped and drifted away from all ears.

"Yo I just secured a gallon for us and I got some ill greenery. I'm about to go see if I can secure another gallon for tonight".

"Yeah that's love. I got some purple, enough for like two spliffs".

"That's right, work your hand". We pounded each other dap as I saw Y-Born walkin' up.

"Yo, Y-Born!!" I acknowledged as Unique spun off to make some moves.

"Damn Sha, I was lookin' all over for you". Y-Born said as he shook my hand and slipped me a small package.

"Yo, what's this I hear that the Gods is at it in your unit?"

"Yeah, it was just a little mishap, it aint really nothin', I got that shit under control."

"I would hope so Sun… I heard niggahs was swingin' and you was in the middle. Y'all need to cut that bullshit out plus I seen Sae talkin' to Mark and shit aint lookin' like it should."

"I got that, I got that."

"O.k. just make sure you got like five packs of Oreos for me in the movies and hold me a seat". Y-Born said as he smiled his toothless smile.

* * * * *

"Romeo Must Die" was definitely all of that and then some, niggahs really enjoyed that movie. As soon as the lights went out and the previews came on, smoke was in the air, drinks was bein' poured and niggahs was gettin' twisted in there. After the movie, we headed back to the units, BET Top 25 Countdown was on, hosted by no other than Jay-Z. Convicts ran to get their headphones so they could check Hova's Top 25, shit was "like that" too. One thing about convicts in prison, that braggin' shit, big spendin' and cats tryna floss and outshine each other is still in effect. Gamblers bet big and small, everyone disputed about one thing or another. Who's still holdin', who's the flyest, arguin' about who's the best in whatever sport, what team is the best; disputes about money, houses, chicks, entertainment and anybody's finances. In the feds, niggahs argue about any and everything a niggah can think of and shit is serious, fights break out, knives get pulled, cats get stuck, gang wars is in effect and at the same time, everything is still everything. You got everything in prison, wanna-be thugs, who are really soft once they're exposed, closet homos, rats, undercover rats, who are eventually exposed and niggahs who was really about big things... and there was all these different types all mixed together in the Federal Penitentiary Lompoc.

"Yo Sha, what's good?"

"I just hung up wit my manz from around my way, Son who wrote "Belly"… niggah is on some shit, he out here workin' wit Jon Singleton and he only lives two and a half hours away, he's on my visitors list and all and still aint make it up here yet… Son keeps a bullshit ass excuse on deck."

"Word?" asked Saekwon.

"Yeah, it makes me wonder about who is really my true niggahs. Niggahs show their true colors when you get locked up."

"I hear you Sun."

"Yo, Unique!" I hollered in Unique's direction and said to Sae "Yo, "I'm about to drink this next gallon. I'll holla!!"

"Be easy Pa!"

"No doubt".

"Yo, you goin' back for the second showin' of "Romeo Must Die?" Sae asked me.

"No question, I'ma be there." I said as I stumbled off to get even more twisted.

Dinner time between movies was the same, they served straight up bullshit so instead of the bullshit, Unique and Black hooked up an ill meal that we all ate while we smoked and got twisted. I didn't even go down to the chow hall to fuck wit them other niggahs cause I didn't want to get out of the zone I was in. I was gettin' ready to go see this movie for the second time plus tomorrow was Sunday, I had to go to the Law Library to review some cases and read the Criminal Law Reporter… then get drunk.

The next day.... Sunday afternoon in the Law Library....

The Law Library was located on the west end of the institution, across from the Barber Shop / Hair Salon, which is what they called it but it was really for convicts who was students, learnin' to cut hair and earn their Barber's License while usin' us convicts as Guinea Pigs. The Education Department was also located in the Law Library, which had about twenty to twenty-five electrical typewriters available and a copy machine. There were three clerks who stood by at a window to deliver whatever Law Books that were requested and the area where the typewriters and tables were was sectioned off by a glass partial and doors so a person could have some kind of quiet to study but it was never that way. Behind the glass partial, was the Leisure Department, which consisted of at least thirty large tables and some tables that seated up to eight or ten people and there were a few two and three main tables too. There were t.v.'s with built -in VCR's sittin' on high tables with stools by the glass partitions that separated the Law from the Leisure part of the Library. There were also twelve to fifteen classrooms that was used to hold classes rangin' from G.E.D. to other Adult Continuing Education (A.C.E.) courses that was available in the Institution, such as parenting, legal research, screen writing, typing, creative writing, foreign languages, it was just too many to name but it was there. It was like goin' to school, they had a regular teachers and some convicts where tutors.

The Leisure Department had a clerk there who ran Ebony, Jet, Essence, FHM, Stuff, Reader's Digest, newspapers from every city in Cali and a few other west coast states. The video tapes for the VCR was also available at the clerk's station. Tapes rangin' from History, Educational, Black History, Science, National Geographic Wildlife and Religious tapes could all be found in Lompoc. Convicts was there workin' on their case issues or continuin' their education but don't let the look fool you. Just because you see niggahs in the Law Library doesn't mean that everything is everything. That was just an illusion thrown out there to the human eye, a lot of shit and different activities popped off in the library as in any other part of prison. Just because you saw someone with a Law Book opened, a pen and paper in hand didn't mean that law work was bein' done.

The Law Library was used to get together or to be by yourself to plan, plot, scheme moves or to put together other activities, positive or negative cause we was in prison and shit didn't stop. The mind still remains active, formulatin' ways to come up and get ahead lawfully or unlawfully. This was also a Hustler's den, there was all kinds of different hustles goin' on from convicts who was proficient typists who was there typin' law work for others chargin' a dollar a page to Jail House Lawyers, who were workin' on other convict's cases. Of course there were dirty moves bein' made as well. Money was replaced by stamps, which is the prison's form of money. A 37 cent stamp was considered a quarter or twenty-five cents Black Market. Just like the importance and value of currency on the outside world, stamps held that same importance and value. Convicts was / is out to accumulate as much stamps as possible and in return, it was so many different ways to get rid of the stamps and change it back into currency. Yeah, stamps is very important and they were easy to hide and move around the institution. You could have no currency on your account but have a hundred books of stamps or a thousand books and still hold the position of havin' money. Transactions can be made more easily cause havin' stamps is "**Money on the wood that made everything good**".

Plots and schemes was goin' down at the library as the thinkers thought extortion schemes and all other kinds of moves to come up with paper. You had convicts in the library in the back classrooms, shootin' dice for anywhere from ten to a hundred books of stamps. Convicts sold any kind of illegal drug ever thought of and wine was available in the library too. Things went so smooth and was done so nonchalantly that to the physical eye, it looked like nothin' wrong was bein' done. What's so ill about the whole format was that the tutors worked amongst themselves and so did the hustlers. Everybody held some type of position to make sure everything was everything (cool, goin' smooth). People were placed as "lookouts" and they even had convicts who were used to keep the supervising officer and teacher busy or lookin' the other way. As long as nothin' got out of hand or no fights broke out, shit ran like a normal day but it was always more to it. Whenever a bust or raid went down, unbelievable things was found that the supervising officer never knew was takin' place, like a seizure of thirty gallons of wine or a dice game where over a thousand books of stamps was seized. So much was goin' on at the same time and done so smooth. They had a big huge bathroom and even one of the stalls was used by a convict with portable hair clippers and beard trimmers to give haircuts. What's so ill was it was when haircuts was being given, there were "no walk-ins", you had to have an appointment and pay in advance type shit.

The smokin' area was where all negotiations went down, that was usually where everyone went for smoke breaks. If you wanted somethin' done as far as lookin' for a good quick typist or a person to break down and explain some legal terminology, "go look in the smoke room area". A hundred different conversations was goin' on at once in there, with every kind of cigarette smoke in the air, niggahs was back there shakin' up the dice too. The library was used for all kinds of things. Lompoc, bein' flooded with gangs meant there was always a meeting or somethin' goin' on in there. At anytime, the Latin Kings, Gangster Disciples, Vice Lords, Black Guerilla Family, Crips, Bloods, Five Percenters and any group that wasn't a religious sect in the sentry file of the prison met in the library cause they couldn't congregate in the Chapel. So mad shit went down in that library, as the ticket man got his gambling tickets typed up and copies made for the day's games and activities.

I could be found in the that Law Library four days out of the week, either workin' on my case issues, discussing legal issues and strategies with convict law technicians or at a typewriter. I could be in the leisure part readin' a magazine, newspaper or Criminal Law Reporter and I could be in the midst of plottin', schemin' and formulatin' a plan. I took classes in the Education Department and I had accumulated certificates in creative writing, screen writing, parenting, poetry workshop, legal research, blueprint reading and other courses. All that and I could still be found in the back sippin' on some Passion Twist Wine (Orange and Grape) like "**What**!!" The Law Library was / is one of my spots.

"Yo Shakim, this shit is crazy "B"!" yelled Eastwood.

We was sittin' at a table in the back of the leisure department. I was browsin' through the "Criminal Law Reporter", lookin' for any new case decisions and court rulings. Eastwood just got through readin' a few cases that was arguing the Apprendi Issue. He was lookin' for a collateral case to use to get in court in the fourth circuit. He caught his case in Norfolk, Virginia and had a cocaine / crack case for which he was sentenced to two life sentences. He vented to me…

"Sha, shit is just crazy ridiculous how niggahs like us can't get back in court. We got issues and all… look at the shit, how this chump got back in court? First of all, he is a racist ass cracker, who shot up in some black people's crib in Jersey. They locked his cracker ass up and he pled out to it, not knowin' that they were gonna enhance him on a "Hate Crime". So he's arguing about that enhancement that gave him five extra years over some shit he pled out to. I got two L's for some invisible drugs, he gets back in court for a hate crime enhancement but I get all kinds of enhancements for firearms, manager / supervisor roles, bein' in a school zone, obstructin' justice and some more shit. Sha, I'm peepin' how they are screamin' how every element of the crime should go to the jury for them to decide, not to the Judge or Probation department. I'm bein' held for drug amounts that the probation department gave me and said I'm accountable for and this bitch ass judge gave me a "L"!! This cracker cryin' over five petty years, gets his case overturned and in the law books and made history so maybe a nigga like me or you can get back in on his argument… this shit got me stressing Pa!!"

I responded by sayin'…

"Believe I know what you're talkin' about Wood. I got oiled up on some hearsay bullshit and they gave me invisible drug amounts too Pa. I just got smashed on my 2244, tryna get a second or successive 2255 motion. I had an affidavit from the main government witness and still got denied with no opinion Sun."

"Sha, shit is ridiculous for sure!"

"Yo, my co-defendant, who got acquitted, the government's theory was that I was managed / supervised by him. I even had an affa from Sun; I just built with his trial lawyer too. He screamed that he could take my case and beat it and it wouldn't be a conflict of interest to the courts, cause he represented my co-dee".

"Which Co-dee?"
"Monday"

"Oh word? So what's up, what's the lawyer sayin'?"

"He screamin' that he can get me back in court, either on a reversal or get me down to fifteen years."

"Yeah?"

"Yeah but he screamin' money figures too. He said he could get me back in court, he is awaitin' that U.S. vs. Cotton case that's in the Fourth Circuit too."

"That's a B-more case, right?"

"Yeah, I know one of dem cats, "Butt-naked" from B-more. We was in the "Hut" together, Son was one of the reasons we got shipped to Marion."

"They case is based on the Apprendi joint too."

"Exactly, so the lawyer is screamin' that I got Apprendi issues too. We gonna see the outcome of the decision on that case so we can get in on that. He also gave me a legal tech from NLPA to scream at so I can work with him on my issues."

"NLPA in Cincinnati, Ohio? Dem niggahs be rippin' cats off crazily!" barked Eastwood.

"They supposed to be ill on legal research and shit."

"Yeah and be chargin' seventy-five hundred to do paperwork."

We both laughed.

"Yo, what's your co-dee's lawyer's name that can help you?"

"Kimball… Keith Kimball."

"Oh word? That was Skeet from Portsmouth's lawyer and shit."

"Yeah but my co-dee had Kimball first, Kimball got his claim to fame beatin' our shit when he was a court appointed lawyer."

"Word?"

"Yeah, now I gotta come up and generate some paper to get him on my shit."

"Yeah Sha, baby, I feel you on that. We gotta keep fightin' for our ultimate freedom Pa. We can't give up at all. Yo, let me ask you this Sun, dem Murder Inc or FUBU cats holdin' you down?" asked Eastwood.

"Sun, I'm at war right now, feel me?"

"I smell you Sun."

"Daymond from FUBU tries to keep shit funky but niggahs aint feelin' my pain or understanding my struggles, don't nobody owe Shakim shit."

"Shits real Pa".

"Definitely!"

"Yo, look at this niggah Fingers, he just came out the smoke room, Sun is crazy Pa!"

Fingers came in our direction with a few Cali Crip niggahs in toll.

"Yo, what's good wit my niggahs?" asked Fingers.

"Nothin' much Sun, just readin' over some cases and shit."
"I feel that, I just got through breakin' the bank over in the smoke room." boasted Fingers while pullin' out dozens of books of stamps and throwin' two books at me and two at Eastwood. Before he and company strolled back toward the smoke room area, Fingers said...

"Cop you some smoke and get your mind right Fam!"

"Son is crazy, he aint lettin' this shit kill him."

"He aint showin' it to us but this shit is killin' him."

"What you sayin'... Son be cryin' on the inside?"

"Shit, he be cryin' when he is in his cell and no one is listenin', shit is Killin' Fingers."

"Shit is killin' me too, I just aint break down yet". I said as I got up to go to the smoke room. For real, for real... shit had me so fucked up that I stopped smokin' twice. Once for two years, another time for about eighteen months. What's so ill is, since I been in Cali, I went from Menthol Newports to smokin' chest bustin' Camels, tell me this shit aint serious.

"Yo Wood, I'ma be back, I'ma go get my smoke on."

"I"ma be right here holdin' the table down" answered Eastwood.

"Ahite fam" I said as I took off towards the smoke area. I went through the partial glass doors and looked outside, all the smokin' jailhouse lawyers was smokin' and talkin'.

Cats in the smokin' area was smokin' and discussin' law and as I said before, there was like ten conversations goin' on at the same time but all about law. Then there was like ten conversations about school and then more conversations about bullshit. As I got a light and looked towards the back, in the corner was a group of cats bunched up as Fingers was rollin' dice.

"Yeah, let me show you how to do this Son!" Fingers shouted as he rolled two dice.

"Yeah!!"

"I got ten stamps say he don't four again."

"Bet!"

"Bet!!"

"Let me show you how to do this Son!" Fingers repeated, as he rolled the dice again.

There was weed smoke in the air as well as cigarettes and wine breath niggahs.

"Yo Sha, what's good? I'm in here rapin' these niggahs!! Oh, no homo!"

Fingers smiled.

"Shit bro, we can play C-Lo too, if that's what you wanna do." said a cat holdin' twelve books.

"Shit, you aint sayin' nothin' niggah, I'm a hustler so anything is good as long as you got flags in your pocket, feel me Son?"

"Son? Fuck outta here homie, I aint no Son."

"No disrespect intended niggah and I aint your homie. I'm from BK, New York niggah!" barked Fingers as he rolled the dice, hittin' his point.

"Bitch ass niggah, pay me!" snapped Fingers... as he went to pick up the stamps that was on the floor under a cat's feet, someone stepped on his hand and said...

"Yo that aint you homie!"

Fingers got up and punched dude in the face.

"Fuck you mean that aint me?" Anything that hit that floor is me, fuck you steppin' on my fingers Bitch ass pussy hole!"

I stepped up in the crowd lookin' to see the reaction and who was next to get it.

"Yo, Fingers what's good?"

Niggahs was backin' away, some was fleeing the smoke area, thinkin' drama was about to pop off.

"Shit, nothin' poppin' God... Game Over!!!"

As soon as Fingers said that, them people announced over the P.A. system…

"One way move back from rec yard and rec areas back to the housing units... This is a one way move only!!!"

It was like they were waiting for some shit to pop off and when it didn't, they called a move… shit was bugged out.

* * * * *

Monday was a slow day as usual. I woke up late with a splittin' headache from all that excessive drinkin' I did over the weekend. My head was throbbin' terribly as I got up and hit the switch to turn the radio the fuck off. Jay-Z's "Song Cry" was on… that song is "like that", I fucked wit it but not at that moment, my head couldn't take hearin' that shit with the way I was feelin' this particular morning. My cell door was locked shut but the others in the unit was locked out, you could get your cell door shut so you could sleep in late. I did that for safety reasons, I'm in prison, not the Holiday Inn, feel me? I took a morning piss to relieve myself, wiped the toilet stool after sprayin' some wanna-be "Lysol" on it then I went to the sink to wash my hands and slay the "Dragon" by brushin' my teeth, gums, and tongue. After I washed my face, I got dressed in my tan prison Khakis and made sure everything was everything in my cell; making my bed and all. I looked out my door window, tryna catch someone's attention to call the C.O.

"Yo, E!!" I hollered to "E", who was standin' on my tier.

"Yo!" E answered.

"Yo Sun, when you get a chance, tell the C.O. cell E-14 wanna lock out!"

"Ahite QB Sha!!" responded "E".

I looked at my watch, it was 10:45am, I was usually up and dressed by 5:45a.m... shit, I slept late. I knew that niggah Unique was up and runnin', I thought to myself, "he probably already smoked a blunt knowin' him". Five minutes later, my cell door opened and I hit the tier, went down to the second tier, lookin' for Unique, who wasn't there. Everyone I fucked wit was gone. Sae, Black was at work, Veto and Inf was on the yard and who knows where the fuck Unique was at. I went to get my radio and headphones so I could catch the videos until lunch.

LUNCH

I went into the chow hall with my unit, they was servin' Spanish rice and Nachos with ground beef and cheese sauce. They were forever servin' that Mexican meal shit and I was already tired of that shit. I only went because they had chocolate chip cookies for desert; I fucks with those hard, so hard I buy a bag of twenty for ten stamps when they were sellin' them in the unit. As I walked from the soda area to sit down at the N.Y. tables, Veto and Infinite was already sittin' there; they came in from the rec yard and made it to chow.

"Peace Sha!" Infinite greeted me.

"What's good Sha?" asked Veto as he moved his tray over so I could have space to put mine on the table.

"Yeah, what's poppin'?" I greeted both of them.

"Yo Sha, you met the new homie?" asked Veto.

"Nah, who is he and where is he from?"

"Some Brooklyn cat who came in from Terre Haute. He said he knows you."

"Yeah? Where he at?"

"I think he's on the yard or maybe at laundry, he wit Mark and dem."

"It figures" I said as I ate my cookies and sat for a few minutes while givin' nods and pounds to fellow convicts then I said...

"Yo, I'ma skate to the yard, I'ma see y'all later"

I knocked on the table and rolled out.

* * * * *

On the yard, convicts was under the shed watchin' t.v....
They were watchin' a 106 & Park re-run from Friday on B.E.T. I
stopped and shook hands and made small talk with a few heads and
started walkin' around the track where I saw a crowd by the N.Y.
section, pull-up / dip bar area. Fingers was at it again, gettin' on
Sincere. A few familiar faces was in attendance but there was one
cat standin' there in freshly ironed Khakis and new boots, meanin'
he was a new arrival off the bus. Fingers was holdin' yet another
debatin' cipher on Jay-Z and Nas, with Sha-Prince, Eastwood,
Sincere, Jimmy and what looked like the whole Baltimore, D.C.
and Philly with a few Bloods and Crips.

"Yo, I'm tellin' your little ass that Jay spits some ill verses Son.
Son said...

**"Got cats on the corner like... don't me and Jigga be soundin'
alike? Nah... not in your fuckin' life... can't nobody pop it like
Mr. Jay-Z..What? You niggahs crazy?... I'm hot like a six...
maybe deep dish wit the grey seats. I flow greater than your
Navigator... I drop through your town...block the data...see
me comin' through in a hot pair of Gators... with a crew wit
rocks the size of crators... can't be touched like hot potatoes,
ya heard?"**

"Then Jay said..."
**"Press your brakes... Feds wanna investigate. Mister. I. don't.
cop. Nothin'. less. than .eight.... anything involvin' my name...
in regards to the fame... its hard..I can't even walk through
Harlem again..charge it to the game I'm Platinum like
American Express..my boy died..and all I did was inherit his
stress..to make every jam tougher...you aint my manz..fuck
ya..I suggest that you live..right? - Negative."**

You heard what he spit on "Do it again?" Son said...

**"Any given moment a hundred gees in your grill..don't come
round talkin' 'bout he got skills..he's al..right..but he's not real.**

Jay-Z's that deal..with Seeds in the field..never fear for war..hug, squeeze that steel."

"Son says the illest shit… like..

"We used to fight for buildin' blocks / now we fight for blocks with buildings / that make a killin'...the closest of friends when we first started / but grew apart..as the money grew...soon grew black hearted / thinkin' back to when we first learned to used rubbers / he never learned ...so in turn I'm kidnappin' his baby's mother."

"That's that "D' Evils" off the classic "Reasonable Doubt" L.P. Son is deep. He spitted...

"I'm tryna be calm but I'ma grow richer / by any means with that thing that Malcolm palmed in the picture / never read the Qur'an or Islamic scriptures / only Psalms I read was on the arms of my niggahs!!"

"Shit, Nas got a new joint called "One Mic" where he says...

"This is my hood, I'ma rep to the death of it / until everybody come home...little niggahs is grown / Hood rats don't abortion your womb / we need more warriors soon / sent from the star, sun and the moon" spitted the new arrival in his fresh Khakis and new boots.

"When Nas said that shit? Matter fact niggah, who the fuck is you?" asked Fingers.

The newcomer stepped up but not too close, just enough to make himself known...

"My name is "Mag", I'm from North Click (North Carolina) but I cause my case up top".

Fingers examined son from head to toe, fixin' his eyes on Mag's shirt barin' a nametag that displayed his name and registration number. The last three digits in Mag's registration number were "053", which meant Brooklyn, Queens or Long Island so this niggah either caught his case or got arrested up top. "Yeah? I'm Jimmy Fingers niggah".

"I heard of you. I'm hip to the "Poison Clan" my cousin was with "Scooter" in Allenwood."

"Mag" was 5'11", 190 solid, brown-skinned with curly hair and several gold teeth; Son looked like he worked out crazily.

"Yeah? Where was you at up top?"

"BK... I was in the East."

"Where in the East?"

"Linden houses, the Plaza (Linden Plaza), P. Worthman, The Blvd, all over that area. I was born up top but moved when I was young... always went back and forth though, my whole fam lives in the East."

"Yeah?" said Fingers, still sizin' Mag up.

"Yeah" as Mag sized Fingers up too.

* * * * *

Saekwon and Mark was spinnin' the track with G.L., who just came in that morning. He came from another Fed Pen, G.L. was a stocky cat, about 5'10", two hundred pounds, he'd been down for over a decade and oh yeah, Son is from the Bed-Stuy section of Brooklyn. He wasn't no hell of a dude in any aggressive way but he was known to make a few power moves in prison to generate money so cats tended to flock around him, tryna get on. G.L. was one of those kinda niggahs that still had connects and peoples on the street who still looked out for him. The prison wolves stayed around, waitin' for a sign of weakness so they could attack and get at son but miraculously, he kept them at bay. I was in Terre Haute with son, he was one makin' promises but not fulfillin' them type of cat but he was semi-cool with me. He, Saekwon and Mark came to the Pull-up / dip bar section and saw a little tension.

"Yo Fingers, what's good?"

"Nuttin, just talkin' to this here bamma ass niggah from N.C., who says he was livin' in the East".

"Yeah?"

Then Sae and Mark came with a series of back and forth questioning, findin' out that Mag just came from M.D.C. Brooklyn and so on...

"Why you way out west then?" asked Mark.

"Shit, they sent me way out here." Mag said as suspicion came across Fingers' face.

"Yo, I'ma have my paper work so y'all can see."

"That's right Son" said Fingers.

* * * * *

Me and G.L. was in another conversation, I hadn't see son in two years so he gave me the rundown of what popped off, leading him to be transferred from Terre Haute to Lompoc. He said the usual, "an investigation" was the reason for his transfer. He told me what unit he was in and I told him I'd get some necessities at him later that day.

"Yo what's good up top?" Sae asked.

Mag got real comfortable with Saekwon...

"Yo, shit is poppin' up top Sun. It's crazy blooded out now, everything is everything but times was ill since that World Trade Center jump off. They got Power 105 and Hot 97 poppin' off on the radio and Nas took over the city."

"What?!!" asked Fingers.

"I said **Nas run N.Y. right now**. Kay Slay and every deejay in N.Y. bows down to the new King of N.Y. "**Nasty Nas from Queens**". He is all over the airwaves, he bodied Jigga with that "Ether" joint."

"Fuck outta here" Fingers already hated this country ass wanna be N.Y. niggah "Mag".

* * * * *

Back at the unit, I got necessities and what nots for that niggah G.L. Sincere and Serious sent over shit to put in the care package and so did Unique, Inf and Veto. That's how shit is done, well, most of the time, when someone arrives from N.Y. to any Fed spot, the N.Y. car usually puts together a care package consistin' of everything from cosmetics, sweat suits, kicks, stamps, cigarettes, radio... all to hold a niggah down until he gets proper, every car does that. So anyway, I put everything in a net bag and went to Saekwon's cell to drop it off, Sae took the bag and was supposed to meet with G.L. on the next move on the rec yard.

"Yo Sha, what's up wit dat niggah Black?"

"Why, what's up?"

"Dat niggah said he aint givin' G.L. nothin'."

I started laughin', Black is a stingy ass little black niggah.

"Yo hold up... Yo, Black!!!" I called down to the second tier.

"Yo!" answerd Black.

"Come up here to Sae's spot little funny, comical ass niggah!" I screamed back.

Black came up five minutes later, I asked son why he aint contribute to G.L's care package.

"Fuck that niggah!" Black answered... "I don't know that niggah to give him shit. When I first got here aint no one give me shit and I didn't expect shit from no one. So what if that niggah is from BK and can make shit happen. I still aint givin' that niggah a mothafuckin' thing. They got generic toothpaste, tooth brushes, deodorant, shampoo and whatever that niggah needs."

Shit was funny, Black continued…

"Plus, I work too hard for mine to just be givin' it away to some strange niggah. I probably won't even like that cat, he could be an undercover homo or somethin'... niggah looks strange and I aint givin' that other niggah "Mag" shit either! Fuck dem cats, my money is for me!!!"

Sae looked at me as I laughed mad hard at this shit. I looked at all that shit in the net bag and thought of takin' shit back... Hell, it was mad shit in there… way too much. Shit looked like he went to the store, I aint no catering service to no niggah either, G.L. is cool and all plus niggahs blessed me lovely when I first touched at Lompoc and any other spot I was in so I brushed that thought and laughed at Black like crazy.

"Yo Sha, for real though, fuck dem niggahs, Black aint givin' up shit!" shouted Black as I laughed at Saekwon's facial expression.

* * * * *

"Mag" was startin' to get a little bit familiarized with cats associated with the N.Y. car, he was on some up top shit and he knew Brooklyn hoods and a lot of cats from around there. He was movin' around with Young Jimmy, they were in the same unit. You could tell that "Mag" was under a lot of well known figures while he was in M.D.C. Brooklyn, he was probably gettin' "Sonned". Fingers was not feelin' this cat one bit and it showed every time "Mag" came around. Son was only on the pound one day goin' on two and was already sittin' at the N.Y. tables, which didn't seem to bother Mark too much, knowin' "Mag" was reppin' and biggin' up Brooklyn and could keep niggahs abreast on what was happenin' in N.Y.C. Sae and Mark was too busy holdin' conferences 101 with G.L., it looked like they were tryna lock shit in with him when the moves went into effect; looks can be very deceiving.

"Yo Mark!" hollered Fingers, who was also with Eastwood, Veto and JaQuan. "I don't know how y'all niggahs is carryin' shit but I aint feelin' that bamma ass niggah for him to be sittin' at the tables. I don't know son and it aint enough seats as it is so how he gonna come over here? N.C. sits with the South!!"
Niggahs was sittin' on the benches on the rec yard in their usual spot.

"Son, the kid just left M.D.C. Brooklyn and is lettin' us know what it is in the town plus we need a niggah like that amongst us." responded Mark.

"Man, fuck outta here! You adoptin' orphans now?" Interrupted JaQuan... "I aint feelin' son like that either, I caught my case in N.C. anybody even seen that kid's paperwork yet?"

Everyone was lookin' around and not havin' the answer that JaQuan was lookin' for.

"That niggah is probably a fuckin' rat or some shit tryna hide behind N. Why niggahs" spitted JaQuan... "Yo Mark, tell ya manz to find somewhere else to sit. I'ma holla at Jimmy cause he runnin' around the unit introducin' this niggah to heads, showin' him his photo album and shit".

"Shit... I aint even seen that niggah Jimmy photos yet!" exclaimed Eastwood.

"Holla at your boy-boy Mark, let son know" said JaQuan.

"Yo, it looks like it's about to rain out here" observed Veto, lookin' up at the cloudy sky, tryna change the subject.

Sure enough, the sky was darkening a bit like it was about to start thunderin' and lightenin' out there. Meanwhile.... Me, Sae, Sincere and Unique was sittin' at the tables in the chow hall when Jimmy came with his tray, followed by his new manz "Mag".

"Yo, what's good Fam-O?" asked Jimmy as he sat down.

"Yeah what's up?"

We watched Mag sit down next to Sae, niggahs had smirks on their faces, especially me.

"Yo, what's poppin'?" Mag greeted us.

"Yo, son, you said you just left M.D.C.?" asked Sincere.

"Yeah, yeah"

"Yo, you claimin' Nasty Nas got the city in the smash?"

"No question, that's the King" responded Mag.

"Yo, son, this niggah knows the words to "Ether"!!" exclaimed Jimmy. "He was spittin' a joint called "One Mic" and ... yo, what's the name of the other shit Son?"
"Which one, "Rewind" or "Second Childhood"?"

"Yo, he spitted a joint where Nas tells a story backwards, son knows all Nas' shit."

"Oh yeah?" Sincere asked, smilin' from ear to ear.

After chow, niggahs wanted to go out to the rec yard to chill plus we knew Mark and dem was already out there. As soon as we came out, I noticed how dark it was...

"Damn son, shit looks like it's about to pour out here."

"Word!! Yo, look at Mark, Fingers and dem at the pull-up bar."

We walked towards them.

"Yo shorty shit stain! I know you don't want it!" screamed Fingers.

"Fuck you!!" shouted Sincere as everyone dapped up.

"Yo, where Jimmy at?" Fingers asked Sae.

"He's comin' out… he was still at the table with his manz Mag".
Fingers' facial expression turned sour, hearin' that his young protégé was walkin' the pound with this bird ass niggah.

"Yo son, I seen that Jadakiss joint wit Mya video… that "Best of me" joint. yo that shit is official Pa" said Eastwood.

"Man, Jigga already killed it on the remix so you aint sayin' nothin' and son killed R. Kelly's "Fiesta" remix too" Fingers scoffed, brushin' off Eastwood's remark.

"Man, Jada is ill though!"

"Fuck outta here son, Jigga shitted on Jada on that remix. I'ma spit the remix for you now that Sin is here. Check it out niggah, the first verse goes...

"Yes… Y'allin..Jigga man be ballin' / leave chicks pigeon toed, some of them be crawlin'/ get the best of you whenever I put my all in / have mommies callin...for the Lord..darlin / Jigga.. a parkin' ass drop coupes wit half the top..expose half my knot / niggah mad when I brag about the cash I got / but I'm used to not havin' a lot...I'm from the gutter and I aint the type to ever chase your box / I'm the type to interior decorate the watch/ I'm the type to slang heavy weight on the block / in every state I pop...work Jigga ya hurt..holla"

"Sun, you sure you aint Jigga?" asked JaQuan.

Fingers wasn't payin' no attention to that shit as Jimmy and Mag walked over and Fingers spitted the second verse...

"5, 4, 3, 2, 1

Carolina blue kicks..hottest niggah on the block / used to wheely bicycles since I was six... / high school, the crossover, waved away kicks / music is the same shit..gave away hits / So ma...get it together..or..forget it forever...when I go at you hard...I can get it through leather..you..act like Jigga can't...get wit whoever.. / Told me you got a man...o.k ma...and?/ that's high school, makin' me chase you around for months / have an affair...act like an adult for once / plus my hand is up your skirt...got damn you flirt / what's a little me on top gon' hurt...? maybe a little..but pain is pleasure,. and pressure busts pipes / and you look like the "I like it rough type" / we can crush tonight...tell me what you like / I got a yellow bottle on a bucket of ice / get right... Young Hova!!"

"Son killed that remix" said Jimmy.

"Word!!"

"But yo," Said Mag...

Everyone stopped for a quick second to see what this niggah had the nerve to say.

"Nas killed Jay".

"Son, first of all, what the fuck is you talkin' about?" asked Fingers.

"Chill" said Sincere, who was really tryna amp shit up "Let son spit a Nas joint to your Jay joint and see what's what."

"Fuck all that shit, I aint feelin' this niggah" spitted Fingers.

"Yo son, this nigga knows all Nas new joints and then some" remarked Jimmy... "Son said he can match any Jay joint and shut him down."

"Fuck that. I tell you what, I'ma spit an ill grimey joint and you spit one and we will leave it at that."

Right then and there, thunder roared and it started gettin' real cloudy and even darker than it already was; rain drops was fallin' as big as quarters.

"Shit!!"

"The Rec yard is now closed, the rec yard is now closed! This is a rec move to return back to the housing units or to the inside gym!!" announced a voice over the loud speaker.

"Yo, lets go down to the gym!"

Niggahs started runnin' to the metal detectors to get off that yard before it started pourin' even harder. On the way to the gym, Sae decided to go back in to his unit. He was slow walkin' with Mark, holding a private conversation with him. Sha-Prince came out of his unit and was also goin' to the gym, which was between the east and west end but more on the west end and huge enough to hold a full court. In the gym, was two pull-up bars, a dip bar, numerous Universal Weight stations in an area and the court had bleachers that could seat about two hundred heads. One thing about the gym, they blasted music down there and the atmosphere was cool, you could listen to the latest tunes while workin' out or playing ball. They also had big mirrors on one side of the wall by the weights so niggahs was always takin' their shirts off type shit to peep the results of their workout or show off. There were leg machines such as stair masters and exercise bikes, treadmills and all that down there. Up stairs had tables for card playin', checkers or chess, they had a t.v. with two Sony Playstations but only sports videogames where available. They even had a band room with drums, a keyboard, amps, speakers and mics, there was another room where you could check out c.d.'s and c.d. players, which was considered the "Listening room" and they had another room with fifteen small t.v.'s with built-in DVD's players so we could check out movies but you had to bring your own headphones to use the c.d. or dvd players. Upstairs even had a full viewin' area where you could look down and watch the game on the court. It was like a private viewin' box in a basketball arena type shit. The gym was opened when the yard was closed, which was 7:45 to 9 p.m. or when the weather was fucked up like now.

Cali being so nice and warm, the yard stayed open, when it closed, the gym was used and that was where activities took place just the same as in the yard. This was where Y-Born had his job and he had it locked down. He ran the c.d.'s, c.d. players and always kept c.d. players available for me. C.d.'s, dvd's, play slot on the Play Station, whatever… Y Born was my manz for real.

As the gym filled up and cats was occupyin' the weights and settin' up a basketball game, we all traveled upstairs to the band room area, it was already ten to fifteen people in there but it had room for like sixty people.

"Damn, I'm soaked and I just washed this shit" said Black, straightenin' out his grey t-shirt.

"Oh shut up complainin', little, cheap ass niggah!" shouted Fingers.

"Yo, what's up?"

Eastwood, Veto, Sha-Prince, Sincere, Me, Unique, Jimmy, JaQuan and Marked stared at Fingers and Mag... other convicts came over to see what was up.

"Yo Slim, turn on the mics, I'ma blaze this niggah" snapped Fingers.

Slim, from Cali, did what he was told, "Yo, J-Bone can play the drums!"

"Word!"

"Yo, check it... I'ma spit one ill joint and that's it" shouted Fingers as he picked up the mic and went for a mic check. "Mic check one, two, one, two... Listen to this niggah!"

J-Bone started warmin' up on the drums, Y-Born looked in and seen us as more cats was coming in.

"Yo Sha, what's this, a talent show?" asked Y-Born who smiled his toothless smile once again.

"Yo, check one, check two, microphone checker, microphone checker, Brooklyn is about to represent some real shit" Fingers gripped and tested the microphone while J-Bone was steady drummin' an ill beat.

"Yo check it, this is from Ja Rule's "It's Murda", where once again, Jay killed it... my manz said...

"Yo, I take a squat then post up with the toast up / I bring beef to a closure / know somethin'? / from the cats stackin' four-somes / I'm loathsome / I scream out "Fuck the world" then I

throw somethin' / Niggahs schemin' hard / but fuck it, it's the God / I leave bullets lodged / leave you leanin' on your broad / and our punks leave you gagged up in your car / slumped Kennedy style with your memory out / what the fuck y'all want?"

Fingers got up close in Mag's face grittin' him.

"Daddio wit the calico / let the gaty blow / leave you bleedin' on your patio / I leave rivals on their backs lookin' up at the sky blue / not only do I leave you...I hide you / I before you / X and Ja Rule / death before dishonor now and prior to / Boss man spy on you / conspire you / me die before you? / you liar you / Niggahs is dead off / hits I approve / fuck it, I got the Feds wearin' wired suits / y'all niggahs don't listen / whether in streets or in prison / when we find them, we twist em / they fuckin' up missin' / y'all don't understand, we want y'all all to hate it / it's murda / murder incorporated / it's murda / in crime we all related / it's murda / see if y'all can take it."

"OOOOOOOOOOOHHHHHHHHHH!!!!!!!!"

The crowd was open off Fingers' performance of Jay-Z's verse from "It's Murda" plus Fingers was movin', spittin' and getting' all up in Mag's face like everything was directed at him with larceny. The crowd was amped! Y-Born had that look on his face like he was tryna tell me to stop shit before it got out of hand.

"Yo Mag, blaze that niggah!" screamed Sincere, as Mag was holdin' his head like he was contemplatin' on what he was gonna spit. Mag grabbed the other mic and looked at the small crowd. He said…

"Yeah? I was gettin' ready to spit Nas joint from the joint he did with G. Rap called "Fast life" but knowin' how this cat tried to bring it, I'ma bring it back. Yo son, give me somethin' ill so I can spit this shit.

J-Bone kicked another ill beat and Mag was rockin' his head, lookin' at Sha-Prince, who was waitin' with Jimmy to hear the ill shit.

"Yo, this is some "Verbal Intercourse" from Rae and Ghost shit" Sha-Prince's face lit up.

"Son said..."

"Through the lights cameras and action, glamour glitters and gold / I unfold the scroll / plant seeds to stampede the globe / when I'm deceased / by then the beast will rise like yeast to conquer peace / leavin' savages to roam in the streets / live on the run / Police payin' me to give in my gun / trick my wisdom with the system that imprisoned my son / smoke a gold leaf / I hold heat, nonchalantly / I'm grungy but the things I do is real and never haunts me / while / funny style niggahs roll in a pile/ rooster heads profile / on a bus to Riker's Isle / holdin' weed inside their pussy with their mind on the pretty things in life / props is a true thugs wife / it's a cycle, niggahs come home some'll go in / do a bullet, come back, do the same shit again / from the womb to the tomb / presume the unpredictable / guns salute life / rapidly that's the ritual"

"Damn son, that niggah spitted that shit exactly how that niggah Nas do, all smooth and shit" said Jimmy.

Fingers wasn't feelin' that shit at all, Sincere was grinnin' from ear to ear. More niggahs was comin' in the band room, it was packed and getting' muggy in there as cats came in to hear the real.

"Yo, I'ma do this next joint for Sin and y'all to show you how Nas bodied that niggah Hov...Check it. Yo son, speed up that same beat, I'ma fall right in." Mag announced.

Mag got in a B-Boy stance, within breathin' distance from Fingers face and held the mic up to his mouth, Black and JaQuan stood by Fingers and Jimmy screamed...

"Yo Sha, peep this joint!

"Yo, son starts off talkin', sayin'... **what's up niggahs. I know you aint talkin' about me dog... you, what? Fuck Jay-Z, you been on my dick niggah, you love my style niggah**..."

As the drums started rollin' and the beat came in, Mag started spittin' one of the illest dis records in Hip Hop / Rap battle history...

"(I) Fuck with your soul like Ether
(Will) Teach you the king, you know who
(Not) God's son across the Belly
(Lose) I prove you lost already

Mag added "For those who didn't catch it, Nas said "I will not lose!"

Check it...

"Brace yourself for the main event / y'all impatiently waitin' / it's like an aids test, what's the results? / Not positive/ who's the best / Pac, Nas or Big? / aint no best, east, west, north, south, flossed out, greedy? I embraced y'all with napalm / blows up, no guts, left chest, face gone / how can Nas be garbage? / Semi-auto to your cartilage / burner at the side of your dome / come outta my throne / I got this...locked since 9-1 / I am the truest / name a rapper that I aint influenced / gave y'all chapters but now I keep my eyes on the Judas / with Hawaiian Sophie fame kept my name in his music / Check it

Fuck wit your soul like Ether
Teach you the king, you know who
God's son across the Belly
I prove you lost already

"I've been fucked over, left for dead, dissed and forgotten / luck ran out, they hoped that I'd be gone, stiff and rotten / y'all just piss on me...shit on me...spit on my grave / talk about me, laugh behind my back but in my face / y'all some well wishers, friendly actin'...envy hidin' snakes / with your hands out for my money man how much can I take? / When these streets keep callin', heard it when I was sleep / that this Gay-Z and Cock-a-fella records wanted beef / started cockin' up my weapon, slowly loadin' up this ammo / to explode it on a camel / and his soldiers I can handle / this for dolo and it's manuscript just sound stupid / when K-R-S already made an album called "Blue Print" / first Biggie's ya man then you got the nerve to say you better than Big / Dick suckin' lips won't you let the late great veteran live?"

Niggahs was makin' all kinds of noises as Mag tilted his head to the side and kept staring at Fingers.

"Y'all niggahs deal wit emotions like bitches / what's sad is I love you cause you're my brother / you traded your soul for riches / My child, I've watched you grow up to be famous / and now I smile like a proud Dad watchin' his only son that made it / you seem to be only concerned with dissin' women / were you abused as a child? / scared to smile, they called you ugly? / well life is hard... hug me / don't reject me / or make records to disrespect me / blatant or indirectly / In 88' you was gettin' chased to your building / callin' my crib and I aint even give you my numbers / all I did was give you a style for you to run with / smilin' in my face / glad to break bread with the God / wearin' Jazz chains, no tecs, no cash, no cars, no jail bars, Jigga..no pies no case / just Hawaiian shirts / hangin' wit little Chase / You a fan / a phony / a fake, pussy, a stan / I'll still whip your ass / you thirty-six in a Karate class? / You Tae Bo Hoe, tryna work it out, what you tryna get brolic? / ask me...if I'm tryna kick knowledge / nah...I'm tryna kick the shit need to learn though / that Ether / that shit that makes your soul burn slow / Is he Dame Diddy, Dame Daddy or Dame Dummy? / Oh I get it...you Biggie and he's Puffy / Rock-a -Fella died of

AIDS that was the end of his chapter / and this the guy you chose to name your company after? / put it together...I rock hoes, y'all rock fellas / and now y'all try to take my spot fellas? / feel these hot rocks fellas / put you in a dry spot fellas / in a pine box with nine shots from my Glock fellas / Foxy got you hot cause you kept your face in her puss / what you think? you gettin' girls now because of your looks? / Neee-gro please / you no mustache havin' with whiskers like a rat / compared to Beans you're wack/ and your manz stabbed "Un" and made you take the blame / you ass..went from Jazz to hangin' wit Kane, to Irv, to Big / and Eminem murdered you on your own shit / You a dick ridin' faggot, you love the attention / Queens niggahs run you niggahs ask Russell Simmons / ha R-O-C get gunned up and clapped quick / J.J. Evans get gunned up and clapped quick / Your whole damn record label gunned up and clapped quick / from Shawn Carter to Jay-Z damn you on Jazz's dick / how much of Big's rhymes is gon' come out your fat lips / wanted to be in every last one of my classics / you pop shit / apologize niggah just ask "Kiss"

Nas is the King!!!"

It was so many "OOOOHHH's" and "AAAHHH's" goin' on from how Mag spitted Nas "Ether" with his body movement and language and Sin was smilin' so hard… As soon as Mag yelled "Nas is the King!!", Fingers hooked off on him with a vicious two piece and Black stomped Mag. Everybody tried to flee the spot cause it was too crowded in that little area due to the overcrowding.

"Yo Chill!!! Chill!!! Chill!!! screamed Sincere. Meanwhile, back in F Unit....

Inf was watchin' Jay-Z's "Girls, Girls, Girls" video, he finally caught it and was happy to finally see it. After the video, Inf was on his way up to the third tier to go to his cell. As he was entering, he didn't notice that G.L. was standin' in a blind spot, with cloth gloves on. Inf walked in to a punch in the eye and G.L.

went to pull out a plexi glass sharpened knife... Inf couldn't do nothin' but grab G.L.....

* * * * *

Back at the Gym, Mag was cleanin' his bloody nose with his Khaki shirt, niggahs was everywhere, playin' the wall and downstairs sittin' on the bleachers, actin' like they were watchin' the game.

"Pussy ass Jamaican ass niggah, I'm tryna see that niggah." Mag said, holdin' his face.

Jimmy had the sorry look on his face as he seen Fingers at the bottom of the stairs with Black, Veto, Sha-Prince, Eastwood and others. Y-Born was tellin' me "Son, you knew that shit was gonna escalate, just make sure you stay out of shit" as he passed me a sharpened plastic with a hell of a point on it.

"I'm good, I'm good." I answered as I took the weapon and put it under my shirt.

Just then, the emergency alarm went off and officers started runnin' toward the west end. I looked and saw Mark with a funny grin on his face.

"Yo, where my little manz Sin at son?" I asked Y-Born.

* * * * *

The Gym C.O. yelled for everyone upstairs to come to the first floor gym area so a crowd was workin' their way down the stairs, it was crowded as convicts angrily moved slowly down the steps. Mag started movin' in that direction while keepin' his eye on Fingers, who was down the steps. Mag had it in his mind that he was gonna hook off on son (Fingers) as soon as he made it down those stairs. He was crowded in as people was in front and in back of him, movin' slow down the stairs. Then as he made it not even three steps from the top going down, an arm came out from the crowd behind him, wrapped around his neck and a razor ripped the left side of his face in a downward motion from his temple to his cheek; blood was shootin' everywhere as convicts pushed to get the hell out the way.

"AAAAAAARRRRRRRGGGGGHHHHH!!!!!!"

"B.K. you bitch ass niggah!!! Never disrespect N. Why Duke!!!"

* * * * *

Shit was crazy, the whole N.Y. car was rounded up within the next three hours, we was all sent to the "Box" and put "under investigation"; they rounded everybody up. We also found out that G.L. moved on Inf on the strength of Sae and Mark. Inf was lucky to grab G.L. and that knife, he only got a cut eye from catchin' that strong right hook and a nick on his shoulder from that plexi but nothin' major. We was all under investigation for possible involvement in a serious assault. The administration wanted someone to break water and inform them who assaulted "Mag" but everyone refused to talk or be interviewed. We sat in the box for three weeks before they started lettin' everyone back out, except for Inf and G.L. "Mag" was history, he couldn't come back either. In the kitchen, niggahs was sittin' at the tables, talkin' shit again… Black was at it with Sha-Prince when Fingers came in.

"Yo Son, what's the deal?" Fingers asked, sittin' down at the table with his tray.

"This niggah tellin' me that Kobe's wife aint white!" shouted Black.

"She aint, she's Italian" stated Sha-Prince.

"What the fuck is the difference?"

"That's what's wrong with you young dudes nowadays, y'all fuss, argue, fight and kill each other in prison over nonsense!" screamed Baltimore "Fatts", an old-head who was highly respected in Lompoc. He was about fifty-seven years old and over two-hundred pounds, bald headed with glasses. He was always in the law library and was hardly ever sighted in the chow hall. "Fatts" had been in for seventeen years. Fatts continued…

"Y'all young niggahs is arguin' about this and that, when none of these people is tryna help you or send you money. Those people don't care about you young bloods but you still argue about them, buy up all these gossip magazines to learn all about them, watch B.E.T. all day and night and you don't know how to get out of jail!!! Go to the law library and study those law books. **GET OUT OF PRISON**!! Go join an educational course, learn to do somethin' constructive young blood! They got computer classes down there… learn how to use a computer. Technology is runnin' the world, everything is computerized nowadays. Didn't all y'all just come out of the hole for some bullshit, rap nonsense? **Fuck Nas! Fuck Jay-Z! Fuck Kobe and his wife**! Them niggahs don't care about none of us prison niggahs!! Start caring for yourself!!! "

After sayin' all that, "Fatts" got up, picked up his tray and walked away.

"Yo, that ol' dude is right son, fuck all that bullshit, we need to get on our shit. Fuck Jay and Nas and all that other shit!" agreed Sha-Prince as he pondered on what "Fatts" just said.

"Man fuck that ol' head, dope fiend ass niggah! He been in prison twenty years now and he still here. How the fuck he gonna give me some good advice? That niggah don't know nothin'!" proclaimed Black.

"Yo Sun, let me tell you what I heard about the 50 Cent - Ja Rule beef, Ja Rule got his chain took and 50 was wit the kid who did it and..................." Will this shit ever end?

REST IN PEACE HARRY "BIG C" HUNT; SUPREME
TEAM'S ILLEST AND CARL "DITCIE" MURRAY; FAR
ROCK'S DON.

* * * * *

CHAPTER 20

"IT IS WHAT IT IS"

I gave you insights and chapters of some of the illest and realest cats of this era and how I saw things. I don't want have anything misunderstood, I'm not claimin' to be the biggest kingpin, killer or any other shit; I'm The Last Illest. Niggahs aint built like me nowadays, I wrote this on the strength of my love for the art form of Hip Hop, in my eyes, from the beginning, to my small involvement, to my street stories... my life.

I only gave you bits and pieces of real eps, it's a lot that I purposely left out. I'm still here, doin' this shit.... Everything is real in the field to the kid… I'm still strivin' to be a better man, father, Son, comrade, friend, ill niggah, God Body and thinker.

"The greatest war is the war within self"

I'm strivin' to come from behind these concrete and steel walls; my goal is my ultimate freedom.

Stay up

P.S. If you don't like my shit.... **Fuck You**
Bring it, I'm still the illest niggah with rhymes, war, whatever!

* * * * *

SHAKIM BIO
& MIKAHS 7 PUBLISHING PRESENT

LOVE HELL OR RIGHT

THE OMEGA JON CHRIST- THE LAST ILLEST

LOYALTY HONOR & RESPECT

ALL TITLES
AVAILABLE
ON AMAZON

GORILLA CONVICT
PUBLICATIONS
Where fiction and reality collide

AVAILABLE NOW! The *Street Legends* series by federal prisoner Seth Ferranti

THE SUPREME TEAM
THE BIRTH OF CRACK AND HIP-HOP, PRINCE'S REIGN OF TERROR AND THE SUPREME/50 CENT BEEF EXPOSED.

SETH FERRANTI

Warehouses of cocaine and heroin, millions in drug money, luxury customized cars, dime pieces galore, bling-bling to shine, multitudes of violence, and vicious murder. . . . These men were self-made stars and their lifestyles are what gangsta rap is all about. Read their stories and ride shotgun with the most memorable figures from the crack era.

"Gorilla Convict is evolving into the most potent voice of the streets. Street Legends is the apple of a street soldier's eye."

Walter "King Tut" Johnson, NYC Original Gangster

"Seth's stories are strong and they resonate with a sense of truth that needs to be expressed."

Kenneth "Supreme" McGriff, NYC Street Legend

ORDER DIRECT: Gorilla Convict Publications /1019 Willott Rd. / St. Peters, MO 63376
$15.00 per book. Shipping and handling: $5.25 for the first book and $2.25 for each additional book.
Postal tracking $1.00 per order. Not responsible for orders without tracking number. Money orders only - no personal checks. All sales final.

Or order instantly online with any major credit card by visiting
www.gorillaconvict.com

ROYAL-T PUBLISHING PRESENT

A MEMOIR

Harlem Heroin(e

MY LOVE AFFAIR WITH HARLEM STREET L
AND THE MEN WHO RULED IT

MS. TEE

Black Hand

Publishing Company LLC

T-Stuckey Talks Hip Hop

Presents
LyQuid Magazine ©™

T-STUCKEY

The PREVIEW Vol. 1

@iamsodeelishis

DEELISHIS

@Ms_CEOPlatinumdiva519
@PlatinumHouseWI
@PlatimumHouseWifesEssentials

Model
@stuckin_my_ways

8 50006 00001 2

FOR MORE INFO CONTACT
313-469-2426

MODEL CASTING CALL
BECOME A PUBLISHED MODEL

ADVERTISE YOUR
ALBUM RELEASE
BOUTIQUE
SALON
BRAND

ARTIST & MODEL
INTERVIEWS
FULL PAGE
$229

SPONSORSHIPS
START AT $100